Irish Eyes

Irish Eyes

THE AMERICAN SONGBOOK SERIES

BOOK ONE

HOPE C. TARR

LUME BOOKS
A JOFFE BOOKS COMPANY

LUME BOOKS
A JOFFE BOOKS COMPANY

Lume Books, London
A Joffe Books Company
www.lumebooks.co.uk

Cover design by George Joseph

Cover photography (historical woman) © Magdalena Russocka/Trevillion Images

ISBN: 978-1-83901-555-7

When Irish eyes are smiling,
Sure, it's like a morn in spring.
In the lilt of Irish laughter,
You can hear the angels sing.
When Irish hearts are happy,
All the world seems bright and gay,
And when Irish eyes are smiling,
Sure, they steal your heart away.

PART I: Brave Beginnings, 1898–1900

If you listen, I'll sing you a sweet little song
Of a flower that's now drooped and dead,
Yet dearer to me, yes, than all of its mates
Tho' each holds aloft its proud head.
T'was given to me by a girl that I knew,
Since we've met, faith, I've known no repose,
She is dearer by far than the world's brightest star,
And I call her my Wild Irish Rose.

Chauncey Olcott, "My Wild Irish Rose"
from *A Romance of Athlone*, 1898

Chapter One

Kilronan, Inis Mór, Aran Islands
August 1898

The letter arrived on an early August day of cerulean skies, golden sunshine, and balmy breezes. It looked as if it had been to battle itself – battered about the edges, the envelope rubbed bald in spots and shored up with copious bits of gumming. The latter doomed any stab at subterfuge I might make, namely steaming open the stickiness. Evaluating its lightness and official-looking United States of America government seal, I hesitated. Opening another's correspondence was a serious breach of my postmistress duties, even if the intended recipient was my own father. But Da was off to the mainland and wouldn't be back before nightfall. Could an impulsive, not-quite-eighteen-year-old girl such as myself truly be expected to cling to patience?

I gave in and tore the thing open.

July 22, 1898

Dear Mr. O'Neill,

It is my sad obligation to report that your son, Private Donal O'Neill, left this world on Friday, July 1st at approximately one o'clock p.m. from mortal wounds sustained in laying siege to San Juan Heights. According to Pvt. Adam Blakely, fighting alongside him, he succumbed soon after being struck down by enemy fire and, mercifully, did not suffer beyond a brief few minutes.

Pvt. O'Neill was a good, honest, and faithful soldier, who had the goodwill of all who knew him. His family and friends have the sincere sympathy of the entire company.

Edward A. Selfridge, Jr.

Capt. 71st New York Volunteer Infantry Com'd Co. K

Tears scored me from cheek to chin. Racing over those brief, blurred lines, I felt as if a chunk of my heart were being broken off and borne away. My chest hurt so badly, I half thought I might be dying myself. In those first fraught moments, I wouldn't have minded if I were. Despite the letter smashed to my breast, a world without Danny was beyond my fathoming.

For the seventeen years and eight months of my life up to that moment, I'd been quietly, uneventfully happy. What did I care if, after Sunday mass, the women congregating in the kirk yard cast sharp eyes my way, clucked their tongues, and lamented what a "puir, motherless wean" I was, the nearest thing to a "wilding"? Let them say what they would, for motherless and wild though I might be, never had I been sensible of any lack. Our mother, Moira Rose, after whom I'm called, passed in childbirth when I was three. Beyond fragments of memory – drawn blinds and black bunting, hushed voices pitched against the backdrop of a newborn's bawling, and the pair of shiny pennies set upon her closed eyes – I don't mind much of the event. Or herself.

From as far back as I can recollect, my life revolved around our family's pub and my father and four brothers: Colm, the eldest; Ronan, who'd decamped to Dublin and wed Keira, a city girl; Killian, the baby of our brood, so small and dark-featured we called him "changeling"; and in betwixt, Donal – Danny. Born with music in his soul and a deft touch for animals, horses especially, he was my favorite and myself his. Even with the great Atlantic separating us, we'd stayed close through our letters. Only now, he was gone, lost, not only to America's New York City but lost... forever.

It wasn't until weeks later that I managed to drag myself from my grief sufficiently to wonder what had become of Danny's comrade-in-arms and best mate, Adam H. Blakely.

Chapter Two

Saturday, September 10, 1898

It was in every way a usual Saturday night, the pub thronged with men arguing over tides and fishes and the price of kelp in Connemara, their raised, rapid speech mostly in Gaelic with the odd English dropped in. Even after all these years, I can close my eyes and conjure that bustling, beloved taproom. The wattle walls stained peaty from centuries of pipe smoke and turf fires, the fishing nets and oilskins slung upon hooks. The damp air thick with sweet tobacco and wet wool. The oil lamps flickering over flushed faces, animated or weary, depending upon whether the week's catch had been bountiful or meager.

Caught up with refilling tankards and passing plates of boiled potatoes and salted herring down the line, I felt him before I saw him, his regard like gentle fingers upon my face. I looked up from the pitcher I was drawing, thinking to find Cam and Brendain O'Conor smiling sloppily at me from over the rims of their pints. Only the brothers were both bent over their beers, too busy arguing over who'd caught the most fishes to trouble me with their awkward overtures. Looking beyond them, my gaze found its way to the front of the room – and the tall, blond stranger, standing hat in hand upon the threshold.

Despite the walking stick he gripped, he held himself steely straight, the crown of his head clearing the lintel, but barely. Even across the breadth of that noisy, smoke-filled room, everything about him was beautiful to me, from the hank of wheat-colored hair fallen over his brow to the lanky grace of his broad-shouldered, long-limbed body, the poverty of flesh at odds with his simple but costly clothing.

Splashing at my feet snapped me back to the bar and the mess I'd made of it.

Beside me, Colm shook off his shoe. "Jaysus, Rose, have a care. You're pourin' out our profit."

The overflowing pitcher and widening puddle upon the floor bore witness to my silliness, as did my beer-stained skirts and soaked-through sandals. Once dried, sure, I'd stink like a brewery.

"I'll fetch the mop and pail," I said, thinking to escape to the kitchen and tidy myself.

But Colm had other ideas. "Hold here, I'll do it. Only mind you keep your wits upon your pourin' and your peepers upon the bar."

He tossed me the dish towel and disappeared into the back.

I spent the next several minutes sopping up the worst of the spillage and refilling the mugs flagged in my face. The sensation of being not so much stared upon as studied had me looking out once more. And then, dear Lord, the thrill of it, the stranger was striding toward me, the hitch to his gait and the satchel slung over his shoulder slowing him not a whit.

Well, 'tis a boozer we're in, and like as not, he's thirsty, I told myself, tucking my nail-bitten hands beneath the bar as he drew up before me.

Setting his cane upon the rail, he eyed the hinged pass-through as though contemplating joining me on the other side. Over the cloud of peat and pipe smoke, his scent met me, conjuring fantasies of finely milled soap, leather-bound books, and another slightly musky aroma I suspected was himself alone. I inhaled, tasting him on my tongue, and for the first time in my life, I understood what it was to be drunk, not on whiskey or beer, but on the elixir of another human being.

The mad mix of feelings, and his nearness, spurred my heart to racing. "*Fáilte.* Is it thirsty you are, stranger?"

A nod answered, the motion sending fair hair flopping over one eye, the iris the same vivid blue as the spring gentians that bloom wild in even the rockiest bits of our island. He lifted a hand and pushed the errant lock back, and it was then that I saw it – the fresh scar slashing one side of his otherwise smooth brow.

"What do you recommend?" he asked, his accent, whilst top-drawer, marking him as a Yank.

Mentally running through the limited libations on offer, I chewed my lower lip, the skin split from previous mistreatment. "A pint of plain suits most," I finally said, fluttering nervous fingers toward the taps.

6

"Beer would be bully, thanks." He leveled me a lopsided smile, drawing my eye to his mouth. The teeth, white and even, might owe to means, but the full lips framing them were a pure and powerful gift of nature.

I reached up and drew a clean pint down from the rack. Keenly conscious of himself minding my every movement, I tilted the glass forty-five degrees, held it under the spout, and slowly pulled down upon the tap handle, filling it just above three-quarters. Tempted as I was to rush, I made myself wait for the beer to settle, the cascade of gaseous bubbles calming to create the perfect cap of creamy foam. Only then did I top off the draft and set it before himself, taking care not to spill so much as a single tawny drop.

Breath in my throat, I let myself look up. "That'll be five p's."

He slid a hand inside his coat and brought out a fistful of coins. "Help a fella out? I'm still learning the currency."

I poked at his outstretched palm and picked out the closest correct coin. "I won't be a moment," I said, turning to the till for his due.

He waved me off and shoved the rest into his pocket, then picked up his beer and took a long swallow. "Holy moly, that's good!" Expression rapturous, he set the glass down. "I should probably introduce myself, if only to save you from calling me 'stranger'," he added, teasing tone belied by the sudden seriousness of the eyes meeting mine. "I'm Adam. Adam Blakely."

I stared, feeling as if the floorboards must be buckling beneath me.

"I'm guessing you're Danny's sister, Rose?"

His polite prodding pulled me back to myself. "Moira Rose, though everyone calls me Rose. It's pleased I am to make your acquaintance, Private Blakely." I held out my hand, still sticky with beer.

He took it, his long fingers and broad palm engulfing mine, his skin smooth, not callused as our men's, the neatly trimmed nails devoid of dirt.

"The pleasure is all mine, though I'm a plain mister now." He released my hand, his warm one sliding away. "For better or worse, my soldiering days are behind me," he added, casting a rueful look to the cane.

"Did Danny speak much of home?" I asked, hoping his answer would be yes.

"He did, fondly and often. Of you, especially."

"What did he say?" I asked, warmed, to be sure, but wary too, for I winced to think the moniker of "wilding" might have made its way to the other side of the Atlantic.

"That you're an ace seamstress, for starters. 'Rare canny with needle and thread' was how he put it." The smile he flashed me didn't quite reach his eyes, shadowed with sadness.

"That's all?" I asked, sensing it wasn't.

"Not exactly, no." He took a deep draft of beer as if calling on his courage. Wiping the foam from his lips, he admitted, "He read me your letters."

"*All* of them?"

I'd dashed off a weekly missive all that May and June, keeping my brother abreast of our wee world's doings – pub happenings and village squabbles and dress patterns I'd copied and sewed. Silly prattle meant for Danny alone.

A sheepish look answered, "By the time we boarded *The Vigilancia* for Cuba, I felt like... well, like I knew this place. This village and all of you. I hope you don't mind."

Had I known, I would have minded. I would have minded terribly. Not so now.

"I'm glad he had yourself to bear him company," I answered, the familiar grief frogging my voice, the sentiment sincere, though it hardly mattered now. "He spoke of you, too. In his letters home."

Adam shot me a mortified look. "That must have been boring."

I shook my head. "Not at all. I think... he looked up to you."

From Camp Black in Hempstead, Long Island, where Danny mustered in, to the training and embarkation camps in Lakeland and Tampa Heights, Florida, not a letter arrived that didn't make mention of his new best mate. Adam scissoring through the lake, cutting a lap fast as any fish. Delivering a "knuckle sandwich" to a recruit he'd caught abusing a horse. Scribbling in his journal, which he meant to make a book of someday. The praise had piled on until Adam Blakely seemed larger than life, a hero the likes of which I'd only ever met in books. Only now, he was here, his flesh-and-blood self but a bar's width away from me.

Changing the subject, I asked, "How do you come to be in Ireland, Mr. Blakely? Are you on holiday with your family?" I stole a glance at his ring finger, happily bare, though not every married man was keen on wearing the proof of it.

"*Adam*, please – *Mr. Blakely* feels like you must mean my father – and no, I'm here on my own, unless you count the lumbering piece of luggage I parked inside your doorway."

8

He shot a glance over his shoulder to a smart campaign case, covered in honey-hued leather and fitted with what looked to be brass handles. A clutch of younger lads gathered round it, taking turns testing its heft.

Rather than break away to rescue it, he turned back to me. "Truth is, I'm here to see you."

Yet another surprise. "Myself? But why?"

He shifted the shoulder bearing the satchel as if suddenly minded of the burden, "Because… well, Danny asked me to. Made me swear, actually." Several silent seconds ticked by, his gaze tethered to mine, and then he shook himself as if awaking. "Pardon my staring, but you're not what I pictured."

Despite the blush scalding my cheeks, I mustered the nerve to ask, "What is it you pictured?"

"More of a kid, I guess. And… skinnier. Fencepost was how Danny put it."

I glanced down at myself and then back up at him. "And how is it you'd… *put it?*"

His gaze veered from mine, dipping to the bar top. "Well, miss, I'd say you were just right. Perfect."

Perfect. I fancied the sound of that, though the wee devil perched upon my shoulder hissed he was only being kind. Wreathed in blushes though I no doubt was, curiosity won out. "What else?"

He looked up. "That you were ginger-haired, same as him, though I'd call yours more of a… burnished copper."

I resisted the urge to run a hand over my hair, the riot of corkscrew curls caught back with a bit of velvet ribbon, trimming left over from the jacket I'd just finished sewing. "Burnished copper, sure, that's very poetic."

Was he in earnest or a shameless flirt? In my inexperience, I'd no way of knowing, though the color climbing his cheeks seemed to favor the former.

Shy-eyed, he shook his head. "Thanks, but I lifted that line. Not that I couldn't come up with one just as good if I had the time. Oh, and he mentioned your complexion – peaches and cream."

"He did not!" My hand flew to my face, the stubborn freckles bridging my forehead and nose a scourge no amount of lemon juice could lighten.

He slanted me a smile. "Okay, you've got me there. He said freckled. The peaches and cream part's all me."

9

From the side of my eye, I saw Cam signaling for another round but pretended not to see. "Anything else?" I asked, hoping to keep this oddly entertaining interchange from petering. Stacked against my usual male company – islanders who expressed themselves with glasses banged upon the bar and single-syllable asks and answers – Adam Blakely afforded a feast of canny conversation. Starved, I stood prepared to devour his every word, no matter that some were over my head.

He tapped two fingers atop the bar, making a show of considering, teasing me as one of my brothers might. "Hmm, let's see." His dancing fingers stalled, and his gaze swept my face. "He said your smile could light up a January sky. Boy, he sure hit the nail on the head with that one," he added, pinning me with eyes so earnest, I forgot to breathe.

"*Rose!*"

I whirled to see Colm bursting forth from the back, blistered cheeks a match for his hair.

Scowling, he dropped both mop and pail and sidled up to my side, "We've a roomful of thirsty men who just got their pay, and a pub down the street that serves Guinness and porter and rye whiskey same as ourselves, only the service is swifter."

Adam rose to defend me, "Please don't blame Rose – Miss O'Neill. The fault's mine for monopolizing her."

Colm's dark look deepened. Ever since Danny had left us for America in '92, he saw Yanks as second to the devil, and the glare he gave Adam bore out the ill feeling. "What affair's it of yours, stranger?"

I laid a hand upon Colm's forearm, fuzzed with copper as Danny's had been. "Mr. Blakely soldiered with Danny in the American war with Spain. You'll recall him from… the letter."

Pulling upon his mustache, he eyed Adam. "You're the lad who fought beside our Danny?"

Adam nodded. "We mustered in together."

Colm opened his mouth as if to ask more. Before he could, our father emerged from the kitchen, an apron tied about his winnowed waist. Since Danny's dying, he'd dropped a stone at least.

"I can hear the pair of you clear to the pantry. What's the trouble?" he demanded, dividing his gaze between my brother and myself.

I gestured to Adam. "Da, this is Mr. Adam Blakely, who served with Danny in Cuba. He's come all the way from…"

"New York City," Adam supplied, sounding strangely shy of it.

My father's craggy countenance softened. "You're Danny's mate? The one with him at... the end?"

Expression solemn, Adam nodded. "I am, sir, and a finer, braver soldier and better friend I've yet to know."

Da's lower lip quivered. For a heart-stopping few seconds, I steeled myself for him to break down, something I'd seen him do but once, on that terrible eve when I'd read him the American army captain's letter.

Rallying, he looked to Colm. "Give the call we're closing early, with a final round on the house." To Adam, "You'll take supper, will you?" Before an answer might be made, he turned to me, "Rose, lass, draw Mr. Blakely another pint – that is if there's aught left of the keg after your watering the floor with it – and we'll hear what the young man's come to say."

The taproom soon cleared of all but a few tenacious tipplers. We left them nursing their final pints and retreated to the kitchen where glasses of whiskey were passed about. I handed mine along, wanting to stay clearheaded, and fetched Adam a chair, rightly supposing that managing a bench with his bad leg might be a trial.

Whilst the men and Killian sat about the rough-hewn table, drinking and making strained small talk, I busied myself with setting out our guest's supper. Left upon the stovetop, the plate of pollock, potatoes, and parsnips was the worse for warming, but when I set it down before Adam, he thanked me with a smile and tucked in as though being fed a feast.

I untied my apron and joined them, nudging Killian over and sliding into the spot across from Adam. Though he ate with gusto, his manners at table were flawless, the coarse napkin laid neatly upon his lap, not tucked into his shirtfront, as was our custom.

Despite Colm's fingers drumming the tabletop, Da waited for Adam to sit back from his empty plate before pressing for his story. "It's a long way you've come, young man, and a sorry tale you carry, for by now, we all know the ending of it," he began, the earlier treble to his tone smoothed out by the whiskey.

Adam opened his satchel and took out a carved wooden rosary box, familiar for all that I hadn't seen it in six years. "Before he... passed, Danny entrusted me with this." Solemn-eyed, he slid the box across the table to me.

It was Danny's all right, down to the "*DONAL*" carved into the front, the wood more weathered than I remembered, but then, it had been to war. Unlike Danny, his treasure had made it safe home.

I lifted the hinged lid to the inscription:

May your troubles be less,
Your blessings be more,
And nothing but happiness walk through your door.

What I wouldn't give to see my brother walk through our door once more! Hands shaking, I took out the rosary, the cube-shaped beads fashioned of Connemara marble, their translucence veined with dark green. Beneath was a stack of letters, mine, tied with twine. I would read them later, alone in my room where I could sob and rail to my broken heart's content, bellowing my angry grief into the pillow.

I closed the box and looked up. "It's grateful I am, we all are, to yourself for bringing something of our Danny back to us."

A splash upon my cheek confirmed I hadn't waited for my room. A handkerchief materialized in Adam's hand. He reached across and handed it to me. Even in my distress, the seamstress in me couldn't help but take note of the fabric's fine, tight weave, "*A.H.B.*" monogrammed in fat, nubby silk letters, the square as freshly starched and pressed as the rest of him. Rather than ruin it with my honking, I used the edge to dab at my damp eyes.

Colm flung Adam a glare. "War isn't a fit topic for tender ears."

Resolved to prove my "tender ears" equal to the task, I picked up my chin. "Danny was… *is* my brother too. I have as much right to listen as anyone at this table."

My father sent Adam a nod. "Do as the lass bids, and mind you don't censor yourself on our account. My Donal was as brave and stalwart and good-hearted as lads come. If he could bear being at war, the least we can do is bear up against the telling of it."

Meeting each of our gazes in turn, Adam began. The happy stories came first. Danny leaning out the window of their military transport train and planting a "smacker" on the lips of a Lakeland, Florida girl who, along with most of the town, had turned out to welcome them. Putting "itching powder" in the boots of a fellow recruit who'd called him a "mick." Volunteering for mess duty and making an entire chest of ice cream sandwiches go missing.

My brother's final moments Adam relayed with great delicacy, calling attention to his selflessness and bravery, assuring us that any pain had been blessedly brief.

"Our K Company lost thirteen men to Cuba, Danny among them," he finished, reaching for his whiskey. "Not that it in any way lightens your loss, but I thought… well, you should know. More were wounded or laid low with malaria and yellow fever." He swallowed the last of his drink and set the glass down.

"You were wounded too," I said, and though my gaze went to his forehead, it was his leg I meant.

He dashed the troublesome hank of hair out of his eyes. "The scratch is just a souvenir. The leg was what forced me from the field. They sent me to the field hospital in Siboney to have the bullet out. I was getting over the surgery when the fever hit. Once I was through the worst, the medics loaded me and a bunch of other fellas onto a medical transport ship to the army hospital on Long Island. Soon as I got out, I booked passage on a steamer to Queenstown. That was about a dozen days ago."

Small wonder he was so pale and gaunt. I picked up the whiskey bottle to offer him more, but he shook his head.

"Why come at all?" Colm asked, though it hardly sounded a question. "With your means, sure you could have shipped the box by post?"

"Fine gratitude, that," I cried out, shamed by his crassness.

"S'truth, isn't it?" Colm swung his gaze to Adam, sizing him up as though he were a mackerel to be weighed, gutted, and filleted. "You've only to look at him to know he's never done a day's labor."

Adam's jaw tightened, otherwise, he took Colm's spleen in stride. "I promised Danny I'd place the box and its contents in Rose's hands, and now I have. If you'll point me to the nearest hostel, I'll say goodnight and be on my way." He took hold of his cane and levered himself to standing.

Panic poured through me, for by then, Adam Blakely was more than a fascinating stranger first brought up in my brother's letters. He was my last living link to Danny, not the boy-man of my memory but the grown one who'd made a home for himself in America.

I shot to my feet, "Stay… please!"

13

Four pairs of male eyes fixed upon me. For a moment, I stood frozen, as shocked by my outburst as any of them.

Recovering, I looked to my father, "Sure we'll not send him off in the middle of the night. Not after he's come all this long way and for our sakes, not his own?"

"Rose has the right of it," Da said in a tone to quell further squabbling. "Any mate of Danny's is welcome beneath this roof, and I'll not hear a word against it."

Resisting the urge to stick out my tongue at Colm, seething in his seat, I swung back to Adam. "It's settled then. You'll bide here. As our *guest*," I added, lobbing Colm a look. "For a fortnight and no less."

I was stretching my luck, and I wasn't the only one to know it.

"A *fortnight*?" Colm cut me a look sharp as any angler's blade.

Giving him my back, I focused on our father. "He can stay in Danny's old room."

"A fortnight it is," Da said, dividing his gaze between myself and Adam. "That is, if the young man's amenable."

Heart in my throat, I glanced back to Adam. "Are you… amenable?" If he said no, sure I'd expire on the spot.

Regarding his walking stick, he silently weighed our offer. "Your Arans are reputed to be in every way extraordinary," he said at last. "I'd be curious to explore them in daylight."

Relief flooded me. Gladness too. "After breakfast, it's happy I'll be to take you about."

Despite the bluish smudges beneath, Adam's eyes shone. "I'd like that. With your permission, sir," he added to my father.

"Suppose we can spare her for a few hours." Da stood, the signal for the lot of us to follow suit. "Kil, lad, light Adam to his room. He's had a long, wearying day, and if Rose has her way – and it's the rare day she doesn't – he's in for another such tomorrow."

Chapter Three

Over the following fortnight, I seized every opportunity to put myself in the path of our American guest. Whisking Adam as far afield from the pub, and Colm, as his wounded leg would allow, I offered up our humble island treasures of holy wells, crumbling forts, and ancient tombs as a courtier might pour precious stones at a prince's feet.

The seal colony that made its home on our north shore was a favorite haunt. By keeping to the coast road, and thereby avoiding the steeper hills, it was also a reasonable ramble for a man with a lame leg. Chewing on a blade of grass beside me, Adam divided his attention between the half-dozen seals sunning on a slab of rock and the little moleskin notebook he carried with him everywhere, jotting down notes at a furious clip then lapsing into long stretches of thoughtful silence.

Presently, he was in one of his silent, thoughtful moods, the stub of pencil stalled mid-page, his gaze upon the scene ahead. I stole a sideways glance, admiring, far from the first time, how long and thick his gold-tipped lashes were, how the sun turned the hank of hair over his forehead from wheat-colored to golden, screening most of the scar. The violent mark made him mortal to me, not the untouchable hero of Danny's wartime letters but a flesh-and-blood friend I might walk about with, laugh with, even tease.

"Penny for your thoughts," he asked, swiveling to face me.

Fearing I'd been caught out gawking, I covered for myself as best I could. "I'm only thinking of the seals, of course, same as yourself. Mind how the wee grayish one keeps angling to join the others, only the lion won't shift over, the great bully. Quite the clannish lot." I punctuated this hastily spun speech with enthusiastic pointing as though the commonplace sea creatures were the world's eighth wonder.

"Aren't we all?" Adam mused. He closed the journal and slid it back into his canvas satchel. "I'm game for a longer walk tomorrow if you have the time. Colm mentioned there's another fort, *Dún Aon*—"

"*Dún Aonghasa*," I said, saving him from struggling over the Gaelic. "Fort of Aengus. Aengus is of the old gods. The god of love," I added in a burst of brazenness.

"Like Cupid?" he said with a smile.

"I suppose so." I forced my gaze up to his, the new, ruddy glow to his face making his eyes seem all the bluer. "Legend holds Aengus fell in love with Caer, the goddess of sleeping and dreams, only she was seized, along with a hundred and fifty girls, all of them cursed to take swan form. Before he might marry her, Aengus must pick her out from the others in the flock. He did, despite them all being like-looking. After, he turned himself into a swan too, and the pair took flight, singing sweet, charmed melodies that put hearers to sleep for three days and nights."

Adam let out a laugh. "They say love makes fools of us all – or in Aengus' case, fowl."

I smiled at the word-play, though my heart wasn't altogether in it.

"Colm said the fort offers the best views of the Atlantic."

The comment acted on me like a match put to paraffin. "Colm wouldn't know his arse from his elbow," I said hotly, inwardly cursing my brother for his meanness. Perched upon a hundred-meter cliff, stone-spiked path meant to protect against invaders, Dún Aonghasa didn't reveal her prized prospect to the faint of heart or frail of limb.

Adam saw through me at once. "Meaning it's too much for me?"

"The last half-mile is uphill and uncommon slippery," I admitted.

His hand resting atop the walking stick stiffened. "You'd have to carry me. Not that you're not equal to it, but I do still have some pride."

I set my hand atop his bunched knuckles. "Your leg's growing stronger by the day. We'll have you climbing the four corners in no time."

He glanced away. "I can't stay on indefinitely, you know, not as a guest."

The agreed-upon fortnight was winding to a close. Lest we lose track, Colm made it known that he too was counting the days. Resolved not to release my new friend so soon, I lapsed into silent scheming.

Inspiration struck, and I said, "What if you weren't only a guest?"

A weary look answered. "I already tried paying for my room and board. Your father won't hear of it."

16

"But if you were to offer something else, something he couldn't refuse?"

"Like what?"

I squeezed the hand I hadn't yet let go of. "This."

We made haste back to the pub and sought out my father. When Adam offered his labor, at first, Da refused, but he was soon brought around, for the truth was, we could do with the help.

And help Adam did. No task was too lowly, no request left unmet. Whether hunting limpets, scraping seaweed from the rocks, twisting rope, mending thatching, or fixing a busted beer tap, he rolled up his sleeves and threw himself into the spirit of the thing. At first, the other cottagers regarded him with a wary eye. But once the story got out of how, in attempting his first milking, he'd slipped off the stool into a steaming cowpat and then risen to laugh with the rest of us, he was accepted as one of our own. He even began dressing as an islander, trading his "cit" clothes for a woolen jersey, loose flannel trousers, and slouched cap.

"How are you keeping?" I called out one fine, warmish afternoon when I came upon him sitting on the pier, legs dangling over the side, the crutch abandoned but still within reach.

He lifted his gaze from the casting net in his lap, and despite seeing him every day for nearly a month, those blue irises meeting mine nearly knocked me to my knees. "Not too shabby for a pin cushion." He held out his hand, the digits peppered with blood where he'd pricked himself.

I tucked my skirts and dropped down beside him, taking in the ravages with tender eyes. "It's a mighty mess you've made of yourself."

"Not as mighty as this." He gestured to the snared netting and blew out a breath. "I don't suppose you'd see your way to straightening out this Gordion Knot I've made?"

I didn't then know what a Gordion Knot was. I only knew I was happy, happier than I'd ever thought to be again. The sun was warm on my back, the sky more of blue than gray for all that autumn was upon us. Most of all there was Adam, settled at my side and, for the time being, seemingly settled into our simple way of life as well.

"Give it here." I reached for the thick needle, lethal-like when wielded by a novice hand.

He flashed me a grateful smile and shifted the tangle onto my lap. "You're an angel."

Ere then, no one had ever likened me to anything in the least celestial. I hid a smile, pretending not to be pleased.

He bent his bad leg and kneaded the stiffness. Looking over in concern, it was then that I saw it.

"Oh, Adam, your lovely shoes!"

The fossils in the limestone had sliced the buttery leather soles to ribbons.

Following my gaze, he grimaced. "Never thought I'd say this, but I miss my army boots."

Brought up on the island, ere then, I'd taken the rough terrain as a matter of course. "A pair of pampooties is what you want for."

"Pam—"

"Pampooties." I reached down and lifted my skirt a finger's length to show him.

His eyes popped, and not only owing to my unseemly display of ankle. "Those are the... most unique sandals I've ever seen. Cowhide?" At my nod, "Turned fur side out?" Again, I nodded. "Is that... fishing line holding them on?"

I jerked my hem back down. "Mind, I've a proper pair of half-boots special-ordered from Galway for Sunday Mass and Holy Days." Cheeks hot, I picked up my mending.

I got through several hitch knots before he nudged me. "C'mon, Rose, don't get your nose out of joint. I think your... pampooties are swell. I wouldn't mind a pair myself, cross my heart. Took me by surprise is all."

That time, I stalled my stitching. "Why's that?"

An awkward pause and then, "I can't help noticing you don't dress like the other women and girls here do. If I didn't know better, I'd think you'd gone shopping on the mainland."

Islander females of every age wore scarlet mostly, their bulky petticoats and boxy jackets dyed from madder root, with a knotted plaid shawl added once autumn arrived. Standing out in my slim wool jackets and dark skirts, I'd been called out for pride on more than one occasion, most often by a mother with daughters to marry off.

"There's a well-heeled Prot widow who summers here. Widow Murphy carries subscriptions on all the top ladies' monthlies." Having first crack at those precious publications, and the fashion plates they contained, was one of the chief privileges of serving as postmistress. "From *Godey's*," I added, moving the mesh to show off my jacket's peplum waist.

18

"Very smart," he said, sounding suitably impressed and wholly sincere.

The compliment, along with the warmth in his eyes, gave me the courage to confide, "I mean to have a dress shop of my own one day. In Dublin. On Grafton Street. I've only been once, to visit my brother and his wife, but someday, I'll go back. When I do, it'll be to stay."

Adam's face lit. "Do it. Promise me you will."

Caught up in his enthusiasm, I admitted, "I've a bit set aside, not nearly sufficient, not yet. But… someday."

"Why wait for someday?" Adam demanded, buoying me along. "Say the word, and I'll stake you."

Horrified to think I'd seemed to be hinting, I shook my head. "I won't take charity."

"It wouldn't be charity. It would be an investment."

"An investment?"

"I'm a businessman, aren't I, or at least that's what I'm bred to be. I'd expect some return. A percentage of your profits," he clarified, rightly reading my confusion.

"You think I'd turn a profit?"

I scoured his face for signs of subterfuge. Friend to Danny though he'd proven himself, I couldn't afford to forget what else he was: a well-heeled Yank on holiday, "playing at peasant", or so Colm never tired of telling me. Good craic, harmless fun – so long as you kept your heart out of it.

A shrug and then, "Why wouldn't you? You're a natural – talented, hard-working, and terrific with people. With the right backing, there's no reason your store – sorry, *atelier* – can't be another House of Worth."

It was the first time anyone had believed in me. My eyes misted. My heart swelled. The fishnet as good as forgotten, I centered my gaze on his beaming one. "I don't know what to say."

Entreating eyes held fast to mine. "Say you'll do it. Say yes to your dream and to me, or at least my piddling part in it."

Yes. With such a man in such a moment, what other answer could there be?

I pulled a long breath. "All right then, yes."

"Put her there, partner." Grinning, Adam grabbed for my hand. Suddenly, he let out an "Ouch!" and snapped back, sucking the side of his hand.

I looked down to the needle I still held onto, tipped in scarlet.

Adam cracked a laugh. "A blood oath, now we've really sealed the deal." He reached for his handkerchief.

Before he could use it, I grabbed his sleeve. "I'll add mine too."

I put the needle tip to my flesh, but Adam stopped me. "Put that thing away. I've already contributed enough for two."

I did as he bid, wiping the needle on the fold of my skirt and then securing it in the hem. Turning back to him, I held out my hand.

He took it in his cut one. "Deal," he said, a husky hitch to his voice.

"Deal," I echoed, chafing my palm against his.

He released me and sat back. I stared down at the scarlet smear, smiling to myself. When he offered me the hankie to wipe it, I shook my head.

He slipped the square back into his pocket. "I'll give you my address in New York. Write me when you're ready."

"Write you?" I asked, hoping I'd misheard.

A blithe nod answered. "So I can wire you the money."

Of course, he still meant to go back to America. New York, the city, was his home, after all. How foolish I'd been to forget that for so much as a moment.

I forced on a smile. "That's grand of you, truly. It's in your debt I'll be."

At my mention of debt, a cloud crossed his features. "It's a business partnership, not indentured servitude. Besides, what's money for, if not to help a friend?"

Friend. Like the mention of his leaving, the word worked upon my spirits like a pin put to a balloon.

One afternoon, wiping down the bar whilst Adam swept up, I came across an old photograph of Danny. Fallen behind a shelf and coated in more than a decade of dust, it was himself as a lad of ten-odd, arm slung about the neck of a favorite goat. The unexpected discovery was like a razor to my heart. Tears burned the backs of my eyes. My throat felt as if an unseen hand stitched it closed.

Flinging down the cloth, I demanded, "Why'd he do it? Why'd he sign on to go off and be shot at? For a cause no concern of his."

Adam's sweeping stalled. He set the broom against the wall and came over to me. Even in my distress, I was keenly conscious of my heart's quickening.

Drawing up to the bar, he said, "Danny might not have been born in America, but otherwise, he was no different from the rest of us. Once war was declared, he got caught up in the romance, the *fever* of the thing. By the time we realized what we'd signed up for, there was nothing to do but see the thing through."

That should have satisfied me. It didn't.

"But it wasn't his fight. It wasn't his country. It wasn't…" I poured myself a glass of water and drank it down.

He reached across the bar and settled a hand atop my shoulder. "You're angry with him."

Angry with my dead brother! "What a heartless, horrid thing to say." I brought the glass down hard.

Shattering shocked me from my fury. I looked down to the bar top aglitter with glass and speckled scarlet.

Adam ducked beneath the overpass and came up beside me.

"It's… nothing, a scratch," I insisted, stupidly struggling to make sense of my gushing hand.

He wrapped his hand about my wrist and held it high. "The hell it isn't," he said, the first I'd ever heard him curse. "You've cut yourself a nasty gash. I'm guessing the nearest doctor's in Galway, more than three hours by ferry, so here's hoping you won't need stitches because, well, you've seen my sewing."

I followed his gaze to the wicked-looking shard poking out from my palm. "Bollocks."

"You can say that again. Now stop your fidgeting and hold still."

Cowed, I bit my lip as he slid the sliver out in one neat piece.

"This next part's going to *really* hurt," he warned, reaching for a bottle of rye.

He guided me over to the sink and doused the wound with whiskey. That time, my pride gave way, and I cried out.

"Easy, give it a minute." He bent his head and blew upon the burning. Tears filled my eyes, and not only because I'd hurt myself. "I'm an idjut."

He looked up at me through his lashes. "No, you're not. You're grieving." Straightening, he took a clean handkerchief from his pocket and used it to wrap the wound. Tying off the makeshift bandage, he said, "If it was in my power to grant you some sort of peace about all this, believe me, I would. But it isn't, and I can't. And… I'm sorry."

I leveled him a look. "Then answer me this: why did *you* sign on?"

He picked up the rag I'd abandoned and used it to brush up the glass. Turning away to dump the bits into the bin, he blew out a heavy breath, "Because I was running away."

I regarded the stiff set of his beautifully broad shoulders. Handsome and brilliant, charming and lettered, he held the world in the palm of his freshly callused hand, or so it seemed to me. "What would you be running from?"

"Expectations, for starters." He faced back to me. "Your turn. Any deep dark secrets you want to get off your chest? I'm a good listener, or at least your brother seemed to think so."

I hesitated. "When the war was still on, I sometimes thought... I might hate you."

Whatever he'd expected me to say, sure it wasn't that. "What the devil for?"

I spotted a glass sliver embedded in the bar and used my newly grown-out thumbnail to pry it free, anything to keep from meeting his gaze boring down upon me. "Danny's letters were full of the great Adam Blakely. I... was jealous." I bit my lip, hating how petty and small and mean-spirited that sounded. And was. "It was always the two of us, Danny and me, no matter that a sea stood between. And suddenly, you were wedged in betwixt, larger than life. A hero."

Color flooded his face, the scar darkening. "I'm the very opposite of heroic. A coward, yellow-bellied as they come. Instead of fighting my corner, I used the war to flee my own family. Not exactly the actions of an Odysseus."

I stayed quiet, then unfamiliar with Homer's mythological hero. I only knew that my real-life one was hurting. And that, for whatever reason, his family was at the heart of it.

His gaze swept over me, settling on my face. "What I said before, about you being angry at Danny, I didn't mean it as any kind of criticism. I was angry with him too, at first. Mad as hell, as a matter of fact."

Yet another thing I hadn't expected from him. "Why?"

"Because he was the one of us to race into danger and die. Because..." He gulped down a breath, the ripple working its way down his throat, a throat I suddenly badly wanted to press my lips to. "Because I failed him."

"Sure that's not so!"

Tortured eyes met mine. "I was supposed to cover him while he took his shot, only the Spanish sharpshooters were hiding in the trees behind us. I was so busy concentrating on the hillside ahead, I didn't remember to look back. Danny paid for my carelessness. With his life. Feel free to hate me all you want. You couldn't possibly despise me more than I do myself."

I moistened my mouth, dry, despite the water I'd downed. "I don't know anything of battle, but I can't think that bullet had your name on it. It was going to strike someone. I doubt the Spaniard who fired it was all that particular about who."

A flicker of a smile answered. "Maybe you're right. Heck, I don't know much of anything anymore. But I know this: I loved Danny like a brother. Still do. From New York to Florida to Cuba, we only knew each a handful of months, and yet I feel like we lived a lifetime."

"It doesn't always take long to love someone," I said, skirting a whisper. "Sometimes a person just... knows."

Caught up in his own grief and regret, Adam didn't seem to see how I wore my heart upon my sleeve, and grateful for it I was. "We talked about how we'd stay friends once we got back to New York, meet up at McSorley's for a beer, and regale everyone with our war stories."

"Would you have?" I asked.

He shrugged. "I like to think so. Guess we'll never know."

A mad notion lifted me from my melancholy. "What if the three of us were to have that beer now? Don't look at me as though I've gone daft. We'll make a party of it, a homecoming party. For Danny."

"Your father won't mind your drinking?"

A less-than-ladylike snort escaped me. "I've been stealing sips of Guinness since I was tall enough to see above the bar, but I'll pour myself a half-pint if it makes you feel better."

He managed a smile. "Rest the hand. I'll do it."

Wary of making even more of a fool of myself than I so far had, when he brushed by me on his way to the taps, I slipped out beneath the gate and pulled out a stool.

He slid the half-pint toward me then took one of the full pours for himself. "To Danny," he said, touching his glass to mine and then to the one on the bar.

"To Danny." I lifted my glass and took a creamy sip.

Our mutual love for Danny was a bond between us and always would be. But with my eyes anchored to Adam's and his to mine, I began to believe my brother's ending might be but the start of our story.

Chapter Four

"Now that you're done with soldiering, what will you do?" I asked a while later, emboldened by the sophisticated sensibility that drinking alone together brought.

On the stool beside me, Adam had finished off his beer and was working his way through Danny's. Most of mine was growing warm in my glass, but then I didn't need it to feel intoxicated. I was already thoroughly, irredeemably drunk. On Adam.

"Go to work for my father, I guess." He shrugged as if the future didn't much matter.

"What sort of work?" I pressed, curious about the family that had such an unhappy hold over him.

"Mining, manufacturing, railroads, hotels – Dad has his fingers in a lot of pies. Someone's got to oversee it all. Someday, that'll be me."

Marking his downturned mouth, I asked, "What would you do if you could do anything, anything in the world?"

His cheeks darkened. "You'll laugh."

"I won't!"

Serious eyes settled on mine. "No, you wouldn't. But then you're not like other girls, are you?"

"I'm a *wilding*," I said, whispering the word, though there was only ourselves to hear.

He furrowed his forehead. "I'm not sure I even know what that means."

But I knew. I'd lived with the moniker all my life and only then did I own how it hurt me.

I laid my good hand atop his. "It means you can trust me. It means any secret of yours I'll carry to the grave."

Gaze on our matched hands, he admitted, "Before the war, I sold an essay to *Scribner's* and another to *Harper's*. Guess you could say I caught the writing bug."

"Danny mentioned you keeping a journal."

He nodded. "It started out as a log of our K Company's exploits. Maybe it was seeing first-hand how fragile we humans are, how quickly our mortal lives can be ended, but I began to believe that if I was lucky enough to come out of Cuba alive, I might have a book in me."

"How far along are you?"

My question drew a laugh, though not an especially happy one. "I've barely begun. And what I do have down is crap, if you'll pardon the expression."

"I don't believe that." I paused, my mind turning over the possibilities. "The diary you carry with you, that's the start of it, isn't it?"

He hesitated, his silence giving me my answer.

"It is!" Forgetting my wound, I caught at his sleeve, my fingers furling about his bicep, thrillingly firm from all the hard laboring.

"Fine, yes." His gaze dropped to his beer. "But take my word for it, it's complete chaos, the most godawful jumble of notes, random recollections, and moribund musings. I thought being laid up would speed things along, but since shipping home, I can barely string together a sentence, at least not one worth reading."

My grip on him tightened. "Writing a book, a *real* book, that touches hearts and opens minds is a grand fine thing. If you don't see it through, sure you'll spend the rest of your life soul sick with regretting."

Tender eyes took in my face. "You really are the most… spectacular girl."

Later, I would savor the compliment in private, spend hours mulling its many possible meanings, but for the present, practicality took precedence. "Maybe it's company you want for."

Sandy brows lifted. "A muse, you mean?" At my nod, "Does this mean you're volunteering for the job?"

"If it helps get your book written, then yes."

"Exactly what would your… *musely* duties involve?"

His teasing smile told me I wasn't the only one of us feeling better. "Keeping your nose to the grindstone for starters." *For starters* – another of his Yank expressions I'd adopted.

"And if I don't have a grindstone or even any particular schedule to stick to?"

"Then we'll set one."

25

"*We* will, will we?"

I aimed my bandaged hand at his chest, "Mind you, I mean to be a very stern sort of muse. No more gadabouts until you've written at least… What *is* a proper number of pages to put down in a day?"

"I don't guess there's any hard and fast rule to it. Heck, one would be one more than I've managed so far."

"Then one page a day it is. And if you set down more, I'll reward you."

The reckless remark did its work. His gaze fastened upon my mouth, and the hunger I read there was real, not feigned, I felt sure of it. "What exactly can I look forward to?"

Not for the first time, I wondered if I wasn't wading dangerously deep. "Write a second page, and I suppose you'll find out," I shot back, the cheeky response at odds with my heart's hammering.

In that instant, I admitted to myself what I'd spent the better part of the past month refusing to face. I wasn't only falling head over feet for Adam Blakely.

I'd landed.

Before I knew it, the 31st of October, Samhain Eve, the start of the ancient Celtic New Year, was upon us. During the day, we played snap apple, sprinkled the barn animals with holy water, and kicked dust beneath our shoes to ward off evil spirits and mischief-making fairies. At sunset, a bonfire was built upon the beach. Bundled against the briskness, we young people gathered about it, the spit and crackle underscoring snatches of laughter and haphazard singing, the occasional rift in the clouds revealing the stars' beacon brightness.

Standing with Adam, our hands held out to the heat, I felt a stab of sadness, and not only because winter's rough seas brought danger to our men and scarcity to our tables. The change of season must mean he'd be leaving us soon, for I had to think he was expected home for the Christmas holiday if not before.

"Bonfire's burning grand-like," I ventured, resolved to make merry whilst we still might.

"It's an impressive blaze," he agreed though his heart didn't sound much in it.

Before I could think what next to say, Úna, a girl I knew from our school days but had never much liked, ran up. "Who is it you're seeing in the fire, Moira Rose? One close by, I'll wager." She cut a look to Adam, and her lip lifted.

Mortified, I stuffed down the urge to slap her. My restraint was rewarded. Before she might say more, a lad she fancied sidled up and hooked his arm through hers, drawing her off to the dancing.

"What was that about?" Adam asked once they'd moved out of earshot.

I forced a shrug. "Staring into the bonfire on Samhain Eve's thought to bring on dreams of your future groom. Or bride."

Adam turned to me, the flames playing upon his face, filled out since he'd first come to us. "Really? What else?"

I hesitated. "A woman dropping a cutting of her hair into the fire will see the face of her future husband in the embers. A silly superstition," I was quick to add. Superstition or not, I'd slipped a cinnamon curl inside my pocket, awaiting the moment when he stepped away.

Eventually, waning flames and gusting winds drove us indoors. But the celebrating was far from finished. Young and old flocked to our pub, where there was drink aplenty as well as music – my father on his mouth organ, Colm on his fiddle, and Da's best mate, Tam McGhee on his button accordion. Tables and benches were pushed aside to make room for the dancing. Adam had scarcely shrugged free of his coat when he was captured and dragged out onto the floor by Úna, no matter that he scarcely knew the steps or that he'd only just left off using his cane. Rather than stand by and stomach her simpering, I slipped behind the bar and busied myself with passing out the poteen, our local malted barley whiskey.

It was there that Adam found me a while later. "All work and no play," he teased, giving my apron a playful pull. "You should be out dancing, not stuck back here."

I dropped my gaze to the pitcher I was toweling dry. "No one's asked me yet."

He lifted the pass-through and held out his hand. "Consider yourself asked."

If I live to reach one hundred, never will I forget the thrill of stepping into Adam's arms for that first dance. Despite it being an energetic reel, despite the mad tempo and flying feet, the spare space stuffed with sweaty-faced couples, despite Adam's missteps as he sought to master the moves we islanders had learned since crawling from the cradle, staring up into his flushed face and laughing eyes, his hands clasping mine and sometimes encircling my waist, I would have stayed there forever if I could, dancing until one or both of us dissolved to dust.

Around one o'clock, the music fell off. Da handed me the keys and went up to bed. A martyr to the drink, Colm followed, unsteady steps causing him to clasp the rail. I stayed below as guests drifted off, husbands and wives collecting sleeping children, courting couples slipping away for a final snog, bachelors helping themselves to the last of the poteen to warm the walk home. Left on my own with Adam, I couldn't have cared if every bottle and keg was drained dry.

Even now, I can't say who reached out first. One moment he was helping me gather the dirty glasses and the next, I was in his arms, my hands anchoring to his shoulders, my face lifting to his. Any hopes I'd harbored that my feelings might run no deeper than infatuation fell away the moment our mouths met. His lips moved over mine, firm yet gentle, knowing yet new, his kiss flavored with whiskey and fueled with an ardor borne of nearly two months' waiting.

I dragged my mouth from his, feeling as if my heart were cracking open and spilling forth, fragile and liquid as a soft-boiled egg. "I don't want you to leave. Not soon. Not ever."

"I don't want to go, either." He slid his hand along my spine, stalling in the hollow just above my buttocks. "But I've got to. Eventually. Just not tonight."

Dipping his head to mine, he brushed the pad of his thumb along the seam of my lips. At the first touch of his tongue, a fierce, sweet craving seized me. Giving way, I closed my eyes and let my body melt into his. An unfamiliar, thrilling hardness brushed against my lower belly. Caught up, I pressed closer, eager for more and yet unsure of what "more" might mean.

But Adam knew. He jerked back as though I'd burned him. "I shouldn't have done that."

I drew back too, feeling his words as I would a slap. "It's my first time being kissed. Next time I'll do better."

"You did... just fine." He thrust his hands into his pockets as though he didn't quite trust them to freedom.

I edged closer. "You liked it, then?"

Fierce eyes met mine. "I'm a man, aren't I? Of course I liked it. But that doesn't make it right. Or mean there can be a next time."

I studied his face, the mouth thinned to a thorny line, the eyes clouded with what I suddenly understood to be remorse. "Why not?"

He blew out a breath. "Because you're still a kid and my dead buddy's sister."

"I'll be eighteen on the eighth of December. And mind, Danny's the one who sent you."

He looked as if I had kicked him. "Because he *trusted* me."

"You make it sound like you stole that kiss. Mind I did kiss you back."

A pained look pulled at his features. "Believe me, I'm aware."

"Sure you've kissed other girls. Do you always feel so melancholic afterwards?" I fished, suddenly, absurdly jealous.

His jaw tightened. "What I've done or not done with other girls is beside the point. After what just happened, the decent thing would be to pack up and take the first ferry out of here."

Feeling as if unseen hands were wringing the blood from my heart, I countered, "The next time you try kissing me, I'll turn away, will I? Or, better yet, smack you sound-like. Pulling pints day upon day brings plenty of occasions for practicing."

His expression slid to amusement as I'd hoped it would. "All right, have it your way. I forget myself again, you deck me, deal?" He struck out his hand.

Slipping mine into his callus-toughened one, I fought the urge to hold on tight. "Deal."

That Friday, the ferry put in as usual, bringing turf and cattle, flour and porter, and, most anticipated of all, the post. Sifting through the sack spilled across the taproom floor, the rarity of a telegram caught my eye. Seeing Adam's name on it, I plucked it from the pile and passed it to him, sitting cross-legged beside me.

"Thanks." Engrossed in an angling periodical he'd ordered, he slipped the orange square into his pocket without a look. "Right now, I'm promised at the pier." He closed the magazine and got up, his hurt leg betraying barely a hint of stiffness.

"The pier?" I repeated, reaching for the Widow Murphy's latest *Godey's*.

"I offered to help Colm tar the currach before it gets any colder."

Fashioned of animal skin and framed in timber, the currach is our traditional fishing trawler, tarring it against leakage a filthy task that few look forward to.

My gaze followed him to the door. "It's glad I am to see the pair of you making peace."

Pulling on his peacoat, he shrugged. "I wouldn't call it peace exactly, but it's a start."

A start. Meaning he was reconsidering leaving? Despite sticking to his vow that our Samhain embrace remain unrepeated, he showed no signs of shunning my company.

The door squeaked closed behind him. Humming to myself, I returned to my sorting, my thoughts going to the hank of my hair I'd flung into the bonfire. Silly superstition mayhap and yet… when I'd dropped my head upon the pillow in the wee hours of All Saints' Day, I'd dreamed of a tall ship and choppy seas.

And Adam slipping a heavy metal band upon my finger.

I didn't see Adam for the rest of the day. When he did return, damp from the rain, supper had passed, the taproom but an hour from shuttering. Wiping down the bar until I feared to wear holes in it, I counted the steps it took for him to make his way over.

Reaching me, he dug inside his pocket and fished out the telegram, the paper wrinkled as an old man's face, the ink running in rivers. Heart in my throat, I took it.

Adam –(Stop)– Father gravely ill –(Stop)– Doctor thinks is his heart – (Stop)– Come home ASAP –(Stop)– Wire your arrival date from shipping co. office in Cork –(Stop)– Mother

He was being summoned home and for a reason he couldn't possibly refuse. Wordless, I handed it back.

He stuffed the sodden square back into his pocket. "Can you get away?"

Other than Tam snoozing in his seat at the settle and my father puffing upon his pipe beside him, we were left to ourselves. Fingers working my apron strings, I nodded, "I'll tell Da and fetch my shawl."

Now that the rain had let up, it was a beautiful if bracing night, the ebony sky shot with stars, the quarter moon golden as a custard, the wind howling like the legendary banshee none of us had ever set eyes upon yet spoke of as fact.

By silent assent, we set out for the wharf. Gazing out to the black bay silvered with starlight, Adam slipped his hand about mine. It was the first time he'd touched me in that way since Samhain when he'd forgotten himself so gloriously.

Linking my fingers with his, I collected my courage. "When will you go?"

Staring ahead, he answered, "There's a Cunard liner sailing from Queenstown on Wednesday. When it does, I'll be on it."

Silent, I calculated the substantial distance to be covered – the three-hour ferry crossing to the mainland and then the railway journey from Galway City to Queenstown, the nearest transatlantic port. "You'd have to set out by—"

"Monday morning." He turned to look at me, anguished eyes meeting mine.

I waited for him to say more, to swear he'd be back and soon, not only for the island and all its treasures but for myself, the girl who worshipped his shadow and had since the moment we'd met.

Instead, silence answered.

Fighting tears, I forced a smile. "That leaves us the two days. We'll make the most of them, won't we?"

Chapter Five

Adam might not have said so in words, but he cared for me as more than a friend. I knew it in my heart, felt it in my bones. Alas, our island was something of a fishbowl, privacy near to impossible. Loath to let him leave without the chance to declare himself, I hatched a scheme to take ourselves away from prying eyes, and off Inis Mór, for an afternoon.

Colm's mended currach wanted for another day to be seaworthy, the tar still soft in spots. That left the Sabbath, our busiest day at the pub, for our Sunday roast was local legend, families clamoring in once Mass finished, many staying past sunset.

I sought out Adam before bed Saturday evening. "We'll take the currach over to Inis Meáin, the next isle over," I whispered as we passed one another in the narrow upstairs hallway. "There's a writer fellow from Dublin, Mr. John Synge, who lets a room in one of the cottages there," I added, shamelessly rolling out my bait. Though the future playwright of *The Playboy of the Western World* had yet to publish aught beyond literary criticisms, he was by far the most celebrated personage in our midst.

Adam's eyes lit. Dared I hope it wasn't only the prospect of conversing with a fellow man of letters that brightened them so? "Any ideas what he's working on?"

I paused, for encountering Mr. Synge was in no way assured. Once autumn arrived, his habit was to decamp to Paris where he bided most of the year.

"A book, I suppose, same as yourself. He's keen on taking down our folklore and customs as well as learning Irish. But should we... miss him, there's a dun set upon a summit not far from the pier. On a clear day, you can see all the way back to the mainland. Oh, and the Temple of the Seven Kings and Diarmuid's Grave," I added as further enticement.

Back braced against the wattle wall, Adam studied my face, his own wearing a worried look. "Shouldn't we ask someone along?"

"A chaperone, you mean? Who exactly do you have in mind? Colm?" I added, falling back upon flippancy to cover my nervousness.

"I was thinking of another girl, a friend."

I shrugged. "I don't have many girls as friends, leastways none I'd trust not to tell." That much was truth.

He shoved away from the wall. "So, we'd be sneaking off?"

Caught out, I conceded, "If you're to leave Monday, it's your last chance to... meet Mr. Synge and have a look at those ruins."

Several times more, he raised objection to my "cloak-and-dagger" tactics, beseeching me to let him go to my father and ask proper permission, but in the end, I prevailed. "No guts, no glory," he finally said, a strange look settling upon his face.

For most of that night, I tossed and turned, torn between feverish excitement and fearful dread that something or someone would prevent our going. The next morning at breakfast, amidst spooning up the porridge, I contrived to cough. Dodging Adam's disapproving look, I claimed a cold and begged off attending mass. As a Protestant, Adam never went with us.

Once the others left, we made our way to the slip where Colm's currach was moored, the pier mostly deserted. Even wearing his fisherman's cap, knit jumper, and peacoat, Adam didn't quite pass for an islander, his smooth face and straight stance setting him apart from our men with their weather-beaten brows and stooped shoulders, the legacy of lives spent buffeted by the Atlantic's biting winds.

He took the food hamper and helped me into the trawler. "Sure Colm won't need the boat today?"

Gaze going to the rope still mooring us, I willed him to hurry. "He never takes it out on Sundays." Boating on the Sabbath, yet another rule I was breaking.

"Let's hope today doesn't prove the exception." He pulled the oilskin over my knees and turned to push us off.

The crossing was uneventful, the wind, though raw, in our favor. Adam worked the oars as though he'd been doing so all his days, and we glided into Inis Meáin under pewter skies.

Beyond an old salt digging for clams, we had the beach to ourselves. I asked him the way to Synge's cottage in Irish, for like most on Inis Meáin, he had near to no English. After some hemming and hawing, he pointed his stick to a sharp outcropping of rock.

We followed the beaten earth track through fallow fields bordered by a low-slung stone wall until we came into the main village of Lisheen, quiet, in keeping with the Sabbath. A half-hour more brought us to a cluster of stone huts, most shuttered for the season. The cottage where Mr. Synge stayed was kept by an old couple, Brid and Paidin MacDonagh. We met the husband at the gate, and he confirmed that his illustrious lodger had indeed departed for the Continent.

Turning back to Adam, I struggled down my guilt. "Are you sore disappointed?"

He shrugged. "Living in New York, there are any number of writers I can seek out if I'm so inclined, but I only have today to spend with you."

The gallant reply, so like himself, saw my step lightening and my guilt lessening. I led us westward to the far end of the island where a succession of natural terraces slanted down to Galway Bay. With Adam's leg as good as healed, we easily climbed the slope to the cliff edge known to be a favorite lookout of Mr. Synge, our breaths forming crystal clouds in the sharp air.

By the time we reached the summit, late morning had melted into midday. I pointed out Connemara, the outline of hills visible through their shrouding of silver mist, and lastly my own Inis Mór. Da and the family would be back from Mass by now. Had we and the boat been discovered missing, I wondered, and then brushed aside the worry to be dealt with later.

Rumblings from Adam's stomach broke in upon our rambles. I might have no thought for food, but he did. We'd brought the oilskin from the boat with us. Each taking a side, we spread it over a stretch of smooth rock and made ourselves comfortable whilst I laid out the lunch, including a flask of tea and a half bottle of whiskey to ward off the damp. Ever the gentleman, Adam insisted upon filling my plate and pouring my tea before serving himself.

Tearing into his sandwich of salted fish, he declared, "You've brought enough to feed an army."

Ignoring the scent of rain in the air, I nibbled my bread and cheese. "Not an army, though it's glad I am a certain soldier brought his appetite."

"*Former* soldier," he corrected, wiping his mouth with the napkin, "and a lowly volunteer at that, yet another black mark in my family's books."

"Are they truly such tartars?"

He took his time in answering, brushing crumbs from his lap. "My paternal grandfather came over from Liverpool to make his fortune, though no one in the family will concede to such common stock now. Mother, however, is a Van Cleese – very proper, very fine. Traces her lineage to the seventeenth-century Dutch who first settled New York – New Amsterdam then."

I couldn't help smiling for what passed as ancient in America seemed nearly new to ourselves. "Our pub was built in the 1500s, and none of us give it a thought, save for when the roof leaks."

Adam chuckled. "I'll take the damp over the frosty civility of good society any day." He broke an oatcake in half and passed me part. "Despite Mother's boast-worthy breeding, she wasn't as fecund as might be wished. There's just me and my sister. If we'd had a brother, he could be the scion."

"And yourself?"

His eyes took on a fevered sheen as if he were tipsy, though thus far, we'd staunched our thirst with tea only. "I'd gladly get by on thin soup and stale bread, living the life of bohème and loving every minute of it."

Daring to see myself in that garret with him, sharpening his pencils and making banquets of our love, I asked, "Why don't you?"

His gaze dimmed. "As the 'son' in Blakely & Son, I'm stuck following my father into the family business as he followed his."

"And your book?"

Thus far, he had a full forty pages set out in his neat, spare script. Based upon the bits he'd let me read, I didn't doubt that once finished, the novel would find a publisher and be a brilliant success, himself lifted to the likes of Nathaniel Hawthorne, Washington Irving, and Mark Twain. Granted, I wasn't close to impartial, or any sort of critic, but I saw the light of him shining through those precious pages, his passion and humor, pain and goodness writ large for a waiting world to laud.

He shrugged. "Relegated to a hobby, I guess."

"Oh, Adam, no."

"Until now, my *scribblings*, as my mother is fond of saying, have been suffered with strained tolerance born of the certainty that I'll fail miserably, give up of my own accord and fall in step."

By then, the oatcake was dust in my fingers. I snared his gaze and said, "But you'd never be happy shut away in an office. You'd... die. Maybe not your body but sure your soul would."

35

Tender eyes took me in. "They don't see it that way. Making money, mounds of it, is what matters in their world. It's *all* that matters. But not to you. Never to you. You really aren't like any girl I've ever known before. I wish we'd met sooner. I wish…"

I leaned closer, as good as feeling his lips upon mine. "What do you wish?"

A fat raindrop struck the bridge of my nose, and we both snapped back.

Adam darted a look to the darkening sky. "Right now, for this rain to hold off."

He rose and walked to the cliff edge. Feeling like I'd awoken from a beautiful but too-brief dream, I followed him over. We peered over the side, a fierce, wet wind slapping our faces, the bay frothing and roaring like a great, cornered beastie, the beach slimmed to a narrow band blanketed by foam, the bruised sky pregnant with purple clouds poised to burst.

He turned back to me. "With luck, we'll make it back to those cottages before the storm breaks and wait it out there."

We packed quickly, the angry air lashing my skirts and ripping the caps from our heads. When we'd finished, Adam took the hamper in one hand and mine in his other. Hands laced, we started down, soles skidding on the wet limestone.

Halfway down, the heavens opened, the pellets striking our skin like stinging bees. Bursts of lightning split the pitch-hued sky, the booms vibrating in our breasts. Though Adam uttered not one word of complaint or recrimination, his hitching gait told me his leg was weakening. More than once, the wind got up beneath me. If not for Adam anchoring me, sure I'd have been carried over the side, my body broken to bits on the rocks below, my story ended.

But like blue sky breaking through the blackness, all at once, my memory dawned. Sliding my hand along the rock facing, I felt about for the hidden hollow. Just as I was about to give up, the rude opening revealed itself. I jogged Adam's arm to show him, and the soldier in him snapped to. He took out his army knife and hacked through the moss and lichen.

"I'll go first," he shouted, dropping down and pushing through.

Fixing a hand to his back, I followed him in.

Darkness entombed us, and with it, a thick mossy scent that, in my terror, tasted of the grave. Suddenly, the earthworks opened, and we fell hard upon our knees. Brushing clumps of wet clay from our clothing, we stood, squinting into the darkness. The cave chamber was squatter than I recalled it being, but then, I wasn't twelve any longer. The conical ceiling scarcely cleared my crown, Adam's not at all.

Hunching, he doffed his cap and drained off the water. "How'd you know about this place?"

"Danny brought me here before he left for America."

Now that our grisly end was no longer a given, my thoughts fled forward. Even were the storm to subside, there'd be no making it back to the north island that night. As much as the sharp chill and my soaked clothing, that fact and its consequences set my teeth to knocking.

Adam reached into his coat pocket and fished out a box of matches, sodden as the rest of us. "Damn," he said, the single curse summing all my guilt and frustration, for though he was too polite to point it out, I alone had maneuvered us here.

But there would be ample opportunity later for lamenting my lunacy. For then, I helped him gather whatever dry wood we could find. He arranged the lot into a pyre, then dropped to his knees and began chafing two twigs together at a furious clip. Tucking my wet skirts, I sat beside him. We lapsed into silence, fixing upon the sticks he never let up on. All at once, they flickered and sparked as if touched by devil's breath. He used them to light the pyre, then stoked it a while more 'til a proper fire took hold.

Only then did he sit back, his gaze going to me. "Better get out of those wet things."

I hesitated, courage curdling. Despite the desire I'd glimpsed in some men's eyes, a part of me still saw myself as the "freckled, skinny fencepost" Danny had described, only now with dripping hair and bluing flesh.

But Adam was insistent. "You don't consider catching a chill in the tropics until it's hurricane season and you're camping rough and the rain's rolling down in sheets. I've seen men hale and hearty felled with fever after a night's soaking. This is no time for modesty."

He was right, more so than he yet realized. Ruined already as I reckoned myself to be, clothed or naked hardly mattered.

I surrendered with a nod, surprised to feel my legs stiffened to blocks beneath me. A few paces carried me to the far side of the cave. Turning away, I peeled off my coat, frock, petticoats, and my heretofore secret vanity, the cone-shaped "bust improver", which I slipped beneath the pile. Parting with my corset took a bit more doing. My numb fingers made for slow going, but being "skinny as a fencepost" brought the advantage of looser lacings.

That left my combination, a single garment of sleeveless camisole and knee-length knickers, the latter cinched beneath my knees by a frill of lace, the damp cream-colored cloth rendering me nearest to nude. Reaching down to unsnap my garters, I saw that not only my nipples and areolas but also my... *Mound of Venus* showed plainly through! Sending up a silent prayer that the flimsy fabric would dry quickly, I braced my right heel upon a ledge of rock and rolled off my stocking, the wet white cotton mud-spattered and clinging like paste. I got it off and stared on the left leg, little suspecting how my "scantily clad silhouette" cavorting upon the cave wall contributed to Adam's agony. Finished, I rejoined him.

Stripped down to his flannels, he squatted over the smoking fire, his good leg raised at the knee and free arm draped across his thigh as a screen for my sensitive eyes, or so I would later learn. Stirring a stick about the fledgling flames, he didn't seem to see me. Like mine, his underclothing was slicked to him, the short-sleeved vest bearing witness to the broad shoulders and sculpted biceps heretofore only hinted at, the above-the-knee drawers displaying leanly muscled legs and a side of taut buttock.

I raised my regard to safer terrain and cleared my throat.

He moved over to make room, his own gaze trained upon the fire. "It's no Samhain bonfire but it's something."

He'd spread the oilskin over the ground as a buffer against the dirt and damp. I tucked my legs and settled in beside him, damp coat overtop.

Holding my hands out to the warmth, I asked, "Did you learn fire-making in the army?"

"It was only the *reserve* army and no, long before that. My uncle used to take me camping in the Adirondacks when I was a kid. Fishing, canoeing, living off the land – growing up, those summers were all I lived for. I'll do the same when I have kids someday."

He took the whiskey from the hamper and passed it to me. Brooding upon the beautiful babies together we might make, I brought the bottle to my mouth and tipped it back. The healthy swallow was more than I was used to. Warmth rippled through me, my tongue and throat instantly, pleasantly afire, my brain buzzing like a hive of drowsy bees. I might have ventured more but before I could, Adam took the bottle back and drew his own coat over us.

The nearness, born of necessity, soon became more. With the loamy scent of ancient stones mingling with the peat smoke and the musk of our own warming bodies, Inis Mór and the world beyond it felt no nearer than the moon. I shifted to face him. Our mouths met as if magnets. Framing my face between his hands, he deepened the kiss, his tongue testing mine. Our previous Samhain interlude had but whetted my appetite. Eager to learn his texture and taste, I met him stroke for stroke, not satisfied 'til he shuddered against me.

He pulled back and rested his forehead against mine. "You're playing with fire, Rose. We both are."

Though the inside of my mouth was sawdust dry, other heretofore unacknowledged bodily parts were profoundly, shamefully moist. "Willing I am to burn if you are." Calling upon every kernel of courage I possessed, I shrugged free of the cover.

Adam's awed gaze swept over me, raw with wanting, terrible in its tenderness. "Are you sure about this, Rose? Really and completely certain?"

I took hold of his hands and guided them to my camisole-clad breasts. "I've never been surer of anything in all my days."

Cupping me, he let out a shaky laugh. "But then you haven't lived all that many days, have you, which makes me an unconscionable cad."

Near to naked though I was, I forced up my chin. "I may be young, but I know my own mind. And heart."

"You do, don't you?" He glided his fingertips over me, the glancing caresses feathering my flesh with delicious tingles. "Once I'm gone, promise you won't hate me?"

He still meant to leave, to take his place in a great, glittering world I had no part in. But for this moment, this night, he was all mine.

I locked my gaze upon his. "I could never hate you."

If I live to be a hundred, never will I forget the simple beauty of that night – the savor of salt on Adam's lips as his mouth moved against mine, the look in his eyes when he slipped a buffering arm beneath me, the weight and warmth of his palm settling betwixt my splayed thighs, the shock of sheer delight when he first fitted himself to me, the swift, piercing pain giving way to a beautiful, bruised belonging. All the while he spoke to me in soft, soothing tones, calling me his sweetheart, his Eve, and lastly and most wonderfully, his love, plying my breached body with kisses and caresses, each thrust and flick of his thumb winding me ever tighter until finally, gloriously, I uncoiled, a keening wail trumpeting my delight. He joined me, calling out my name and sinking deep into me, his damp face falling to the curve of my shoulder, his fast-beating heart a mate for my own.

Chapter Six

Afterward, we lay in each other's arms, my head pillowed upon Adam's shoulder, our dried coats serving as blankets. Thinking back to my minutes-ago outburst, I knew my first blushes since parting with my purity.

Staring into smoky shadow, I found my voice. "That terrible keening I let out, I didn't mean to make such a fuss."

Raising himself up on his elbow, Adam regarded me a long moment, expression at turns tender and amused. "Sweet baby, don't you know you *making a fuss* is the whole point, not to mention about the best-damned compliment you can give a man?"

I hadn't known. But then how would I have?

"Truth is, I'm looking forward to what other delicious sounds you'll make once we get *really* good at this," he added, the devil's own grin lighting his face.

I reached out to swat him when it struck me. "Adam?"

Solemn-faced, he took hold of my hand and pulled me to sit up beside him. "Moira Rose O'Neill, will you do me the honor of becoming my wife?"

The yearned-for words were like a lit match to my guilt, for though it was my conniving that had marooned us here, I was no mantrap. "I won't see you sacrifice yourself for my sake."

He pierced me with a sharp, shocked look. "*Sacrifice* myself?"

I bit my bottom lip, still tender from his kisses.

His frown slid back to a smile. "Sweetheart, don't you know by now I'm head over heels for you? And not just for that pretty face and luscious body," he added, dropping a kiss atop my bare shoulder. "I was halfway to being in love before I ever laid eyes on you."

"The letters?"

He nodded. "Those weeks I was laid up in that field hospital on Long Island, I must have reread them a least a hundred times. Your letters to Danny saved me, Rose. *You* saved me." Taking both my hands in his, he drew me to him as though I were a lifeline indeed.

"We saved each other," I said with feeling, for I didn't like to think what state I'd be in had he forsworn his vow to Danny and stayed in the States.

His stark gaze scoured my face. "Even if I'd never made Danny any promise, even if there'd been no rosary box to return, I like to think I'd have found some excuse for getting myself to you. You're my soulmate, after all."

His declaration was beyond my most dizzying dreams. I launched myself against him, showering his lips and throat with clumsy kisses.

Pulling back, he swept his adoring gaze over me, making me feel more a fairytale princess than the barmaid I was. "Am I safe in taking that as a yes?"

"Yes, yes, *yes!*" I threw my arms about his neck, too caught up to care that the coat covering slipped indecently downward.

He let out a whoop and kissed me again, a long, deep draft that left both of us breathless. "Oh, Rose, my sweet, loyal girl, with you at my side, I know I can make a success of... *everything!*"

He tore off his university ring, reached for my left hand, and slipped the heavy, engraved circlet onto my finger. The band swam on me just as it had in my Samhain dream.

"It's a shabby offering, I know. Soon as we get to New York, I'll buy you the biggest, most perfect diamond Tiffany & Company has to offer."

I shook my head, the happy tears skittering across my cheeks. "All I want for is yourself, loving me as you do now."

The look he sent me had me feeling as if I'd stumbled upon Solomon's gold. "Swear you'll stay like you are now, sweet and unspoiled? Swear Manhattan won't change you?"

For the first time since accepting his proposal, I hesitated. "But it must, mustn't it, otherwise I've no hope of fitting in and making you proud."

"I couldn't possibly be any prouder, only..." His eyes dimmed. "If Dad really is on his last leg, springing a bride on him might push him over the edge, Mother too. Probably better if I go on ahead and pave the way. You understand, don't you?"

I suffered a stab of unease, my first since the storm had stranded us. "Of course I do, only... Must we be parted for long, do you think?"

42

He gave my hand a reassuring squeeze. "A month, six weeks tops, to square things, then I'll send for you." His gaze searched mine. "I'm asking a lot, I know. You'll be leaving behind your home and family for a place the exact opposite of how things are here."

Mad in love as I was, resolved we would be perfectly, gloriously happy, I summoned a smile. "Don't you know by now I'd follow you to the ends of the earth?"

"Darling girl." He caught my wrist and kissed it. Lips lingering on the tender inside, he fixed his gaze upon my face. "Not the ends of the earth, more's the pity. To most who live there, New York's more like the center of the universe."

Alas, we couldn't remain happy castaways forever.

"Do you think we'll ever come back?" I asked Adam early the next morning, closing the lid on the picnic hamper from which we'd broken our fast.

"Let's hope not." He rolled his shoulders. "Those rocks make for rough going."

I cast a sentimental eye to the oilskin, our bridal bower, or so I saw it. "I'd think you'd have some fond feelings."

"Course I do." He helped me to my feet, hands keeping hold of mine. "But I am very much looking forward to being with you in a real bed, a big, feather-stuffed four-poster. In New York."

"It'll fit in the garret, will it?" I asked, only partway teasing.

His smile clouded. "We'll have to wait and see about that."

We stepped out to clear skies and calm waters. Miraculously, the currach was where we'd moored her and seemingly in one piece. Closer inspection revealed a pinkie-sized hole in her hull. Adam used his army knife to cut up bits of the oilcloth, which we used as a temporary plug.

"So long as we take it slow and bail as we go, she should hold to Inis Mór," he assured me, pushing off from the pier.

Sitting across from him as he rowed, myself busy with the bucket, I steeled myself to weather a different sort of storm. Wounded war hero or not, Danny's best mate or not, Adam stood to be gutted and filleted like a fish once we put in. I said as much, but he waved off my worries.

"I met plenty of fellows like Colm during the war. Strong as oxen and just as stubborn. A man like that makes a hell of a fighter, not only because he's big but because he's loyal. I can handle myself with the Colms of the world. Strange as it sounds, I admire their honesty."

I finished dumping the pail over the side before saying, "It won't matter whose idea it was to sneak off. It's yourself he'll come at."

"I wouldn't respect him if he didn't. You're his sister, after all. But it won't come to blows, I promise."

One of the fishermen must have sighted us and signaled back to shore, for we pulled in to find Colm and my father waiting at the pier. Mounting the wooden steps, I took in their haggard faces and rumpled clothing and felt a stab of guilt.

Da took me in his arms. "Lass, I thought sure you were drowned." Releasing me, he slung his gaze to Adam, who'd come up behind me. "If you've done aught harm to my girl, I'll murder you with my own hands, and they can hang me for it after." He held out his hands, still broad of back, lethal looking, despite the gnarled fingers.

Colm stepped up to Adam. "Give me one reason I shouldn't break your fookin' neck?"

For a fitful moment, I thought he meant to shove Adam into the shallow water. Not about to give him the chance, I stepped between them. "Going off on our own was my idea entirely."

Adam faced my father. "We were in the wrong to deceive you, and for that, you have my sincere apology. But you should know I love Rose and mean to make her my wife."

My father looked to me. "This is true, child?"

"It is." Before leaving the cave, I'd taken the ribbon from my hair and used it to tie Adam's token about my neck. I lifted it from my collar then, revealing the ring.

Colm was the first to recover. "Grand. I'll row to the mainland and fetch the priest."

I shook my head. "Adam's been called home. His father's grave ill, mayhap dying. He must leave today if he's to make the next ship for New York."

Colm snorted. "Wheesh, that's neat, isn't it?"

I wheeled on him, "It's truth! I saw the telegram with my own eyes."

Gaze on Adam, Da said, "You love my girl, do you?"

"With all my heart," Adam replied without pause, the words warming me, though by then, I had heard them many times.

"And you mean to bring her over to America as your bride?"

44

Solemn-eyed, Adam inclined his head. "Just as soon as I see to my father, I'll send the remittance for Rose's passage, you have my word." He held out his hand. "Do we have your blessing, sir?"

An agonizing moment passed, my suitor and father locking eyes, Adam's outstretched arm unwavering. "You do." Clasping Adam's hand at last, Da looked over to Colm, fuming but beaten. "Let us back to the pub to toast the happy couple."

Later that morning, the six of us stood at the ferry landing, Colm stony-eyed and still seething, Killian, sleepy-faced and sporting pillow creases upon his cheek. And Adam. He'd changed into the traveling suit he'd worn the night of his arrival. Seeing him in his city clothes, the past two months seemed almost a dream.

Da, bless himself, stepped into the awkward silence. "Colm, lad, shake hands with your soon-to-be brother-in-law and wish him Godspeed, for I'll see the pair of you part as friends."

I tensed as Colm wrapped his big hand about Adam's and leaned in until they stood nearly nose-to-nose. "Make no mistake, Yank, if aught ill befalls her, I'll cross that great pond and murder you meself."

Killian came up next. "You'll bring Rose back to visit, won't you, Adam?"

Adam laid a hand upon Kil's shoulder. "You bet I will, sport. And you'll come and stay with us in New York."

Eyeing the approaching ferry, Da herded my brothers away. "Come along, lads. We'll leave the lovebirds to themselves."

Once they'd stepped away, the brave face I'd worn to the pier crumbled. Clutching Adam's coat front, I shook my head. "A month, maybe six weeks, how will I bear it?"

He gathered me against him. "The time'll fly, you'll see."

I didn't believe that but then neither, I think, did he.

I hesitated, gnawing at my lip. "You should know that other than the bit set aside for Dublin, there's no... no dowry." Not for the first time since accepting his proposal, I worried what his family would think of me, a penniless barmaid with but one pair of shoes to her name.

Gaze tender, he shook his head. "Don't you know by now you *are* my gold?"

He tipped up my chin and brushed his mouth over mine. I kissed him soundly, letting myself pretend the embrace was of greeting, not goodbye.

The ferry horn called us back to ourselves. Out of the side of my eye, I saw the gangplank lowering and stifled a sob. "You'll write, won't you?"

Adam held me at arm's length as if mapping my every feature and freckle. "Every day, pages and pages until you're sick of hearing from me." He released me and reached for his traveling trunk. "Goodbye, darling."

I caught at his sleeve. "Not goodbye. It's bad luck. Better we say go safely for now."

He lapsed into the crooked smile I couldn't get sufficient of. "Is that any luckier?"

I thought a moment. "Sure, it's less... permanent."

"All right, sweetheart, 'go safely for now' it is." He dropped a last kiss upon my lips and turned to board.

Nursing tears, I didn't hear Colm come up until he stood directly behind me. "A man such as that one can tell as many lies as four men when he wants something, or *someone.*"

Wound tight as a top, I whirled on him. "That's my betrothed you're speaking against, and brother or no, I won't hear another word. Instead of spoiling my happiness, it's your own affairs you ought to be sorting. Nuala O'Grady won't wait forever. It's a mercy the poor girl hasn't given up ere now and taken the veil."

I had the satisfaction of seeing him turn the purple of a pickled turnip. "Is it a sin to want the best for my only sister?"

"Adam is the best. He's a dream come true."

Colm's eyes drilled into mine. "The thing with dreams, little sister, is sooner or later you've to wake up."

Chapter Seven

Manhattan, New York City
November 24 – Thanksgiving Day
"Adam?" Beatrice Blakely speared her son with a look. "Have you heard a word I've said?"

Adam paused in pushing a candied yam about his plate. "I did, Mother. You received a postcard. From Paris. Vanessa and her parents will be back. For Christmas. I wasn't aware you required a response. Your question about it being 'splendid news' struck me as rhetorical."

She set her silverware on the side of her plate with a sigh. "You've been crabby from the cradle, but ever since Ireland, you're positively abominable to be around. And for heaven's sake, eat your turkey. It's unnatural to subsist on fish alone. Tell him, Horatio." She cast a plaintive look to her husband at the other end of the massive, polished mahogany table.

Recovered from what had turned out to be a bilious attack brought on by an exceptionally volcanic ulcer, Adam's father ladled more gravy onto his plate. "Tomorrow, you'll join me for lunch at Delmonico's. A good bloody steak is just the thing to put the color in your cheeks."

"Any ruddier and people will mistake him for a farmer," she protested. "And those hands, I can't bear to think what you did to create such calluses."

Adam reached for his patience – and his wine glass. "Honest labor, Mother. To my best knowledge, it's never killed anyone." Done with the pretense of eating, done with pretense at all, he divided his gaze between them. "I have an announcement, and I guess now's as good a time as any."

"Please don't tell us there's another war on," Beatrice pleaded. "There isn't, is there?" She darted a look to her husband, who shook his head.

Adam girded himself. "I'm staying put – and getting married."

His mother met the news with a blinding smile. "I'm so relieved you're seeing sense at last! We'll start planning the moment Vanessa's back."

"I'm not marrying Vanessa."

Her face froze. "If this is some sort of—"

"It's no joke. The girl I'm marrying is Rose. Miss Moira Rose O'Neill."

"*O'Neill?*" His father glared over his glass of claret. "Have your Bridget on the side if you must, but the Carlston girl is the one you're wedding."

Adam squared his shoulders. "No, sir, she's not."

Beatrice lifted her water glass and took a swift sip. "We had an agreement. We would indulge you with this last overseas jaunt, and you would propose to Vanessa as soon as you returned."

Horatio tore the napkin from his collar. "Vanessa's a fine-looking girl, bloodlines of a thoroughbred. If I were a young man in your shoes—"

"But you're not, are you?" Adam snapped. "You've lived your life. You *are* living it. Shouldn't I have the freedom to do the same?"

A snort answered. "In my day, we didn't demand our freedom. We did our *duty*. When I was your age, I stayed put on my native soil, married your mother, and took up the reins of my father's business so our children, and theirs, would have a legacy of which they might be rightfully proud. So *you* would have a legacy. Is this how you repay me, frittering away your university education scribbling sonnets and now this – proposing to some Irish trollop?"

Adam felt his temper spiking. "Rose is no trollop, Dad. And I don't scribble sonnets. I write *novels*." It was only the one novel, the draft nowhere near complete, though since returning, he'd stayed faithful to our custom of sitting down to write at least one page every morning.

Face mottling, Horatio stabbed a finger into the air. "You can't feed yourself on dreams, my boy, much less a family. Break things off with Vanessa, and you'll find yourself turned out without a red cent."

Beatrice gasped. "Horatio, please, it's Thanksgiving!"

"Holiday or not, I'm done with mollycoddling his mulishness. He marries Vanessa, or he's out." He got up and limped to the doorway, gouty leg dragging. "If I must, I'll hand Blakely & Son over to Bess's husband when the time comes."

"That's a capital plan, Dad," Adam called after him. "Give it all to Roger, lock, stock, and barrel. You'll be doing me a favor."

The door slammed.

Adam shoved away from the table, prepared to go upstairs and fling his few things into the traveling case. The time on Inis Mór had taught him how little he needed to get by on. What better time than the present to put the lesson to use?

Beatrice fitted a hand to her forehead. "Do sit down so we can talk this over rationally."

"What's left to talk about?"

"If you've set your sights on this… Irish girl…"

Adam subsided into his seat. "She has a name – *Rose*."

"Very well, if you're certain this… Rose is the right girl for you—"

"She's the *only* girl for me."

"Then give me time to smooth things over with your father. He'll be brought around. Eventually."

Still skeptical, he said, "I thought you had your heart set on Vanessa too."

"It's no secret I'm very fond of her, but you're my flesh and blood. There isn't anything I wouldn't do for you. I only ask one thing in return."

He steeled himself. "What's that?"

"Hold off on sending for your Irish bride, your… Rose until you can speak to Vanessa in person. Yours aren't the only feelings at stake, you know. Surely, the daughter of our dearest friends deserves to hear the news from you and not some society wag?"

Adam paused. Eager as he was to send for me, "paving the way" was, after all, the point of his returning on his own. "All right, I'll wait until I can tell Vanessa face to face. But the minute I do, I'm sending for Rose."

"Of course." She reached over and patted the top of his hand. "Now, don't look so glum. Scowling only makes that unfortunate scar stand out. If yours is indeed a love match, what difference can a few weeks possibly make?"

Inis Mór
December 8 – Rose's 18th Birthday
"Jaysus, how many weeks along are you?" my sister-in-law, Keira demanded. Digging into her apron pocket, she pulled out a handkerchief and passed it to me.

I lifted my head from the bucket holding the better part of my birthday breakfast and took it. "Not a month even. But it was only the one night and my first time."

Keira rolled her eyes. "And how many times do you imagine it takes?" she asked, helping me to my feet. "I've seen something was off with you from the moment we got here."

Visiting from Dublin with Ronan and their little boy, Keira was the only other woman in our household and the only female in whom I dared confide. Leaning on her, I gained the edge of the bed and sat. Now that she'd called me out, the bouts of nausea, sensitivity to smells, and tenderness in my breasts took on sudden, frightful meaning. And then there was the canniest clue of all.

I'd missed my monthly.

In luring Adam to Inis Meáin, I'd played at a woman's game, but in so many ways, I was a child still. Adam had warned we were trifling with fire. Mayhap I should have listened.

I snatched my mother's Bible from the bedside table and shoved it toward her. "Swear you won't tell a soul."

She drew back. "As if I would."

Steadying my gaze upon hers, I kept the Bible out.

She gave in, laying her hand atop the cracked leather cover. "Fine, I swear."

I took the holy book back and collapsed against the headboard. "Oh, Keira, what am I to do?"

"The only thing you can do." She dropped down beside me. "Take yourself to America, quick as you can."

I stared down at my bare toes, too ashamed to admit the truth.

She took hold of my chin and turned my face up to hers. "His last letter, when was it?"

Swallowing my shame, I admitted, "He sent a telegram from the ship, but nothing since. I've posted two letters of my own but... his father's taken sick, dying mayhap. Still, not a word in all these weeks! And himself a *writer*."

She released her pinching grip but not her eyes, which held fast to mine. "Then you'd best write again, and mind you don't mince words. If his father's dead, he's dead; if he's dying, then that's that. Either way, your man made you a promise. It's up to you to hold him to it."

Her common-sense advice was the antidote to my weepiness. "You're right."

"Tell me something I *don't* know. Now dry your eyes and have a lie-down. I'll bring up tea and biscuits to help settle your stomach. And try not to fret yourself. It's bad for the baby." She got up to go.

On impulse, I called her back. "You won't be thinking less of me now that I'm... ruined?"

"Don't be daft! Did you never wonder how it is our Conall came in seven months, not nine?" Smiling, she let herself out into the hallway.

Left alone, I took out the pen and paper purchased from a fancy stationer on Grafton Street. Pulling a chair up to my sewing table, I gathered myself and began:

My dearest, darling Adam,

I have the grandest surprise, the most wonderful news...

Cunard Berth, Pier 54, New York Harbor

"Check again – this time, try *Moira* Rose O'Neill," Adam demanded, scanning the cabin-class passengers stepping off the steamship barge. Whenever a Cunard or White Star passenger liner called, he'd rushed down to the Battery to meet it. Despite posting the remittance for my passage weeks ago, he'd yet to hear from me.

The purser shook his head. "No O'Neill listed anywhere in cabin class."

"There must be some mistake, a misspelling, maybe?"

"Afraid not, sir. Logged in the names myself."

Adam pressed a fist to his forehead. "Try Blakely."

The man's eyes widened. "Spelled same as yours, is it?"

"Just look, will you!"

More shuffling of ledger sheets and then, "No 'Blakely' either. Will there be anything else, sir?"

"No... thanks." Adam took out his money clip, peeled off a dollar, and passed it over.

"Cheers." The seaman slipped the bill into his pea coat. Eyeing Adam, he hesitated, then added, "You wouldn't be the first to pay some jilt's passage."

Turning away, Adam didn't answer.

His carriage was close by, curbed at the intersection of Broadway and Whitehall Streets. He cut through Battery Park, the trees stripped down to sticks, the path littered with dry, dead leaves. No, not littered – *paved*. The crunching sound beneath his soles seemed to admonish him further. If only he might transport himself back to early November, there'd be no brave-faced goodbyes on the Kilronan pier, no returning to New York alone to "pave the way." Given a second chance, he'd find his courage from the first and bring me over as his bride, to hell with his stuffed-shirt family.

"Yoo-hoo, *A-dam*!"

He swung about to a slender female in a plum-colored carriage costume, picking a path toward him. Vanessa Carlston.

Adam met her midway. "Vanessa, what are you doing down here?"

"Don't I merit a 'welcome home' at least?" she asked, pulling a pout.

"Sorry, welcome back. How was Paris?"

"Sublime," she said, the word punctuated by a dramatic draw of breath.

"I'll bet. I'd give an eye tooth to see Mr. Eiffel's tower up close. Did you get to take one of the lifts to the top?" Built on the Champ du Mars as the gateway to the 1889 World's Fair, the four-legged iron latticework pyramid soared more than one thousand feet, dwarfing all other constructions in the city.

"That awful eyesore! We passed by in the carriage when it was illuminated for night, but I hardly cared to stop, let alone go up inside the vulgar thing."

Adam's eye went to her hat of purple-dyed rooster feathers, silk flowers, and faux fruit, and he fought down a less-than-kind laugh.

"The shopping was divine," she barreled on. "We came back with trunks and trunks. Oh, and the best part, we brought back one of the girls from the hotel to be my new lady's maid. Mademoiselle Bellerose is a marvel with hair and so clever with clothes. I can't think how I ever got on without her. She did say what Bellerose means in English, but I forget."

"Beautiful Rose," Adam said, swallowing against his throat's sudden thickening. "You never said what brings you downtown to Bowling Green."

"I've just come from touring my namesake. Papa's newest ship, he's christened her *The Vanessa*." Beneath the rich brocade, her narrow chest puffed ever so slightly.

"That's terrific. Congratulations."

Her father, Andrew, kept an office in Steamship Row. Adam had as good as forgotten. Still, finding her here, unescorted, struck him as strange. It *was* strange. For well-bred women such as Vanessa, venturing below 14th Street simply wasn't done, no matter that the funds for French lessons and debutante balls and shopping trips to Ladies' Mile came from the very warehouses, gasworks, and shipyards they were expected to shun.

"You must ask him to have his captain take you aboard. He's positively perishing to show her off."

"Another time, thanks. I'm on my way home. Can I drop you somewhere?" he asked, dreading her answer.

"What a lifesaver you are! I sent the carriage back to Mother, thinking I'd come home with Papa, only he's stuck in some dull old meeting." She hooked her arm through his.

Thinking wistfully of our rambles, Adam shortened his stride to match her mincing steps.

She cast him a sideways smile. "Your limp, it's scarcely noticeable now."

"Exercise, not lying about turned out to be the cure. I gave up the cane... while I was in Ireland."

She mulled that a moment. "You were gone quite a bit longer than you'd said. Two whole months. I put Papa and Mama off on going to Paris for as long as I could but finally—"

"You were right to go," he cut in, for he hadn't wanted her to wait for him, not even then.

He had his landau in sight. Brewster Green, it was hard to miss, a standout from the black carriages and dun-colored commercial carts lining the curbside. He'd had it repainted a couple of months before signing on for Cuba, the bold color choice an act of rebellion back when such silliness had still seemed to matter.

He handed her up, then crossed to the driver's side and climbed in.

She settled the carriage blanket over her knees and turned to face him. "You can kiss me if you like. We're as good as engaged, after all."

He braced himself with a brisk breath. "We need to talk."

Topaz-blue eyes pinned his. "My, you do sound serious."

"I am. What I have to say I've put off for too long."

Her features froze except for her mouth, the smile slipping away like the icing on a cake set out in the summer sun. "Very well, if you're determined to break my heart, get on with it."

"How did you—"

"Know?" A brittle laugh and then, "How could I *not* know? I've been back for more than a week, and you've yet to call."

"I can't go through with marrying you, Vanessa. I thought I could, but I can't."

Her mouth flattened. "You make marrying me sound like going to war, only you *like* going to war."

He regarded the reins looped about his glove. "I can't tell you how sorry I am about... well, everything."

She picked at the sable edging her sleeve. "Sorry? That's rich. When you

53

ran off to Cuba, I stood by you, waited for you, *defended* you no matter what anyone said. When you came home, lice-riddled and filthy, wounded and fevered, I sat by your bedside. When you left for Ireland, I waited again. It sometimes feels, Adam, as though I've waited for you my whole life."

He forced his gaze back to her stony one. "To be fair, I never asked you to."

"Maybe not in so many words, but your father assured mine you'd come up to scratch just as soon as you got back. And your mother predicted we'd be announcing our engagement at Christmas and marrying after Easter. All the shopping in Paris was for my *trousseau!*"

"I never meant to hurt or mislead you. If nothing else, I hope you'll believe that."

She raised her chin to the road ahead. "Before you left for Ireland, you were set to marry me, and now you're not. You met someone over there, didn't you?"

Adam hesitated. She was cannier than he'd credited.

"At the very least, I deserve to hear who it is you're throwing me over for."

"There is… someone, a girl from the Arans, the sister of a fellow soldier, a friend, who didn't make it back. Falling in love wasn't anything we planned, it just… happened. Before I left, I asked her to marry me."

Pale brows lifted. "Marry a Bridget? Is this some sort of joke?"

He sent her a leveling look. "I've never been more serious in my life. And her name is Rose."

"*Rose.*" Her mouth pursed as though she tasted something bitter. "What do your parents have to say about all this?"

"Mother's coming around to the idea. Dad, too." It was a week since his father last threatened to cut him off – progress even if, second to me, disinheritance was his dearest dream. "Trust me, before long, you'll see this for the lucky escape it is."

"Lucky for you, perhaps. I'm the one left out in the cold."

"How do you figure that? We never made any announcement. Heck, I didn't even get around to giving you a ring."

"There may not be a formal engagement, but everyone expects it. Oh, you'll be fine, men always are, but I… I shall be leavings. *Your* leavings." Eyes filling, she rifled through her handbag for a hankie.

For the first time since they were kids at Bailey's Beach and her nanny slapped her bottom for dirtying her dress, Adam felt sincerely sorry for her. It wasn't her fault her parents and his had pushed her into his path since he'd traded short pants for trousers. She was as much a pawn to their matchmaking as he, more so. As a female, she wasn't free to chart her own course, not to Cuba or Ireland, or anywhere else.

Feeling like a heel, he said, "What can I do to make it up to you?"

Dabbing at her eyes, she said, "The Bellevue Hospital charity ball is Friday. Your mother assured mine we could count on you as my escort, and it's too late to come up with anyone else."

"I'll do it. I'll go." Inspiration struck, and he added, "And I'll do you one better. What if I make myself out to be drunk and... jealous? And you flirt and fill up your dance card and say how you wouldn't marry me if I was the last bachelor on earth. That way, I'll be *your* leavings."

Scrunching the hankie in her hand, she looked over. "You'd do that?"

"I would. I *will*." He stopped there, studying her. For a girl who'd just been jilted, she seemed to be recovering at a remarkable rate. "But afterward, we go our separate ways, agreed?"

The smile slanting her mouth didn't quite reach her eyes, but at least the latter were clearing. "Yes, of course."

Relieved, he drew back on the reins and flicked the whip. "Capital, I'll come for you at six o'clock."

Chapter Eight

The ferry upon which Adam took his leave now bore me to the mainland. It wasn't until the mooring rope was released that the depth of my decision descended upon me. I was running away from home, the only one I'd ever known. Standing at the rail as the bay waters lengthened, the pier and village swallowed by mist, I felt tears welling.

Three hours later, I stepped ashore at Rossaveal. I scoured the harbor for familiar faces. To my relief, I saw none. If anyone marked me as a runaway, and sure my oatcake-crammed pockets and overstuffed carpet bag stood as strong clues, no one approached.

After inquiring at the ferry office, I found my way to the coaching station and bought my ticket to Galway City. The twenty-odd mile journey was a bumpy, barreling ride over mostly dirt-packed roads, my backside bashing against the wooden seat every time the driver hit a rut. By the time we reached the railway station at Eyre Square, I felt like bruised fruit.

Inside, I made haste to the ticket-seller's booth. "One fare for the southbound train to Queenstown, if you please," I said to the uniformed agent.

"What class?"

Unused to managing such matters for myself, I hesitated. "Whatever's least dear."

"One third-class carriage it is," he said, punching the keys of his machine.

He slid the ticket and timetable card toward me. According to the latter, the eighty-five miles to Queenstown, with stops, would be covered in four hours and twenty minutes.

Something else snagged my notice, and I snapped up my head. "It says the next train won't come 'til morning!"

That night, I slept rough, making a bed of one of the station benches. Every approaching footfall or screech of brakes brought me to gasping wakefulness, braced to find my disappointed father and furious brother looming over me.

The next morning, bleary-eyed and stiff as a board, I pushed onto the third-class rail compartment. Every seat was taken, obliging me to drop my bag and take hold of one of the leather straps. An infant's high-pitched wailing drew covered ears and glaring looks. Mindful of my own babe, still pea-sized inside me, I sent the harried mother a smile.

At Ennistimon, a seat opened, by a window no less. Finishing off my remaining oatcakes, I stared out the smudged glass and made a game of silently ticking off the remaining stops. Ennis. Limerick City. Mallow. The last would be Queenstown, my destination. Other than my one visit to Dublin, this was the most of the mainland I'd seen. How ironic, and sad, that running off to America should be the occasion for my adventuring.

But once I set sail, there'd be time aplenty for mourning all I'd miss. For the moment, I fixed my mind upon my purpose: getting myself aboard the steamer to New York. And Adam.

The Waldorf-Astoria Hotel, Fifth Avenue at 34th Street
The annual charity ball to benefit Bellevue Hospital was the crowning glory of the winter season, that year, more so than any other, for it was held at the new Astoria Hotel, opened the prior November and connected by corridor to its erstwhile rival, the Waldorf. No fewer than three orchestras were engaged for the ball that would begin at nine o'clock.

But first, boxholders were led into the blue, gold, and silver Astor Gallery for a lavish five-course supper – Beluga caviar and a collation of cold canapes, green turtle soup, lobster cutlets drenched in cream sauce with German asparagus, foie gras, and mixed cold meats and finishing with an array of desserts. Seated across from Vanessa at a balcony table for two, Adam chewed and swallowed, smiled and sipped, doing his level best to digest her ceaseless stream of chatter. Amongst the upstate resort villages, did the Tuxedo Clubhouse live up to its boast of offering the best toboggan slide? Now that sleighing season was in full swing, didn't Adam agree Sundays in Central Park were being overtaken by the working classes? Speaking of which, what *had* the organizers of the current fete been thinking to sell "ball only" tickets, allowing in nobodies and ne'er-do-wells? What riffraff they might meet on the dance floor she didn't care to contemplate.

57

Looking up from the half-eaten éclair weeping custard across his plate, Adam sprang from his seat. "Let's go find out, shall we?"

They descended the gilt-railed stairs to the sea of couples flooding into the French Baroque ballroom. After the obligatory opening dance, they went their separate ways, Adam to the bar, Vanessa to flirt outrageously. Only as the evening wore on, it became clear she wasn't sticking to their script. She kept her distance from the dance floor, turning down every bachelor who approached and chatting up women only.

By eleven o'clock, the blazing electric lights, the buzz of competing conversations, even the orchestra's playing all seemed to press in upon Adam. Fed up and tipsy, he pushed through the throng to where Vanessa held court among a clutch of women gathered, thick as flies, about her, all reporters, judging from their faded finery and drab, refurbished day dresses.

"A word, if I may," he said, reaching her.

"Of course." She slipped her hand into the crook of his arm. "Ladies, it seems my... escort cannot be parted from me a moment more."

A well-known society wag with a profusion of wilted rooster feathers stuck into her sagging salt-and-pepper pompadour remarked upon "the ardor of youth", drawing chortles and sly smiles.

Face warm, Adam looked about for an escape route. An arcaded alcove forested with potted palms caught his eye, and he steered Vanessa toward it. Judging from the other couples sheltering in nearby niches, the spot was serving as a lovers' lane of sorts, but at least there, he could escape being on display.

He disengaged Vanessa's hand and rounded on her. "We had a deal."

"Heavens, Adam, stand any closer, and someone may feel obliged to fetch a parson to do the deed here and now."

Stepping back, he resisted the urge to give her a good, sound shake as he had a time or two when they were children. "I don't know what game you're playing but—"

A camera's flash and crackle sent him swiveling about.

"Evelyn Moon for *The New York Herald*. How are you two lovebirds faring this evening?"

Adam peered past the bloom of black spots to a boxy, bespectacled brunette, a notepad and pencil in plain view. He'd seen her amongst the other female society reporters, but until now, she hadn't merited more than a passing glance. With her was a lanky man in a baggy day suit, wielding the source of the spotting – the latest Kodak box camera, the aperture aimed squarely at Adam's face.

"Any impending *announcements* to share with our readers?" she pressed, gaze flitting from Adam to Vanessa.

Vanessa opened her mouth to answer, but Adam no longer trusted what she might say. "You'll have to excuse us," he said, taking her hand and stepping into the open. "Miss Carlston has a headache, and I've called for the carriage."

By the time Adam's carriage drew up outside the Carlston's Fifth Avenue mansion, most of Adam's wine had worn off but none of his outrage. Considering the champagne he'd put away, it was probably a good thing he'd given into his mother's plea to leave the landau at home and take the town carriage. Only the regular driver was laid low with the flu, and their Irish butler, Davis, had taken his place on the box. Mindful of Davis, and his sharp ears, Adam kept a tight lid on his temper. As for Vanessa, her flippancy had fled the moment the carriage door closed. She spent most of the snowy ride knitting her gloves to threads.

Signaling Davis to stay put, Adam climbed out and circled to Vanessa's side. The slate sidewalk was iced over in patches, the walkway and marble front steps in not much better shape. More than once, Vanessa's thin-soled slippers sent her skidding, obliging him to hold onto her.

Reaching the entrance, he dropped her hand. "I don't know what that was tonight, but any debt I owed you is officially cleared."

She looked up at him, her plaintive expression as good as putting him in the wrong. "We were having such a lovely time, I couldn't bring myself to spoil it."

A *lovely* time? Was that how she saw it?

She fished in her beaded bag for the key. "Come inside, and we'll hash everything out."

"Thanks, but no thanks." He turned to go.

"Not even if I have my father join us?"

He stalled in his steps. "Kind of late, isn't it?" Between the time taken up waiting in line at the cloakroom and then in the carriage queue, it must be after midnight.

"He'll still be up reading. We can break the news together. That way, you shan't shoulder all the blame, only half." She hugged her fur-lined cape tighter. "Come in before we both catch our deaths."

Torn, Adam glanced back to the carriage. "What about Davis?"

"He's Irish, isn't he?" She turned away and fitted the key into the lock. "He's sure to have a flask on him."

They stepped into the foyer, the gasolier and sconces turned down to dim, the leather and platinum-covered walls melting into murkiness. "This way," she whispered, striking off though they still wore their coats.

Adam followed her through, thick carpets muffling their footfalls as they passed through the ornate front parlor and cavernous dining and breakfast rooms to an informal sitting room at the rear, rarely used by the frosty feel of it.

Vanessa moved to the mantel and turned up one of a pair of Tiffany lamps. "I can get a fire going if you like."

Adam stuffed his gloves into his pockets but kept his overcoat on. "Don't bother, I won't be staying long." He glanced back to the hallway, imagining the murky scene from a parent's point of view. "Us alone like this, what will your father say?"

"Don't be a stick-in-the-mud. We were alone in the carriage."

"Davis was on the box," he pointed out.

"Yes, lucky for me."

"Lucky how?" he asked, the comment striking him as off.

She crossed to the spirits cabinet and pulled the crystal stopper from a decanter of what might be brandy. "Your regular driver is deaf as a doornail. Having Davis close by kept you from ringing a peal over my head."

"What happened to getting your father?" he asked, seeing her pour just two snifters.

Looking back over her shoulder, she sent him a smile. "I thought we'd have a private toast first. To the shortest engagement on record."

"We were never actually engaged," he pointed out, taking the drink she passed him. Eyeing the generous pour, he hesitated. "I've already had enough champagne to sink a battleship. We can sit down with your father tomorrow when we all have clear heads."

She studied him, one corner of her lip lifting. "Afraid you might forget yourself? Or is it your Bridget you're in peril of putting out of your mind?"

He leveled her a look. "Her name's Rose, and I could down the whole damned decanter and still not forget her. I'm that crazy about her."

"Then you've nothing to worry about, do you? One last drink and then if you still want to leave, I won't hold you."

One drink and then walk away to freedom. As dares went, it sounded a cinch.

"No strings?" he asked, just to be sure.

"None at all."

Adam knocked back the brandy in a single stinging swallow.

He was in the hospital on Long Island, sweating and fevered, shaking and terrified. Faces floated above him. A worried-looking nurse mouthed, malaria, *and a doctor wielded a wicked-looking syringe, the stab of thick needle, a minor price to pay for the mercy of morphine.*

Adam awakened to a seismic shifting, the cruel canting seeming to come from outside himself. Chugging filled his ears and pounded his head, firing through every fiber and filament until he feared he would split open.

Pictures from the previous evening paraded past his mind's eye. Vanessa smiling at him from the other side of the ballroom. The carriage ride home through the snowy streets, his feet frozen and his stomach tight. And lastly, the press of chilly crystal into his palm, the deep draft setting his throat afire. All at once, he understood. He was sick for certain, not of malaria but of a malady of his own making.

A hangover.

He cracked open gluey eyes. The room was foreign to him, well-appointed but closet-size. The bed he lay upon took up most of it. But more than not knowing where he was or how he'd got there, it was the sideways glimpse of pale hair pouring over the pillow next to his that sent him bolting upright.

"Vanessa!"

She rolled onto her side and faced him with a satisfied smile. "Sleep well?"

"Christ, what are you... we... Where are we?"

She wrapped the sheet around herself and sat up beside him. "An Empire State Express train headed for Niagara Falls. Surely you remember?"

He scrubbed hard knuckles across his forehead. "I don't. Not a thing."

She narrowed her eyes. "You were certainly keen on eloping last night. Don't tell me you've got cold feet already?" She kicked out a foot from the covers and held it out as if making a study of her rather bony toes.

Panic slammed him. "Are you telling me we're... *married*?!"

She flinched as though he'd cracked a whip with the word. "Not yet but soon. Once we check into the hotel in Niagara, I'll have a bath, and then we can seek out a justice of the peace."

Adam stared, dumbstruck. He hadn't left the ball exactly sober, but he'd been a far cry from three sheets to the wind.

Her mouth softened into a smile. "But we have hours yet before we need bother with all that, plenty of time for... getting better acquainted."

She laid a hand on his shoulder, the movement sending the sheet slipping. He pitched back. "Christ, cover yourself!"

Rolling her eyes, she pulled up the covers. "I suppose I must accustom myself to love, honor, and *obey*."

A knock outside the cabin door nearly sent him seizing.

Draping her evening cape about her, Vanessa went to answer it. "That will be the breakfast we ordered."

Suddenly sensible of his own lack of clothing, he snapped the covers up to his chin. "Send it away."

"Really, darling, I do hope you're not going to be one of those loutish, bellicose husbands who thinks only of his own needs. You may have sated your... *appetites* last night, but I'm starved."

Up to that point, he'd told himself he had to have passed out without touching her. But if he hadn't, if he'd... *known* her, the situation wasn't only dire. It was irredeemable.

Holding the cape closed, she flicked the bolt free. "Come in," she called out, a happy trill.

"Morning ma'am, sir." Eyes on the floor, the porter entered carrying a cloth-covered breakfast tray. "Where'd you like it, Mrs. Blakely?"

Mrs. Blakely! Had Adam really been so stupid as to book their cabin using his real surname, a name known not only in New York but throughout the north-eastern United States?!

"Put it down anywhere," Adam snapped.

"Yes, sir." The porter pulled out a table on casters, set the tray down, and backed out.

Vanessa lifted cone-shaped metal covers off plates heaped with bacon, eggs, and buttered toast, the greasy scent filling the compartment. "Train food isn't ever very good, but I do believe I'm too hungry to mind." She carried a plate to bed and squeezed in beside him. "You should have something. You'll feel better once you do." She picked up a strip of bacon and wiggled it under his nose.

Stomach flipping, he shook his head. "No thanks."

"Suit yourself." Biting into the bacon, she eyed him. "You really don't remember?"

"I remember everything up to us going back to your parents' house, then... nothing."

She fell back against the pillows, licking her fingers. "You did have quite a lot to drink."

"Tell me something I *don't* know."

He gained his feet, bringing the bedsheet with him. Wrapping it about his waist, he searched for his small clothes. The crumpled heap at the foot of the bunk had all the makings of garments discarded in passionate haste. Spying his trousers, he snared them with his foot. Only once he'd managed to pull them on did he drop the sheet.

Shoving his arm into a shirtsleeve, he turned back to face her. "Tell me everything."

Light brown brows arched. "*Everything?*"

"Yes."

"Very well, you didn't have only the one brandy. You insisted upon... several. Suddenly, you smashed your glass into the fireplace, swore you'd been a fool to break it off with me, and begged me to run away with you. I never considered myself the eloping sort, but you can be quite persuasive when you're in a passion."

In a passion? For Vanessa? A girl he hadn't always liked and certainly never loved.

He glanced to the one small window, the half-raised blind affording a view of frozen countryside whizzing by. "Where are we?"

She shrugged. "Near Buffalo, I think."

Adam willed his bursting brain to focus. With a top speed of eighty-two mph, the new express trains could clear the distance between Buffalo and New York City in just over seven hours, including the stops.

He looked back to Vanessa, a slick of bacon grease on her chin. "Get dressed. We're getting off at the next stop."

63

* * *

A shriek of brakes brought us into the red brickwork railway station at Queenstown. I collected my carpet bag and stepped off with the others, doing my best to ignore the refreshment carts lining the lobby. Outside, hackney cabs covered the curb, porters rushing across the pullup and loading luggage onto carts. I stopped one and asked the way to the waterfront.

The tang of fishes and the mewling of seagulls heralded me to Harbor Row. By then, my feet were frozen inside my boots, and my gloved fingers not much better off. I pressed on, passing a solicitor and notary, several wine and spirits dealers, grocers, lodging houses, and a merchant tailor and outfitter. Just as I was sure I must have taken a wrong turn, I came upon No. 3 Scott's Square. A placard stuck inside the moisture-spotted window announced:

The Cunard Steamship Company, Limited
Steamship passage to
NEW YORK, BOSTON, PHILADELPHIA &
BALTIMORE
at lowest rates.

The air within the shipping company office was stale and thick, and the seating scarce, the backless benches taken up with travelers, many clutching their orange passage tickets as if fearful they might be snatched away. The less lucky perched upon their trunks or camped upon the straw-covered boards, coats serving as blankets or rolled into pillows. A few sported smart, store-bought clothes, but most were rustic folk, their garments homespun, their sparse belongings borne along by makeshift means – potato sacks, pillowcases, straw baskets, whatever would serve.

Murmuring apologies, I picked a path through to the ticket counter where a mustached man in a company jumper and felt cap flipped through a copy of *The Irish Times*. "I'd like to book passage to America. New York City."

He let out a yawn, treating me to a close-up view of a cottony tongue and yellowed molars. "Cabin passage starts at twenty-six pounds for first class. Second class runs from twenty-one pounds to eighteen pounds, depending on size and whether you want private or shared."

The sums sent my jaw dropping. "Is there a... third class?"

"That'd be steerage." He straightened and looked down his nose at me. "Twelve guineas including steward's fee and provisions."

I reached for my money, the knotted handkerchief still serving for a purse. I loosened it and began counting out the coin. "I'm gasping for a cuppa. Is there time for tea before we sail?"

The mouth beneath the bristles twisted. "Time enough for the whole blinkin' pot. *The Brittanic* don't depart 'til tomorrow."

"Tomorrow?!" I repeated, praying I'd misheard.

"Put in from Liverpool this morning. She's still to be provisioned and fueled, cleaned and inspected by the maritime commissioner before she's given the go-ahead to shove off." He paused, "Fancied you could just stroll aboard, did you?"

I had indeed.

He let out a snort. "This may be Queenstown, but you ain't Her Royal Majesty. Step aside and wait to be called up like all the others."

Following his gaze back over my shoulder, I saw that a queue had formed behind me, snaking nearly to the door.

A big-boned blond bent to my ear. "Do not give them the reason to single you out. They do not desire to send the makers of trouble to *Amerika*."

Cheeks burning, I gave the surly agent my name and then went off to wait. Finding a free corner, I set down my carpet bag and used the toe of my boot to scrape away the soiled straw. I'd just settled when the blond walked up, a hamper hooked over her forearm and a substantial-sized traveling trunk dangling from her other hand.

"We sit together, *ja?*"

Still stewing over the dustup with the agent, I snapped, "I've no claim upon this spot, so I suppose you must suit yourself."

Unruffled by my rudeness, she dropped the trunk and plunked down beside me. "Gerta Müller." She stuck out a hand, broad of back and bare of glove.

Grudgingly, I took it. "Rose," I said, leaving off my surname for truly, what affair was it of hers?

"Like the flower, *ja?*"

I gave a curt nod.

"In Deutsch, it is the same – Rose." She dipped a hand into her hamper, took out a wax paper-wrapped sandwich, and handed me half. "*Essen.*"

A prisoner to hunger though I was, still, I didn't like to be beholden. "Thank you, but I had something at the station."

My belly's rumbling made a liar of me. She looked at me askance. "Pride makes for the poor dinner." Again, she held out the half. That time, I took it with a mumbled thank you. It was some sort of sausage dressed in pickled cabbage, heavier fare than the fishes I was used to but welcome, nonetheless. I tucked in, devouring it down to the crust.

Licking my fingers, I leaned back against the wall. "What you said before about them not sending troublemakers to America, what did you mean?"

She swallowed her last morsel, then wiped her mouth on the back of her hand. "They are looking for a reason to... weed out the peoples who may make the... troubles *before* we sail."

"But I'm no charity case," I protested. "So long as my passage is paid, what do they care what mischief I might get up to in a foreign land? Not that I mean to get up to any," I added, lest one of the patrolling agents overhear.

She darted her gaze to the room's four corners. "The shipping company agent must sit down with each passenger before we leave port. You, me, all the peoples in this room will be asked the same eleven questions, and he will write down our answers on the ship's..." she stopped, groping for the correct word.

"Manifest?"

"*Ja.* If they do not like your answer to any of these questions, they will not take you to *Amerika.*"

I felt a frisson of fear. "Surely not!"

"My *brüder*, he is in... Cincinnati, Ohio five years. He writes to me of how it first was for him and his wife. Once we land in New York, we will be taken to the... emigrant receiving station and asked these same questions again. If the inspectors there do not like our answers or if we give to them one that is different from what is written on the... very important paper—"

"Manifest," I supplied again, wishing I'd asked Danny the particulars of his passage when I'd had the chance.

"*Ja*, that. They can send us back. If they do, it is the shipping company that must pay our passage as well as a fine – *one hundred* American dollars."

Dropping my voice, I asked, "What sorts of questions will they put to us?"

She reached beneath her bulky coat and showed me a folded paper wedged into her waistband. "From *mein brüder*."

Not once during my school days had I so much as stolen a glance at another's exam paper. But this was no schoolroom. It was the real world, and a cold, callous one it was showing itself to be. When she palmed me the paper, I didn't think twice.

I took it.

Chapter Nine

It was dark out when the cab Adam hired from Grand Central pulled up at the Carlston mansion. Any hope he had held onto that the dreadful mistake might be put behind them shriveled the moment he and Vanessa set foot inside the foyer.

"Miss, your parents and Mr. Blakely's are waiting upstairs in the library," the butler announced, relieving them of their coats.

Feeling as though he mounted scaffold steps, Adam followed Vanessa up the crimson-carpeted staircase.

Her father, Andrew, met them on the library threshold. "Get in and sit down, both of you."

Before crossing the equivalent of the enemy line, Adam took a moment to surveil the scene. His father at the Chinese Chippendale desk, fisting a glass of what looked to be whiskey, cherry cheeks proclaiming it to be far from his first. His mother and Vanessa's perched upon the horse-hair-covered sofa like china-doll bookends, Mamie sniffling into a lace-edged hankie, Beatrice cooing soothing sayings into her friend's ear. Vanessa crossed the Persian carpet and joined them, slipping in beside her mother who subsided into fresh fits at the sight of her.

Carlston carried the door closed with a slam and spun about to Adam. "I trusted you. More than trusted, I saw you as the son we never had." He brought his face to Adam's, so close Adam spotted the spittle congregating at the corners of his mouth. "And this, *this* is how you repay me." He flung a hand toward Vanessa, finger-combed hair spitting pins, periwinkle ballgown a crush of creases. "Be glad your last name is Blakely. If you were anyone else's son, I'd put a bullet in your brow."

Adam's father approached. "See here, Andrew, I know you're upset, and you've every right to be, but don't go losing your head. Young people are prone to impetuousness. There's nothing so broken here it can't be mended."

Vanessa popped up from her seat. "Mr. Blakely's right, Papa. Adam didn't steal me away. We... eloped."

Carlston punched a fist into the air. "Then where's the marriage license? The ring?" He bounded over and took hold of her left wrist, flagging her bare hand for all to see. "There is no license, and there is no ring because there's been no *marriage*. But by God, there will be!"

Vanessa's shoulders rounded. Her bottom lip commenced quivering. "He said... he'd had a change of heart that he wanted us to marry after all. I see now it was only the strong spirits speaking, but at the time, he seemed so... sincere. I never would have gone off otherwise, and now that I have, I'm... ruined!"

Adam could but stare. Could a man, any man, really do that degree of damage and not leave a wrinkle of recollection? And how was it that the woman who'd cavorted with bare-assed boldness just that morning suddenly sounded closer to twelve than twenty?

Fury fading, Carlston patted her shoulder. "No, Vannie, you're not." Turning away, he ground his gaze into Adam. "For all any of us know, my daughter may be carrying the next Carlston Blakely heir, and I damn well expect you to step up and do your duty."

Adam looked to his father, his final, fragile hope, but the set expression on his sire's face told him he'd find no champion there, either. "Sorry, my boy, but you've flouted the rules one time too many. Time to pay the piper."

His mother passed Mamie a fresh hankie and stood. "This marriage will be the making of you, Adam. Soon you'll see this... unpleasantness for the blessing-in-disguise it is."

Vanessa came up to his side and slipped her hand in his. "Your mother's right. We're going to be marvelously happy."

Meeting her eyes, clear despite the moments-ago crying, Adam owned that any hope of happiness with me was dead now. Going forward, he would look upon the great Atlantic as an unbreachable barrier. Even if my silence was nothing more than a fluke of spotty posts and bad luck, even if I loved him deeply and truly as ever, there was no honorable offer he might make me. As much as his heart would always belong to me, his Wild Irish Rose, his body, his very life, belonged to Vanessa.

With her hand still lying in his, he heard a wooden voice, *his* voice, ask, "Vanessa, will you do me the honor of being my wife?"

Her sparkling gaze rose to his. "Yes, Adam, I will."

Gerta and I spent the night on the straw, huddled against the damp. The next morning, we and our fellow steerage passengers were ferried out to Lynch's Quay, the berth for Cunard's transatlantic steamships. Clutching our passage tickets, we stood at the rail, conversations dropping off as *The Brittanic* came into view. Ere then, the biggest boat I had taken was our mainland ferry. The four-funneled, triple-decked behemoth before us was like nothing I'd ever imagined – a floating city. And, for the next ten to twelve days, my home.

Boarding was managed with admirable efficiency, but then the cabin-class passengers had been brought on earlier and settled into their quarters. For ourselves, there was still the roll call to be got through, a last chance for the shipping company to pick off the weak or infirm before pulling up anchor. Paraded up the starboard gangway to the upper deck and then back portside to the main deck under the eagle eyes of the ship's officers, it was hard not to feel like cattle. Afterward, we were grouped according to sex and led below deck, the women and children put up at the forward end of the vessel, the men and older boys quartered in the aft.

Our dormitory was squat, stifling, and noisy, the adjacent boiler room contributing both heat and intermittent clanging. Metal-framed bunks, three to a column, lent it a warren-like quality. Gerta and I clung close with the happy result that we were assigned adjoining berths. As we were below the water line, there was neither ventilation nor plumbing. We were each given a bucket to relieve ourselves, which we were responsible for carrying on deck and dumping over the ship's side.

Once in open waters, one day bled into the next. The stench of unwashed bodies, tobacco – several of the women smoked pipes – and human waste seemed to worsen by the hour. Those who tried keeping themselves and their children decent used the slop buckets to wash themselves and their clothes, the latter dried upon lines strung between upper berths. Meals were weevil-riddled porridge or watery stew ladled onto tin plates and served with a hunk of coarse bread. Most were too seasick or, in my case, pregnancy sick to muster much of an appetite.

The terrible tedium tested us all. Women and girls well enough to leave their berths passed the time with needlework or reading, praying, or cards. To lift the melancholy, those with musical instruments played them, the rest of us singing or humming along. Pilgrimages to peer out the smeared glass porthole revealed the same vista day upon day – endless sea but nary a scrap of sky.

I don't know how I would have got through were it not for Gerta. Her booming laugh drew scowls from those seeking to sleep through the sickness, but for me, her unflagging good nature was a godsend. From the start, she demonstrated a steely determination to look out for me, installing me in the lower bunk so I could reach the privy pan with ease, spoon-feeding me my rations when I was too ill to leave my berth, and diverting my mind with learning German words and phrases.

When I pointed out that English, not German, was the language of America, she shook her head. "There are many Deutsch in *Amerika*. It is *gut* to know other tongues, especially in a big city such as New York."

On clear days, we bundled ourselves into our coats and scarves, hats and gloves and took a turn about the steerage deck, talking until the cold drove us back below. Mostly I liked to listen, a state of affairs that suited us both, for despite her limited English and my lack of German, Gerta was more than equal to carrying both sides of a conversation with the result that I soon became acquainted with her history.

"I was born in Baiersbronn," she told me the afternoon of our second full day at sea. "It is a village in the Black Forest. *Mein vater*... my father was killed fighting for Prussia in the war with France."

Thinking of my mother, whom I'd never known, I murmured my sympathies.

She shrugged. "I was little. I do not remember much."

Like myself, she'd grown up in the inn her mother managed, tending the vegetable garden, chatting up guests in the taproom – *stube* – and helping in the kitchen where she learned to make *maultaschen*, a rich beef broth of raviolis stuffed with beef and pork.

"Unlike my *brüder* and *schwestern*, I was content to remain at home, *ein spinster. Mutter* despaired I was too *wählerisch* – choosy," she translated with a grin. "And then two *brüder*, carpenters from Cork, came to stay on holiday. Sean looked at me, and I at him, and we took the fall... how do you say it... 'head over feet'?"

71

Carried back to my first time setting eyes on Adam, I felt my throat thicken.

"*Mutter* gave us her blessing, and we married within the month. We were to leave together for *Irland* when she sickened. I stayed to nurse her."

"What happened?" I asked, stomach pitting for, traveling alone as she was, hers could not be a wholly happy tale.

She glanced down at the thin gold circlet upon her left ring finger and sighed. "When I came to Cork, Sean was dead. A crane dropped some wood and…" Looking out to the gray blanket of sea, she made a quick swipe of her eyes.

I set a hand upon her shoulder, wishing I might offer more in the way of comfort. "What do you mean to do once we reach New York?" I asked, thinking that perhaps Adam might help her find work.

"I will take the train to Ohio – Cincinnati. *Mein brüder…* brother and his wife have a *biergarten* in the city. They have asked for my help with it and the *kinder*."

She pulled a cardboard postcard holder from her pocket and passed it to me. It was a standard studio photographic portrait, the subjects stiff and unsmiling, posed against a painted canvas backdrop. Gerta's mustached brother sat enthroned in an elaborately carved wooden chair, his toddler son upon his lap, whilst his wife stood beside him, the infant in her arms.

Pointing proudly, she said, "A beauty, *ja?*"

At first, I thought she meant the sour-faced sister-in-law, but then I saw it was the babe. Dimpled and chubby-cheeked, the child was indeed a perfect little cherub.

Mindful of my own baby, still a seedling inside me, I passed the picture back. "She is," I said, hoping the biting air might be blamed for my misting eyes.

Gerta's damp eyes were still sharp as tacks. "You are missing your Adam?"

The story I'd given, that I was meeting my American fiancé in New York, whilst thin on details was true so far as I knew. Tempted as I was to unburden myself about the lack of letters and now the baby, I held back. Brief as our time together was, I couldn't bear for my new friend to think badly of me.

Christmas arrived, marked only by a tot of whiskey sponsored by the ship's captain. I gave mine to Gerta and lapsed into homesickness. Were Da and Colm and Kil celebrating as always? I hoped so, and yet I had to think Danny's dying and my running off must throw a pall upon their merrymaking.

On the tenth day, shouts of "Land ho!" saw my spirits lifting. Ahead lay Sandy Hook lighthouse, the gateway to New York Harbor and my new life, or so I hoped.

A cutter carrying immigration officials met us at the harbor mouth. Inspectors, accompanied by an entourage of clerks, interpreters, and doctors, boarded and began processing the first- and second-class passengers, the interviews and physical examinations conducted in the privacy of their cabins. Meanwhile, we in steerage were called up on deck as in Queenstown. Despite the freezing wind, we were told to take off our hats and open our coat collars and then made to march about.

Shivering, I leaned into Gerta. "If we aren't sick already, we will be after this."

Afterward, we were allowed back below to gather our belongings. Seated upon the bottom berth, I surveyed my reflection in Gerta's moisture-spotted hand mirror, scarcely owning the sunken-cheeked, sallow-complexioned stranger staring back as myself.

Handing back the looking glass, I said, "What if Adam doesn't know me?"

"He will know you." Dropping her voice, she asked, "The baby sickness, it is better today?"

I stared up at her, shock making a mute of me.

"My friend in Deutschland has four, and every time, she looked as you do – green as lettuce and pale as a ghost."

So much for hoping her mirror was overly harsh. "All these days, you never said a word."

"You must have *gut* reason for keeping the secret. *Gut* or no, it is yours to keep." She brought down my carpet bag from the rack and set it at my feet. "Now let us leave this big, oh-so-smelly ship and greet our new *vaterland*."

73

Chapter Ten

When we stepped back out onto the steerage deck, passengers were piled three-deep. All at once, the fog thinned, and the sun broke free of its screen of clouds. Cheers swept the deck, the privations of the past ten days forgotten as young and old jockeyed to gain precious proximity to the rail for a glimpse of Lady Liberty. Crowned head high, torch aloft in what I fancied was a welcoming wave, and copper flesh, weathered a warm nut brown, she rose from the white-capped waters, as grand a sight as ever I've been privileged to set eyes upon.

Overcome, I gripped Gerta's arm, "We've made it!"

We passed the tiny teardrop of land known as Ellis Island, the only sign of habitation an American flag flapping in the wind. The federalized emigrant receiving station was wrapped in scaffolding, its Georgia pine buildings having been razed by fire the previous year. The eerie stillness put me in mind of the ghost villages we whispered of back home.

I turned away to the protruding toe of shoreline. As we closed in upon the bustling harbor, Gerta pointed out a low-slung circular sandstone fortress, Castle Garden, in use as the city's aquarium, and a turreted gray building, the Barge Office, where a makeshift landing depot was set up to receive us.

A double-decked government barge drew up to ferry us to shore. As in Queenstown, the cabin-class passengers were let on first. Whatever space remained would be filled by as many in steerage as could be squeezed on. The less lucky would stay behind until the tug returned.

Finally, the ropes were removed. Like caged animals set free, we charged the exit stairs, families and couples struggling to stay together. Gerta grabbed my elbow and pushed us forward. We cleared the gangplank but barely, the ropes replaced as soon as we crossed over. Stacked like cordwood, we stood on the lower deck, belongings in our arms.

Fortunately, it was a short trip to shore. After ten days at sea, the pier seemed to pitch beneath me. Nor was I the only disembarking passenger with wobbly legs. Before we could find our footing, shipping officials known as groupers herded us toward a roped-off promenade, barking for us to fall in line. Policemen patrolled the queue, whistles about their necks and clubs dangling from their belts. More than once we were warned that shoving or stepping away, even to answer calls of nature, would be repaid with exile to the rear.

The waiting stretched past an hour, the wind off the water racking us no matter how close together we stood. Those who could afford the twenty-five cents turned their bags over to handlers to be stored or sent on to addresses in the city. Most of us settled for dragging our trunks and baskets and sea chests along with us. Craning my neck, I could just make out the signage above the depot's main entrance:

Commissioner of Emigration
Of The State of New York
Emigrant Landing Depot and Offices

We entered to a maze of boarded-off chutes, the wood partitions stained from the press of bodies and whittled with messages, some in English, most not. Sheets of iron netting hung from floor to ceiling, creating makeshift pens. Arrowed signs pointed the way to the various departments: Registry, Exchange, Telegraph, Letter-Writing, Information, and Railroad. Before disembarking, we were each handed a card with our passenger identification number and a letter indicating the aisle where we were to stand. I stepped into the aisle marked "A", Gerta into the "B" one beside me.

Fenced in like farm animals, the foulness was ferocious. The respite in the open air had taken away my tolerance, and I held Adam's handkerchief to my nose and mouth, grateful my breakfast had come up earlier.

Beside me, Gerta warned, "Do not be sick, not here."

I followed her fraught gaze to the row of white-jacketed doctors ahead. Stethoscopes ringing their necks and holding clipboards and stubs of chalk, they monitored our approach.

Mouth to my ear, she added, "If they find you are pregnant with no husband, they send you back."

"Back home, you mean?" At her nod, I felt my legs turn to jelly. "They can do that?"

"It is their country, *spatzi*. They can do as they wish."

I stuffed the hankie back in my pocket just as a bespectacled nurse drew up beside me. "*You*." Before I could answer, she hooked her hand about my upper arm and marched me toward a screened-off area.

Inside, I wrenched free. "What have I done?"

"It's plain as the nose on that Pole's face you're pregnant," she hissed, jerking her chin to a blond clutching a carpet bag even more threadbare than mine.

I forced up my chin. "I'm queasy from the ferry is all."

She leaned in, her sour breath testing my stomach's resolve. "Breeding or not, one word from me into a doctor's ear, and he'll chalk you '*Pg*' and put you on the next boat back."

To have broken my poor father's heart and struck out all this way only to be sent back without seeing Adam was too terrible to contemplate.

"You want me to pass you, it'll cost."

Back in Queenstown, I'd exchanged my Irish pounds for American dollars, incurring the shipping company's hefty handling fee, another naïve mistake. Hands trembling, I brought out my money scarf, unknotted it, and drew out a dollar.

"You expect me to risk my position for this pittance?" she spat, spittle landing upon my lips.

Too late I saw my foolishness in letting her see all I had. Cowed, I handed her a five-dollar note.

She shoved it into her pinafore. "Back in line and keep your mouth shut."

Shaking, I stepped out and resumed my place.

Gerta took one look at me and muttered, "*Hündin*. She wanted money, a bribe, *ja*?"

I nodded.

She must have seen the tears I struggled to hold in, for she tightened her lips and said no more.

Heading our queues, we were called up together. Gerta's examiner, a whiskered doctor of middling years, poked his chalk stub at her midsection. "Someone likes her bratwurst and beer a little too much, eh, Fraulein?"

The crass comment made me yearn to point out his own paunch. Before

76

I could, Gerta cut me a warning look. Turning back to her inquisitor, she smiled sweetly, though I could as good as feel her heart's racing.

"Ah well, Herr Doctor, a little... sausage never hurt anyone, *ja*?"

Flushing, he set his stethoscope to her chest.

I turned to my examiner, younger and clean-shaven. "How are you feeling today, Miss O'Neill?" he asked, not unkindly.

"Grand," I lied, wishing for a sip of water to moisten my mouth.

"Good, good." He made a few ticks upon the chart. "I need to have a look at your eyes." A slender buttonhook instrument materialized in his hand.

He brought the device up to my right eye, and I shrank back. "I see you plain as day."

"Nonetheless, I need to check you for trachoma." Reading my no doubt blank look, he elaborated, "A highly contagious illness of the eye that, if left untreated, can lead to blindness. I can't sign off on you entering the country without ruling it out. It's the *law*," he added, tone ominous.

Praying I wouldn't greet Adam with a gouged eye, I forced myself to stand perfectly still, suffering him to use the nasty thing to roll up first my right eyelid and then my left.

"Good, good." He slipped the instrument back into his coat pocket without wiping it. "Stick out your tongue and say, 'Ahhhhh.'"

I obeyed, opening my mouth wide whilst he held down my tongue with a short, flat stick. Next, he had me open my coat. I did, albeit with reluctance, and he set his stethoscope to my chest and bade me take several deep breaths. Lastly, he probed me with his hands, looking for lumps. When he came to my belly, I tensed.

Stepping back, he shook his head, and my heart dropped.

"For the future, I urge you to resist the lure of feminine vanity before it damages your health."

"Doctor?"

"Your corset, Miss O'Neill, is constricting your lungs and digestive organs. If you persist in lacing yourself so tightly, over time, you may well do yourself an injury. But for the present, you give every indication of being a healthy young woman." I held my breath as he raised the clipboard and scratched his pen across the medical certificate.

I took it and met up with Gerta, who'd been passed as well. We continued to the Registry where uniformed clerks stood behind lectern-like desks. One by one, we were called up, our identities verified by matching the name and identification number on our tag to the ship's manifest, our freshly written medical certificates given thorough, final scrutiny. As Gerta had foretold, the eleven questions posed back in Queenstown were repeated, our replies compared with those on record, our faces and bodies scrutinized for signs of dissembling.

"State your name," the inspector said to me after a glance at the paper.

"Moira Rose O'Neill."

"And you've come over from Ireland?"

"Inis Mór – Inishmore you'd know it as," I answered. "My family has a public house there," I added, meaning for him to know I wasn't a pauper.

Unimpressed, he asked, "Final destination?"

"New York City."

"Marital status?"

"Betrothed… sorry *engaged*," I said, mindful of matching the American–English word taken down in Queenstown.

That time, he looked up, gaze raking me. "Your fiancé, is he meeting you here?"

"He is," I lied, praying he wouldn't press for particulars.

He continued down the list, ticking off the remainder of the questions. "Are you literate, Miss O'Neill? Can you read and—"

"I'm familiar with the word, sir, and indeed, I am." There it was again, that streak of brash pride that has so often been my undoing.

A grunt and then, "Have you ever resided in an almshouse or otherwise been supported by charity?"

"No."

"Do you suffer from any crippling illness or deformity?"

Patience thinning, I touched my coat front, free of chalk. "Sure your doctor wouldn't have passed me if I had."

His cold look seemed to cut clear through me. "It's not unheard of for coats to be turned inside out or chalk to be brushed away. The tricks you people pull would fill a book, so do yourself a service and simply answer the question."

"No, I'm neither crippled nor deformed."

"Are you a prostitute or likely to become a public charge?"

Though it was my second time being asked, I felt my face flame. "Certainly not!"

"Welcome to America." A stamp upon the manifest ledger and a tick mark on the tag pinned to my coat followed the grudging greeting.

Farther down the room, Gerta was suffering the same. Though translators were supposed to be made available, from what I could tell, when faced with non-English-speaking passengers, the clerks simply shouted. Fortunately, Gerta bore up and was cleared as well.

Grateful to have the ordeal over, I squeezed her hand. "We made it."

The corners of her mouth kicked up. "Willkommen Zuhause."

Owing to her shipboard lessons, I recognized the German. Welcome home.

We continued to the Railroad Department, where Gerta bought her ticket to Cincinnati, and then to the telegraph office so that she might wire her brother of her safe arrival. Thinking of Da and the lads, no doubt sick with worrying, I was tempted to do the same, but cables cost money, and thanks to the wicked nurse, I was down to my last dollar.

The lines were long, the scant seating taken. The stuffiness saw my queasiness returning. At Gerta's urging, I left her and made my way outside. We would meet up at the main gate by the fruit-seller's stall.

Late in the day though it was, the pier still teemed with people, for ours wasn't the only steamer to make port that day. Migrants of all ages, ethnicities, and walks of life circulated, many clothed in the costumes of their native countries. Catching sight of a Dutch family shod in wooden clogs, I wondered how my pampooties would be received here. Not so well, I thought.

Nor was it only we newcomers filling the place. Sober-suited missionaries stood on soapboxes, preaching and pushing their tracts on passersby. Baggage masters, counting house clerks, translators, boarding house runners, agents from the adjacent Labor Bureau, police constables, and members of various immigrant aid societies all milled about as well. Moving through, I found my way to the main gate and the old Irishwoman fruit-seller, her glistening wrapped apples and plump pears making my mouth water.

To take my mind off my belly's emptiness, I played naughts and crosses against myself in the gravel, using the toe of my boot to mark off the x's and o's. The sensation of being watched had me looking out across the courtyard. A lanky man in a tall beaver hat cut through the crowd toward me, his checker-cloth suit and white wingtips marking him as a man of means if not taste. Wondering if he might be an inspector sent to sniff out my story, I took up my carpet bag, prepared to run if I must.

He reached me, his snaggle-toothed smile sunshine itself. "Aren't you a pretty Colleen?" he cooed, looking me up and down. "From Dublin? Or is it Belfast?"

"Inishmore," I answered, careful to say no more than I'd committed to paper.

"Gerry Flanagan's the name. On behalf of the Irish Aid Society, welcome to New York." He bowed as if in a ballroom.

I set the carpet bag back down. "If you'll pardon my saying so, you don't speak as any Irishman I've ever met." His clipped vowels and occasional dropped "r" marked him as a Yank, though crude of speech, at least compared to Adam.

Tobacco-stained teeth bared themselves in a grin. "I'm Bronx born and bred, but my dear old dad was a Dublin man and my ma a black-eyed lass from Sligo. They came over during the Great Hunger and settled in Bainbridge, may the Lord rest their sainted souls," he added, clapping a hand to his heart. "It's out of respect for their memories that I undertake this noble work."

"What work would that be, sir?"

"Why, the work of Catholic charity, of course, steering daughters of Erin such as yourself to gainful employment and respectable lodgings in our fair metropolis."

"That's good of you, but I'm to be married shortly."

"Well, isn't that grand," he exclaimed, gaze going over me. "Whoever he is, he's a lucky son of a... fella. But seeing as none of us knows what life has in store, no harm in taking one of these." He peeled off a sheet from his stack and passed it over.

Not wishing to be rude, I took it.

Boarding house for young ladies of good character.
Primely situated, in the heart of Mulberry Park.
Room & board at reasonable rates.
Irish welcome. Catholic preferred.

Gerta's walking up ended the odd interlude. At her approach, my would-be benefactor tipped his hat and scuttled off.

80

"Who was that?" she asked, looking over my shoulder to the paper.

I gave a shrug. "Someone from the Irish Aid Society." Already Mr. Flanagan was fading from my mind, my attention on the plump pear she held out. I pocketed the paper and linked my arm with hers. "I'll walk you to the ferry, will I?"

Chapter Eleven

We shared Gerta's pear whilst waiting for the ferry that would carry her across the Hudson to the Erie Railway Depot in Jersey City. We'd just finished when the boat came into view, "*Erie Eisenbahn*" called out in bold black letters.

She tossed the fruit core into the water and turned to me. "My *brüder* says there are so many of our peoples in Ohio, I won't miss Deutschland at all."

"Sure he's right," I said, a catch to my voice. "But oh, Gertie, how'll I get on without you?"

After nearly a fortnight together, we were more than traveling companions. We were bosom friends. I wasn't Rose anymore, not to her. I was Little Rose – *Röschen* – herself Gert or sometimes Gertie.

She smiled. "The three of you will 'get on' very well, I think. This night, you will be back with your Adam."

"Adam Blakely," I supplied, for the first time saying his surname aloud.

"Tell me, Frau Blakely, where in this city of New York will you live?"

"I'm not altogether certain, but for now, you can reach me here." I felt in my pocket for the slip of paper with Adam's direction and passed it to her.

The boat was closing in. Eager as I was to reunite with Adam, I felt a sinking in my stomach. Another goodbye. Another chapter of my young life closing.

I hugged her hard. "Don't forget to write."

Drawing back, she tried for a smile. "*Gott sei mit dir*." God be with you.

Tearing up, I gave her hand a squeeze. "Go safely for now."

With Gerta gone, I'd no reason to tarry. Following a handful of fellow arrivals who seemed to know their way, I cut through Battery Park, my soles slipping on snow, the twilight turning the barren tree branches into witches' claws. An elevated railway bridge lay ahead, its steel girders blocking the darkening sky. Beneath the trestles, several single-horse livery cabs queued up, fresh coaches pulling up to replace the full ones.

My turn came, and I stepped up, calling out Adam's address to the driver. Hand on the door handle, I thought to ask, "How much will it be?"

"Thirty cents up to the first mile, seventy-five cents after that up to the first hour," he recited, clearly impatient to be off.

I hesitated, unsure if my single dollar would see me to Adam's door.

The cabbie cut me a look. "See here, Irish, get in or step aside. You're costing me fares."

Reasoning Adam would surely make up any shortfall, I got in. I'd scarcely settled on the cracked leather when we shot forward. Righting myself, I drew back the carriage curtain and scrubbed my fist over the frosted glass, clearing a circle so I could see out. Streets whizzed by, their names meaning nothing to me. The lamppost-lit views, however, stupefied and enthralled me. Never had I imagined buildings might be so towering and yet so closely stacked, that streets might be so thick with horses and carts and carriages and people, scores of them out and about despite the evening hour.

We turned onto 79th Street and jolted to a halt at the high curb. Staring out, I caught my breath. Twin lampposts flanked a tall wrought-iron gate propped upon stonework pilasters. Beyond was the house, six stories of gleaming white limestone, trimmed with scrollwork masonry, so fine, it put me in mind of the lace on a ladies' sleeve.

Making money, mounds of it, is what matters in their world. Adam's words echoed back to me, and only then did I understand they'd been meant as a warning.

I'd barely handed over the fare and gotten my twenty-five cents due when the cabbie cracked the whip and sped off, leaving me standing with my bag on the slate sidewalk.

I pulled open the hinged gate and entered. A short path led to a flight of circular marble front steps. I held tight to the rail, my light head owing as much to nerves as to how little I'd eaten. On the portico, I took hold of the doorknocker, a fierce-faced brass lion polished to a blinding sheen, and cracked it upon the carved maple.

83

The door was opened by a distinguished man of middling years, his salt-and-pepper hair center-parted and pomaded, his collar stock spotless, his dark suit without a speck of dust.

"Mr. Blakely, sir, an honor it is to make your acquaintance. And may I say what a relief it is to see you looking so fit." I set down the carpet bag and held out my hand.

His mouth curled in a not-very-nice smile. "I assure you the Messieurs Blakely do not waste their valuable time interviewing the help. Come back in the morning to the tradesmen's entrance on the east side of the area and ask for the housekeeper." He dropped back, drawing the door closed.

Before he could, I shoved my shoe into the gap.

"It's Mr. *Adam* Blakely I've come to see," I said, forcing up my chin. "Kindly tell him Rose – Miss O'Neill – is waiting."

His brows rose as if my name registered familiar. "I don't know what game you're about, my girl," he said, lapsing into the brogue of our northern counties. "Mr. Adam ain't at home and won't ever be to the likes o' you. Now shove off before I call in the coppers."

"I'll not budge, not 'til I'm brought to Adam." Eyeing the agape door and his substantial frame, I weighed my chances of striking past him.

Just as I'd steeled myself to make my move, a woman called out, "Heavens, Davis, whatever is going on out there?"

The butler, for so I now knew him to be, looked back over his shoulder. "Forgive me, madam, but there's a… *person* claiming to be an acquaintance of Master Adam's. I've told her he's not at home, but she refuses to leave," he answered, any trace of Irishness erased.

His mistress took his place at the threshold. Tall and elegant, her pompadour piled higher than I would have thought hair could climb, her slender figure adorned in claret-colored velvet, the skirts of which billowed out beautifully, the regal woman before me could be but one person. Adam's mother, Beatrice Blakely.

"Begging your pardon, missus, but I'm not Adam's acquaintance. I'm Rose O'Neill, his betrothed."

Her lightly lined oval face turned gray as an oyster shell. Blue eyes, paler than Adam's, raked over me, missing nothing – not my battered hat, worn coat, nor scuffed half-boots.

"Come in," she finally said, falling back for me to enter.

I reached for my carpet bag, sagging on its side, but Davis snapped it up, holding it aloft as if the faded needlepoint carried contagion.

The scene I stepped into might have been one of the opulent interiors pictured in Mrs. Murphy's magazines. Fluted columns supported a soaring plasterwork ceiling painted to resemble a cloud-covered sky. Suspended from the room's center was an enormous gas chandelier, its etched glass globes supported by stems of gleaming gold leaf. A central staircase spiraled upward, its polished mahogany banister crowned with a flourish of carved acorns. Floor-to-ceiling windows, outfitted with stained-glass panels flanked the room, the ruby and milk-white roses making prisms of the man-made light.

Mrs. Blakely followed my eye. "Designed by Lois Comfort Tiffany."

"The gent with the diamond rings," I said, pleased with myself for remembering.

Grimacing, she turned to Davis. "Send up tea, otherwise, I'm not to be disturbed."

She struck out for the stairs. Following her up, I peered over the rail, catching glimpses of sumptuous furnishings, carpets, and porcelains, each hallway graced by a gilded mirror and fronted by a bank of windows draped in velvet and festooned with fringe.

We stepped off into a third-story gallery lined with gilt-framed portraits. I stopped before the largest, a family scene. A younger Mrs. Blakely stared haughtily down from the canvas, slender white arm draped along the back of an elaborately carved armchair occupied by an iron-eyed gentleman with a neatly clipped beard – Adam's father, it seemed safe to presume. A blond boy and girl filled the foreground, the girl dressed all in pink, the boy in blue. I focused on the boy – Adam – hair combed back from his unblemished brow, blue eyes glinting with what I could only think must be mutiny. Though he held a toy soldier in one hand, there was little in his demeanor to suggest he'd come from playing.

Mrs. Blakely followed my gaze. "Painted when the children were seven and nine. I had them dressed as a nod to Gainsborough's Blue Boy and Thomas Lawrence's Pinkie. I don't suppose you're familiar?"

Though my blushing face likely answered for me, I shook my head.

She continued down a long corridor ending in a paneled mahogany door carved with alternating clusters of fan-shaped leaves. "My sitting room," she said, producing a key from her pocket.

A twist of cut-crystal knob brought the heavy door open. I followed her in, a shiver shooting through me though the house was well-heated, and I still wore my coat.

It was a woman's room, the dainty gilded furnishings covered in rose and gold, the walls hung with silk paper in a repeating rose-and-trellis pattern, bow-and-arrow wielding Cupids peeking out.

"Sit, won't you?" She flicked a ruby-and-gold-wreathed wrist toward a pair of low-backed chairs, their slender wooden legs inlaid with what might be abalone or mother-of-pearl.

I lowered myself onto the satin-covered cushion, lightly, so as not to leave a mark. "Your husband, he's recovered, I hope?" Had he passed, sure there'd be black bunting at the door and herself in widow's weeds.

"He is." She slipped into the opposite seat. "You're very well-informed on my family."

"I spotted your telegram when I was sorting the post. The ferry brings it twice a week," I added, nerves bringing out the babbler in me.

She adjusted the lace at her cuffs, Brussels, or so I surmised. "Remind me where in Ireland you're from."

"Inis Mór. My people have bided there for seven generations."

"Your *people* – how quaint." A frozen smile fought the frown furrowing her forehead. "And what do they do?"

"Do?"

"Your father, what is his *occupation*? How does he come by his *money*?" she added as though explaining herself to a halfwit.

Caught off guard, I fumbled, "Well, I can't say that there's all that much money to speak of but what bit comes our way does so through the pub."

"Saloon owners," she muttered, more to herself than to me.

"Pubs, we say." I looked to the door, willing Adam to walk through. Following my gaze, she said, "They aren't expected back for a while yet."

"They?"

Her gaze pricked mine. "He and Miss Vanessa Carlston. His fiancée."

Blood rushed my ears. The room seemed to sway. I gripped the chair arms, past caring that my damp hands left finger marks in the fabric.

"Adam and Vanessa have had an understanding for some time," she continued. "Had he not hared off to Cuba to fight in that foolish war, they would have married last year."

I shook my head. "But he promised himself. To me." I reached into my coat collar and pulled out my proof – the ribbon bearing Adam's school ring.

"A friendship token, nothing more." She sent me a pitying look. "I've no doubt my son can be quite the convincing Casanova when it suits him. If it's any consolation, I'm sure he was quite taken with you at the time."

I shot to my feet. "Adam's not like that. He's good and honest and *true*. You should know – he's your son. You *would* know if ever you troubled to hear him out."

Face firming, she stood as well. "If you won't accept my word, surely you'll not repudiate the proof of your own eyes."

She strode over to a mahogany secretary desk and lifted the lid. I followed her, looking on as she sifted through the green baize-lined drawer.

"See for yourself." She plucked a newspaper clipping from the stack and held it out.

Heart drumming, I snatched it away. On the masthead: *Town Topics: The Journal of Society*. Willing my hands to steady, I read the rest.

Heir to the Blakely fortune, Mr. Adam Horatio Blakely attended the annual Bellevue Hospital Foundation Charity Ball held at the Waldorf-Astoria, his manly arm adorned by Miss Vanessa Elizabeth Carlston, daughter of shipping magnate Andrew Beauchamp Carlston and his wife, Meredith "Mamie" Carlston, nee DeVries.

Blinking back tears, I continued...

The golden couple, who began as childhood playmates frol-icking upon the sanctified sands of Newport's Bailey's Beach, was a frequent fixture on the social circuit before B's departure to Cuba for the Spanish war. Hark, what's that ringing sound, you ask? Wedding bells? Whispers of an impending announce-ment do indeed abound. According to a Reliable Source, plans for an Easter wedding are in the works. Rest assured, a full reportage shall follow as the delectable details unfold. Until then, I remain...
    Yours,
    The Saunterer.

A pen nib scratching across paper brought me back to myself. I looked up to my tormentor tearing a bank draft from a leather-bound ledger. "Three hundred dollars, more than enough to cover the cost of your passage back to Ireland or anywhere else you desire."

Three hundred dollars, a minor fortune to one such as myself, a sum sufficient to set up shop on Grafton Street, and still I shook my head. "Keep your money, missus. Whatever poor opinion you have of me, my heart's not on offer, not at any price."

She looked from the draft in her hand to me, and her lip lifted. "A winter's night on the city streets will have you changing your tune."

"I won't. And I don't care what some scandalmonger has to say." I tore the newspaper article in twain and let the halves float to the floor. "If Adam's had a change of heart, then let him say so. To my face."

"Stupid slut," she said with a shake of her head. "Get out before I have you thrown out. Don't show your face here again," she added, hers mottling to match her wallpaper.

I backed toward the door. "Oh, I'll be back. Back for Adam, and then it's his face you'll never see again."

I turned and yanked the door open, knocking into the parlor maid on her way in with the tea. The side of the heavy silver service slammed me, sending china rattling and biscuits flying. I sidestepped the mess and bolted through the gallery to the stairs, the carpeting muffling my fleeing feet, my pulse pounding like surf in my ears.

Descending to the front hall, I spied my carpet bag still by the door. I snatched it, shouldered open the heavy door, and skidded down the front steps to the gate. Only once it closed behind me did I stop to catch my breath and consider my circumstances.

I had nowhere to go.

I began walking, blindly at first but with increasing purpose, the street-lamps guiding my way. Tomorrow, I would decide what to do. For the present, I must find shelter and soon.

Light from the lamp of an oncoming carriage wrenched me from my reverie. I leaped into the snow-covered bushes as the gaudy green convey-ance sailed by, splashing slush from the gutter. Primed to give the driver a proper piece of my mind, I stuck my head out of the frozen foliage and froze.

Adam. The silk top hat was considerably smarter than the wool fisher-man's cap he'd favored on the island, but the clean-chiseled profile beneath was unmistakably his. I opened my mouth to call out, then glimpsed the taken seat beside him. *She* was with him. Vanessa Carlston. The woman, the *lady* he'd meant to marry all along.

Sealing my lips, I watched as he slowed the landau to a stop. The woman, Vanessa, turned and brushed her mouth over his.

With that one kiss, my baby was made fatherless and myself the nearest thing to widowed. One kiss and God help me, I hated her. If looks might do murder, sure mine would have sent her crumpling to the carriage floor.

Fortunately, human life is not so flimsily fashioned. Instead of slaying my rival, I stayed crouched in the hedge, peering past icicles, as Adam turned the gig over to a groomsman and ferried them both inside. Only once they'd disappeared within did I step out from my hiding place.

A coal cart barreled by, so close I felt the wind of it. "Jesus, lady, watch where you're going!"

Shaken, I laid my hand upon my belly and the sweet sapling of a life that sheltered there.

Bide easy, my wee one. I already love you sufficient for two. Once you arrive, I'll be as good a mother – and father – as any child could wish for.

Provided I didn't freeze or starve to death first.

Chapter Twelve

I followed the cable car tracks along Park Avenue, trusting them to lead me back downtown. By then, it wasn't only pitch dark but fierce cold, the biting air making a meal of my coat. Inside my thin gloves, my fingertips burned. The carpet bag might have held bricks, so heavy did it weigh upon me. Nose dripping, I reached into my coat pocket for the hankie. Instead, I came across the flier from the Irish Aid Society.

The paper was dishrag limp, as thoroughly wrung out as the rest of me. Stopping beneath a streetlamp, I looked it over, wishing I'd picked up a map of the city when I'd had the chance. A white-clad dustman happened by, pushing his cart of brooms and brushes. I showed him my paper, not missing how his eyes bugged at the Mulberry Street direction.

"The Bend may be a park now, and most of the old Five Points cleared, but the area's still plenty chancy," he told me.

I shoved the sheet back into my pocket. "All the same, how do I get there?"

"The El. Elevated Steam Engine. It'll take you anywhere in the city for five cents."

He directed me to the nearest station, not so far as I feared. A ten-minute walk took me there. I bought my nickel fare from the booth attendant and crouched against a column to break the bitter cold. Late as it was, the platform was piled with people, most lugging lunch pails, buckets and brooms, and tool satchels.

A short while later, the train rumbled in. I brazened my way aboard, scattering apologies as I went. The conductor called out a message, his speech too thick and rapid for me to decipher, and then the doors bumped closed, and we rattled forward onto the thin ribbon of railway. Caught in the aisle, I seized the nearest leather strap and hung on for dear life.

I got off at Canal Street and Bowery as I'd been directed. Descending to street level, Croton Brewery lay on my one side, Bowery Mission on my other, both landmarks I'd been told to look out for. After several passes of the same stretch of poorly lit, cobbled street, I retraced my steps, and that time, I spotted the crooked, half-hidden signpost for Mulberry Street. The latter led me to a low-slung clapboard house that matched the number on the paper, if not the pious description. In no position to be *wählerisch*, choosy, I pulled back the weathered door and walked in.

The taproom was narrow and sour-smelling, a mix of spilled beer, unwashed bodies, and a pungent, grassy scent I would later know as hashish. A battered bar ran the length of one wall. A few backless stools stood before it, but most patrons stood over their glasses of whiskey and beer. A blousy blond, face painted like a fair dolly's and her décolletage indecently low, held up one corner, arm slung about the neck of a dead-eyed man; otherwise, I was the only female.

I shuffled across the straw-strewn floor to the barman working the taps, his rolled-up shirtsleeves showing off thick forearms, inked from wrist to elbow. "The Catholic hostelry on this street, do you know it?" I asked, thinking the address on the flier must be a mistake.

His gaze flickered to the paper I took out and then back to me. "You're looking at it."

"But this is a... saloon," I said, remembering the word Adam's mother had spoken with such disdain.

He snorted. "*Was* a saloon. Thanks to the good Senator Raines, we're officially a *hotel*."

Named for its sponsor, Senator John Raines, The Raines Law prohibited the sale of spirits on Sundays by establishments other than hotels. Saloon keepers skirted the regulation by adding a modest menu and offering ten lodging rooms for let. But I wouldn't learn all that until later.

"How much for a room?" I asked, hoping that at least the flier's promise of "reasonable rates" could be relied upon.

"Three dollars for the month, collected on the first. You'll share with two other girls, Frankie and Fiona over there." He jerked his bristled chin toward the blond minding me with narrowed eyes.

Three dollars! Considering I had but twenty-five cents to my name, it might as well have been three hundred, and yet...

"I'll take it." I reached for my carpet bag, eager to feel a mattress beneath me.

"Not so fast. Half upfront." He held out his hand, the palm crusted in the creases, the nails long and blackened.

I stepped back. "I'll pay you soon as I find work."

"Will you now?" He spat, shooting an arc of tobacco into the cracked crockery on the counter. "What kind of work is it you do?"

I almost answered barmaid, but glancing again to the blond, I gathered that must mean something very different here. "Seamstress," I said instead.

Chewing on his cheek, he thought a moment. "Seems you're in luck. Fiona could do with a new frock, Frankie, too."

"Provide the material, and I'll fashion whatever you fancy."

He dipped a hand into his apron pocket and took out a key. Only when I reached for it, he snapped it back. "I'll need collateral. In case you take it into your pretty head to skip out."

Sweat dampened my armpits for all that I'd been frozen moments ago. "But I haven't anything of value."

His eye honed upon my throat. "What's on the other end of that ribbon?"

I touched my open coat collar. In my nervousness, I must have unfastened the top button. "A... ring," I admitted. As soon as the words were said, I would have parted with an eyetooth to call them back.

His face brightened. "Give it here," he said, reaching that disreputable hand toward me.

I pulled the ribbon over my head and passed Adam's ring over.

"Princeton, huh?" He fingered the engraved metal. "Fetch more once it's melted."

"Melted, but you mustn't!" A college ring wasn't much of a legacy, but it was all I had of Adam's to pass down to our child.

He studied me a moment. "What's it to you? Whoever you nicked it from got his rich papa to buy him another."

"I didn't steal it. It was a... gift."

"Sure it was, sweets. And I'm President McKinley."

I hoisted my chin. "That ring's worth far more than three dollars, and I'm not the only one of us to know it. Once I pay you, I'll expect it back – un-melted. Have we an understanding? Or shall I bide my time 'til morning and take it to the shops to pawn?"

My bold bluff bore fruit. He shoved the ring and ribbon into a pocket and passed me the key. "You'd better be the seamstress you say you are, otherwise that ring's getting melted, and you'll be paying for your room and board in flesh, not flimflam."

I carried myself and my carpet bag up the crooked back stairs to the top. Crossing the threshold, I set down my bag and took stock. The mean little cubbyhole was hardly a proper bedchamber for one person let alone three, the sole furnishing an ironwork bed wedged beneath the sloped ceiling. I took off my coat and spread it over the mussed covers, then laid myself atop. Despite heartbreak and hunger, exhaustion soon claimed me. I slept, dimly aware of muttered curses and boozy breaths and blowsy bodies shoving in beside me.

Gnawing in my belly brought me waking early. Cracking open an eye, I saw how it was I spent the night so toasty. A dark-skinned brunette with a beauty mark painted aside her mouth purred on the pillow beside me. On my other side, the blond, Fiona, had her tousled head tucked upon my shoulder, her beer-laced breath sending my empty stomach seesawing.

Keeping an eye on my two bedwarmers, both dead to the world, I crawled out and made my way over to the smudged window. In daylight, the derelict block looked more forlorn than it did frightening, the street littered with ash barrels, beer bottles, and more than one passed-out reveler. Resolved that no child of mine would be born overlooking what was little better than a drainage ditch, I turned away and set about making myself as decent as I might.

Slipping my key into my pocket, I went below in search of sustenance. From the near-bare pantry, I scrounged some lard and two eggs, which I cracked into a skillet. Ravenous, I devoured every morsel, using my thumb to mop up the last lick of yolk.

My next order of business was to secure myself a position, one that didn't entail following my roommates into their tawdry trade. I found a rolled-up copy of the previous day's *New York Times* in an ash barrel outside, saving myself the nickel price. I brought it inside and perused the classified advertisements whilst sipping my mug of unsweetened tea. One boxed advert caught my eye, filling me with foreboding.

Wanted, a Cook and a Chambermaid. They must be
Americans, Scotch, Swiss, or Africans; none others need apply.

The following four days, I presented myself at one business upon another. The male foremen and shopkeepers were all smiles until I opened my mouth to speak, then the advertised vacancies were miraculously met. The women were less civil, turning up their noses as if I carried the stench of rotten eggs and stale beer. Considering where I lodged, mayhap I did.

What hours I didn't spend wearing my soles thin in search of work, I devoted to fashioning Fiona's frock. Scowling down from the stool I'd stood her upon, she let out a huff. "My feet are murdering me."

"Quit your bitching," Frankie – Françoise – bellowed from the bed. "I need my beauty nap."

Fiona snorted. "Cats don't nap as much as you do."

Crudities were batted back and forth albeit without much in the way of real rancor. Coarse-spoken and fond of drink though they were, they weren't bad girls. Like myself, they'd come to New York in search of better lives, Fiona from Liverpool, and Frankie from New Orleans. Both had been let down by the men in their lives, Fiona by an elder brother whose new wife had shown her the door, and Frankie by a sailor father who'd walked out on her mother when Frankie was four. Looked at it in that light, we weren't so very different.

Fiona went back to admiring herself in the moisture-spotted wall mirror, a castoff from the bar below. "Blimey, I look a proper lady."

The garish gown the saloon keeper, Big Rick had selected, scarlet bomba-zine edged in black lace, was a far cry from the sophisticated creations I'd copied from Mrs. Murphy's magazines, but I'd seen to it that the fit was perfection.

I stuck the last of the pins into the skirt's hobble hemline and stood. "It doesn't hurt that your figure's a perfect hourglass."

The compliment, sincerely meant, saw her softening. "You're not so bad yourself. Drop some of them buttons, and let Frankie make up your face, and you'd do all right for yourself downstairs. Virgins go for ten dollars a toss."

A virgin – if only she knew. Feeling a fraud, I busied myself with gathering up the rest of my sewing things. "If I don't find work soon, I may have to. I spent my last nickel on the El this morning. I'm officially penniless."

Frankie rolled out of bed and padded over. "Cheer up, *chérie*. You'll find something."

"Until you do, I've got just the thing to perk you up." Fiona stepped down from the stool and began rooting through the clutter. "It's here somewhere. Ah, knew it!" She pulled out a stained magazine from a week-old heap and held it out to me.

Town Topics. The very publication from which Adam's mother had torn out the clip of him with Vanessa Carlston at the ball. Feeling sick, I tried giving it back, but Fi wasn't having it.

"That Saunterer really dishes up the dirt on the hoity-toity," she said with a grin. "He's always good for a laugh."

"*Il est très drôle,*" Frankie concurred, coming up on my other side and opening the periodical to the dog-eared page.

I gave in and took it, the words painting quite a picture.

CHILDHOOD SWEETHEARTS TIE THE KNOT

The wedding of Adam H. Blakely, son and heir of A. Horatio Blakely II, and Miss Vanessa Elizabeth Carlston, only daughter of Andrew V. Carlston, will be celebrated on Monday next at Grace Church, with a champagne luncheon to follow in the Octagon Room of The Windsor Hotel. No fewer than two hundred guests are expected, all from the crème de la crème of Manhattan society.

The oh-so-hasty announcement has taken New York society by storm, for it was generally understood that the couple, bosom friends since babyhood, would not tie the knot until Easter week. Alas, the ardor of youth!

Yours,
The Saunterer

Adam went through the wedding at Grace Church and then the reception at The Windsor like a sleepwalker. Worse than the public farce was the one he must play out in private. Retired to the bridal suite, wedding finery exchanged for nightclothes, a brocade robe over striped silk pajamas for him and a cream-colored silk peignoir trimmed with Valenciennes lace for Vanessa, he lingered over the room-service supper, knowing he but delayed the inevitable.

Vanessa looked up from picking at the lobster on her plate, her waxen prettiness exulted by the candles in the silver epergne set between them. "I didn't realize you had such exquisite taste," she said, stroking the double strand of champagne-colored saltwater pearls, his wedding present to her picked out by his mother.

"Glad you like them." He lifted the champagne bottle from its chased silver ice bucket and topped off her coupe. "They look... very fine on you." Like the candlelight supper for two, the tepid compliment was a step toward making the best of things.

She took a sip, her gaze flickering to his empty glass. "You're not joining me?"

"I did my drinking downstairs, but don't let me stop you."

Throughout the multi-course luncheon with its wearying succession of toasts, he'd imbibed sparingly. On that score, at least, he'd learned his lesson.

She set her glass aside. "On second thought, it wouldn't do to nod off on our first night as man and wife."

Like an actor picking up his cue, Adam pushed away from the table and went to her. Taking her hand, he led them over to the turned-down bed. Beyond their robes, he didn't bother with undressing. Joining her on the bed, his one thought was to get through the thing as quickly as he could. Bittersweet memories flogged him – flame-colored curls fanned over an oilskin blanket, tawny eyes aglow with passion, milky white thighs widening to welcome him. Only by closing his eyes and conjuring my face and form did he manage to do his duty. When at last he released himself, it was my name he moaned into the pillow.

She shoved him away and bolted upright, fair hair flinging into her face, fury radiating from her slight, bristling body. "How dare you!" She hauled back and slapped him.

Flopping back against the banked pillows, he fingered his stinging skin. "It won't happen again."

"See that it doesn't." She flung off the sheet, feet hitting the floor.

"Where are you going?" he asked, watching her cut across the carpet to the call bell.

"To ring Yvette and have her draw me a bath."

Imagining the years ahead, myriad evenings filled with festering bitterness, he let his miserable gaze drop to the empty space beside him. It was then that he saw it, the rusty blot upon the bottom sheet.

Gaze glued to the spot, he elbowed himself upright. "What the hell?"

Halfway to the en-suite bathroom, Vanessa turned back. "My monthly. It's early, but then with all the hubbub over the wedding..."

Had their marriage begun otherwise, Adam would have taken her explanation on faith. As it was, he read the fear in her eyes, heard the tremor in her tone, and shot up from the bed.

"I never laid a hand on you on that train, did I? Until five minutes ago, you were a virgin, weren't you? Answer me, dammit!"

She didn't have to. Her silence confirmed his conclusion as well as any words.

He rounded the footboard and seized her by the upper arms. "Why'd you do it? Why would you even *want* to?"

Defiance fought the fear on her face. "What does it matter? We're married now. You may not be happy about it, I can see you're not, but the fact is I'm good for you. Everyone sees it – our parents, our friends, even the hacks who pen those silly society columns. Everyone but you. You only needed a little push."

A little push.

He shook her then, just once, just a little, not because doing so would get the story out of her any faster but because it felt too good not to.

Holding her at arm's length, he drilled his gaze into her widened pupils. "You're going to tell me everything, starting with what you gave me to get me on that train."

97

Chapter Thirteen

The Great Blizzard of 1899 began as the continuance of a bitterly cold winter. Commencing in Canada on the 11th of February, it swept the eastern half of the continent from Saskatchewan to Cuba, bringing record snowfalls and below-freezing temperatures to every U.S. state. For three days, New York City was as good as shut down. Floating ice blocked the ferry that ran from Wall Street to Brooklyn. The cable car tracks iced over. Water pipes froze then burst. The newspapers recounted the weather-related tragedies, such as that of Brooklyn artist James Coakley, who lost his shoe in the snow and stood to lose his foot to gangrene.

Unsavory as my saloon abode was, at least it kept me warm and safe. Unless I found work soon, I'd not stay that way. My February rent was a fortnight past due. I'd staved off Big Rick by starting on a second frock, this one for Frankie, but it too would be finished soon. I was halfway resigned to joining my two roommates at the bar when I came across an advert for what seemed the answer to my prayers.

The Windsor Hotel at 575 Fifth Avenue, long established as the most comfortable and homelike hotel in New York City, seeks a chambermaid of good character, sound sense, and neat and respectable appearance. Prior experience employed in hotels a benefit. Young women of American, English, German, French, and Scots–Irish origins invited to apply...

Situated on Upper Fifth Avenue, the seven-story brick-and-brownstone hotel stood amongst some of the city's grandest mansions – the brownstone flanked by mayoral lampposts owned by heiress Helen Gould at No. 579; William K. Vanderbilt's "Petit Chateau" at No. 660 and the brick-and-limestone palace covering Nos. 640 and 642 built by his father, William Henry.

The next morning, standing on the shoveled sidewalk, I studied the canopied main entrance and asked myself if I ought to use the baggage door on 46ᵗʰ Street instead. With my coat brushed, half-boots blackened, and hat smartened up with salvage from Fiona's and Frankie's frocks, I fancied I looked neat and respectable. Still, my origins were humble, my speech and manner unmistakably foreign. *Irish.* Before coming to America, I hadn't thought any of that mattered. Now, I knew otherwise.

I might be dithering there still, shivering in my shoes, if not for the doorman pulling back the double doors and ushering me in. Moving through the main lobby, I took in the domed plasterwork ceiling and magnificent marble spiral staircase and wondered how it would feel to work in such a place. Though not yet nine o'clock, a goodly number of guests milled about, several accompanied by personal servants. Nannies minded their charges; one pert ladies' maid took advantage of her employer's distraction to bat her eyes at a well-built bellhop.

I soon sought out the octagonal salon where Adam's wedding luncheon was held. Entering the empty chamber, I pictured it abuzz with two hundred divinely dressed guests, the linen-draped tables set with china and crystal and silver. Filling out the fantasy, I conjured the sumptuous feast that would be served, not all at once but proper-like, in courses. On a dais banded with fat satin bows would be the musicians – a string quartet, I felt certain. As the first sweet strains of a waltz filled the room, Adam would lead his bride onto the dance floor, not Vanessa but myself, wreathed in pearls and smiles and wedding white. Closing my eyes, I stopped where I was and twirled.

"May I help you?"

I snapped open my eyes.

A dapper gentleman of middling years smiled at me from the threshold, his fleshy countenance clean-shaven save for a salt-and-pepper walrus mustache, his bullish neck banded by a boldly patterned bowtie. "Warren F. Leland at your service."

The hotelier himself! I forced my eyes up to his. "Rose O'Neill. I've come about the chambermaid's position."

He led us back through the lobby to his private office. Closing the door, he installed me in one of the armchairs and then sat himself at the mahogany desk fitted with brass pulls and topped with tooled leather. Several silver-framed photographs sat out atop. Seeming in no hurry, he pointed out the people in the pictures: his wife, Isabella, and their four grown children, Charles, Ralph, Helen, and Frances, called Fannie, an invalid to epilepsy. The boys were back in Chicago; his wife and girls lived with him at the hotel.

Smiling over at me, he asked, "Tell me, young lady, what makes you want to work at The Windsor?"

I took a breath. "Why, my uh... experience in doing so."

Granted, I was guilty of gilding the lily, casting my family's pub as a "boutique hostelry for the discriminating traveler", a line I'd lifted from a travel advert and rehearsed until I could say it just so. All the while, I watched his face, pleased when he didn't appear put off by my speech, but then his native Chicago was home to a considerable community of Irish, or so I'd later learn.

A top-to-bottom tour followed. Taking the lobby lift floor-to-floor, I understood that The Windsor was a small city unto itself. All the practical amenities were provided on the premises – barber's shop, grocery, telegraph office, and restaurants serving three meals a day. And such splendor! Rosewood paneling, inlaid with satinwood and black walnut, festooned the public rooms and main hallways. The guestrooms, five hundred in all, were kitted out in curtains, bed hangings, and carpets of crimson, blue, or purple velvet.

Standing inside a vacant fourth-floor guest suite, Mr. Leland pointed out its features as if a proud parent. "A two-bedroom with full parlor and private bathroom such as this runs to two hundred dollars a week," he said without so much as blinking. "But it's not only luxury that has our guests paying top dollar. It's peace of mind." He crossed to the window and pulled back the drapery, displaying the coil of rope anchored to the sill. "In the event of an emergency, guests can lower themselves to ground level, though I'm proud to say there's never been the need."

Back in his office, I'd no sooner resumed my seat when he began rattling off his terms. "As a junior maid, you'll start at $30 monthly, bed and board included – three meals a day taken in the kitchen between shifts. Every other Sunday off, otherwise holidays and leave are granted by seniority. Do you find these terms satisfactory?"

Overwhelmed, I gave a vigorous nod. "I do, sir. Very much so, sir. Thank you, sir."

The corners of his mouth kicked up. "Welcome to The Windsor, Miss O'Neill."

My first week passed in a flurry of early mornings and late evenings, my days bookended by hauling my cart of brushes and cloths, soaps, and polishers to and from the basement. Each guestroom had its own fireplace, and it being winter, cinders must be swept up, fire bars, fenders, and fire irons cleaned and polished and the grate reassembled, and a fresh fire laid. Next, the carpets were brushed, the furniture dusted, and any messes tidied. Once a week, the wood furnishings were polished with the hotel's special recipe of clarified beeswax and turpentine, and the beds stripped and remade, the soiled linens stuffed into laundry bags and sent down to the basement by way of the service lift.

The exacting standards spoke to the loftiness of the patrons we served. Touring opera divas, captains of industry, financiers, politicians, and visiting heads of state were among those who treated the hotel as a second home. Abner McKinley, brother to the President, occupied a suite of rooms on the third floor with his wife and invalid daughter.

Not all hotel guests were of the champagne and caviar set. Among our long-term residents was Mrs. Dora Gray Duncan, a divorcee from San Francisco who gave children's dance classes in a fourth-floor parlor to support herself and her brood of four, including the future dance sensation, then twenty-two-year-old Isadora.

Like Mrs. Duncan, I too must find the means to keep myself and my child without husband or kin to rely upon. Other than the telegram I'd sent Colm and my father to let them know of my whereabouts, and the streetcar fare to Sunday Mass and back, I squirreled away every cent I earned. Whenever the other maids asked me along on their pleasure jaunts to dime museums, kinetoscope parlors, and shopping arcades, I found an excuse to stay behind. As a result, I acquired a reputation for stand-offishness. It didn't help that my progressing pregnancy obliged me to duck behind the dressing screen to change and bathe.

One day, as I was pushing my cart to the basement stockroom to replenish my supplies, Fate delivered what I accounted to be the most welcome and wondrous of surprises.

"Gertie!" I abandoned the cart and flew forward to meet her.

"*Röschen.*" Her arms wrapped about me.

Hugging and laughing, we rocked side to side.

Finally, I let go to look at her. Seeing the same hat and cloak she'd worn on the ship, the same heavy trunk at her feet, I could almost believe it was hours since we'd stepped ashore at the Battery instead of six weeks.

"I thought you were in Cincinnati... with your family."

She hesitated, gaze going to the laundry room. "A story for later, I think. I am here to work."

"That's grand." I clasped her hand. "Let's see you settled."

The maids' dormitory was deserted when we entered, it being the middle of the day. Taking advantage of the rare privacy, I led her to the vacant bed by mine.

"We'll be roommates again," I said, helping her lift the trunk upon the mattress.

Amidst pointing out the washstand and clothespress and the other shared necessities, it struck me that Gerta didn't seem at all surprised to find me here. Tamping down my curiosity, I left her with the mutual promise that we'd talk later that night.

The remainder of my shift crawled by. Out of the blue, the dotty Texas oil dowager in No. 536 announced she fancied brandy with her bedtime mug of warm milk, an order her paid companion countermanded in the strongest of terms. The bachelor lawyer on the sixth floor complained the pipes in his bath yielded naught but cold water. A colicky infant bawled 'til dusk, raising complaints from the adjacent rooms. It was that sort of day.

Let off at last, I made haste to the basement. Tiptoeing into the dormitory, I saw that most were already abed, sleeping, or speaking softly in pairs. A single lamp burned on the bedside table between my cot and Gerta's. Hoping she was yet awake, I shucked off my uniform and dropped the nightgown over my head, for once dispensing with the dressing screen.

"Gerta?" I whispered, coming up to her.

Her lids lifted, and her eyes met mine. "I thought you would never come." She picked up a corner of the blanket and moved over to make room.

Slipping in beside her, I briefly recounted the night's trials. "But what happened in Ohio? When we parted, you were off to help your brother's family with their..."

"*Biergarten.*" She let out a sigh. "I was, as they say, the third wheel. My *schwägerin* likes things one way. I like them another. Nothing I did found her favor. Always my *brüder* took her side, which is as it should be. She is his wife. I was sad to say goodbye to *die kinder*, but I could not stay." Though her face was in shadow, the pain in her voice was plain.

I gave her hand a squeeze. "Someday, you may meet and marry another such as your Sean and have children… *kinder* of your own."

"We will see. I am not a beauty like you, *Röschen*. The men like the dainty doll. I am more the draft horse."

It would be false modesty to claim myself as plain, and yet I rather thought beauty made too much of me. "If you saw me out of this corset, sure you'd change your tune about my daintiness."

She hesitated. "I saw the wedding announcement in the newspapers. I could not read all the *Englisch,* but what I understood was… enough. That is when I knew I must find you."

"But how did you know to seek me here?"

"I remembered the man from the Battery and his Irish boarding house. I went there but you were gone. Two *mädchen* – girls – took me aside. They said you had taken work here. The brown-haired one gave me this."

From beneath her pillow, she brought out a knotted handkerchief. I pushed up on one elbow and opened it. A metal circlet fell out onto the mattress.

Adam's ring. I'd never thought to see it again. Once I'd announced I was leaving, Big Rick had refused to give it up. "Thank you." I tucked the ring into the bodice of the corset I kept on beneath my night rail.

Her eyes met mine in the darkness. "The baby, he is growing, *ja?* When is your time?"

"End of July, I think."

Already, I'd let out the waist of my uniform as far as it would go. Despite my lacings, every week, the fabric stretched tighter.

A frown fretted her forehead. "Soon the bump will be too big to hide. What will you do?"

Suddenly, powerfully weary, I sent out a sigh. "Go to Mr. Leland and beg him to keep me on up to my time, I suppose." That he didn't appear put off by Mrs. Duncan's being divorced gave me hope he might be persuaded, especially if I volunteered to work out of sight in the kitchen or laundry.

She thought a moment. "There is a home for... fallen women on Bank Street run by the Little Sisters of Mercy. I have heard the sisters sometimes take in unwed mothers. If that is so, it would be a safe, clean place for you to bide until the babe is weaned and you can leave him to work again."

I'd racked my brain for weeks, and inside of an hour, my canny friend had come up with a plan. Not only a plan but a solution. "You think they would take me in?"

"I cannot say for certain. We will go there and ask for ourselves."

Moved, I reached for her hand. "Oh, Gerta, I do believe you're the best friend I've ever had."

We agreed to meet up after church that Sunday, Gerta from services at St. Mark's Evangelical Lutheran Church and myself from Mass at St. Brigid's in the Lower East Side. In the meantime, there were two workdays to be got through, and busy ones they promised to be, for that Friday was the 17th of March. Saint Patrick's Day. A grand parade was planned along Fifth Avenue. The hotel was booked to capacity with out-of-towners eager to avail themselves of our prime views.

We said our goodnights, and I slipped from Gerta's bed back into my own. I'd scarcely settled in when I heard my friend's none-too-soft snoring. Smiling, I turned onto my side. For the first time since discovering Adam's duplicity, I faced the future with more hope than fear. Weary as I was, my thoughts galloped on, and it was a good while before I too drifted off.

Chapter Fourteen

Friday, March 17, 1899

Drums and bagpipes announced the parade's approach. Drawn out by the warmish weather, thousands stood three-deep along the roped-off sidewalks of Fifth Avenue, many with shamrocks pinned to their hats and lapels and waving miniature Irish flags.

Unfortunately, the fifth-floor room I hadn't finished making up was on the hotel's 47th Street side and thusly out of view. Stripping off a pillowcase, I glanced at the wall clock. Three o'clock. Telling myself there was no harm in having a peek, I slipped out into the hallway and made my way through the connecting corridors to the closest concourse. A broad bank of windows faced onto Fifth. Quite a few hotel patrons and several staff were installed there already. I glimpsed Gerta standing off to the side and made my way over to her.

Her gaze flickered to me. "It is just reaching us."

Standing on tiptoe, I peered past one lady's feathered hat to the avenue below as the first of several brass bands marched by, instruments and gold braid gleaming in the soft March sunshine. Next came the fire wagons wrapped in green and orange bunting, the strapping firemen in their steep helmets, riding inside or marching along, decked out for the holiday in dark blue dress coats with double-breasted silver buttons.

"O'Neill, over here! You too, Mueller."

Gerta and I shared a look. That baying bellow could belong to but one woman. We turned to the head housekeeper, Mrs. Tolley, bearing down upon us.

"What do you two think you're up to?"

For once, I was the first to speak up. "Watching the parade, missus."

Her pinched face puckered. "How many times must I tell you, it's not missus, it's *madam*?" She turned to Gerta. "You, you're paid to launder, not loiter." Swinging back to me, she added, "And you to clean. I know for a fact No. 536 remains to be made up."

I swallowed. "Sorry, Mrs. Tolley. It won't happen again."

"See that it doesn't. Now back to work, both of you."

Gerta waited for her to walk away before asking, "It is only the one room to finish?"

I nodded. "Cleaning's done, but the bed's still to be made. When I knocked this morning, the lady's maid said missus – *madam* – was sleeping in."

Gerta grimaced. "These lazy peoples, do they not know it is your Irish holiday?"

I smothered a smile, for the celebration, the parade especially, was an American invention entirely. In Ireland, we observed the saint's day quietly and mostly soberly, for it fell during Lent.

"I'd best be getting back. You can tell me about it later." I dragged my gaze from the window and turned to go.

Gerta's hand on my arm stayed me. "I will bring the linens from the press and meet you there. With two of us, the work will go very fast."

"That's good of you, but I couldn't."

But Gerta was adamant. "Friends, this is what we are for."

Rushing back to the room, I caught a whiff of something charred but gave it little mind. Some gentleman's smelly cigar, most likely. Mindful of the ticking clock, I picked up my step and let myself back inside No. 536. I'd just shucked off the bottom bedsheet when garbled shouting from the street sent me hurrying over to the window. Sure enough, another chant rose, and that time, there was no mistaking the crowd's caroling.

"*Fire!*"

Heart hammering, I flew across the room and set my palm upon the door, the panel warmish. Inching it open, I peered out. The corridor I'd only just come through was choked with smoke and fleeing people. A few guests had on their coats, several more carried precious pets or cherished possessions, but most wore only their indoor clothes and were empty-handed.

I fell back inside. Willing myself to calm, I told myself all I need do was dart down the hall, gather Gerta, and together, we'd descend the nearest stairwell to safety.

I rushed to the washstand, snatched up a facecloth, and dunked it into the washbasin I hadn't gotten around to emptying. Covering my nose and mouth with the wet cotton, I slipped out into the hall and joined the stampede.

"Gerta!" I called, my raised voice barely making a dent in the din. "Gerta!" With luck, she was safe outside, as worried for me as I for her.

Ahead, someone got the stairwell door open. Flames flared, beating us back. Though I held to the rear, I felt the blistering upon my brow. We whipped about and charged toward the opposite end of the corridor.

A wall of fire met us there as well. Flames licked our faces. Smoke choked our lungs. I felt as if my flesh must be melting. The fear ratcheted. Pushing and shoving broke out as the terrified sought to break free of the bottleneck. Screams rose to the rafters. A baby wailed. Ceiling beams crackled, the flame-riddled wood buckling. The hallway carpet was by then a river of fire. More flames roared from the elevator shaft. People scattered, ducking into rooms and rushing the windows. I watched in mute horror as one by one, guests climbed onto the sill and stepped off, their screams echoed by the onlookers outside.

I beelined back to the room from whence I'd come. Perspiration poured off me, skirts plastered to my sweaty legs. Bracing my breath, I lowered the towel from my face and used it to turn the doorknob, the brass now molten.

I shut the door and stepped back. My gaze lifted to the lintel and the transom window above it where smoke spilled in through the slats. Coughing, I dragged over a chair and climbed onto the cushion. Arms stretched above my head, I strained to close the casement.

Flames gusted through. I fell back, my howl lost to the chair's crashing. The carpet cushioned my fall but barely. I curled onto my side, cradling scorched hands to my chest.

Lying there, suddenly I remembered – the safety rope – one for every guest chamber! Sobbing, I used my elbows to push myself upright and scrambled over to the window, left open to air the room.

My heart dropped, my hopes with it. Black smoke banded the four floors below me. Lost cause though I likely was, for my baby's sake, I mustered myself and screamed.

Fire company foreman, Captain Joseph Kavanaugh liked nothing better than a parade, and New York's annual procession in praise of Saint Patrick was his hands-down favorite festival. Marching down Fifth Avenue with his fellows from Engine Company No. 6, he was anticipating the string of Bowery saloons where they'd finish out the day when the familiar stench stopped him in his tracks. He swiveled to the hotel on the opposite side of the avenue. Fire blanketed The Windsor's lower four floors, black smoke blowing forth from the windows fronting Fifth as well as those on the 46th and 47th Street sides.

The band stalled to a scratchy stop. Spectators stood dumbstruck, staring up at the hotel, its cornices and fire escapes crawling with people. More of the trapped stood at the open windows, wailing to be saved.

Just then, a life-sized doll dropped from one of the front-facing windows and crashed onto the sidewalk. Only the bloodied, broken carcass belonged not to a doll but a woman. She'd chosen suicide over burning. Joe couldn't blame her, but Jesus, how he wished she'd waited. Several more jumpers followed, the shriek of sirens joining the screams of onlookers helpless to do other than stand by and watch.

Only Joe Kavanaugh had never been helpless a day in his thirty-two years, and he wasn't about to begin being so then. Dumping the daffodils from his presentation trumpet, he lifted the mouthpiece to his lips.

"Liam, pull the engine as close to the Forty-sixth Street side as you can get 'er. Pat, put in the butt! Gordie, send up the aerial ladder! Work her lively, boys. Pump her hard."

Vanessa flung herself into the parlor chair across from Adam's. "How close is it?"

Not for the first time since she'd called him home from work, blubbering into Mr. Bell's acoustic telephone, Adam sought to soothe her. "Not close at all. No farther than Forty-seventh." He reached for the coffee she'd insisted on calling for and poured himself a cup.

"But the smell," she said, hugging herself.

Though their Fifth Avenue mansion was nearly twenty blocks up, the plume of purplish smoke was visible from the upper floors, the acrid stench stealing inside despite the maids sealing all the windows.

"Why not go up and have a nap?" he said, more kindness than he usually showed her.

She narrowed her eyes. "Me, fast asleep with the four walls afire, that would solve all your problems, wouldn't it?"

Stirring sugar into his coffee, Adam didn't dignify the accusation with an answer.

He hadn't shared a bed with her since their wedding night when she'd admitted to managing their "elopement" by dosing his drink with her mother's laudanum. The brandy would have masked the opiate's reddish-brown hue and bitter taste even if he hadn't let her goad him into gulping it. Davis, in on the scheme, had helped get him into the carriage, then driven them to Grand Central. Though Vanessa maintained the butler had acted solely on his own, motivated by the money she'd slipped him, Adam's gut said there was more to the story.

"I'll stay as I am, thank you," she added, spearing him with a look. "Someone needs to see that the curtains and carpets are beaten once the ash clears."

Adam set down his coffee untasted. "People are *dying*, Vanessa. Some have jumped to their deaths to escape burning. Neighbors, like Helen Gould, are opening their homes to the injured."

Her forehead furrowed. "Why not take them to the hospitals?"

As usual, she'd missed his point by miles. "Every facility is flooded with survivors. Some cases require immediate attention – triaging."

"That's awful," she conceded. "But it's not as if there's anything we can do about it."

Adam thought for a moment. The mansion had how many bedrooms? Even living there, he'd lost count. And then there were the public rooms, closed off except for entertaining, which, according to Vanessa, they didn't do nearly enough of. With the furniture cleared and the ceiling fixtures already converted to electricity, the dining room would serve as an ace operating theater, the side parlors as examination rooms and dormitories.

He stood, infused with a foreign and altogether heady feeling. Purpose.

"Where are you off to?" she demanded, following him out into the hallway.

Headed for the butler's pantry, Adam didn't spend a single precious second looking back. "To place a telephone call and see if we can't put this mausoleum to actual use."

Sirens pierced the pandemonium. Fire trucks sped to the scene. Help was on its way. All I need do was stay alive to receive it.

"Lady, down here. *Here!*"

109

Choking on ash, I looked down. Breaking through the blackness, a big man in a dark blue uniform coat and steep fireman's helmet balanced upon a ladder's uppermost rung, a boot braced upon the scrollwork masonry.

"Stand clear," he ordered.

I dropped back. A moment later, a wicked-looking hook struck, cinching onto the window ledge.

He heaved himself up and stuck out his gloved hand. "Grab hold."

I held up my hands, my fingers fat and black as burned sausages. "Can't."

The mouth beneath the thick walrus mustache firmed. "You can. You *will.*" Dark eyes, not a trace of pity in them, fixed upon mine. "My men are working a hose on this wall, but it won't hold for long." His big, gloved hand grasped my elbow. The other struck out to steady me. "Don't look down, look at *me.*"

Steely arms banded about me, bearing me backward out the window. For a few panicked breaths, I felt only air beneath my flailing feet, then my right sole met a ladder's rung, followed by my left.

"Wasn't so bad, was it?" his smiling voice sang into my ear, his breadth binding me to the bricks, his thick coat shielding me from the worst of the steam and spray. "Now, we just have to climb down. Nice and easy. Slow and steady does it. Not too slow, though," he added in that same sunshiny tone.

"H-hurts," I whimpered, pain flaring in my fingers.

"I know, sweetheart, but we're almost there. Lock your arms, and I'll do the rest."

Rung by rung, he guided us down, his strength unflagging as Samson's, his steps unerring as a tightrope walker's. Only I seemed sensible to the blistering heat, to the sparks and ash spitting in our faces as the grand hotel gave way, its mighty walls crumbling like crackers.

We touched down upon the street. A whoop went up, firemen and well-wishers crowding about. My rescuer swung me into his arms and shot off, shouldering his way through. Burying my face in his damp neck, I closed my eyes and surrendered to the luxury of limpness.

Chapter Fifteen

The ambulance bore me to St. Vincent's, the downtown Catholic charity hospital at 195 West 11th Street. Frenzied hours followed, most of which I spent lying upon my gurney, abandoned to the corridor whilst others worse off were worked upon. Eventually, my turn came. A gray-haired doctor bent over me, assisted by a young nurse who held out a tray of bandages, antiseptic, tweezers, and surgical scissors.

"I won't lie to you, young lady," he said. "This is going to hurt."

At his nod, an orderly I hadn't noticed came up from behind and held me down by the shoulders. The first touch of metal to my scored skin set me screaming. The doctor calmly worked on, scraping away my scorched skin, setting bit by bloodied bit upon the tray. It was slow going, agony beyond bearing. And yet bear it I did. They gave me no choice. No matter how pitifully I pleaded or how fiercely I fought and cursed and threatened, they kept on, the nurse cooing soothing sayings I was too wild to heed until finally, mercifully, I fainted.

Later, a knifing sensation in my lower belly brought me back to myself. I was in a ward of metal cots occupied by women and girls wearing light cotton hospital gowns as did I. My hands were wrapped in thick bandages; lighter gauze covered the lesser lesions on my calves and thighs. I swung my gaze to the wall clock. In the lowered light, I could just make out the hands. Five minutes past midnight. Amidst trying to stitch together the missing hours, another stab struck. I howled, hugging my knees to my belly. Something was wrong, horribly wrong, with my baby. Frantic, I pulled myself up and felt about for a bell.

"Nurse! *Nurse!*"

The young nurse, Cynthia, who'd assisted the doctor earlier, materialized at my bedside, her blue-and-white striped cotton uniform dress and white muslin apron rumpled as though she'd slept in them, one starched white cuff bearing a rusty red stain that might be blood or carbolic, her fluted organdy cap askew, as if pinned on in haste. She took one look at me, and her groggy gaze sharpened.

"Where's the pain?" she asked, bending over my bedrail.

I motioned to my belly. "Please don't let me lose my baby."

Peeling back the covers, she looked down – and her pupils popped. "I'll get the night duty doctor right away."

What followed is a blur of pain and fear. The orderly lifting me onto a padded table and wheeling me away. The operating theater with its glaring electric lights and carbolic reek. The mask placed over my nose and mouth despite my thrashing, the connecting hose pumping the ether that would send me tumbling into mindless, merciful oblivion.

When I next awakened, I was tucked beneath crisp cotton sheets in a tiny private room. Bit by bit, recent events trickled back – the horrible heat and fumes, the torture of having my burned flesh sheared away, and lastly the warm, sticky ooze between my thighs. Even drugged, I felt as if a horse cart had rammed me.

Two women stood at the foot of my bed. The younger I recognized as Nurse Cynthia. The elder, about thirty, was bareheaded, her dark hair pulled severely back from her plain, pale face, her somber black gown trimmed in starched white collar and cuffs, her only ornament, a crucifix hanging from her neck on a fine gold chain.

"I'm Miss Katherine Sanborn, Directress of the hospital's School of Nursing," she said, coming closer.

Wondering why such an important person would be at my bedside, I asked, "W-what did I have?"

Nurse Cynthia bit her lip. "A… girl."

I smiled, for hadn't I as good as known it? "She's to be called Mary after my mam." Mary, the English for Moira.

Silence splintered my bliss. Something was missing. Something was wrong. The tiny room was altogether too quiet, too still. True, the births I'd been party to had all happened at home, and yet babies were babies. Lusty bawling followed that first slap upon the bum, but from my sweet Mary, not a mewl.

I lifted my head and looked about for the crib. I saw none. One of the other nurses must have taken the baby to the nursery for washing up. "How soon can I see her?"

The two exchanged glances. Cynthia came to the head of the bed. "Would you like some water?" she asked, reaching for the cup and pitcher set out on the night table.

Parched though I was, I shook my head. "My baby, please bring her to me."

Mute gazes sallied back and forth. I could see the terrible truth writ across their strained features, in the pitying eyes dodging mine.

My baby, my Mary, was dead.

I began to cry.

Still stationed at the foot of the bed, Miss Sanborn spoke up. "Unfortunately, the baby was too premature, her lungs insufficiently developed to survive outside the womb. The doctor will be by later. He can answer any questions you have then."

Not due until summer, of course, Mary would be too tiny and under-developed to survive on her own. Ere then, my mind hadn't admitted that terrible truth.

"I want to see her." Tears streamed my cheeks, but from my voice not so much as a quaver, for I hadn't the luxury of breaking down, not yet.

Miss Sanborn's plain features firmed. "I'm not sure that's wise."

Nurse Cynthia smoothed back my hair with her cool, roughened hand. "You've had a shock. You need rest."

"Don't tell me what I need," I lashed out, poor payment for the kindness she'd shown me. "I need to see my baby. I want to see her. It's my *right*."

Miss Sanborn studied me. "We would need the doctor's permission. If it isn't already... too late."

I gasped. "You've burned her, haven't you?! Tossed her in the furnace, like so much rubbish?" After all I'd been through, had my sweet girl gone up in flames anyway?

"Calm yourself, Miss O'Neill. I'm certain no one has done anything of the sort," Miss Sanborn said, not sounding certain at all.

Nurse Cynthia spoke up. "I could go and... inquire?"

Her superior hesitated, then nodded. "Very well, go. I'll wait with her."

A short while later, the nurse returned, carrying a tiny, pink-wrapped bundle. Pitifully small, more like a miniature doll than a baby, Mary was settled in the crook of my arm.

Desperate to memorize every detail, I scoured her wee, winsome face. She looked so peaceful, eyes closed, rosebud mouth softly parted as if in sleep. Downy hair dusted her head – impossible to tell if it would have turned copper-colored in time or stayed blond as Adam's. Her tiny pink fingernails were a marvel to me. Her nose wasn't yet fully formed, and yet it turned up at the tip as mine did. The ears and chin were Adam's entirely.

I chafed my cheek against her petal softness. "Dinna fret, my wee one. Mummy will have you plump and rosy-cheeked soon enough."

Nurse Cynthia edged closer. "Let me take her now."

I stiffened, handless hold firming. "I'll see her baptized first." I'd die a hundred deaths before I'd turn over my darling to be dumped into a potter's field, unshriven and unmarked.

The directress's face shuttered. "The hospital is flooded with fire victims. Father's going bed to bed, in some cases, administering last rites."

I set my jaw. "Baptism's a rite."

"Yes, but in this case, the child... When the ambulance driver brought you in, there was no ring."

"What does it matter?" I snapped. "Isn't every child a child of God?"

"Of course, but no priest will baptize a baby conceived out of wedlock. As a Catholic, you must know this?"

I did, and yet the prospect of my darling passing an eternity in Purgatory sent a different sort of panic pouring through me. "Have pity!"

"Ladies, what seems to be the problem?"

Our gazes flew to the open doorway. Filling it was the fireman who'd brought me out. He'd exchanged his dress uniform for a camel-colored wool coat, red shirt, and rolled-up boots. Soot-covered as he was, I could just make out the print upon his helmet's white shield plate:

Americus 6
foreman
Jos. Kavanaugh

At Captain Kavanaugh's insistence, a senior sister was called in. "This is most irregular," the nun announced, looking from the dead baby in my arms to himself.

He'd taken off his helmet, which he held tucked beneath one brawny arm. Sweat plastered his short, blue-black hair to his head, the sheen putting me in mind of a raven's wing.

Catching my eye, he flashed me a smile, the effect spoiled by a chipped front tooth. "If you'll pardon my saying so, sister, it's by way of being a very *irregular* kind of night."

Cradling Mary, I said, "I mean to make sure my baby goes to Heaven, sister."

She shook her cornette-covered head, her expression pained. "The Catechism suggests we can entrust the child to God's mercy, for in the scriptures, Jesus said, 'Let the children come to me.' Take comfort in that and be at peace."

Suggests didn't satisfy me. I wanted assurances, absolute, indisputable assurances that my girl's soul would find a host in Heaven. "My only comfort will come from seeing her baptized."

A put-out sigh answered. "The sacrament of baptism is for the living. Father won't consent to do it."

A cough from the corner drew our attention back to the fireman. "If the priest won't budge, then you could do it, couldn't you?"

"That would be most—"

"Irregular," he persisted, eye trained upon me. "And greatly appreciated, not only by me but by the whole of Engine Company Six. As foreman, I have a bit of pull when it comes to deciding where our annual Christmas donation goes. Being a Catholic myself, I've always had a soft spot for St. Vincent's. We all know the good work you sisters do, serving the poor and homeless. But with so many worthy charities, it can be hard to settle on just one."

The nun turned back to me, wimpled face flushing. "In the event of a stillbirth, the grieving parents may find solace in the Church's *Book of Blessings*, 'The Blessing of Parents After a Miscarriage.' If the body of the child is present, as it is here, the mother or father may also bestow a name and trace the sign of the cross on its forehead."

It was as close to the rite of baptism as I could hope to come and a far greater concession than I could have won on my own. "Thank you," I said, more to himself than the sister.

The nun looked to Captain Kavanaugh. "You're the father?"

He flushed, his strong jaw dropping. "Er, no, I just, that's to say—"

"Her father is… passed on," I broke in.

The lie was no lie but my soul's purest truth. After all my months of pining, finally, Adam felt as dead to me as our child.

The blessing was said, and then the sister asked me, "What name would you give her?"

"Mary," I answered, pushing past the knot in my throat.

If she objected to me naming my love child after Our Lady, to her credit, she showed no sign but nodded for me to continue.

Praying my voice wouldn't break, I looked down upon my daughter. "I baptize thee, Mary, in the name of the Father, Son, and Holy Ghost." I sketched the cross upon that sweet, tiny brow and sealed it with a kiss.

The nun's stern demeanor softened. "I'll say a novena for her soul. And yours as well, my child."

Spent, I squeezed my watering eyes closed and nodded.

Nurse Cynthia returned. Watching her walk out with my baby, I fell back upon the pillow, silently praying for God to take me too.

Captain Kavanaugh stepped up to my bedside. "Thank you, sister, and be assured the Christian kindness you've shown here today won't be forgotten by Engine Company Six at Christmas time or any other."

The nun answered with a nod and left us.

Alone with the fireman, I found my voice, gravelly with grief. "For what you did just now, what you said to the sister, I thank you. But not for saving me. I can't thank you for that, not now, not ever. I wish... I wish you'd left me to burn."

He rested his big hand on the bedrail, the knuckles shiny with scars. "Look, kid, you've had a tough break, no doubt about it, but you weren't the only one to lose a loved one yesterday. Leland, the hotel owner, lost both his wife and their daughter, Helen."

Helen Leland hadn't been much more than twenty. Accomplished and kind-faced, she'd been set to continue her studies abroad. Not so now.

"Poor Mr. Leland." My thoughts leaped to Gerta, still missing so far as I knew. "I was with a friend just before the fire broke out, a German girl a few years older than myself. Gerta Mueller. She would have been on the fifth floor as well."

"I'll see what I can find out. Right now, I've got to get back and help wet down the site." He set his helmet upon his head and turned to go. "I'll come again when I can."

Chapter Sixteen

Sleep was my solace, the morphine they dosed me with my gateway to oblivion. Drifting in and out of consciousness, I had vague recollections of a man's face floating above mine, the blunt features lit by earnest dark eyes and a smile peeking out from a walrus mustache, the one top tooth broken nearly in twain, the others perfect as pearls. It was the fireman, Captain Kavanaugh. In my dreams, I wanted to smile back at him. Only once I awakened did I remember why smiling for me was all in the past.

Periodically, the dressings on my hands were changed, the bandages allowed to go from wet to dry and then peeled away, the process – debridement, they called it – meant to remove the topmost layer of my ruined skin so that healthy pink tissue could grow in. It was agony and yet unlike that first time, I neither begged nor railed. Instead, I lay silent and blank-faced as a porcelain doll, or so they told me later. Likewise, when Nurse Cynthia suggested shearing my singed curls to shoulder length, I sat statue still as hanks of charred hair landed in my lap.

Anger was the only emotion I could trust myself to feel. What wasn't turned inward I directed at my savior, Captain Kavanaugh. He'd risked himself to save me, but to what purpose? I was without kinfolk or country, position, or home. Worst of all, I was beyond God's grace, or so I saw myself.

My bandaged hands kept me from killing myself outright. That left starvation, a slower path but the only one open to me. Resolved to take it, I refused the meals rolled up to my bedside. Porridge and clear broth, heavily sugared tea, and squares of twice-burned toast – invalid fare – and still I swore I couldn't stomach it.

"Eat *something*," Nurse Cynthia pleaded, holding the spoon of bone broth to my lips.

I locked my jaw tighter.

She set the bowl back on the tray with a sigh. "Oh, Rose, what I am to do with you?"

Let me die in peace? Rather than say so and distress the poor woman further, I peered past her to the bedside table. My gaze caught on a clutch of daisies arranged in a mason jar, the first I'd seen them there, and a lump landed in my throat. The petals, so white and soft seeming, put me in mind of wee Mary cradled against my cheek.

Following my eye, she smiled. "That nice Captain Kavanaugh brought them. He comes by every evening to look in on you, quiet as a mouse, great big man though he be."

So, the dreams weren't dreams at all. I elbowed myself upright, shocked at the effort even that small action took. "Please, take them away."

She drew back. "But they're so pretty and cheerful."

Pretty and cheerful – as if a fistful of field flowers could chip away at the chill enclosing me. Bandages be damned, I hauled back and struck, my forearm hitting the side of the jar, my mothers' grief felling it to the floor. The girl in the bed nearest mine let out a shriek. Nurse Cynthia hurried off to fetch an orderly. Alone, I stared down to broken glass and floating flowers. *Damn Joseph Kavanaugh. Damn him to hell.*

Every day for the following week, the fire headlined all the newspapers, not only in New York but across the country. As workmen sifted through the ruins, revised rosters of the dead and injured were printed daily. I scoured the lists for Gerta, hoping to find her amongst the survivors. I never did. But by then, the fifth floor was known as the death floor for good reason.

An inquest was held to determine the cause of the fire. In its course, the following official story emerged. At 3:00 p.m., John Foy, a head waiter at the hotel, was passing through the hall on the parlor floor on his way to the bank of bow windows to watch the parade. Ahead, he spotted a gentleman light a cigar and toss the match out the window. According to Foy, the strong breeze blew the lit stick back into the lace curtain, within seconds, setting it and the surrounding draperies afire. Foy tried smothering the flames, but they swiftly spread to the corridor. He then rushed to the fire alarm box, but the pull-chain broke. Leaving it, he raced down to the main floor to alert the front desk and lastly to the basement laundry, crying, "Fire!" as he went.

The careless smoker story had its skeptics. As reported in *The New York Times*, third-floor guest Colonel C.B. Cowardin, President of the Richmond Virginia Dispatch Company, had detected a charred odor as early as nine o'clock that morning, suggesting the fire had smoldered all day in the walls or flues running from the third to the top floor on the hotel's south-eastern side.

Beyond dispute was the outcome. Forty-five bodies were recovered from the rubble, not all of them identifiable. Another forty-one remained missing. It was assumed the unclaimed would be buried in a potter's field, but Mr. Leland pronounced the notion sacrilege. The coffins of sixteen unidentified corpses and a seventeenth filled with sundry body parts were laid to rest at Kensico Cemetery in Westchester at that good man's expense.

Not all the news was a testament to tragedy. Daring rescues were reported. A bicycle policeman, Charles Liebold, singlehandedly rescued five men from a lower floor, one of whom he had to haul over his shoulder. Nor were all the rescuers two-footed. *The Mail and Express* printed a picture of Nell, the Dalmatian mascot of Hook and Ladder No. 21, who came through the fire but narrowly.

But by far the gallant heroes of the day were the firemen. Fire Chief Binns singled out ten of his top men to be placed upon the Roll of Merit, but only one did he recommend for the coveted James Gordon Bennett Medal for exceptional bravery in the service of saving lives.

Captain Joseph Kavanaugh.

Adam poked his head inside his father's office. "A word?"

Horatio looked up from the stock reports scattered across his green baize desk blotter. "I'm headed into a meeting. Can it wait?"

Adam held his ground. "I'm afraid it can't."

His father blew out a breath and flagged Adam inside. "Very well, but be quick."

Adam pulled up a straight-back guest chair. "About the fire at The Windsor, did you read the *Times* article I put on your desk?"

Horatio nodded. "Terrible tragedy, but does that justify targeting every business owner in this city? Labor reform will bankrupt us all. Once we're forced to close our doors, who will put bread on their tables then, hmm?"

Adam girded himself. "If we implement minor modifications now, install fire stops and sprinkler systems, and ensure that all exits are kept unblocked and the fire escapes are in working order, the existing hotels and factories can be rendered fireproof within the year. Not only will we court the goodwill of our workers and the public, but we may prevent another tragedy."

A sour look answered. "Must I remind you that we're answerable to our shareholders? They expect us to make money, not spend it unduly." Horatio sat back, signaling the subject as closed.

Only Adam wasn't ready to give in. "I admit profits will take a hit in the first few quarters, but in the long run, we'll more than make back any monies laid out in increased productivity. Look at it as an investment in the future, not a capitulation—"

"I assure you our competitors won't be *capitulating* to the demands of the ragged rabble. We can't afford to either."

"Damn it, Dad, we're talking about human lives, not only figures on a ledger sheet."

"There are sufficient honest, hard-working, God-fearing men and women in this country only too glad to give a fair day's work for a fair day's wage. The next thing I know, you'll be pushing me to reduce the shifts from ten to eight hours! Whoever heard of an eight-hour workday? I don't work only eight hours. Why should they?"

Adam raked a hand through his hair. "The majority of machinist accidents occur in the tenth hour. Men and boys maimed for life, in some cases killed because they nod off while working the equipment."

"If they're tired, then let them go home at the end of their shift and not to the saloons."

Such bullish prejudice, such callous disregard for the plight of one's fellow man! How was Adam to reason with such a person? The plain answer: he wasn't.

"The workers in this city have grown soft, Adam. This fire, while regrettable, is being exploited by the yellow press to stir up the populace for no purpose other than to sell papers."

"At least let me present my proposal to the board. Why not put it to a vote and let the members decide?"

It was his father's turn to lose his temper. "This chair isn't yours yet. Your time will come, and when it does, you'd better hope you're man enough to fill it."

Adam rocketed to his feet, nearly setting the spindly chair on its side. "If you despise my ideas so much, release me. I'll gladly walk away from all of it tomorrow, make that *today*."

"Ungrateful whelp! Whether you want it or not, whether you're fit for it or not, Blakely Enterprises is your birthright. Now take yourself home to your wife. If you won't make yourself useful here, the least you can do is sire me a grandson."

Day upon day, Captain Kavanaugh turned up at my bedside, usually in the early evening when the supper trays were delivered. "You'll feel better with a hot meal in your belly. I know I do," he said when, once again, I refused to touch a morsel.

Propped upon pillows, I regarded him in hostile silence.

He pulled the wooden visitors' chair up to my bedside and straddled the seat. "You don't want 'em to have to resort to the feeding tubes. Nasty business and painful, too."

The veiled threat saw me leaping to life. "Let them try!"

"Easy now, no cause to get your back up. Skinny as you are, you just might crack a rib. Instead of starving yourself, maybe clear out the pipes with a good cry?"

"What would you know of it?"

He sent me a long look. "I have four nieces and nephews, five, counting the baby. It's a rare day one of 'em isn't howling his head off about something or other, and as far as I know, they're all healthy as horses."

What an insensitive clod to prattle on about children, babies especially! If only I might have use of my hands, I'd slap him silly. I pushed myself onto my elbows, or so I tried to. My wasted muscles gave way, my arms buckling.

He was on his feet in an instant. "If you don't start eating soon, your next bed will be a pine box. Is that what you want?"

Collapsed upon the bedstead, I felt tears welling, my first in more than a week. "What if it is? When will you get it through that brick of a brain that I'm none of your concern?"

"Like it or not, being the one to pull you out makes for a kind of bond between us."

"Sure you must be expecting a medal," I shot back, not then knowing he'd been recommended for The Bennett.

Too modest to say so, he settled for a shrug. "A kind word every now and again wouldn't hurt." He handed me a rolled-up copy of *The Times* I'd asked him for and reached for his coat. "I'll come again tomorrow. In the meantime, take a good look around. You're not the only one who's lost something or someone."

His words ate at me. After he left, my gaze went to the full beds about me. Some patients I knew from The Windsor, by face if not name. My nearest neighbor, a waitress in the hotel restaurant, had burns over three-quarters of her body, one side of her face swathed in bandages. Another I recognized as one of the maids from my dormitory. She'd jumped from a lower window, crushing her right leg so badly the doctor had amputated above the knee. Looking on as she played solitaire, a dip in the blanket where her calf would have been, I felt a stab of shame.

That evening, when I turned up my nose at the supper tray that arrived, my grumbling gut made a liar of me.

"Somebody's feeling better," Nurse Cynthia said. "I can help you if you like."

Not yet willing to surrender, I shook my head.

She set the tray on the night table. "Suit yourself. The orderlies will be by in the morning to collect it." She turned on her heel and strode off.

Around me, my fellow patients tucked in. Surrounded by smacking lips and scraping cutlery, I steeled myself to stay strong.

The call for lights out should have brought relief, only I couldn't sleep. The longer I lay awake, willing myself to think of anything, absolutely anything, but the food within reach, the more my mouth watered. Finally, I pulled myself upright, twisted my torso, and made a clumsy grab. The spoon I dropped on the first go. Swinging my legs over the bedside sapped what strength I still had and brought the hem of my hospital gown riding my thighs. Glancing down at myself, I gasped. My limbs had withered to sticks, for all that they felt lined with lead, my knees knobby as a crone's. I leaned toward the tray, the small movement sending the room reeling. Sucking down air, I tried again, that time hooking my left arm through the metal bedrail and reaching out with my right.

The congealed stew was the consistency of glue and the color of ash. I caught myself smacking my lips and darted a look about. Fortunately, my ward mates all seemed to be sleeping, the dormitory filled with snores, sighs, and the odd moan, the night nurses out in the hallway too busy to look in. Satisfied, I released the bedrail and braced the bowl betwixt my hands. Like an animal frantic to feed, I dropped my head, lapping up bits of briny beef and morsels of mushy carrots and brownish potatoes. When, chin dripping, I finally lowered the vessel to my lap, there wasn't a drop left, not of the stew and not of my pride either. The broth might have been beef, but it was crow I'd eaten. Owing to Joe Kavanaugh, I hadn't only forsworn my fast.

I'd decided to live again.

Chapter Seventeen

Adam walked in from butting heads with his father to find Vanessa waiting. He'd scarcely handed over his hat and coat to their butler when she popped out from a side parlor.

"I need to speak to you," she said, sounding grave.

In no mood, he started for the stairs. "Can't it wait 'til dinner?"

She followed him to the landing. "It can't."

Adam set his briefcase on the step and turned around. "All right, I'm listening," he said, aware he wasn't the only one.

Out of the side of his eye, he spied Yvette Bellerose, Vanessa's lady's maid-cum-companion, holding back by the parlor pocket doors. Since the wedding, the women were inseparable, Yvette hovering over her charge like a voluptuous mother hen.

Wound tight as piano wire, Vanessa bolstered herself with a deep draw of breath. "I need you to break things off with the tart you've been seeing."

So, she'd found out about his Friday-night forays to Longacre Square. The intersection of Broadway and Seventh Avenue was a hub for theaters and variety saloons, lobster palaces – and brothels of the better sort. He had a regular girl he saw, a redhead who went by Sally. Though her hair was helped along by a dye bottle, and her eyes were hazel, not brown, she bore a passing likeness to me – so long as he kept the lamp low.

"Aren't you even going to deny it?" she demanded when he still hadn't spoken.

Adam shrugged, gratified that at last, his loathing had dulled to a distant dislike. "What would be the point?"

She fastened her furious gaze on his face. "The point is I'm… *we're* having a baby."

Another lie, it must be. He hadn't gone near her since their wedding night. Pregnancy was possible, of course, but the odds had to be slim.

He folded his arms across his chest. "Given our history, I admit to some skepticism."

"Speak to Dr. Holtz if you like. Why else do you imagine I'm so ill all the time?"

He thought back over the last month – her keen distaste for certain foods down to their smells, her late-morning lie-ins. "Why delay the happy declaration?"

She hesitated, a bright pink blotch crowning either cheek. "I've had some… irregularities in the past. Dr. Holtz warned I might have difficulty carrying a pregnancy to term."

Adam studied her, taking in the chalky pallor, the smudges beneath her eyes. Some women did still die giving birth. Puerperal fever and hemorrhage were but a few of the things that could go wrong, and Vanessa had just admitted to a history of female problems. She might be a heartless bitch, a dauntless dragon, but her constitution was on the delicate side. As children, she'd always seemed to be laid low with one ailment or another.

But no, this was wicked! This was wrong! Whatever else Vanessa was, she was his unborn child's mother. He was to be a father. Strictly speaking, he *was* a father. For the first time since he'd awakened on that train, he saw a glimmer of hope breaking through the bleakness.

"How are you feeling?" Instinctively, he reached a hand toward her still-flat belly, then caught himself and pulled back.

The laugh she let out could have cut glass. "If I didn't know better, I'd think you cared."

Adam did care. He cared deeply – for his unborn child. "No more late evenings until the child is delivered."

She eyed him. "If you expect me to sacrifice the pleasures of civilized company, then I'll expect a similar sacrifice in return. Your forays to Longacre Square end as of now."

His standing Friday-evening rendezvous with Sally was the one bright spot in an otherwise bleak existence, her gaudy boudoir his sole sojourn from pretense and duty and numbness. But now that he was to be a father, he couldn't very well continue as he had.

"Very well. You have my word."

She blinked as if startled by his easy acquiescence. "I mean it, no more sneaking around."

That he hadn't *snuck* at all was a trifling point. Rather than argue it, he stuck out his hand. "Rest easy, Vanessa. It looks like we've struck yet another deal."

Gaze going over me, Joe flashed a smile. "We'll have you back to your fighting weight in no time."

"You don't have to look so pleased with yourself," I said sourly, spooning up the last of the jacket potatoes in gravy, my thick mitts replaced by lighter bandages.

"Can't help it. You don't look like the same woman from three weeks ago."

"Burned toast, you mean?"

His smile flattened. "You were lucky."

I let the spoon drop. "Ah, yes, lucky me," I said, the sarcasm salted with self-pity.

"I'm sorry about the German girl. And... the baby. I heard the nurses talking amongst themselves. The doctors say you can have more."

"I don't want more," I said, voice faltering. "I want *her*."

He rested his forearms on the bedrail. "That's how you feel now, and who could blame you? But you may change your mind... in time."

"I won't. Besides, who'd have me now?"

"You might be surprised," he said softly, and for a hitching heartbeat, I thought he meant to kiss me. Instead, he straightened and drew back. "You and him, is it over?"

I didn't have to ask who he meant. "I haven't had a word from him since before I left Ireland, and I don't wish to." Men such as Adam didn't plight their troths with poor publicans' daughters. I understood that now, albeit too late. Brooding on the easy mark I'd made, I eyed him. "What of yourself? Are you promised?"

Gaze on mine, he shook his head. "Nope."

"A sweetheart, then?"

Another headshake.

"Why's that?" I asked, resolved not to let my guard down, not ever again.

He frowned. "Well, it's not for lack of interest or opportunity if that's what you're getting at."

126

"Ladies' man, are you?" I pressed, watching him closely.

"Keeping fireman's hours doesn't leave much leeway for courting. But for the right girl, I'd make the time."

I studied him. Brawny, broad-shouldered, and buff, he cut an impressive figure. And while the broken nose and chipped tooth spoiled any pretense to prettiness, rather than detract, the roughness seemed to add... *something*.

"So, Miss O'Neill, you see before you an honest bachelor, free as a bird." Amusement flickered in his gaze, but I saw something else there too, something stronger and altogether more dangerous.

Hope.

"Top of the morning to you, Miss O'Neill." Smiling ear to ear, Captain Kavanaugh sidled up to my bedside the following Sunday, hat in one hand and clutch of camellias in the other.

He still wore his church clothes, a three-button waistcoat and striped flannel suit, decent, if too tight in the shoulders, his pomaded hair center-parted and combed back from his brow. Seemingly blind to the swoony looks trailing him, he dropped the bouquet into the jelly jar and pulled up what I had come to think of as *his* chair.

Catching a whiff of the Florida Water in which he must have all but bathed, I said, "You do know that actual Irish never greet each other that way?"

"Really? I'm Irish on both sides of the blanket, and I say it all the time." He drew closer, the scraping of chair legs setting my teeth on edge.

"Captain Kavanaugh, if you've taken it into your head to—"

"Joe's the name... Joseph, after my dad. Joe or Joseph, I answer to either."

"I don't want you to answer at all. And I'll thank you to wipe that silly grin off your face."

"Is my face really so offensive?" he asked with the confidence of one who knows the answer to be in his favor.

Lifting my gaze from my secret weakness, his manly chin, squarish and cleaved by a dashing dimple, I concentrated on his walrus mustache, the style made popular by Theodore Roosevelt, now state governor. "That bristly bush, I'm surprised it hasn't caught fire ere now."

He sat back, turning his face side to side. "Would you like me better if I shaved it off?"

"Who's to say I like you now?" I tossed back even as I wondered about the firm-looking lips beneath the fringe.

His eyes met mine, and in their dark depths I detected a challenge. "Oh, you like me all right."

I snorted. "Sure, that's one person's opinion."

"You're just too stubborn and ornery to admit it."

Resolved to give not so much as a crumb of encouragement, I answered, "You remind me of my older brother, Colm."

Put out, he pondered that. "Handsome feller is he?"

"Not particularly. But you're both big as bulls and thick as two planks. And he has one of those crumb-catchers, too."

"It's not every man who can grow one so full and thick," he bragged, stroking his upper lip. "Soft, too. Fancy a feel? Oh, right, the hands. I suppose I could be persuaded to settle for your lips instead."

"Captain Kavanaugh!"

He toyed with one waxed tip. "Don't get your hackles up, I was only joshing – teasing," he translated. "But seriously, think I'd be handsomer without it?"

"You wouldn't be any uglier."

And so our interchanges went.

Even for an Irishman, he could fill up a stretch of silence like nobody's business. Beneath the bluster and blarney, there was a beautiful sincerity underscoring even the tallest of his tales. Sometimes he spoke of his prize-fighting days, the origin of both the broken tooth and scarred knuckles, but mostly, his stories centered upon his family – his sister, Kathleen, who'd raised him after their parents passed, her fireman husband Patrick – Pat – and their brood.

And then one evening, he didn't turn up at his usual time.

"No gentleman caller tonight?" asked the girl playing solitaire in the cot next to me.

Her stump was healing nicely, they said. Like me, she'd be discharged soon.

I glanced up from the fashion magazine I couldn't seem to concentrate on. "Seems not."

She pulled another card from the deck. "That's too bad."

"He can come or not, it's all the same to me," I said, making a show of turning the page.

128

She snorted. "Fine-looking feller like that can park his boots under my bed any day."

I shot her a look and went back to reading – or tried to.

Nine o'clock came, and the ward lights flickered to dim. Around me, patients put away their puzzles and books and settled down to sleep. Restless, I slipped out of bed. Pacing the empty aisle, I owned how much Joe's visits had come to mean to me. With Gerta gone, he was the closest to a friend I had, our sparring a more potent tonic than any drug the doctors dosed me with. Coming up with cutting comebacks and fresh insults gave me a reason to wake up mornings. Only it seemed I'd tested him one time too many. Finally, he'd seen sense and washed his hands of me.

"Careful, you'll wear holes in the floor."

I swung to the doorway. Joe leaned on the side post, helmet tucked beneath his arm, his face smudged and hair sweat-soaked, a stronger-than-usual smokiness clinging to him.

"Thought I'd poke my head in and see how you're doing," he whispered, both feet planted out in the hallway. "Now that I have, I'll be on my way."

"But you just got here," I protested.

"If they catch me loitering, they'll kick me out for sneaking in after lights out."

"I don't believe you snuck in at all," I said, tamping down a twinge of jealousy.

More likely, he'd sweet-talked his way past the nurses at the front desk. Ordinarily, such staunch sentinels, they seemed powerless against his cheeky charm, the younger ones especially.

A flash of white teeth answered. "Could be Nurse Flannery's got a taste for lemon drops. And Nurse Stevens isn't opposed to a chuck 'neath the chin now and again."

Wondering if Nurse Stevens' chin was all he had... *chucked*, I said, "Still, we'd better hide you, hadn't we?"

He followed me over to my cot, and I drew the curtained divider closed around us.

Turning up the bedside lamp, I whispered, "Take your coat off at least."

He obliged, shucking off the heavy tan garment and dropping it over the chairback. His back was a beautiful thing, the red wool shirt stretched taut across broad shoulders and a tapered torso, a waterfall of rippling muscles marking the terrain between.

129

He turned to face me, and that's when I spotted it, the corner of a bandage peeking out from the cloth knotted about his throat. "You're hurt. Burned." Amongst all the dangers the world contained, fire now held a special, sinister significance.

He touched a hand to the side of his neck. "Bit of blistering is all. A burning board thwacked me good. One of the medics fixed me up." His gaze burrowed into mine. "If I'd known you'd look at me like you're doing now, I'd have taken a match to myself weeks ago."

"That's a horrid thing to say. And I'm not looking at you any different than I ever do."

Solemn eyes stayed upon mine. "Oh, that's where you're wrong. You're looking at me like maybe you care. Like maybe I matter something to you."

"Of course you matter. We're friends, aren't we?"

"Friends, huh?" he said, looking less than pleased.

Reminded I wore only the thin hospital gown, the hem hanging at mid-calf, I slipped back into bed.

He dropped into the chair, gaze going to the food tray by my bedside, untouched beyond a bite of biscuit. "Back on your hunger strike?"

"Wasn't hungry is all. You have it. It'll go to waste otherwise."

I didn't have to offer a second time. He pulled the tiny table closer and tore in. Even the cold soup disappeared, spooned up amidst accounts of the earlier fire.

"Ah, Rose, it was a close thing, the blaze fierce as Lucifer's breath. Took near a full tank to make a decent dent in it, and just when we did, one of the hoses gave up the ghost."

Hugging my knees, I asked, "Aren't you ever... afraid?"

He tugged the napkin from his collar and tossed it atop the cleared plate. "I figure when it's my time, it's my time, and that's that. Until then, might as well do what I'm cut out for."

It was a curiously comforting thought. If he was right, then maybe Mary's loss wasn't my fault or even Adam's. Maybe, our Maker had called her home to serve some higher purpose.

"Thought about where you'll go after you're let out of here?" he asked, pulling me back to the present.

I plucked a loose thread on the wool blanket. "I'd go home to Ireland, but my savings went up in smoke along with the hotel."

As had my clothing and other possessions, including Adam's school ring. It had escaped melting by Big Rick only to suffer a similar fate at The Windsor.

"If I stay on in New York, I suppose I could take holy orders," I added though, to be truthful, the prospect of consecrating my life to Christ was lessening in appeal of late.

By the looks of him, he didn't much fancy either alternative. "Don't do anything hasty. Give yourself time to think things over."

I let out a low laugh. "And how do you propose I keep myself whilst I do all this fine thinking? Until my hands heal, I won't be any use for working."

Earnest eyes met mine. "You could come home with me."

"Captain Kavanaugh!" I exclaimed, well and truly shocked. Granted I wasn't exactly respectable, but I hadn't sunk so low as to set up housekeeping with a man not my husband.

To this day, I've never met a man who could match the swift, deep blushes of Joe Kavanaugh. He went pink from the points of his collar to the center part in his hair.

"Cripes, that came out all wrong. I meant to my sister and brother-in-law's. Kathleen and Pat's flat's no palace, but it's clean and safe and not the worst place to hole up while you find your footing."

"That's good of you, but I won't impose."

"You wouldn't be. With four kids and now the baby, Kathleen could do with the female company." He hesitated, looking as though he'd something more on his mind. "I know your life's been turned inside out, and you're feeling all alone in the world, but you don't have to be, leastways not unless you're set on it."

Unsure of what to say to that, I stayed silent.

He stood. "I'll say my goodnights now and let you get some shuteye." He collected his helmet and coat and reached for the curtain.

Even knowing he'd be back the next evening, I couldn't keep from calling out. "Joe?"

He turned back, face wearing a rawness I recognized as longing.

Meeting his eye, I forced out the words that had stayed stuck in my throat for far too long. "Thank you."

Chapter Eighteen

It felt strange to be out in the world again. A siren or passing paddy wagon sufficed to send me quaking in my borrowed half-boots – and seeking refuge at Joe's side.

The tenement at 97 Orchard Street, where Joe lived with his family when he wasn't on call at the stationhouse, was a five-story brickwork building of twenty-odd flats with a striped canopy sagging over the entrance and a beer dive in the basement. The interior entryway was dimly lit and sour-smelling, the pressed leather wall covering peeling in places. A narrow set of wooden stairs led upward. Still weak, I kept my arm linked with Joe's.

On the way up, he gave me what he liked to call "the lay of the land." There were four flats and two toilets to a floor, the washroom shared by adjacent families and accessed through a connecting door. Each flat was outfitted with a kitchen tap, running cold water, and a single window that opened onto the airshaft. Despite the close quarters, neighbors generally got along.

At the fourth floor, we stepped off into a narrow corridor, low-ceilinged and surprisingly quiet. Fishing in his pocket for the key, Joe led us to a door at the far end, its chipped brown paint making it indistinguishable from its fellows.

He poked his head inside and called out, "We're here."

I peered past him to the tiny kitchen where a man, stripped down to his flannels, sat at the table shuffling a deck of playing cards. "Hiya, Rose," he said, as though we'd met before. "You look a sight better than you did that day at The Windsor."

Joe shot him a look then turned back to me. "That diplomat would be my brother-in-law and fellow smoke-eater, Patrick."

Tucking my hands inside my coat sleeves, I murmured a hello.

A sturdily built brunette stood at the cast-iron stove covered with cookpots, a baby swaddled to her breast. "I'm Joe's sister, Kathleen, and this one's long-suffering missus." Wiping floury hands on her apron, she looked me up and down and then over to her brother. "What are you thinking to keep the poor girl standing out in the hallway? Bring her in."

I'd no sooner set foot inside when children seemed to come out of the woodwork, two boys and two girls, all talking at once. Joe's whistle quieted them. From eldest to littlest, each youngster was called forth and introduced: Patrick, after his dad, though he went by Paddy, Garrett – Gary, Maureen – Mo, and Norah, just turned five.

I felt the tug of tiny hands upon my skirt, and a lisping voice piped up, "Pretty."

Draped in hand-me-down homespun and an oversized coat, my shorn hair stuffed inside a shapeless cap, the piecemeal ensemble provided by the good sisters of St. Vincent's, I'd never felt less pretty in all my life. Still, looking into little Norah's upturned face, I couldn't help but smile.

"Thank you, darling. You're very pretty yourself."

Kathleen sidled up. "This is our Katharine," she said, pressing a kiss atop the baby's downy-dusted head, "though she goes by Katie."

Raw from my recent loss, the sight of that sweet, perfect infant ripped at my heart. "She's lovely," I managed, a catch to my voice.

Kathleen jerked her chin to her husband. "Pat, my love, do you think you might hoist your arse from that chair and bring in the bags?"

Face warm, I admitted, "I'm afraid I lost all I had to the fire."

Kathleen flagged a hand in the air. "No worries, we'll fix that soon enough."

"Please don't put yourself to any more trouble on my account. It's more than kind of you to take me in."

She snorted. "Kind, my foot! I'm desperate for another woman to talk to."

Joe shot me a wink as if to say *I told you so.*

Laying a light hand upon my bandaged one, Norah asked, "How'd you hurted yourself?"

Kathleen frowned. "That would be 'hurt', and how many times must I tell you it isn't polite to ask personal questions?"

"I don't mind." I turned back to the child. "A big building, a hotel, caught fire, and they were burned, but they're much better now."

"Did Uncle Joe save you?" This from the middle boy, Garrett.

Out of the corner of my eye, I caught "Uncle Joe" watching me. "He did. He was very brave."

"There's not a fire anywhere he can't beat." The boast came from the eldest boy, Paddy.

"Uncle Joe's the bravest smoke-eater in the whole city," Maureen put in.

I looked over at Joe, ears pink and eyes on the floor.

Kathleen gestured to the nook that served as a kitchen. "Go wash up. Dinner's done."

Norah looked back to Joe. "Afterwards, will you tell us a story?"

Reaching down, he chucked her beneath the chin. "I will, provided you mind your ma and eat your green beans."

"A ghost story?" Gary put in.

Kathleen rolled her eyes. "I'd like to sleep a wink tonight, if you don't mind."

"I have a story even better than ghosts," I blurted out, surprising myself as much as anyone.

Paddy stared at me askance. "What's better than ghosts?"

I thought for a moment. "I'll tell you a tale of the fairy folk. Unlike ghosts, they're real."

His brother frowned. "Fairies aren't real."

Catching Joe's eye, I said, "Sure, that's what they *want* you to think. But first, mind your mam and wash up."

They filed into the kitchen, little Norah bringing up the rear. Almost to the sink, she whipped about and rushed back to me. "I'm glad you got saved," she said, hugging my legs.

Throat thick, I reached out a bandaged hand and touched her cap of reddish-brown curls. "So am I," I said and realized I meant it.

97 Orchard Street, No. 4A, New York, NY
20ᵗʰ April 1899

Dear Da, Colm, and Kil,

By now you may have read of the fire that razed a grand New York City hotel. Whilst I was indeed at The Windsor on that dreadful day, I am amongst those fortunate to have escaped with my life. Barring a few burns and bruises, I am well, though without a permanent home or situation. For the time being, I am

lodging with the Mulraneys, a fine family of Catholic faith and
Irish origins, my room and board given in exchange for helping
the goodwife to keep house and mind her five children. 'Tis herself,
sister to the fireman who carried me out, who takes down this
letter – alas, bandaged hands make for poor penmanship! It may
be some while before my next letter – in my own hand, I do hope.
Until then, I ask that you send news of yourselves, and home, to
the above direction.

Your devoted daughter and sister,
Rose

Humbled by the hearty welcome I'd received, I resolved to make myself as useful as I might. On my first day, I took up the broom and managed to sweep most of the main room until Kathleen beckoned me over to the kitchen table where she sat breastfeeding the baby.

"Take her, will you?" She held Katie out to me, the child's chubby legs pedaling air.

"My bandages," I protested.

"If you can hold a broom, you can hold a baby." Before I could beg off again, she shoved Katie into my arms. I tried handing her back, but Kathleen was adamant. "You'll be a regular little mother inside of a day," she assured me, buttoning her shirtwaist.

The tug-of-war was repeated over the following few days. Whatever housekeeping task I took on, Joe's sister always brought me back to minding the baby. Tending that sweet, perfect cherub day in and out, I began to consider that one day I might have another child. Both Adam and our Mary were lost to me, but was it too much to hope that I might have a second chance for an ordinary woman's dreams? A baby to love, a hearth of my own, and a good, steady man to share it? A good, steady man like... Joe Kavanaugh?

Weeks went by. Spring slipped into summer. Accustomed to mild summers softened by bay breezes, the heat and humidity took getting used to. My flannel underthings clung to me, chafing in the most inconvenient places. If not for the men about, I would have stripped down to my shift as Kathleen and the girls did. Instead, I stayed dressed, suffering beneath my buttons.

On the 21st of July, the city's newsboys went on strike. Thousands rallied under the charismatic Louis Ballett, dubbed Kid Blink for his blind eye, to demand a return to fifty-cent bundles. During the Spanish war, when newspapers were flying off the stands, publishers had raised the cost of a hundred-paper bundle to sixty cents. Most had since returned to the pre-war price with two notable holdouts: Joseph Pulitzer's *Evening World* and William Randolph Hearst's *New York Evening Journal*. The stand-off turned ugly. For days, the boys and their supporters blocked the Brooklyn Bridge, cutting off newspaper delivery to northern cities. Pulitzer and Hearst retaliated by hiring strike-breakers and protection men to rough-up the protesters.

A longstanding member of the Knights of Labor, Joe stood solidly with the strikers. One evening, he walked in with split knuckles and an ear-to-ear grin. Peace was restored on August 2nd when Pulitzer and Hearst agreed to buy back any unsold stock.

More than once during that steamy, contentious summer, I found myself thinking of Adam and not kindly. Born to riches, did he ever stop to consider how we, the Other Half got on?

But I had more pressing worries to occupy me. Since the fire, my life had been in the hands of other people entirely, the doctors and nurses of St. Vincent's and now, the Kavanaugh-Mulraney clan. If I were to stay on at Orchard Street, I couldn't continue as a charity case.

Once again, I scoured the classifieds and struck out in search of work, my pink, peeling hands hidden inside white cotton gloves. That time, instead of downplaying my Irishness, I laid the blarney on thick as butter, talking up my experience as a "hospitality hostess" in my family's "restaurant" in Galway as well as my "intimate acquaintanceship" with the dressmakers and milliners of Dublin's Grafton Street.

Within a week, I secured a situation as a sidewalk saleslady on the stretch of Division Street from Chatham Square to Clinton Street known as Millinery Lane. Competition amongst the twenty-odd haberdasheries was cut-throat. Rain or shine, I stood outside the shop entrance, keeping a sharp eye out for potential patrons.

"Fancy a stylish hat, missus?" I'd call out. "We've some lovely selections inside. Nip in and have a look, won't you?"

Privately, I was horrified by the overwrought creations I hawked, pyramids of peacock feathers and yards of twisted and trailing tulle and chiffon in the most garish colors and styles. One sticky day, when I was perishing for a turn in front of the fan, I let slip my sentiments to my employer.

"You think you can do better?" he huffed, perspiration pearling the bald pate not covered by his yarmulke.

Mustering my boldness, I stared him square in the eye. "As it happens, Herr Silberstein, I *know* I can."

I steeled myself to be sacked. Instead, he hauled me through the shop to the curtained-off rear and sat me down at the Singer sewing machine.

"You have one hour," he said and then walked off, snapping the curtain closed.

Turning my face to the fan, I took a moment to gather myself. My scarred fingers weren't as nimble as they once were, much of the feeling lost. Fortunately, Mr. Singer's latest model greatly reduced the need for hand stitching. Encouraged, I got to work, my foot pumping the cast-iron pedal.

Inside of an hour, my employer returned to find me adding the last bit of tacking to a hat, not of any pattern but my own creation. He held it up whilst I looked on, scarcely daring to breathe.

Setting the hat back on the form, he broke into a grin. "Fraulein O'Neill, it is pleased I am to offer you the position of head seamstress."

I tucked my trembling hands under the table and brought up my chin. "And it's pleased I'll be to accept, Herr Silberstein, just as soon as we settle upon my new salary."

Chapter Nineteen

Amongst tenement families, the kitchen was the hub of homelife. Along with cooking, it was there we washed not only our dishes and laundry but ourselves. On Saturday evenings, Pat or Joe would roll out the heavy copper-lined tub whilst Kathleen and I heated water on the stove.

One Saturday evening, I walked in on Joe shaving. He had on his trousers and bracers but no shirt, a towel about his neck.

"Sorry! Kathleen asked me to put the kettle on and... Oh, never mind." Face afire, I began backing out.

"No need to run off like a scared rabbit," he said, the wicked gleam in his eyes confirming he well knew the havoc he wreaked.

"I won't be a moment." I brushed by and busied myself with putting on the kettle.

He turned back to the hand mirror propped upon a pile of old books. "Don't rush on my account." Lifting the razor, he scraped a sure, smooth swathe down one lathered cheek.

He'd shaved off the mustache weeks ago. Its absence transformed his face, drawing attention to his dark, flashing eyes and rugged jawline. Even the broken-toothed smile seemed softened, framed as it was by full, firm-looking lips.

Whoever first said that a watched pot never boils had the right of it. He was nearly done shaving, and still, the kettle hadn't sounded.

Turning away from the stovetop, I watched him work the blade along his jaw and chin. "What's in shaving lather, anyway?" I asked, mostly to fill the awkward silence.

"Heck if I know. Looks like whipped cream, don't it?" He touched a finger to an unshaven patch and dabbed a dollop onto his tongue. "Don't taste like it," he said, making a face.

"Idjut!" I dealt his arm a swat, the bicep like flesh-covered steel. "Sure, you've gone and poisoned yourself with your showing off."

His laughing eyes met mine in the mirror. "Would you miss me if I had? Would you cry if I croaked?"

I forced a shrug. "What if I did? You wouldn't be here to see."

He finished toweling off and turned to face me, his broad shoulders and barrel chest in full view, the flat nipples a surprising baby pink. A queue of dark hair began below his breastbone, bisecting his muscled belly and disappearing into the waistband of his trousers. Imagining all the ways I might trace that tempting trail brought perspiration beading my brow.

"Not unless I came back as a ghost. Late at night when you're abed, your fine hair spilled across the pillow and that prim pucker of yours softened with sleep – that's when I'd haunt you."

The kettle's shriek sent me all but leaping out of my shoes.

He chuckled. "Nervous as a cat, aren't you?"

I swung away to the stove, picked up an oven mitt, and lifted the kettle off the burner. "You're a devil, Joseph Kavanaugh. I can't think why I let you draw me into your nonsense."

"Because you like me more than you let on?"

I did, not that I'd give him the satisfaction of saying so. "I wouldn't wager on it."

He tossed the towel aside and bridged the spare space between us. "I'm not the gambler – Pat is – but I might lay down a bet or two if I had reason to think the odds were in my favor. Are they, Rosie?"

Before I could think what to answer, Kathleen walked in. "Was that the kettle I heard?" she asked, looking between us.

Heat hit my face, my fledgling desire shriveling to shame. Avoiding her eyes, I nodded. "I'll make the tea." Grateful for the excuse to turn away, I opened the cabinet and began taking down mugs.

"Pour a cup for me too," Joe called over, reaching for his shirt from the back of the chair.

"Since when do you drink tea?" Kathleen asked. "It's been coffee for you since you were old enough to see atop the table, and beer soon as you started shaving," she added, shooting a wink my way.

Slipping an arm into the sleeve, he smiled. "A man can change, can't he? I've a powerful thirst for tea these days, and a mind to learn how Rose here likes hers."

Privacy in a three-room flat was always in short supply, but especially so on Sundays, everyone's only full day off work. The Free Reading Room and Library at 135 Greenwich Street was my sanctuary. Slipping inside the cool, spare space, I'd select my newspaper or magazine from the rack, pull up a chair, and lose myself in the blessed quiet.

"*Reading*," Joe scoffed when I admitted where I disappeared to after mass.

"You're welcome to join me. You too, Pat," I made certain to say.

As soon as the invitation was out, I regretted it. Open Sundays only, the reading room was the one place I could claim as my own.

Kathleen answered for them. "Unless they serve beer, I wouldn't count on these two darkening the door."

Expressions sheepish, the men beat a hasty retreat to their chosen watering hole. I helped Kathleen settle the children, Baby Katie and Norah put down for their naps, the others given Pat's playing cards with strict instructions not to dare bend or soil them, then went to fetch my hat and gloves. The reading room carried quite a few foreign newspapers, *The Irish Times* amongst them. I was eager to see if they'd got in any new issues.

"Rose?" Kathleen called me back.

I paused in pinning on my hat and turned about.

"Might you stay behind for a bit? We can have a tipple of our own and some women's chat without the men underfoot."

Heart sinking, I stuck on a smile. "That'd be grand."

I set down my things and went to the kitchen table where she set out a bottle of sherry and two glasses. The latter she filled beyond the usual three fingers.

"Happy Sunday," she said, raising hers in toast.

"Happy Sunday," I echoed.

We sipped in silence, and it struck me that, kind as Kathleen was to me, we hadn't all that much in common.

She studied me over the rim of her glass. "This is nice, isn't it?"

I agreed it was.

"You must get homesick for Ireland and your family, though?"

"I do," I admitted. "Inis Mór will always be home to me."

"Still, New York's not so bad, is it?" she went on. "Suppose I'm prejudiced, being born here, but I can't imagine living anywhere else."

"Sure, it's an exciting city and a big one," I agreed. Entirely too big at times, but I kept that thought to myself.

"But you're finding your way, aren't you, settling in?"

"I am, thanks to yourselves."

She waved off my praise. "We Irish have to stick together. Setting an extra plate at supper, passing out another pillow and blanket are the least I can do."

I protested she'd done a great deal more than that, but as usual, she wouldn't hear of it.

"Now, my brother, Joe, well, he's the crusader of the family. I've always said he ought to go into politics. With that fine, deep voice and prize-fighter's physique, he's built for the bully pulpit, wouldn't you agree?"

I hesitated, for the Joe I knew seemed wholly happy fighting fires and saving lives. "If that's what he wants."

My answer didn't satisfy her, I could see that. "And what is it *you* want, Rose?"

"Sorry?"

Her gaze honed upon mine, and much as I might want to look away, I couldn't. "Woman-to-woman, tell me, what do *you* think of my brother?"

I should have seen this conversation coming. Joe hardly made a secret of his feelings for me, and Kathleen had practically raised him. Since the episode in the kitchen, I'd acknowledged she wasn't above playing matchmaker. After supper, she often contrived to clear the kitchen so that Joe and I were left to do the washing up. At mass, she made certain we sat side by side.

Caught, I considered my words. "He's a fine man and a brave one. A hero. If not for himself, I wouldn't be sitting here."

She nodded, but again, I could see she wasn't entirely pleased. "A woman could search the earth's four corners and not find a better man than my brother. Mind you, I'm not saying he's perfect," she carried on. "He has the Kavanaugh temper, same as me, and come Saturday night he's been known to take a drop too many, but show me the Irishman who hasn't? If he had a wife to come home to, the *right* wife, and a babe of his own to bounce upon his knee, he'd settle down tame as a lamb, I know it."

The Joe I knew had a good deal more lion than lamb in him, but I buttoned my lip and listened.

She pinned her gaze upon mine. "There isn't a woman in this ward between sixteen and sixty who wouldn't be over the moon to have him court her."

Among the denizens of the Lower East Side, firemen were the hands-down local heroes, and Joe was a particularly splendid specimen.

Uneasy, I hedged, "Sure, he'll make some woman a fine husband."

She rolled her eyes. "He doesn't want 'some woman'. He wants you. The question is do you want him back?"

"I don't know what to say."

Truly I didn't. When it came to Joe, my thoughts were a muddle. Whilst in hospital, I'd stopped thinking of him as my rescuer and started seeing him as my friend. These past weeks, I'd faced that what I felt for him was more than friendship but less than love, leastways not the romantic sort I'd known with Adam. And yet, beyond heartache and grief, what had that fraught first love affair truly brought me?

She set down her empty glass with a sigh. "It's no business of mine, I know, only I see the way he looks at you, and it pulls at my heartstrings."

"Kathleen, I—"

"Don't decide just yet. Give yourself time to consider. Whatever course you come to, you've a home here for as long as you need it."

From the back room, the baby's bawling broke the tension between us. We stood in unison, Kathleen waving me off. "Run along to your reading room."

My disloyal gaze edged to the door. "If you're sure?"

"I am." Hand resting atop the chair back, she paused, then added, "Only promise me you'll think over what I've said?"

On the way to the reading room, I thought of little else. I might not be in love with Joe, I was reasonably certain I wasn't, and yet there was something about him, something that... *stirred* me. His hands especially held me in a sort of thrall. Square-palmed and thick-fingered, the backs dusted with black hairs, the knuckles webbed in white scars, they forced their way into my fantasies. Watching him run his thumb round the lip of his coffee mug, a habit of his, I felt a warm, answering tug within me. Much as I might lash myself for it, the wicked longings I thought I'd put away for good after Adam were making themselves known again.

Later, whilst sitting at one of the library tables, flipping through a months-old copy of *The Sunday Illustrated Magazine*, my mind was as good as made up for me.

Mr. and Mrs. Adam H. Blakely, recently returned from their honeymoon tour of the Continent, have taken up residence on Upper Fifth Avenue, the five-story brownstone mansion a wedding gift from Mr. Blakely Sr...

The accompanying photograph of Adam enthroned in an ornately carved, high-backed chair, Vanessa posed beside him, her flaxen hair piled into a pompadour and slim figure fitted into a Worth gown, was harsh tonic, but it did its work. Closing the magazine, I was resolved.

It was high time I ceased grieving the past and got on with living again.

The following Saturday evening, Joe and Pat were out at the saloons, Kathleen and the kids visiting an ailing parishioner. With the flat all to myself, I decided to see to some sewing. In the middle of darning a stocking, panic seized me. I was back at The Windsor, the fire buckling ceilings and consuming curtains and carpets, the smoke-choked corridors crammed with guests and staff fleeing for their lives. Wringing my scarred hands, I paced the four corners, seeking to anchor my mind to safe, humdrum sounds. The cuckoo's ticking. The wail of a police wagon from the street below. Footfalls out in the hallway.

The key turned in the flat door, and Joe walked in. Taking in his open shirt collar, askew cap, and rolled-up shirtsleeves, I gathered he'd drunk quite a bit. One sleek strand of slicked-back hair fell forward over his eye, reminding me improbably of Adam.

"You're home early," I said, resisting the urge to run to him.

Even three sheets to the wind, he had the loveliest smile. "Pat got himself goaded into arm wrestling. He was down two dollars when I left, and he swears he won't come home 'til he's won back every plug nickel. Kathleen will murder us both if he loses the rent money again."

The faint purplish blotch upon his right wrist told me Pat wasn't the only one who'd spent the Sabbath eve wrestling. Only judging by the smile wreathing his face, Joe had won.

"His wagering is hardly your fault," I said, wishing my voice were less wobbly.

"If I've learned anything from watching those two go at it over the years, the course of true love rarely runs smooth, but it always runs deep.

It's easier to stay sore at a brother than a husband." He came closer, and his smile slipped. "You're white as a sheet. What's happened?"

I hesitated. How to explain cowardice to one who knows only courage? "Sometimes, my mind falls back to the fire, and suddenly it's as if smoke's filling the room, and the walls are running with flames, and I find myself fighting for breath. I wouldn't fault you for thinking me mad. Sometimes, I wonder myself."

His kind-eyed look cut me off. "What I think, *know*, is you've come through a terrible trial, one that'd drive a less strappy girl cuckoo. But not you, Rosie. You're a fighter. I saw it in you from the first."

I chewed my lip, past caring what I'd look like for Mass on the morrow.

"No wonder you're thinking of fire, it's like an oven in here." He walked over to the window and hoisted the sash higher. Cool air wafted in, cleansed by the recent rain. "Let's get you some air."

Beyond him was the fire escape, a slender platform of spindly metal steps onto which I'd yet to venture. He swung his torso and legs over the sill and climbed out, lithe as an acrobat for all that he was big as a bear. Facing back to me, he stretched out his hand.

After a long, heart-pounding pause, I took it and climbed out, my soles pinging upon machine-cut metal, my gaze glued to his. A waist-high rail was all that separated us from the street below.

Joe stepped behind me and slipped both arms about my waist, anchoring me against him. "The flat may be scarce bigger than a biscuit tin, but it's no firetrap – I made sure of it before I let Pat move my sister in. If a fire should ever break out, take those folding stairs straight down to the street."

I looked down to the thick forearms banding my waist and felt a frisson of something other than fear.

As if sensing the shift in me, he firmed his hold. "You're safe. I've got you. I'll always have you – so long as you let me."

The thickness pressing into my backside promised he was prepared to do considerably more than cradle me, but to his credit, his hands didn't stray.

"Joe, I don't know—"

"But *I* know. I've known you were the only girl for me since I first set eyes on you in that hotel window."

Resting back against him, I stared up at the night sky. As a child, I'd searched the stars for answers. Answers and my mother. I'd felt certain she must live somewhere within the heavens, mayhap as a star herself, guiding and protecting me. Now, I had a living, breathing, flesh-and-blood protector in this big, brave, beautiful man. All I need do was give myself leave to accept him.

Joe's lips brushed over my hair, calling me back to the answer I owed him. "Let me court you, Rosie. The chance to win you fair and square is all I'm asking."

That Monday, I used my lunchbreak to post a letter to my father, the first penned in my own hand since the fire. In it, I explained I'd found well-paying work as a seamstress in a millinery shop. I continued to lodge with the same upstanding Irish–American Catholic family, a charity case no more, but as a bona fide boarder. Lastly, I wrote that a good, honest Irish Catholic man, the fireman who'd saved me, had asked to court me. And that after considerable soul-searching I'd given him my answer.

And that it was yes.

Chapter Twenty

Coney Island, August 1899

I looked over to Joe sprawled on the beach blanket beside me, nose and cheeks dabbed with Pond's cream, as were mine. "Another sandwich?" I asked, though he'd had three already.

He paused from blowing into his empty beer bottle. "Maybe just one more."

He loved to eat almost as much as he loved to drink. Fortunately, he was the most energetic man I'd ever met. Even at home, he seemed always to be in motion, whether it was "roughhousing" with his nephews or tinkering with one of the many household items forever in need of fixing. Whatever he took in went to muscle, not fat, as his swimsuit-clad physique attested. The sleeveless, striped tank top and above-the-knee small pants stretched across his muscular torso and powerful thighs like a second skin, not to mention other, more personal parts where he seemed to be equally... *blessed.*

I raised my regard to the safer terrain of his face and pressed my thighs firmly together. "So it must be, for that's all that's left." I reached into the hamper and handed him the last napkin-wrapped sandwich.

Resting back upon my palms while he wolfed the thing down, I stared out to the white-capped waters, the crashing waves swarming with navy-suited sea bathers, their costumes the same ones we'd let down to the women's thick knit hose. Savoring the salt on my tongue, I drank in all the lovely warmth like a thirsty sponge.

"Wouldn't it be grand to let a cottage here for a few days or even a week?" I ventured. "Kathleen could do with the break, and the little ones would love it."

"Pat would never go for it," Joe said, cracking his knuckles.

Casting him a sideways look, I asked, "And yourself?"

"It'd be all right, I guess." His gaze went to the hamper. "Say, is there any more beer?"

I shook my head, for the three bottles I'd brought for him were drained dry. "Next time, I'll pack more. If we come again," I added, not wanting to presume.

Since we'd started stepping out, Joe had proven himself the perfect suitor, treating me to boxing matches and concerts at Madison Square, vaudeville acts, and even Broadway plays. No ticket cost too dear so long as it pleased me.

He reached out and tweaked the tip of my nose, tender from all the sunshine. "You love it here, so, of course we're coming back. Only Kathleen will have my hide if I bring you home all burned. What say we change out of these suits and stroll the boardwalk for a bit?"

We gathered our things and hot-footed it toward the changing huts, zigzagging through blankets and chairs, beach hammocks, and brollies.

"What's that you're humming?" I asked, pausing beneath an abandoned cabana to pick out a pebble from my slipper sole.

Joe shrugged. "Just a little ditty I can't get outta my head."

Ever eager to expand my limited knowledge of American music, I asked, "Does it have a name?"

"...*Rose, Sweet Rose.*"

I swatted his arm, rock hard as the rest of him. "Joseph Kavanaugh, you are making that up."

"Cross my heart, it's been on the playbill at Hammerstein's Olympia since '97."

"Sing it for me?"

His face went from sunburnt pink to blazing red. "*Here?*"

I summoned my most winning smile, curious to test the hold I had over him.

"All right, but remember you asked for it." He braced himself with a breath and began:

"All the sunshine is brighter, and my heart is lighter, I'll tell you why,
I'm in love with the fairest, the sweetest, the rarest of maidens shy.
Not a flower that grows is as dainty as Rose is, I've bought the ring,

And every night in the twilight to her I sing,
And every night in the twilight to her I sing:
You are my own little fairy, oh, Rose, sweet Rose;
Sometimes a trifle contrary, Rose, sweet Rose."
He paused there and cut me a look.
"Ah, but you're never airy, Rose, sweet Rose,
Eyes that are bluest and heart that is truest, my Rose, sweet Rose."

He had a fine voice, deep and true. Though I'd heard him sing Sundays in church, having him serenade me when it was just the two of us was an altogether different, dare I say it, *romantic* experience.

I waited for him to finish before pointing out, "My eyes are brown, not blue, in case you hadn't noticed."

Staring down into them, he eased into a smile. "Oh, I noticed all right, only I wouldn't call 'em brown. I'd say whiskey-colored, tawny, and rich."

It was my turn to feel self-conscious. Pretending interest in a little girl descending the boardwalk steps, carrying a cone of pink cotton candy, mouth and chin gummed with the stuff, I remarked, "There must be a great many Roses in New York."

"Can't say. I'm only interested in the one." The look he sent me brimmed with barefaced longing, and I was suddenly sensible to a funny, fluttery feeling low in my belly.

Lest I lose myself to it, I shifted my gaze to the pier. "Race you to the shower stalls. Last one there's a..." Like her music, I had yet to master America's idioms.

Joe's amused gaze flickered over my face. "Rotten egg."

One Sunday in early September, Joe and I stood on the tenement stoop to catch the late-morning breeze, himself stationed on the step below me, putting us at eye level. Despite the heat, he still had on his suit, the gray flannel with the burgundy stripe he'd finally let me fit for him.

"You're looking very dapper," I remarked, as much in praise to my tailoring as the fine form filling it. "Where's it to be today – Central Park, the fights, or perhaps tea with the queen?"

The latter made him laugh. "That would be the *First Lady* but no, even better."

"Give me a hint?"

Settling his hands upon my hips, his twinkling eyes touched mine. "Someplace I've never taken you before."

"That's not a hint. That's a tease."

He slanted me a look. "Now you know how *I* feel."

We descended to the sidewalk, packed with pushcarts. Ordinarily, Joe wouldn't pass up the opportunity to chat up the sellers, but today, a sense of single-minded purpose seemed to seize him. Holding my hand, he bore us along, deaf and blind to those who hailed him.

We left the busy block behind and turned onto Broome Street.

"Where's the fire?" I quipped, lengthening my steps to keep up.

"That's for me to know and you to find out," he shot back, his teasing tone at odds with his sober looks.

We made a left onto Allen Street. Owing to the absence of peddlers' stalls, the foot traffic was far thinner here, and yet Joe held fast to my hand, almost as if fearing I might slip away. No chance of that, for by then, I was burning with curiosity to discover our destination.

We turned left again, that time onto Grand Street. The shopping corridor was shuttered for the Sabbath, and yet goodly numbers of people sauntered along in their Sunday best, families and courting couples out for a stroll, mostly working people as were we. One young man sped by on a bicycle, nearly losing his straw bowler when the front wheel bucked on a broken patch of paving. A trio of young women swanned down the sidewalk toward us, parasols hoisted, a silly affectation considering the El train platform blocked all but a slim snatch of sooty sky.

Stuck at a street corner whilst a bevy of buggies, horse carts, hired carriages, and lastly, a streetcar sailed by, I spotted a couple ogling the display window of the corner shop, their fashionable clothing at odds with the gritty surrounds.

"Dan, darling," the woman trilled, "see that sweet sterling silver tea service on the left? You'd never know it wasn't from Tiffany's. Do say I can come back tomorrow with one of the footmen and pick it up. I'm sure they're selling it for a song."

Joe's hold on my hand stiffened. "Slumming it," he said beneath his breath, and before I could reply, there was a break in traffic, and he steered us swiftly across.

We walked a half-block more, stopping at the last in a terrace of shops, its striped tarp sagging and sun-faded, the display window covered over with brown craft paper. Nailed above the door, a simple wooden sign bore the message "*For Rent*", a line lashed through the words.

Joe produced a ring of keys and fitted the largest into the moisture-speckled lock. "I know the proprietor," he said in answer to my look.

We stepped inside. Dust motes flitted like snowflakes in the dark, dank air, making my nose itch and my throat prickle.

"Hold tight," Joe said.

He left me on the threshold and went off in search of a light. The next few moments were silent save for drawers being pulled opened and banged closed. A few muffled curses and then a match struck.

Joe stood at the counter holding a kerosene lamp aloft. "What'd you think?"

I stepped further inside and looked about. Display cases and equipment buried beneath dustsheets. Sawdust-covered floorboards and rotting wood beams. Barrels stacked against a wall, giving off a faint scent of brine. Floor-to-ceiling shelves, white with dust and crowded with cobwebs. At the rear, a natty curtain was drawn across what I supposed must be the stockroom.

I turned back to him. "A good top-to-bottom scrubbing and it'll be grand." I swallowed, throat tight and not only from the dust. "It's yours, isn't it?"

He nodded, face splitting into a grin. "Kavanaugh's Dry Goods Emporium. Sign's being delivered tomorrow." He set the lamp on the counter and came toward me. "Course, with me at the firehouse, I'll need a partner to run things until I can quit the company."

"You'd give up firefighting?"

"I would. I *will*." He stepped closer, sealing the space between us and clasping both my hands. "I have dreams, Rosie, big ones, and the ambition to back 'em up. All I need, all I've ever needed, is the right girl at my side. And now I've found her. I've found you." Before I could catch my breath, he went down on one knee. "Marry me, Rosie. Make me the happiest man on God's green earth and say yes. If you do, I swear I'll ask for no greater glory than the honor of being your husband and having you as my helpmate. No, not just helpmate. Full partners, that's what we'll be."

Though I'd known this day was coming, hearing the words, seeing himself kneeling at my feet, rendered me momentarily mute.

"I'll work hard for you, Rose, harder than I've ever worked in my life. Oh, I know you don't feel the same about me, not yet anyways. How could you when your heart's still mending? But I'm a patient man when I've the need to be, and a woman like you is worth waiting for. Say yes, and I swear I'll never give you cause to regret it."

"Oh, Joe, it's you who may end up regretting."

His beseeching gaze stayed steadfast upon mine. "Answer me this and no more: do you think you could learn to love me?"

Heart hammering, I took stock of all he offered, this big, rough man with the scarred knuckles and chocolate brown eyes that melted whenever he looked at me. He wasn't Adam, and he never would be. But he was strong and gentle, capable and kind, loyal to his core, and braver than any man had a right to be. Above all, he loved me without condition.

Looking into his upturned face, I said, "I think so, yes."

He carried my scarred fingers to his lips, my deadened flesh feeling next to nothing, my heart pounding so violently I feared it might break forth from my chest. "Then you'll marry me?"

"Yes, Joe, I will."

And with those simple words, the die was cast, my destiny decided. Adam was in my past. The man gazing up at me as if I were an angel fallen to earth was in every way my future.

PART II: Roots, 1900–1914

Privacy is something that few of us in the United States desire, and that none of the very rich can have for any price. As for the scions of a pampered and corrupt nobility, it is our duty and pleasure to revile, insult, gibe, sneer at, stare at, and crowd them as much as we can. Thus, we demonstrate the superiority of our political position and of our manners.

The Saunterer, *Town Topics: The Journal of Society*

Chapter Twenty-One

1900–1901

Time sped by. Before I knew it, I'd been married four months. Kathleen had spoken true. Despite the long hours Joe put in at the firehouse, he was as devoted a husband as any woman could wish for.

That's not to say we didn't have our differences. Born and bred to the city, he never seemed bothered by the noise and dirt and pushing and shoving as I still sometimes was. Our increasingly rare seaside Sundays invariably ended with him peevish and fidgety. All the fresh air muddled his mind, he insisted, and I'll admit he did seem more relaxed once the Manhattan skyline came back into sight.

And then there were politics. Fiercely proud of his Irish roots, he read *The Irish World* and the weekly *Freeman's Journal* cover to cover, taking every word as though it came from the Bible, whilst mainstream dailies like *The New York Times* merited only a grumbling glance-over.

That spring 1900, we went head-to-head in our first-ever fight over, of all things, ice. In those days, ice was an essential household commodity, for most tenement dwellers couldn't afford a proper ice safe to store perishables, instead making do with a wood box stuffed with rags or newspaper to slow the ice block's melting. Fortunately, unlike so many staples in the city, ice was inexpensive.

Until Maine native, Charles W. Morse, pooled his sundry ice interests into one large trust, the American Ice Company. Morse lost no time in offering cut-rate shares to city officials, including Mayor Robert Anderson Van Wyck and Boss Richard Croker of Tammany Hall, the municipal Democratic party machine. In return, Morse's ships received privileged access to the city docks, enabling American Ice to drive most competitors out of business.

In April, just as the weather was warming, American Ice doubled its prices and announced it would no longer sell the five-cent chunks upon which tenement households relied. Mid-May, temperatures spiked to ninety degrees Fahrenheit. Milk spoiled. The health consequences for infants and young children prompted a public outcry. Bowing to pressure, American Ice went back to selling five-cent blocks, again sending its wagons to the tenement districts, ours included.

The concession came too late. The press took up the battle cry. Joseph Pulitzer's *The World* ran a cartoon of a tiger-tailed Boss Croker waving an ice block whilst a sad-eyed mother saw to her sick baby. I made the mistake of showing it to Joe over breakfast one morning.

He cast me a cold look, a feat, considering we were burning up even with the fan going. "Think that's funny, kicking a good man when he's down?"

Stunned, I stared at him across the table. "A *good man*, Richard Croker? American Ice is bad enough, but it's come out he's invested in two other big companies, Manhattan Elevated Railroad and U.S. Fidelity & Casualty Company – both with city contracts."

"So what?"

"Croker's a crook, that's what. He lines his pockets whilst pretending to protect working people."

It was the worst thing I could have said. Bearded, big-bodied, and the son of Famine immigrants, Croker was Joe's sort of fella. That he was willing to overlook Croker being a Protestant spoke to the steep pedestal upon which he stood the man.

"Tell me, Missus High and Mighty, if the day comes when you find yourself with a husband too wounded to work or worse, left a widow, who do you think'll pay the landlord, the grocer – the funeral director? It won't be any muckety-muck reformers, that's for damned sure. I'll tell you who it'll be – Tammany!"

He shoved away from the table and stormed out. Though we made up later that night and into the wee hours, I couldn't but feel that our marriage, so shiny new, bore an indelible dent.

That June on Medal Day, Joe finally received his Bennett. Standing beside him on the dais outside City Hall as Fire Commissioner John J. Scannell pinned the medal upon his breast, never was I prouder to be his wife.

More and more, my brief time with Adam took on the haziness of a dream. Owing to the newspapers, I didn't have to wonder how he was keeping. Neither he nor Vanessa could sneeze without the Saunterer putting it in print. Recently, he'd become a father. His son, Robert Horatio Carlton Blakely, was christened before a cadre of Manhattan's elite. Reading of the princely presents bestowed, amongst them an eighteen-karat gold rattle with mother-of-pearl handle from Tiffany & Company, I felt a stab of the old bitterness.

That Thanksgiving we had the Mulraneys over for dinner. It pained me to see how not only the kids but also Kathleen and Pat went about the flat in wonder. The icebox was a marvel to them all. Given the recent shortage, I felt ashamed to have it.

"To think you don't have to go to market every day," Kathleen exclaimed as we stood at the kitchen sink, doing the washing up, herself elbow deep in soapy water, myself relegated to drying. "And so much space for just the two of you," she added, glancing out to the parlor where Joe and Pat were settling in for a smoke. "It is still just the two of you, isn't it?" Her gaze dropped to my belly, pancake flat despite all my praying.

Throat thickening, I admitted it was. "But we're trying," I added, forcing a smile. "Joe's determined, and so am I."

She dunked another plate into the suds. "Enjoy the peace and quiet while you can. Not to mention all the 'trying'," she added with a wink.

Later, after they left, I walked out of the water closet and burst into tears.

Joe took my face between his big, rough palms, so gently you'd think I was made of china. "Tears on a holiday! Rosie, sweetheart, what's the matter?"

Eyes running, I searched my empty pockets for a hankie. "My courses came. Oh, Joe, what if I can't have another baby? What if the… miscarriage *broke* something?" There, I'd voiced it, the terrible fear bedeviling me.

His mouth firmed. Always in robust health himself, he couldn't credit frailty or defect in others. "That's foolish talk. You're healthy as a horse. The doctors at St. Vincent's said so."

"What if they're wrong? What if it's only ever just the two of us?"

He thought for a moment. "Well, it's been just you and me since September, and it's not been so bad, has it? Apart from my snoring, I mean?"

"No, of course not, but—"

"No buts." He wiped the tears from my face with the pads of his thumb. "The way I see it, kids are like the cherries atop an ice cream sundae. Sometimes the soda jerk gets in a rush and forgets to add 'em, but so long as there's plenty of ice cream and chocolate sauce and whipped cream, I

157

don't ever much mind. Don't get me wrong, I like cherries, I like 'em a lot, but I *love* whipped cream."

"Oh, Joe!" I hugged him hard, closer to loving him than I'd ever come.

He swung me up into his arms and bore us toward the bedroom.

"But I have my—"

"As if I mind about that!" Sitting me on the side of the bed, he shoved up my skirts, his hands fast to follow.

Losing myself to our love play, I set my worries aside.

A new century was upon us, and it was impossible not to get caught up in the centennial madness sweeping the city. Throughout December 1900, *The World, The Journal, The Herald, The New York Tribune,* and *The Brooklyn Eagle* ran special Sunday pullout sections featuring reviews and timelines of the soon-to-be bygone century. Many of the great literary minds of the day, including Emile Zola, H.G. Wells, and Mark Twain, weighed in on what life might be like a hundred years hence, in 2001.

The much-anticipated night arrived amidst a steady snowfall. Undaunted, revelers bundled up and flocked to City Hall Park for the fireworks display. Farther downtown, the more somber-minded congregated outside Trinity Church. Thinking of the baby we still hoped to make, I suggested we join the latter group. Joe overruled me, a state of affairs becoming more and more commonplace.

"We can hear church bells any day," he pointed out. "But how often do we get the chance to see fireworks over City Hall celebrating a new century, no less?"

It was bitterly cold. Standing amidst the crowd congregating in City Hall Park, Joe's arm about my shoulders and the whiskey I'd sipped from his flask warming me from within, I reminded myself what a lucky woman I was. Since stepping ashore at the Battery two years earlier, I'd gone from penniless and secretly pregnant migrant to respectably wed proprietress of our own shop. It was quite a turnabout.

At the stroke of midnight, City Hall went dark, and then the power was switched back on, a marvel of fancy electric lights. Fireworks shot forth from behind the building's central cupola, splashing the marble façade with a kaleidoscope of colors. Churches, including nearby Trinity, sent up a city-wide symphony of chimes, a joyous joining of secular and sacred.

Joe pulled me to him and planted a lusty kiss upon my lips. "Ah, Rosie, so long as I have you at my side to see me through to the new century, I can't help but feel lucky, no matter what the future brings."

Shortly after midnight, the trouble started. Those dispersing from City Hall and Trinity converged at Broadway. Soon, that street and other connecting ones were bottlenecked by those fighting their way toward the Brooklyn Bridge, whilst others headed for transportation points to bear them uptown. Cursing and shoving broke out. Bottles were smashed, as were several store windows. Nearby, a siren blared.

Steering us through, Joe held tight to my arm. "Stay with me."

Half a block later, he shoved me into an alleyway and ducked in behind. "You all right?" he asked, shifting to shield me with his big, warm body.

Back flattened against the bricks, I managed a nod. "Seems you're always saving me."

He wrapped an arm about me, bringing me flush against him. "Love, cherish, and protect – that's my job, remember?"

He smelled of the whiskey we'd both drunk too much of, shaving soap, and clean flannel. Despite the scuttling of cockroaches and rats, I couldn't fathom moving away.

His hungry mouth took mine. Slipping a hand inside my coat, he found my breast.

"Joe, we're in public," I protested albeit weakly.

He rolled his eyes, or so I surmised, for his face was in shadow. "We're in an *alley*."

"What if someone sees us?" A lit match or hand lantern would reveal us all too clearly.

"They'd be pea green, for I'm a fortunate fella indeed."

Beyond the reach of streetlamps, it was the darkness as much as the whiskey that made us bold. He grabbed a fistful of my skirts and hiked them high. The frillies I wore beneath, a Christmas gift from himself, had a slit front unencumbered by buttons or hooks. Now, I understood why. He lifted me off my feet, one arm banding my bum. I wrapped my arms about his neck and my legs about his waist and held on tight. Braced against the bricks, I surrendered to him filling me, my lust a match for his, our cries lost to the crowd's clamoring.

I spent most of the following New Year's morning retching into a washbasin. Dropped to my knees, I swore I'd never touch whiskey again.

159

Standing at the sink, Joe shook his head. "Sure you're really Irish?"

"Hush up and hand me that towel," I snapped, scarcely able to meet his eye for thinking of our alleyway encounter.

He turned on the tap, wetted the cloth, and passed it to me. "Seriously, Rosie, whoever heard of getting soused on two measly mouthfuls of Jameson's?"

I stifled a groan, for the mere mention of the stuff sent my stomach seesawing. "It was four, if you must know. My father always says a drunken man is a sorry sight, but a drunken woman is only a disaster."

"Stop flogging yourself, will ya! All I've ever felt is proud to have you at my side – not to mention all the other positions."

I winced. "Please, don't remind me."

"You certainly whistled a different tune last night. Would you rather we'd stayed on the street to be run over?"

Earlier he'd read me the newspaper report of the previous night's chaos. One child was trampled to death. Several adults began the new century with bad cuts and bruises.

"No, of course not. I only meant we shouldn't have... well, done what we did. What if someone saw us, someone we *know*? It could be bad for the store."

He gave me a hand up. "Tell me this," he said once I'd gained my feet. "Are you sore because I liquored you up and led you astray – or because you liked it?"

"Both," I admitted, biting my lip.

His expression softened. "We're man and wife, Rosie. Between us, there's no such thing as sinning, no right or wrong. Only pleasure. Speaking of which..." Taking me by surprise, he lifted me onto the counter. "I'll put a baby in that belly of yours yet, Mrs. Kavanaugh."

Hiding my smile in his shoulder, I owned that whilst marriage to a thick-skulled Irish brute could be an infuriating state of affairs, it had its moments.

Chapter Twenty-Two

The culprit for my queasiness that New Year's Day wasn't the whiskey after all, but our son and daughter, twins, who made their appearance on the 27th of July 1901, the same day the new USS Maine battleship was inaugurated in the Port of Philadelphia, three years after the explosion of its predecessor in Havana Harbor set off our brief, bloody war with Spain. For once, my joy was such that I refused to spoil it by thinking of Danny. Or Adam.

We named the girl Moira. From her first breath, Moira was a force of nature, a black-haired bruiser in the spit of Joe, down to the dimple dividing her chin. She slept all day and cried all night, great, racking wails that reached to the rafters until, wrung out, we scooped her from her crib and brought her into bed between us. Our son, the tinier of the two, we baptized Joseph, though, from the start, he was Joey to us. Whereas Moira was Joe entirely, Joey took after me, a tawny-eyed ginger, slow to anger and swift to love.

The assassination of President McKinley put a damper on our bliss. On the 6th of September, the President was greeting guests at the Pan-American Exposition in Buffalo when Leon Czolgosz, an avowed anarchist, shot him twice. McKinley seemed to rally, but after a week, he worsened, his gut wound gone to gangrene. In the early hours of the 14th, he slipped away. Vice President Roosevelt rushed to Buffalo to take the oath of office. The hawkish "hero" of San Juan Hill was now President.

Such grand-scale tragedies and triumphs felt far removed from my daily life, which revolved around opening and closing the store. Every morning, I brought the babies down in their bassinets and set them behind the counter. There they stayed until we closed at seven, slumbering through the register's dinging.

161

Kavanaugh's quickly became a hub of activity for the neighborhood and not only amongst our fellow Irish. It wasn't uncommon for Mr. Lee from the laundry to stop by for a hand of pinochle or Mrs. Katz from the kosher bakery to nip in for a sack of flour and a chat. I was glad of the company. The old saw that firemen only came home to eat supper and make babies proved truer than I'd prepared for. Joe's shift schedule – twenty-one hours a day with one twenty-four-hour leave granted each month – didn't leave much time for a home life. Beyond all, I worried for him, for well I knew how dangerous his job could be. Not a day passed that I didn't pray to St. Florian, patron saint of firefighters, to see him safe.

Still, rearing my children and running the store, I was closer to contentment than I'd ever thought to be again. And yet, when I lowered myself into the bath late at night and all alone, slipping my hand beneath the screen of soapsuds and closing my eyes, the head I imagined ducking beneath the water to join me wasn't raven-black but sun-kissed blond.

Adam was just back from reading Robbie to sleep with *The Tale of Peter Rabbit* when moaning from Vanessa's side of their shared wall reached him. He made his way over to the dressing closet door connecting their bedrooms and set his ear to the paneling. Was she ill? In the grip of a nightmare? Vanessa was at best a manipulative opportunist, at worst a conniving bitch, but above all, she was Robbie's mother. When she didn't answer his knocking, he turned the key and walked though.

Vanessa sprawled on her back in the center of the four-poster, pale hair pouring over the pillows, naked, save for the pearls about her throat. A buxom, bare-assed brunette knelt between her tented legs, one fleshy buttock marked with a crescent moon-shaped mole.

"Yvette?" he said, struggling to make sense of the scene.

The Frenchwoman bolted off the bed. "Monsieur, it is not... what it seems."

Vanessa pushed herself upright. "Darling, do shut up. *Monsieur* may be lacking in many attributes, but he does have eyes."

Adam turned back to the maid, who'd managed to wrestle on her shirtwaist but not much else. Clutching her remaining clothes, she dove for the door.

Adam waited for it to close before turning back to Vanessa. "I take it this is a standing arrangement?"

Yawning, Vanessa stretched slender arms above her head. "Yvette's always been skillful with massages – my feet after a night of dancing, my lower back when I was carrying Robbie – but we didn't take up until after he was born. If you were ever going to come around, it would be then. Only you didn't. What had I to lose?" She had the audacity to smile. "Now that you've found us out, what do you intend to do about it?"

The question smacked of a challenge. At the very least, he should dismiss Yvette. And yet, what would it serve?

"I haven't decided," he answered in all honesty.

Now that the shock was wearing off, other subtler details seeped into his awareness. The wrecked bed, the sheets twisted and damp-looking, one corner made into a makeshift knot. The cosmetic pot open on the nightstand, the pale cream bearing the imprint of hastily dunked fingers, the rose-scented reek mingling with that of sweat. And sex. He hadn't been with anyone since Sally, hadn't left a bed looking like this one did in quite some time. Years.

Hoping to hide his weakness, he said, "What do you think the Saunterer would write were he to discover that Vanessa Carlston Blakely was a secret Sappho?"

She didn't so much as blink. "I'd be finished, a pariah, but it's a moot point since you won't say a word."

Her cockiness set his teeth on edge. It also made him hard as hell. "And why is that?"

"Because whatever else I am, I'm also your precious son's mother. The whispers would follow Robbie all his life."

She had him there. Robbie was everything to him, his Achilles Heel, his one absolute weakness. The depth and breadth of his love for his child exalted and terrified him. That she might strike out at him through his boy was never far from his thoughts.

He folded his arms across his chest. "You really are amoral, aren't you?"

"Not all of you is so disapproving, it seems."

He followed her gaze downward to the protruding front of his pajamas. Loathe her though he did, the hard-on weighing between his legs didn't lie. He might not want her for herself, but he badly wanted what she offered. Sex without strings, desire without dignity or caring.

Meeting her eyes, he said, "I'll go back to my room if that's what you want."

Her regard riveted on his cock. "It seems a pity to waste... all that."

The suggestion disgusted him. It was also savagely and undeniably exciting. He took a step toward the bed, then another, stopping at the edge. "If I stay, we do this my way."

"Meaning?"

Rather than answer in words, Adam dropped onto the mattress. He registered a fleeting glimpse of her shocked eyes and then flipped her over onto her belly.

Not having to see her face helped inestimably. She was no longer a person, not even one he hated. He reached between her thighs and shoved two fingers inside her. She wasn't only drenched, she was hot. Burning up.

"On your knees."

She obeyed, twisting to look back at him. "Is this how you did it with your whore?"

"Sally? I didn't mind looking into her eyes, but then I *liked* her."

She gasped when he entered her, greeted each fast, deep thrust with moans for more. Giving it, he drew back and swatted her buttock, hard enough to leave his handprint. Shuddering seized her, seeming to roll through her in choppy waves. Hating himself, he pulled out and spent himself on the sheet.

Vanessa turned onto her side and stared over at him, face softer than he'd seen it in years. "That was—"

He rolled away and rose from the bed. "Yvette can stay. But take your trysts to her room from now on. And lock the damned door."

1904–1905

The 27th of October 1904 saw the opening of the city's first Subway line. Covering nine miles and twenty-eight stations, the underground train carried riders from City Hall in Lower Manhattan all the way to 145th Street and Broadway in Harlem in just fifteen minutes. Heretofore midtown, not downtown, would be the commercial hub of the city, a shift I knew must figure into Kavanaugh's future.

On the 31st of December 1904, the newly completed *New York Times* headquarters opened in Longacre Square, rechristened Times Square after its prestigious publishing tenant. Clad in pink granite and crowned by a searchlight, the twenty-three-story Italian Renaissance-style office building would welcome the New Year with a ticketed rooftop gala.

164

Joe and I made plans to bundle up the twins and join the hundreds of thousands expected to assemble for the free fireworks. Only at the last moment, Joey spiked a fever. Joe pressed for us to go anyway. Though a husband's word was second to law in those days, when it came to my kids, I was a tigress. Joey wasn't leaving his bed, and I wasn't leaving him. I expected Joe to relent and stay home so that we might see in the New Year as a family. Instead, he took Moira and went off to the fireworks. Meanwhile, I sat up, dosing our sick boy with cough syrup and rubbing Vick's Magic Croup Salve into his sore chest. Just before dawn, his fever finally broke. I left him and crawled into Joe's and my bed to snatch a few hours' sleep.

The trouble between us was brought to a boil in the murky morning of that New Year's Day when Joe's seeking mouth dragged me from my dead-to-the-world slumber.

I pushed back, my elbow meeting his chest. "Joe, please." At that moment, I would have sold my soul to Satan for twenty more minutes' sleep.

Plastered to my backside, he nuzzled my neck. "That's what I'm trying to do, sweets." He rolled me onto my back and moved atop me.

By then, wide awake, I dealt him a sharp shove. "I said *no!*"

He froze. "This is a fine way to ring in a new year." Resting back upon his heels, he stared down at me as if I was a stranger. "You'd deny me my rights, then?"

His rights. I hauled up on my elbows. "Whilst you were out *ringing* in the New Year, I was up with Joey."

"Is it my fault the boy's sick?"

Leaning back against the headboard, I pressed a hand to my thrumming head. "Of course not, but seeing as he is, maybe you could help out a bit, wash up the dinner dishes at least?"

He scowled. "That's woman's work."

"You didn't seem to think so when we were at Pat and Kathleen's." Keen on courting me, he'd been only too eager to pitch in, anything for time alone together.

"We're married now."

"So we are," I agreed, my flat tone surprising even myself.

His face darkened. "If you think you can do better, I'm sure the hotels are still hiring chambermaids and the haberdashers' seamstresses."

I pretended to consider. "Come to think of it, I wasn't altogether unhappy at the hat shop. Or the hotel. The hours were better, and so was the pay."

The look he lanced me could have cut glass. "All these years, I've never known you to be altogether unhappy or *happy* with anything or anyone, least of all me."

The accusation struck too near the truth. "I'm not unhappy, I'm exhausted. I need a rest."

"Rest up to your heart's content." He swung his legs over the side of the bed and got up. "If you won't abide by your marriage vows, I'll find comfort elsewhere." He reached for his shirt, as usual, left hanging on the bedpost, and punched an arm into the sleeve.

Falling back against the pillows, I threw my arms in the air. "You'll do as you please, I'm sure. You always do, no matter who's hurt by it."

Pulling on his pants, he twisted to face me. "*I'm* the one who's hurting us? To hear you tell it, it's me who's spent the last five years mooning over somebody else. Oh, don't bother denying it. I see in your eyes how you still pine for him, your precious lover boy who left you in the lurch."

I should have refuted him then and there, no matter that it meant lying. Instead, I sealed my lips and let angry silence stand as my answer.

Defiant eyes drilled into mine. "Don't fret, missus. From here on, I'll leave you alone to get all the goddamned rest you want. Just remember, it was *you* who turned *me* away."

Chapter Twenty-Three

The following few months were uneasy ones. Though Joe and I still shared a bed, we slept facing away from each other. Every morning, I rose feeling as though I walked on glass.

In the early hours of the 14th of March 1905, I woke to the wail of sirens. With Joe at the station, my first, frantic thought was that the store was afire, the twins and myself trapped as I'd been at The Windsor. I bolted out of bed to the window, steeling myself for a blaze below.

There was none. For the first time since awakening, I let myself breathe. Tiptoeing out, I poked my head into the alcove where we'd set up the twins' cots. Both were sleeping still, all well within their wee worlds. But there was a fire somewhere and judging by the charred odor wafting in from the partially open window and the alarms blaring, it wasn't far off.

I threw my coat on over my nightgown, bundled up Moira and Joey, and rushed them over to Mrs. Katz's. Good neighbor that she was, she put them in bed alongside her own children. Unencumbered, I picked up my heels and followed the siren the several blocks to Allen Street.

105 Allen Street was a tenement of mostly Jewish migrants from Eastern Europe. The surrounding sidewalk was crowded with spectators and escaped residents still wearing their nightclothes. How many more lives stood at stake I didn't then know. The life I focused upon was Joe's.

One of the crew, his face blackened and sweat-streaked as I'd seen Joe's many a time, approached and tried steering me aside. "You shouldn't be here, ma'am. We need to keep the area clear."

Seeing the "6" on his helmet, I stood my ground. "Joe Kavanaugh, is he in there? I'm his wife."

Realizing I was one of their own, he released me. "There's a kid trapped inside. We tried talking him out of it, but he was dead set on going back in for her."

Numb, I listened to the rest. The mother and two older children had managed to drop the baby and themselves to safety from the fire escape. But the toddler, asleep in a second room, walled off by flames, was unreachable, or so Joe's fellows were convinced. Stubborn as a bull and fearless as a lion, my man was not one to give up so easily.

The fireman looked back to the building, scarcely visible for the smoke. "I've gotta get back. Do everybody a favor, and stay behind the chalk line."

"Fine, only let me help. I'm a fireman's wife, after all, and... thanks to brave men like my husband, a survivor of the Windsor Hotel."

At my mention of the by-then famous fire, he relented. "There's a group of wives laying out sandwiches and coffee over there." He jerked his chin toward a handful of women gathered at a trestle table beneath the Second Avenue El platform, commandeering a coffee urn and spreading lard on thinly sliced bread. "They could probably use an extra pair of hands."

Grateful for an occupation beyond worrying, I joined them and spent the next hour handing out wax paper-wrapped sandwiches and tin cups of black coffee to exhausted firemen.

Never will I forget the rush of relief I felt when I spotted Joe's strapping silhouette emerge from the black plumage, a small child clinging to his neck. Heart in my throat, I held back as he laid the little thing upon the ambulance gurney as once he'd done me, the weeping mother all but prostrating herself at his feet. I waited until she was settled into the ambulance carriage along with her child, and then made my way over.

Sitting on the curb, a blanket about his shoulders, he stopped quaffing coffee and looked up at me. "Rosie, what the devil are you doing here?"

"Never mind about that. Let's get you looked at," I said, helping him to the medic's station.

Standing by as his fractured wrist was wrapped, I reminded myself it wasn't only Joe who'd been lucky. I had as well. Whatever else my husband was, he was foremost a hero. I made myself a promise to remember that the next time he tested my patience.

Back at the flat, I broke down. "You great, thick-skulled lummox," I wept into his chest, one of the few parts unscathed. "What did you think you were about back there, nearly making orphans of our kids and a widow of me?"

Expression tender, he tucked his good arm about me. "Careful, Rosie, I might get it into my head you love me a little."

Eyes running, I looked up at him. "Mind we do have six years and two children together, or is your head too stuffed with smoke to recall them?"

He reached down and tipped up my chin. "Oh, I recall them all right. What would you say to us getting to work on making a third?"

A while later, we reclined together in the new porcelain bathtub. Cradling him between my tented legs, I sponged the soot from his bruised back.

"Like old times," he said, and though he faced away from me, I heard the satisfaction in his voice. "I've missed you, Rosie."

"I've missed you, too. And I don't want to lose you. Quit the company, not someday, but now."

He was coming on forty, not a pensioner, surely, but not a young buck either. And he'd put on weight, not a lot but… enough.

He stiffened against me. "I'm foreman. The fellas look up to me."

I set the sponge aside. "And why wouldn't they? You've given them every reason to as well as a dozen years of your life. But it's time someone else stepped up."

Silence answered, the nearest thing to a "no."

"I'm serious, Joe. After today, I've had sufficient of fires to last me a lifetime. At least think on it."

"Right now, there are plenty of other things I'd rather think about." He glanced back at me over his shoulder, expression unmistakable.

"So soon?"

The smile he sent me might have melted metal. "They didn't call me the Ox of Orchard Street only for my fist fighting," he said, a boast that by then, I knew to be borne out.

He wasn't the only one of us game for another go. Now that we were reconciled, I was as eager to make up for lost time as he was.

"Let me get the towel, otherwise you'll make a river of the floor."

"Screw the floor." Hands about my waist, he flipped us so that I was astride him.

Beneath the water, I drew him to me. Too caught up to care for the porcelain cutting into my knees or the sooty suds sopping the floor, I anchored my hands to the tub's curved edge and took him deep, not stopping until he bellowed his pleasure to the rafters.

169

Later, lying abed, my head upon his shoulder, I admitted to myself it wasn't only our lovemaking I'd missed. "I got a letter from my father the other day," I said, happy to share day-to-day happenings again. "Would you believe Killian's wed, with a babe on the way?"

More shocking still was his choice of bride. Úna, my old schoolmate, who'd teased me so mercilessly that Samhain Eve.

Joe turned to face me. "Think we made a baby tonight?"

Caught off guard, I hesitated. "We'll have to wait and see."

"But you want another kid with me, don't you?" he asked, an edge to his voice.

"Of course I do, only… between minding the twins and running the store, I don't know if I'm coming or going."

He lifted his head from the pillow. "We could hire someone to help out."

"Can we afford that? Never mind, I know for a fact we can't. And your job, it's so dangerous."

"Back to that, are we?"

"You're a grand firefighter and the bravest man I know, but how long can you keep it up? No one's luck lasts forever."

Several silent moments slipped by. Rather than risk another rift, I closed my eyes.

I was just drifting off when he blurted out, "I'll do it. I'll quit."

I opened my eyes and turned to face him. "Mean it?"

A nod answered. "In a few years, I'll be too old and fat for scaling buildings and running up stairwells, and then what? Your widow's pension won't begin to cover the rent on this place."

Finally, we could be full partners, not only in marriage and family but the business too. "Oh, Joe, you won't regret it! This is a new beginning, a new day for us, I know it!"

He pressed a kiss to my forehead. "Keep smiling at me like you're doing now, Rosie Girl, and I won't be able to hold back from giving you all the new days you could want."

All the New York dailies reported Joe's daring rescue of the little girl given up for a goner. His heroism at the Windsor Hotel was recalled as were his glory days in the boxing ring, the latter accompanied by a grainy photograph of his younger self, bare-chested and buff, his tapered torso accentuated by a satin sash splashed with green shamrocks.

I worried the press attention would have him reneging on resigning, but to my relief, he kept his word and gave notice. A fortnight later, the two of us were taking the quarterly inventory, the shop sign turned over to closed, the evening hour creeping toward seven-thirty.

Trailing me along the aisles, he said, "Let's call it a night. We can pick up first thing in the morning. The kids are starving, and so am I."

I looked up from my clipboard, again losing count. Truth be told, I wasn't yet used to having him around, not to mention underfoot. "Honestly, you're worse than Moira and Joey. Them I can bribe with sweets or the promise of a bedtime story. And I... *we* won't be picking up anything in the morning. There'll be customers to wait upon, all in a rush to get off to work."

"A break then." He stuffed his hands into his trouser pockets and looked down at his feet. "I need to talk to you."

His serious tone sent my heart sinking. If Joe wanted to talk, something was afoot.

I steeled myself and took a seat atop a turned-over crate. "I'm listening."

He pulled up the stepping stool and plunked down beside me. "Big Tim Sullivan and Tom Foley stood me for a pint the other day."

Timothy Sullivan and Thomas Foley were Tammany Hall bigwigs. A former U.S. Senator representing New York's 8th district, Sullivan ran virtually all jobs, and vice, in the Bowery. Saloons, vaudeville theaters, nickelodeons, racetracks, athletic clubs – and prize-fighting rackets – were all in his wheelhouse.

A successful saloon owner, Foley was district leader for the Lower East Side and in thick with the big boss, Charlie Murphy. It was whispered he was in league with Jewish gang leader Monk Eastman and Eastman's rival, Paul Kelly, founder of the Italian Five Pointers, playing the two factions off one another to further his purpose: getting out the vote for Tammany candidates.

"So that's where you disappeared to," I said, hating what a scold I sounded, and yet with Joe, a pint never meant only one. It was past midnight when he'd walked in, three sheets to the wind.

"Don't give me that look. It was a business meeting."

"What sort of business?" I asked, half afraid to hear.

Eyes on mine, Joe admitted, "They're offering to back me as ward leader for the Seventh."

It was the very last thing I expected to hear, and yet in hindsight, it shouldn't have shocked me. In those days, fire companies were fertile fields for party recruiters. Tammany's notorious kingpin, Boss William Macy Tweed, had founded Joe's Americus Fire Company No. 6, serving as its first foreman. Tammany's mascot, the Tammany Tiger, was taken from the tiger's head painted upon the back of every Big Six engine.

Finding my tongue, I said, "Sure that's very... flattering. You told them no, of course?"

His jaw tightened. "What, you think I'm not cut out to be a pol?"

Joe's courage and leadership abilities were without question, but he was also blunt-speaking and bull-headed. Nor was he above using his fists to drive home his point, as I'd seen for myself during the newsboys' strike.

Weighing my words, I answered, "You're the bravest man I know and a born leader. The men under you trust you with their lives. But a politician? I'm not so certain."

He shot to his feet. "Folks are fed up with fast talkers who grandstand and then do zip once they're in. I'd be a dark-horse candidate, a man of the people, which's exactly why they wanna run me."

I suspected Tammany's motives for courting Joe had more to do with shoring up its sagging voting base. Once almost entirely Irish, our seventh ward was home to migrants from other parts of the world, many of whom, like Mrs. Katz and Mr. Lee and the grocer, Mr. Bianchi, had set up successful small businesses. A city-wide celebrity and bona fide hero, Joe was a popular figure to rally votes around.

He began pacing, the dragging feet of minutes ago pounding the floorboards to pulp.

Following him with my eyes, I asked, "When must you give them your answer?"

He stopped at a shelf of soap powder. Lining up the boxes, he acted as if he hadn't heard.

Knowing better, I rose and walked over. "Don't tell me you've already said yes?" And then, "You have, haven't you?"

He didn't deny it.

"What of the store?" I demanded.

From the start, our plan had been to run Kavanaugh's together. But over the past weeks, I'd come to see that Joe liked the idea of being a shopkeeper more so than the reality. The "daily grind" bored him. Bookkeeping and inventorying were beyond him, or so he swore. Those parts he did fancy, chatting up customers, "kibitzing" Mrs. Katz called it, took place at the register, where all too often, he let his pals purchase on credit whilst holding strangers to the penny.

He turned to look at me. "I'm doing it for the store. For us. Once I'm rubbing elbows with the Tim Sullivans and Tom Foleys of the world, doors are going to open for us, big ones." Bruised eyes brushed over my face. "Don't you see, Rosie, this is my chance to be somebody, to prove I'm more than just another used-up mick boxer?"

I gripped his shoulder. "You're already somebody. You've naught to prove to anyone."

His gaze searched mine. Hesitant. Hopeful. "So, you're with me?"

If only I'd been able to put aside my past with Adam and love Joe as he deserved, he wouldn't have to ask. He'd know he had my support along with the whole of my heart. If a place in city government could bring him the happiness I hadn't, who was I to deny him?

"Yes, Joe, I'm with you."

Chapter Twenty-Four

Tammany Hall, 14th Street between Irving Place and Third Avenue
Tuesday, November 7, 1905 – Election Day
We spent that first election day at Tammany headquarters, the main auditorium decked out in red, white, and blue bunting, Bayne's 69th Regiment Band keeping boredom at bay. Well before the polls closed at midnight, Joe's landslide victory was declared. Jaws stiff from all the smiling, I joined him onstage with Joey and Moira, cheers of "*Killer Kavanaugh*" ringing through the room.

Pat and Kathleen and their kids came out to help us celebrate. I turned the twins over to Norah, then eleven, and joined the adults at the punch bowl. Eventually, Joe and Pat drifted off to the balcony for a smoke, leaving Kathleen and me to ourselves.

She turned her face up to mine, thinner and paler than before but beaming. "This is a proud day, isn't it Rose? I only wish Joe's and my dear parents were alive to see it."

I bit my lip, for I rather thought the course of Joe's political career remained to be writ. From what I'd so far seen, his Tammany handlers were the ones wielding the pen.

"And the headquarters, it's all so elegant, don't you think?" she added, shooting an awed glance to the gilt-coffered ceiling.

Thinking of the money working people such as ourselves poured into the place to make such pomp possible, I sipped my punch in silence.

"Rose, what is it? What's the matter?"

"A bit knackered is all. It's been a long day. How's Norah getting on in school?" I asked, hoping to turn the topic.

But Joe's sister was nothing if not stubborn, a Kavanaugh trait, or so I'd come to see it. "Something's off with you," she insisted, raking me with sharp eyes until I finally relented.

"I worry this position might not be the best thing for Joe. For any of us," I admitted.

Her gaze narrowed. "How's that?"

"Since the campaign started, it's been one boozer after another. We see him less now than we did when he was at the station house."

If I'd thought to pour my troubles into a sympathetic ear, I was to be swiftly and sorely disappointed.

"So he takes a nip more than he ought. Show me the Irishman who doesn't. Honestly, Rose, are things that bad? From where some of us sit, they look pretty prime."

Stunned by her waspishness, I could do naught but stare.

But Kathleen wasn't done yet. "He's done all this for you. To make you proud."

"But I *am* proud."

She looked at me askance. "Are you? I wonder. All these years, he's never left off trying to prove himself to you. You must see it, or are you that blind?"

Joe and Pat walked up with Moira, sparing me from answering. Judging from their cherry cheeks and whiskey breaths, smoking wasn't all they'd got up to.

"Look who we found playing hide-and-seek in the committee room," Joe said with a chuckle, the twirled and waxed handlebars of his recently regrown mustache putting me in mind of a villain in a movie-house melodrama.

I dropped my gaze to Moira, holding fast to her father's hand. Just four years old, already she had the makings of a minx, the very opposite of my gentle Joey.

I left Kathleen and went over to them. Addressing Moira, I said, "Gave your poor cousin the slip, did you? Why am I not surprised? And where's Joey?"

"With Noo-Noo," she answered, meaning Norah.

"My girlie wanted to be with her dada on his big day, can you blame her?" Joe said, effectively sticking a pin in any further scolding.

He swept her up into his arms and spun her around, her Mary Janes coming close to clipping more than one hapless bystander.

Coming to a halt, he asked, "What d'you think of your old dad now, princess?"

Plucking at the Bennet medal on his breast, she beamed up at him. "When I'm big, I'll vote for you too, Papa."

Joe set her down. "Thanks, sweets, but voting's not for ladies."

Over our daughter's head, I sent him a look. "Your father's right – to a point. Women aren't yet permitted to vote, though a great many are working hard to change that."

Joe scowled, for female suffrage was yet another subject upon which we disagreed. "*Agitating*, you mean."

Like as not we'd have it out later once the kids were abed, but for the time being, I let the subject languish. Not so Moira.

Screwing her face into a scowl, she stamped her wee foot. "I will too vote."

"If ever there was a female with the head for it, it's my Moo-Moo," Joe conceded, smoothing things over as he'd never deign to do with me.

Norah rushed up, breathless and red-faced, her hand holding fast to Joey's. Seeing Moira safe and sound, her fraught expression eased somewhat. "Auntie Rose, I'm *so* sorry. One minute she was beside me and the next—"

"Moira could throw a Pinkerton detective off the scent," I said, settling a hand upon her shoulder. Gaze circuiting our family circle, I forced a smile. "Now that we're all here, let's have some cake, shall we?"

1906–1907

Joe's victory signaled the end of life as we'd known it. More and more nights were spent in the company of his Tammany cronies. A favorite haunt was the Pelham Café, a ragtime piano joint in the heart of Chinatown run by Mike Salter, a Russian Jewish gangster who'd made a name for himself as Tom Foley's chief election captain. Stuffing ballot boxes, bribing and coercing constituents into casting multiple votes, and old-fashioned skull-cracking were all in his wheelhouse. In return, Tammany granted him carte blanche in running the vice trade in Chinatown. Prize-fights, cockfights, dice games, and opium parlors, "The Prince of Chinatown" had his fingers in many pies.

A typical night saw Joe staggering home from the Pelham, singing show tunes beneath his boozy breath. Only by then it wasn't *Rose, Sweet Rose* he crooned but *Marie From Sunny Italy*, the ditty written by Salter's singing waiter, a skinny Russian Jewish kid with a knack for crafting catchy lyrics. Izzy Baline, the future Irving Berlin.

One early morning, the bedroom door squeaked open, and Joe soft-footed it inside.

Awake, I pulled the chain on the bedside lamp and sat up. "Blessed Mother, you reek like the inside of a whiskey barrel."

He swung away and tugged off his necktie. "Foley and I had important city business to discuss."

I folded tense arms across my breasts, fragile armor for my heart's hurting. "I kept a plate for you in the kitchen."

Dropping his cufflinks into the drawer, he didn't bother looking back. "I ate at the club."

I caught another whiff of him, and that time I detected not only whiskey but something else entirely. Violets, jasmine, and wood. Perfume. Not just any perfume but Guerlain Fleur Qui Meurt from Paris. The other day, in taking inventory, I'd come up a bottle short. Now, I knew why.

I snapped upright. "I didn't know you had a nose for French fragrance."

He turned to face me, rumpled shirt open to the waist, rippling muscles still there but softened by a rim of fat, the skin dusted with the same springy dark hair I'd once trailed my fingers through. "Jealous?"

I was, as well as horribly hurt, not that I meant to give him the satisfaction of saying so. "Disappointed and… disgusted, to be sure. But jealous? Don't flatter yourself."

"Believe me, I don't. You've seen to that."

"This is *my* fault, is it?" Part of me wanted to box his ears so soundly they never stopped ringing. The other part ached to launch myself at his chest and cling there until he swore never to stray again.

He came up to the bed. Punched in the heart though I felt, out of habit, I moved over to make room.

He sat with a sigh. "You give me the pleasure of your body and take your pleasure in mine, but that heart of yours you keep locked up tighter than a bank vault. Even now, it's only your pride that's hurting."

I felt my eyes filling, for there was more than a grain of truth in what he said. "I've been a good and faithful wife to you, Joseph Kavanaugh, and a good mother to our children and well you know it. If you believe even half of what you just said, it's the drink and your own guilty conscience talking."

Bloodshot gaze holding mine, he blew out a breath. "I'm drunk all right and more than a little guilty, but what I'm not is a fool. Maybe you can still pull the wool over your own eyes, Rosie Girl, but not mine. Not anymore."

To salve my wounded pride, I began thinking of our marriage as a business arrangement. Joe had given me a ring, a roof, and respectability. In return, I'd given him two bright, beautiful, healthy children and my unpaid labor as housekeeper, bookkeeper, shop clerk, and store manager. I told myself it was a bargain well met. On my better days, I came close to believing it.

And then one winter night, I awoke to find Joe missing from bed though he'd come home early, unusually so considering the night owl hours he kept. I turned up the lamp, put on my robe, and padded out into the flat's main room. No Joe there either. Thinking he must have stepped out for a smoke or a nip from his flask, I was on my way back to bed when banging from below brought me up short. Heart in my throat, I grabbed a brass candlestick from the dining table and slipped down the back stairs.

I stepped off into a rush of chilly air, the bluster rustling the stockroom curtain. Drawing it back a bit, I saw that the rear door for receiving deliveries stood propped open with a brick. Muffled male voices and what sounded like crates being shoved about reached me from out in the alley. We were being burgled! And yet what sort of thieves bothered with bolts of fabric and boxes of dry soap when the plum prize, the till, sat out in plain sight?

Not about to wait to find out, I brandished the candlestick and sprang forward. "Get the bloody hell out of my store!!!"

Three men, rough-looking and bundled against the cold, whirled on me, one clenching a crowbar. For the following few heartbeats, horror made a mute of me, for the largest and tallest of the trio was Joe.

"Relax, fellas, it's just the wife." Gaze flickering to me, he said, "Put that down before you hurt someone, and go back to bed."

I let the arm holding the candlestick drop, but my feet I kept planted. "I won't, not until you tell me what's going on."

I stared past him to the haphazard clustering of crates, several with the lids pried open and weeping straw upon my fresh-swept floor. They weren't carrying stock out. They were carrying it *in*. As my gaze adjusted to the dimness, the contents began to take shape. The sunken circle with numbers upon its periphery and a spinner at its center – a roulette wheel! The metal and varnished wood tabletop chest I'd first mistook for a till – a slots machine!

I looked back at Joe. "How could you?"

His gaze shuttered, the rest of his features solidifying to stone. "It doesn't concern you."

"The hell it doesn't," I said, rare though it was for me to curse.

He closed the few paces between us, hands drawn into fists. "Get upstairs, woman, or I won't answer for the consequences."

Though it shames me to admit it, I retreated. Scrambling up the stairs, I took the steps two at a time, not stopping until I reached the top. Perspiring, I dared a look back down. The stairwell was empty, the stockroom curtain pulled back in place. Beyond it, the sounds of heavy objects being shifted told me they'd resumed their work. Heart hammering, I slipped inside the flat and drew the door closed behind me. Leaning back against the painted wood, I wondered if I oughtn't to bolt it. But against who? Joe had a key, and the two hooligans below were there at his invitation. In the end, I set the candlestick back on the table and drew out a chair. Gaze on the cuckoo clock, a wedding gift from Pat and Kathleen, I waited.

Twenty minutes later, Joe came up. Behaving as though nothing untoward had taken place, he locked up and went to hang his coat on the hook.

I shot to my feet and cut across the parlor to him. "Trafficking in illegal betting, what are you *thinking*!?"

He had the audacity to shrug. "You're making a mountain out of a molehill. The... equipment belongs to a friend. I'm just keeping it for him until... the heat's off."

The heat – meaning the police. I folded my arms over my fast-beating heart and lifted my chin. "One of your Tammany cronies, you mean?" The question was no sooner out than I recalled that the sides of several crates were chalked "*PC*." "Those betting machines are from the Pelham Café, aren't they?"

He didn't deny it. "Salter's Foley's right-hand man. Now, he and Big Tom both owe me a favor."

Blood boiling, I demanded, "And if it gets out that you're abetting the vice trade, what then? We'll be ruined, that's what. Not only yourself but me, the kids. The *store*."

"That's not going to happen."

I shook my head. "That's not in your power to promise, and even if it were, this is *wrong*."

He rolled his eyes, whites bloodshot from all the late nights, the irises black as coals and sharp as tacks. "You weren't born here. You don't understand how things work. One hand washes the other, that's how things get done."

"By greed and graft, you mean?"

His gaze drilled into mine. "There's a difference between honest and dishonest graft, and I'm not the first to say so."

More Tammany rhetoric! If only I might go back to closing my eyes and stoppering my ears to all of it. But it was too late for that.

"If there were true justice, you'd be on your way to Sing Sing and the rest of that thieving, lying lot with you. I won't stand for it."

He brought his face close to mine. "You'll stand for it because I'm your husband and I say you will."

Gone was the tender-hearted husband who'd kissed my scars on our wedding night. In his place was Killer Kavanaugh, out for blood from anyone who crossed him. I braced myself for his blow, daring him to hit me, half-hoping he would, if only for the excuse to take the kids and leave him. A black eye or broken tooth would be a small price to pay for such guiltless freedom. But walking away wouldn't only be the end of our marriage. It would be the end of Kavanaugh's, not only the present dry goods emporium but the grand midtown department store I'd begun envisioning.

"If you want to deck me, then do it. But so long as I've breath in my body and life in my limbs, I'll fight you on this."

His brow knitted, thick-fingered hands flexing like a fisting heart. "Fight me, how?"

Though the flat was chilly, the undersides of my robe sleeves were damp. "I'll take myself to the police precinct and turn you in."

Color flooded his face. "You wouldn't."

"Try me."

I marked the moment the fight went out of him. His gaze veered away, breaking the deadlock between us. "It'll be gone by Saturday." He turned and headed for the bedroom.

I flung out a hand and caught at his sleeve, surprising us both. "What you said the other night... Am I to blame for bringing you to this?"

He turned back to me, love and hatred warring over the craggy terrain of weathered flesh and busted bone. "You mean because no matter how high I rise in your eyes, I'll never measure up to *him*?"

I opened my mouth to deny it, to swear I loved him with the whole of my heart and all the rest of me, but the declaration stayed stuck in my throat.

He grimaced. "No matter how good I am to you and the kids, you'll never see your way to loving me, not a hundred percent. I made my peace with that after the kids came along. What I can't let go of *isn't* you not loving me." A deep draft of air and then, "It's that all these years, you let me go on believing one day you would."

The dozen crates marked "*PC*" vanished from the stockroom early that Saturday morning, spirited away quick as they'd come. When I came down to open the store, not a single slip of straw remained to show they'd ever been there.

The next year, 1907, the Prince of Chinatown would be taken into custody, not for illegal gaming but voter fraud. The Pelham was shut down, boarded up like a coffin. Out on bail, Salter hightailed it to Canada. Not even his closest associates would hear from him for three years.

The episode marked a turning point in my marriage. Any lip service to Joe and me being partners was all in the past. Going forward, we lived by an unspoken understanding. Whatever schemes he got up to, whatever women he dallied with, I would turn a blind eye – so long as he kept them clear of Kavanaugh's.

Chapter Twenty-Five

The annual Timothy D. Sullivan Association picnic at Donnelly's Grove in College Point, Queens was a highlight of Tammany's summer social calendar. The morning began with a parade through the Bowery from the Occidental Hotel to the foot of Clinton Street, where nearly five thousand Sullivanites boarded two steamboats, each outfitted with a gaming salon. Joe made a beeline for the craps table before we even cast off, leaving the kids and me on the bow deck, which was fine by me. Those crates from the Pelham were never far from my thoughts, and I was happy to steer clear of anything to do with gambling, sanctioned or otherwise.

Once arrived at the picnic grounds, there was plenty to keep everyone entertained – sack races, a football match that pitted married men against bachelors, and a clam bake. Now, the day was winding to a close. Bellies full of fresh seafood, sweetcorn, and grilled hotdogs, as well as the bottles of free beer passed about, most adults had settled in for a rest before packing up.

Stretched out on the checkered cloth, I flipped through the latest copy of *Vogue* whilst keeping an eye on the field where Moira had joined a group of boys playing tag. Kitted out in a miniature version of my own pale blue-gray linen lawn dress, my little tomboy was looking the worse for wear, hair ribbons unraveling, frock grass-stained and sporting a rip.

Joey, in contrast, played a quiet match of marbles with a few other boys, his sailor suit showing nary a crease, his hair smooth but for the cowlick sticking up at the back, a casualty of the humidity. Watching him, brow furrowing as he lined up his shot, I felt my heart fisting. Already, he'd fallen afoul of a schoolyard bully, who'd stolen his milk money and knocked him down. I'd kept the episode from Joe, not for the bully's sake but for Joey's, for well I knew how my former prize-fighter husband disdained physical weakness of any sort.

"Rosie, over here!"

I looked over to Joe cutting across the lawn toward me, Sullivan at his side. Both wore light-colored linen suits and straw bowlers, the standard menswear for summertime. I closed my magazine and stood as the pair sidled up.

"Rose, meet Congressman Timothy Sullivan. Big Tim, my wife, Rose."

Though married, Sullivan was said to have an eye for the ladies. The intensity of his scrutiny – nary a freckle of mine seemed to miss his notice – bore out the rumor.

"Congressman," I said, craning my neck to look up, for tall as Joe was, Sullivan topped him by several inches. "Thank you for the lovely afternoon. You've spoiled us all."

I offered my hand, and he took it in his damp one, holding on a whit too tight and long. "Glad to hear you're enjoying yourself," he answered, letting go at last. "But why haven't we met before?" He shot a look in Joe's direction. "Keeps you chained up at home all to himself, does he? Can't say I blame him."

I put on a smile, uncomfortably aware of his regard brushing over my bosom. "Truth be told, it's minding our twins and store that keeps me occupied."

"Nice little place, I hear. I'll have to send my missus by for a look around."

"That'd be grand," I said, reckoning his money was green as anyone's. "Only, we're not so little any longer. We've taken over the two side-by-side storefronts and expanded to carry ladies' readymade accessories – hats and gloves, mostly. It's my... our hope to buy the building next year," I added, ignoring Joe's quelling look, for he hated when I "ran off at the mouth" about the business.

Sullivan cut Joe a sideways glance. "Beauty *and* brains." Swinging back to me, he said, "Keep him straight, Mrs. Kavanaugh. It's a fortunate feller who has a woman like you backing him." Something farther afield caught his eye, and he took a step back. "Jimmy Oliver's headed for the beer tent. He promised to stand for the kids' ice creams, but by the looks of him, he may need reminding."

Sullivan started to walk off, but Joe halted him with a hand on his shoulder. "I'll get it."

I sent him a look, a silent reminder we hadn't money to burn.

Sullivan eyed him. "That's swell of you, Kavanaugh, but are you sure? Judging from your missus's mug, she has other plans for that money."

Not about to appear hen-pecked, Joe made a funnel of his hands and belted out, "Who wants ice cream!?!"

Every child on the field froze in place.

"Good man." Sullivan slapped Joe on the back. "I'll leave you to it, then." He tipped his hat to me and wheeled off as the first wave of kids covered us.

Looking over a sea of snatching hands, I said, "Have you lost your wits? There must be close to two hundred children here."

For once, Joe didn't argue. "All with fathers who vote, some more than once."

Taking in his smug smile, I demanded, "You can't honestly think they'll vote you in as assemblyman over free ice cream?"

"Why not?" He pulled out his money clip, the spring straining to hold a wad of bills. "A favor granted is a favor earned," he parroted, passing out the notes.

"Says who?" I demanded, helpless to do other than stand by as our money melted away.

Even as I framed the question, I owned I already knew the answer. Tammany.

146 Men and Girls Die in Waist Factory Fire;
Trapped High Up in Washington Place Building;
Street Strewn with Bodies; Piles of Dead Inside
—The New York Times, March 26, 1911

The fire at the Triangle Shirtwaist Factory hit me hard and not only because it brought back The Windsor. Our Nora worked as a sewing machine operator on the factory's ninth floor, a good job for a girl of seventeen, or so Pat and Kathleen saw it.

Around a quarter to five, I heard the first of a succession of sirens. I finished giving my customer her change and stepped outside to better discern their direction. Seeing Mrs. Katz pacing outside the bakery, I made my way over.

"A four-alarmer at least," I said, for my years as a fireman's wife had trained my ear. "Any idea where it is?"

She turned to face me, flour on her cheek and fear in her eyes. "The Triangle. My Lilith works there."

I braced a hand to the bricks, feeling as if I'd been gutted. "So does our niece."

We took a taxi to Washington Place, the plume of smoke in the sky thickening with every passing block. Our driver pulled up to the adjacent Washington Square Park, and my chest tightened, for the scene playing out was the Windsor Hotel, only worse.

The Asch building, which housed the factory on its upper floors, was banded by flames and belching black smoke. The first fire trucks had arrived. It was painfully apparent that the hoses were too short to reach the ninth floor, where most workers, including our girls, slaved for pittance pay.

Helpless, we waited in the park, cordoned off and packed with people, many of whom, like ourselves, had loved ones within. Anytime I spotted a man in uniform, I rushed up and demanded news, but not even the policemen stationed onsite seemed to know much.

"Auntie Rose."

Nora pushed through the barricades and rushed up, Lilith with her. Neither girl seemed to have suffered so much as a singed eyelash. At the sight of her child, Mrs. Katz dissolved into a puddle, the tears she'd bravely held back rushing down her cheeks.

I clasped Nora close, my own eyes swimming. "I thought for sure…"

"The foreman sent Lily and me out for sandwiches. When we got back—" She pulled back to show me the crushed brown bag and burst into tears.

Nora and Lilith were among the fortunate few. Most of the fire's one hundred and forty-six casualties, nearly all immigrant women and girls from Eastern Europe and Southern Italy, would come from the ninth floor. Some victims succumbed to the flames; others jumped. Clasping hands for courage, girls leaped in pairs, tearing through the rescue nets too fragile to hold them. Meanwhile, the factory owners, the so-called Shirtwaist Kings, Max Blanck and Isaac Harris and their coterie, climbed out their tenth-floor office and escaped onto the rooftop of the adjacent law school.

The fire dominated the news for months. It came to light that the factory had experienced *four* prior fires and been reported as unsafe to the city's Building Department due to an insufficiency of working exits – fire escapes blocked by equipment and bolts of fabric – as well as workroom doors locked from the outside to prevent unauthorized breaks. Owner avarice, including denying employee requests to practice fire drills, had greatly contributed to the calamity.

For once, political allegiances took a back seat to justice. Nativist or newcomer, Christian or Jew, Protestant or Catholic, Republican or Democrat – the aggrieved public gathered in churches, synagogues, and, lastly, the streets. The International Ladies' Garment Workers Union lobbied for a city-wide day of remembrance for the dead, no, *murdered* girls. Labor unions, religious communities, social reform organizations, and political groups, including Tammany, joined forces to demand real progress in worker protections. Within a month of the fire, the New York State Factory Investigation Committee was created to review conditions in factories and sweatshops across the state. Joe lost no time in wrangling himself a seat on it, not that I begrudged him the appointment. With his first-hand knowledge of firefighting, he was ideally suited to do some good.

Looking back, I can't say I was happy, but having finally given up the tug-of-war with Tammany for my husband, I was more at peace than I'd been in years.

And then, one damp December evening, everything changed.

Chapter Twenty-Six

My thirty-first birthday began as any ordinary day. Joe offered to take me out to a fancy supper at Rector's, but knowing it would almost certainly turn into another evening of his hobnobbing, I begged off. A family party was planned instead, supposedly in secret, though maintaining stealth in a four-room flat is fair near impossible. I went about my workday as usual, pretending not to notice the high whispers, spilled flour, and brown paper-wrapped bundles spirited in. If the smell of burned cake was any indication, preparations were progressing apace.

Stationed at the front counter, I took advantage of the rare time alone to give the ledger a good going over. The shop bell clanging caught me unawares. I looked up to a tall gentleman in a silk top hat and evening cape dripping rainwater inside my doorway.

"I'm closed, sir," I called out, "but if you'll tell me what it is you need, I'll see if we have it in stock."

"I was hoping you might make an exception. It's rather urgent." He swept off his hat and stepped into the light.

I stared across the shop floor to Adam Blakely.

Blood rushed my ears. The air in my lungs stuck. My heart thumped so violently, I feared it might burst. All at once, I felt sick and happy, queasy and elated. The years fell away. For a few glorious seconds, I was that girl again, bold and brave, untainted and untried, standing behind my father's bar drawing beer into an overflowing pint, spellbound by the most beautiful boy I'd ever set eyes upon.

A few more footfalls carried him to the counter, his gaze widening as he took me in. He hesitated, then set down his soaked hat, the moisture fogging the glass. "Is it really you, Rose? Or am I dreaming?"

Mute, I dragged my gaze up to his face, making note of the changes – the hint of silver at his temples, the fine lines bracketing his mouth, the sadness clouding his eyes, the irises grayed from the brilliant blue I remembered. And yet, he was still Adam, the handsome Yank to whom I'd given the whole of myself without a care for the consequences. Even with all the years and all the hurt between us, I couldn't look at him without wanting to feel his hands on my body.

My pencil pinging to the floor brought me back to myself. "No, you're not dreaming, not unless I'm dreaming with you."

His gaze lowered to my left hand. Out of habit, I tucked my fingers to hide the scarring, the movement bringing into prominence the gold band Joe had put there.

Bruised eyes lifted to mine. "You've married."

"I have."

He cleared his throat and made a show of looking about. "All this is yours?"

I nodded. "Ours, yes."

He brought his gaze back to mine, gladness suffusing the sadness. "Your dream, you've done it!"

After all these years, he still remembered. "Grand's no Grafton Street, and we don't sell dresses, leastways not yet, though those ladies' hats on the shelf are mine and the evening purses too," I added, not above pride. "What of yourself? Your writing?"

Beneath the mantle of black cape, broad shoulders shifted. "These days my authorship is confined to stockholders' reports and staff memos, and those I have my secretary take down and type up. Between work and… family, there isn't time for my scribbling."

Scribbling – his parents' word, not his, and certainly never mine.

A thunder of feet overhead tore me from my trance. "What brings you to Grand Street?"

"I – we're – just back from Brooklyn. A tea to benefit the new central library."

We, meaning he had his wife with him. "The one to go up at Prospect Park Plaza?" I asked, pleased by my cool, even tone.

He nodded. "Carnegie's bankrolling the lion's share, but we Blakelys are chipping in as well, though our endowment's small potatoes. A humble entrance hallway."

The matter-of-fact mention served as a reminder of how far apart our circumstances yet were.

I crossed to the front of the counter, careful to keep my distance. "What can I help you with?" I asked, my brisk tradeswoman tone meant to put an end to further reminiscences.

"My… wife, we rushed back for the opera, only she tore her dress getting into the car, and it won't do to be seen at The Met with… Christ, Rose," he said, dropping any pretense of our being former friends only, "I stop in for needle and thread and instead, I find… *you*."

Heart in my throat, I admitted, "I've been here these twelve years."

"*Twelve* years?" He scraped a hand through his damp hair, sending the troublesome hank falling over his forehead. Even after all those years, I had to fight the urge to reach out and smooth it back. "My God, to think you've been in my own backyard all this time."

Before I could answer, Joey burst through the parted stockroom curtains and ran up to us. "Mommy, it's your *birthday*. Why are you still *work-ing*?"

Adam's anguished eyes met mine. "December eighth, I remember now."

"My thirty-first," I admitted.

"I just celebrated my thirty-sixth. I suppose that makes us rather grown up," he mused.

"I suppose it does. That and being parents." Feeling as if I were strangling, I gestured to Joey, "My son, Joseph." I ran my fingers through Joey's ginger curls, their springy texture bringing me back to some semblance of sanity.

Joey lifted curious eyes to Adam. "I go by Joey, so folks don't get me mixed up with my papa. He's Joseph *Senior*."

Shocked, Adam looked to me. "You're married to Joseph Kavanaugh, the Tammany assemblyman?"

"I am," I answered, cringing to think what he might have heard. Training my gaze on my son's upturned face, a tangible reminder of the blessings the last dozen years had brought, I said, "I'll finish helping this gentleman and come up straightaway."

He eyed me. "Promise?"

I cupped his cheek. "Cross my heart."

Addressing Joey, Adam said, "I apologize for interrupting the festivities."

The curtain flew back again. "You're not interrupting," Moira said, tromping toward us. "You're *delaying*. They're not the same at all."

She had a sharp tongue, my girl, and an even sharper mind, not to mention a penchant for eavesdropping I'd so far been unable to break her of.

I hastened over to the aisle of sewing supplies. "What color?" I called out to Adam, burying my flaming face in the shelving.

"Sorry?" He peered after me, hazy-eyed as one who'd just awoken.

"What color is your *wife's* dress? So I can match the thread."

"…Light blue, I think."

I scooped up every shade of blue thread we carried and a packet of sewing needles and scissors and brought them to the counter. Barricaded behind it, I wrapped the lot in brown paper and tied it with twine, hoping to hide my hands' shaking.

Adam took out his money clip to pay.

Throat thick, I shook my head. "Compliments of Kavanaugh's."

A dozen years and one dead child stood between us. Weighted against that, of what account were a few spools of thread? A packet of sewing needles?

"But Mums!" Moira exclaimed, coming up to the counter. "You have a fit when Dad forgets to charge people."

"It's my birthday, and I'll do as I please." I slid the sloppily wrapped parcel across the counter toward Adam.

Looking between us, Joey asked him, "Wanna come to Mommy's party? There's a great big cake with chocolate icing and—"

"Quiet, numbskull!" Moira hissed, jabbing him in the side. "It's supposed to be a *secret*."

"Moira, that will do!" I said, hating how she bullied him. To Joey, I added, "I won't let on I know. It'll be our secret."

Over the children's heads, Adam and I exchanged a look.

"That'll make it a double secret, won't it?" Joey asked.

Blinking back tears, I admitted, "Why yes, my love, I suppose it will."

Rubbing his ribs, Joey frowned. "I don't like secrets. Keeping 'em is too much work."

To be so young and so altogether wise. "I don't like them much myself," I said.

"Then we'll tell Dad?" Joey asked.

"Yes, we'll tell him." Flanked by my kids, it was hard to fathom that moments ago, I'd fancied myself seventeen again.

Joey brightened. "But we'll still have cake, won't we?"

I nodded. "We will."

"Yippee!" He did an about-face and charged toward the curtain. Conscious of herself as a budding young lady of ten, Moira excused herself and followed him through.

Watching the drapery drop into place behind them, I turned back to Adam. "Will there be anything else?"

His gaze raked mine. "Before I go, I want you to know—"

Ringing cut him off. Our gazes swung to the entrance and the striking blond sweeping inside. Vanessa Carlton Blakely.

I was keenly conscious of the contrast between us, herself draped in diamonds and fur, her carefully coiffed hair seemingly impervious to the damp, myself in a plain shirtwaist and practical dark skirt, my pinned-up curls untouched since that morning.

Recovering, I called out, "Good evening, madam. Welcome to Kavanaugh's."

Ignoring me, she dropped her brolly into the porcelain stand and approached Adam. "I was beginning to fear you'd fallen through the floorboards."

Stiffening, he snapped, "We agreed you would wait in the car with Frank."

"I know, but it's so dismal outside. And in this dodgy part of town, who's to say what might happen." She flicked her gaze toward me. "Do they have it or not?"

Passing her the package, Adam offered me a strained smile. "Thank you for staying open... Mrs. Kavanaugh. We've kept you long enough. Many happy returns." He turned away and steered them to the door.

Chapter Twenty-Seven

Regrets, Adam was awash in them. Whatever had passed for peace all these years shattered the moment he stepped over my shop's threshold. Ere then, he'd likened the loss of me to his war-wounded leg. The ache was always there, the dull pain ever threatening to flare, but he'd learned to live with it.

Seeing me again changed that. It changed everything. But then, unlike the half-finished novel shoved into a drawer, he'd never put me away, not really. Facing me after all those years, any thought for his waiting wife with her ripped gown and short temper, everything that was mundane and material and small, fled him.

The following Monday, he left the office at lunchtime and took the El to Grand Street. Standing outside our shop, the smart, electrified sign announcing "Kavanaugh & Company", our new, modern moniker, he stuffed down his scruples and entered.

Joe stepped out from behind the counter, a cigar wedged into the side of his mouth. "Can I help you?"

Apart from the occasional newspaper photograph, it was the first Adam set eyes on my husband. A muscle jumped in his jaw. Were those the days of old, he would have gladly challenged Joe to a duel to the death. Then, at least, he would have a fair and honest way of winning me.

As it was, he looked beyond Joe to the shelves stocked with ladies' hats and delicately beaded evening bags. "I'm looking for a gift. For a lady."

Eager to get back to his card game, Joe turned to the stockroom and bellowed, "R-o-s-e! *Cus-to-mer.*"

I stepped out, an apron about my waist and my hands tucked into the gloves I wore for cleaning. Seeing the two of them side by side, I felt sure my legs would fold. Adam, straight-backed, clear-eyed, and not a thread out of place. Joe, chomping on that awful cigar, a five o'clock shadow blanketing his jaw and gut straining his shirtwaist buttons, the very image of the dissipated, loutish Irishman the newspaper delighted in lampooning.

Squelching that disloyal thought, I forced my feet forward. "Welcome to Kavanaugh's," I said, barely able to meet either's eye.

Adam spoke up. "I'm searching for a present for my sister, and I'd appreciate a woman's point of view." Only the determined glitter of his gaze gave away he was no ordinary customer.

I sent Joe a swift sideways glance, but his attention had strayed back to the stockroom. "I'll leave you two to it," he said, heading off.

I waited for the curtain to fall into place behind him before looking back at Adam. "You shouldn't be here," I hissed, shaking with anger and something else, something more. Fear.

He strode over to the hats upon their forms. "Tell me, Mrs. Kavanaugh," he said in a carrying voice, "what's in vogue for ladies' headwear these days? I confess I'm hopeless when it comes to female fashion."

Left with little choice, I followed him over. "These... hair fascinators are extremely popular for evening." Dropping my voice, I added, "Leave – *now*."

An infuriating smile answered. "A hat for daywear seems more suited to my sister's immediate needs. Something a lady might wear to... afternoon tea." He reached across me under the pretense of lifting one of the hats from its form. Instead, he set his hand atop mine. His mouth hovered at my ear, the brush of his breath resurrecting my shameful, long-ago longing. "The tearoom of the Plaza. Tomorrow. Two o'clock."

I had a keen dislike of hotels, though, of course, Adam wouldn't have known that.

The red-and-green-striped motorized taxi left me off at The Plaza's canopied main entrance. Standing at the foot of the crimson-carpeted steps, monogrammed with back-to-back P's, I girded myself to go inside. Why had I come? What was it I hoped to find here? Once I listened to whatever excuses Adam meant to make and gave him a proper piece of my mind, could I finally close the door on our painful past?

Decorated for Christmas, the main lobby, with its crystal-globed chandeliers and gleaming grand staircase, carried me back to my first setting foot inside The Windsor, shivering in my shabby coat. How far I'd come since then. Too far to risk everything I'd built.

More than one corridor led off from the lobby. I stopped a passing porter, who pointed me to the tearoom. The strains of a string quartet and a hive-like humming brought me to an atrium of Grecian-style fleur-de-pêche marble pillars and mirrored doorways. Palm trees, ferns, and sundry flora festooned the arched alcoves. A stained-glass dome soared from the salon's center, its soft yellow-and-green panels painting the wan winter light a sun-kissed gold.

I spotted Adam at a table for two in one of the rear alcoves. He saw me too, his mouth lifting in the lopsided smile I'd once loved so dearly. Courage curdling, I looked away, contemplating bolting down the hallway from whence I'd come.

Before I could, the maître d' looked up from the seating ledger he'd been poring over. "Good afternoon, madam. Reservation, please?"

"The lady is with me."

Adam stepped swiftly behind me. In a blink, my coat was whisked away and handed off to a heretofore invisible hotel employee.

Cupping my elbow, Adam guided us back to his table. "You came. I wasn't sure you would."

Cheeks warm, I admitted, "That makes two of us."

He drew out my chair. "You look beautiful, by the way. Very stylish," he said, taking in my suit of charcoal worsted, simple but smart, and tailored to make the most of my still slender figure.

With it, I wore one of my millinery creations, a plaited black felt hat covered in gray chiffon and trimmed with black piping, a single black rooster feather festooning the band. The two times he'd shown up at the store, he'd caught me by surprise and found a frump. Not above vanity, I'd set out to show him exactly what he'd been missing.

I settled into my seat. "Surely you didn't ask me here only to shower me with shallow compliments."

"Not shallow at all. Wholly sincere." He eased into his chair and took up his menu, the tooled leather holder embossed with those peculiarly appealing back-to-back P's. "But you're right. I asked you here to set the record straight."

I steadied my gaze upon his. "You have five minutes."

He closed his menu with a smack. "I'll make the most of them, then."

Our waiter walked up. "Shall I pour the champagne, sir?"

For the first time, I noticed the bottle on ice at Adam's side. Champagne was for celebrations – and seductions. Our sad little contretemps hardly qualified as either.

At Adam's nod, the bottle was pulled from its silver pedestal bucket and swaddled in white cloth, uncorked, the cork sniffed, and the contents tasted and approved by himself. Finally, our crystal coupes were filled, and the bottle returned to the ice.

Leaving my fizzing glass lie, I waited for the waiter to walk away. "Four minutes. One of us works for a living."

The unkind comment met its mark. Looking at me through wounded eyes, he said, "Very well, marrying Vanessa was a mistake, the biggest of my life. How's that for unvarnished honesty?"

"And yet marry her you did. Your betrothal was announced in every newspaper, your wedding the talk of the town. Even that horrid *Saunterings* columnist reported on it." I glanced at my champagne, tempted to fling it in his face, though, of course, I didn't dare draw the attention.

"I didn't have a choice."

"There's *always* a choice," I countered, not about to let him off so lightly.

His eyes flashed then, the stark blue fire banishing the broken man I'd met again on that rainy evening in my shop. "Very well, then tell me this – why the change of heart?"

"*Change of heart*, not I," I answered hotly, shocked to my shoes, for never had it occurred to me that in coming here, I'd be put in the position of defending myself.

"I sent you three letters in all, four counting the telegram from the ship, none of which you answered. At first, I tried telling myself Colm must have kept them from you, then I remembered it was you who sorted the mail."

"I wrote you too." I stopped there, memory stumbling to catch up. How many letters had I sent? Strange how certain details grow fuzzy with time whilst others remain razor sharp. "After the telegram, I never heard from you again. What was I to think but that your family had talked you out of marrying me?"

"They tried and failed. Miserably. For weeks, every time a passenger liner made port, I rushed down to the docks to meet it." He stopped there, eyes beseeching me to believe him.

Believe him I did, not that it mattered now. "I came over in steerage." Dark blond brows snapped together, bringing the faded scar into prominence. "But I enclosed the money for your passage in my letter. More than enough for you to come over in the finest first-class stateroom the ship offered."

"And yet you married Vanessa. The two of you had an understanding *before* you set out for Ireland." For whatever reason, I couldn't bring myself to mention the humiliating sit-down with his mother.

He had the decency not to deny it. "I broke things off with her after she got back from Paris. I'd made up my mind to book myself on the next steamer to Queenstown and bring you back myself."

Anchoring my gaze to his, I leaned in, by then, too caught up to care what any onlooker might make of us. "But you didn't, did you? You stayed in New York and went through with the marriage." Whatever trumpery or ill luck had kept us apart, the swiftness with which he'd moved on still stung.

His hand holding the champagne glass tightened. "I let her talk me into taking her to one last event, a charity ball, so she could save face. Afterward, we'd go our separate ways. Suffice it to say, the evening didn't turn out as I planned."

I brought the glass to my dry lips. "I'm listening."

"I saw her home, thinking to deposit her at her door and be done. But she coaxed me into coming inside, promised to fetch her father so we could tell him together we were calling things off. When she handed me a brandy, I downed it to get the ball rolling. The next thing I knew, I was on a train to Niagara with a splitting head and... Vanessa beside me. She'd drugged my drink, not that I knew it then."

"Oh, Adam." Feelings flooded me, shock and fury on his behalf, bottomless sadness on my own.

He finished off his champagne. "It wasn't until we were... together on our wedding night that I knew for certain I'd never touched her on the train."

By then, both our glasses stood empty. The server returned, but Adam waved him off and refilled them himself.

"My son was conceived on our wedding night before I found out. Hard to believe one time can make a baby, but it's true."

Thinking of our Mary, I reached for my glass and stole a swift sip.

"Despite everything, I can't regret Robbie. From the moment I learned she was carrying him, I loved him. Sounds crazy, doesn't it?"

Throat threading, I shook my head. "It doesn't." Much as I'd never gotten over Adam, and surely now, never would, I couldn't for a moment regret Moira and Joey.

He sent me a warm look. "This is going to sound like a fond father talking, but a sweeter, brighter, better-hearted boy you'd be hard-pressed to find. He may be half Vanessa, but he's also half me – the *better* parts. But here I am rambling on. You have children of your own, a little boy and girl. Are there others?"

"Just the twins."

"Twins, huh? I would have guessed the girl to be older."

"She is by all of four minutes, a fact she lords over her brother without shame."

We shared a smile.

He lifted the sweating bottle and poured out the last of it. "Truth will out... even if it does come twelve years late."

"Timing never was our strong suit," I agreed. "Though I suppose it's all worked out," I added, the feeble lie ringing hollow, even to me.

Cradling his coupe, he sat back to study me. "Has it?"

I dropped my gaze to the timepiece pinned to my jacket. My planned-upon five minutes was stretching toward an hour. "I should be off."

He glanced to an adjacent table, topped with a tiered china tray laden with savories and sweets. "Why not stay for that tea I promised? From the looks of it, they put on quite a spread."

I shook my head. "I couldn't manage a morsel."

"Me either," he admitted. "Though I could do with a stiff whiskey. Join me?"

With half a bottle of champagne buzzing through me and my heart on my sleeve, I didn't dare. "I won't but thank you."

"A cup of tea, then?"

Before I could refuse that too, he signaled the server and ordered himself a whiskey neat and a pot of Darjeeling for myself. The whiskey didn't last long, whereas most of my tea turned tepid in its gold-rimmed china pot.

His gaze scoured mine. "I've never stopped loving you, you know."

A sigh, a searching look, and next I knew, I was spilling my soul, the pent-up longing too potent to pull back. "I love you too and always have.

197

Even when I told myself I loathed you, I knew it for a lie. No matter how hard I tried to put you in the past, you were always with me. *Always.*"

I'd scarcely finished declaring myself when the waiter circled back with the check. Like a sleeper abruptly awakened, I glanced about, surprised to see the other tables empty, the serving staff setting up for the supper service. I lifted my napkin from my lap. "By the looks of it, we're about to be tossed out."

Adam hesitated. "I feel like a cad admitting it, but I've... taken a room upstairs. You have every right to slap me soundly for so much as suggesting it, but would you consider... coming up for a while? We can talk freely there."

Were I to accept, there'd be precious little talking done, and I wasn't the only one of us to know it. Star-crossed lovers though Adam and I were, thwarted by powerful forces and duplicitous doings, did we have the right to thumb our noses at the laws of God and Man?

And yet a voice, mine, answered, "I will, for a while."

The look Adam sent me swung to rapture. He dug a hand into his jacket pocket. Beneath the table, I felt the press of metal against my palm. A key. "Number 546. I'll settle here and meet you upstairs in ten minutes."

Chapter Twenty-Eight

I stepped off the lift and hurried down the hallway, following the numbered wall plaques. Beyond a chambermaid, pushing her cleaning cart as once I had done, I met no one. Nervous as I was, I found Adam's room without incident and slipped inside.

I left the outer door ajar and took off my winter coat, which I'd gone through the pretense of collecting from the coat check. Draping it over a chair, I cut through the sitting area to the marbled bathroom, unpinning my hat as I went. Inside, I ran the cold tap and bent over the sink, sluicing my face. Reaching for a linen hand towel, I caught my reflection in the gilded wall mirror. My cheeks were pink, my eyes chicory dark, and my lips berry-colored though any trace of rouge had rubbed off. The unblemished girl of Adam's memory was forever gone – along with the scars from the fire, my body bore the marks of two pregnancies – but the woman looking back at me from the beveled glass was altogether more glowing, more alive than I'd seen her in a decade.

I took down my hair and shook it out, leaving the pins in a pile upon the rose marble countertop. I'd collect them later. *Afterward.* Finger-combing the loosened tresses, I heard the outer door open and stepped out.

Adam stood upon the threshold, hat in hand and overcoat slung over one arm. "You're here." His look of wonderment made it seem almost a question. "I've been watching the infernal lobby clock like a madman, telling myself I'd come up and find the room empty, that you'd had second thoughts and gone home."

Heart thrashing, I crossed the carpet toward him. "I should have. I tried to. I... couldn't."

And then we were in each other's arms, mouths meeting and hands seeking the flesh beneath clothing. The bed seemed leagues away. We backed into the bathroom, kissing our way to the counter. Adam lifted me onto the chilly marble and shoved up my shift. Slipping both hands beneath my bottom, he drew me to the edge.

Not yet ready to be taken, I sank firm fingers into his scalp, guiding him lower. Burying himself between my thighs, he pleasured me with deep, damp kisses whilst I braced my back against the mirror and raked my ruined fingers through his hair. Only after I'd cried out my pleasure did he stand and fit himself to me. He came into me hard, his length and thickness filling me in a single stroke, piercing the last of my armoring.

Afterward, he moved to the bed, a king-size four-poster draped in velvet and dressed in satin sheets, the pillowcases monogrammed with the back-to-back P's. Slipping beneath the covers, we embarked upon a more leisurely relearning of each other's bodies. His had changed but slightly. His shoulders were broader whilst his torso remained trim and flat, his scars faded but in all the spots I remembered. Only now, he wasn't the only one of us marked.

He captured my hand and lifted it to his mouth, lavishing kisses on my fire-licked fingers.

"To think once, I fretted over a few freckles," I said, surprised to feel tears springing.

He stopped and looked up at me through those thick, long lashes. "I saw that first night in the store, but I didn't dare ask then. I'm asking now."

Letting my hand lie in his, I settled back upon the banked pillows. "I was working at the Windsor Hotel as a chambermaid when the fire broke out."

His eyes widened. "My God, if I'd any idea you were in it, that you were there, I'd..." Words failing him, he broke off.

"Joe was one of the firemen marching in the parade. The others had given up on those of us trapped on the fifth floor, but he climbed up and brought me out."

There, I'd done it, not only addressed the elephant in the room but brought the beast into bed with us.

Adam stiffened. "I'm grateful to him for that much."

"It's not him who's in the wrong," I pointed out, slipping my hand from his.

Fierce eyes found their way back to my face, all but pinning me to the pillows. "You were mine first."

200

I slid my fingers through his hair, pushing it back from his brow as I'd done a thousand times at least. "I've never stopped being yours, not really. Hard as the years have worn on us, they've worn even harder on him."

He considered that. "Why is it I feel like you're leaving something out? Whatever burdens you've shouldered, it's past time I took up my share."

"After you left Inis Mór, I learned I was with child."

"Your twins, are they—"

"Moira and Joey are Joe's. The other, our Mary, I... miscarried after the fire."

His free hand fisted. "Just when I thought I couldn't possibly despise Vanessa more than I already do..."

"I shouldn't have told you. It was selfish of me."

A handkerchief, crisply monogrammed and perfectly pressed, materialized in his hand and passed into mine. I used it to blot my eyes and blow my nose, the result more bugle's blast than the ladylike sniffle I'd always aspired to. I caught Adam's smile and managed one in return. Not everything had changed.

"No, you were right to tell me." He dropped a kiss atop my shoulder and drew back to look at me. "Only, no more secrets between us, not now, not ever."

He spoke as though we had a future together. Alas, I knew better. "Ever is a terribly tall order, don't you think?"

"Maybe so, but *forever* with you sounds exactly right." He moved to cover me, his lean-muscled body flush with mine, his kisses making me forget aught beyond the present moment.

Evening pressed in, dappling the ceiling with shadows. The twins would be home from school, and their cousin Norah, whom I'd left minding the shop, expected back at Orchard Street. I untangled myself from Adam, pushed off the covers, and sat up, swinging my legs over the bedside. Once on our feet, it was as if an enchantment was lifted. I wasn't brave Rose anymore, the heroine of my own tale, but Mrs. Joseph Kavanaugh, a hapless housewife and shopkeeper who'd pawned her freedom for a gold band and the patina of propriety.

We dressed in sober silence. With every stitch of clothing I put back on, it was as if I added another chink to the unseen shackles mooring me. By the time I'd buttoned the collar of my shirtwaist and replaced the

201

final pin in my hair, a future beyond the four walls of that hotel chamber was back to feeling exactly what it was. Impossible.

We agreed to leave separately, though Adam insisted on having his driver, Frank, take me home. I refused at first but when I saw how late it was, after seven, I agreed to let him bring me as far as Broadway.

Adam walked me to the door. He caught me to him, mouth covering mine.

Drawing back, he searched my face. "How soon can I see you again?"

"Adam, I don't think—"

"Good, *don't* think. If we'd done less thinking thirteen years ago, we'd be married and happy now." He locked his eyes upon mine. "I'm going to work something out. Until then, we'll be careful. Next time, we'll meet somewhere less conspicuous, less—"

Framing his face between my gloved hands, I shook my head. "Oh, my darling, don't you see? There mustn't be a next time."

His gaze burned into mine. "But there will be. There *has* to be. I won't settle for wasting what's left of my life on a loveless marriage, and neither should you."

And so the bittersweet weeks of stolen afternoons began.

Chapter Twenty-Nine

The following week was Christmas. Watching Joey and Moira tear into their gifts whilst Joe sat sipping whiskey-laced coffee, I wondered how Adam was keeping the holiday. Later, Joe and I hosted the usual holiday family dinner. Kathleen came, despite a racking cough, another of her frequent chest colds, though the blood I glimpsed on her handkerchief suggested something more serious. Once, I would have dragged her to the doctor myself, but ever since that first Election Day, she'd treated me with a chilly, arm's-length civility.

Before I knew it, another New Year was upon us – 1912. Less than a month had passed since that rainy birthday night Adam had happened back into my life, and yet I felt as though I'd lived a lifetime. My mood at any given moment might seesaw between despair and delight, remorse and rapture. Every time I went to him, I swore to myself it would be the last – only it never was.

One early January day, Joe made a rare afternoon appearance in the store. Looking up from counting out the till, I saw Adam's handkerchief in his hand, and my heart fell to my feet.

"Who's A.H.B.?" he asked, fingering the fine Egyptian cotton.

Closing the cash drawer, I took a moment to muster myself. "A customer, I suppose."

Day upon day, I'd determined to launder, press, and return the handkerchief to Adam, and day upon day, I'd found some reason for putting it off. Giving back that slight square of cloth would signify saying goodbye once and for all, and that I wasn't yet prepared to do. Our illicit love affair was just that – dangerous and sinful and *wrong* – but it also gave my life zest.

I held out my hand, willing it to stay steady. "Why don't I keep it up here by the register in case its owner comes looking for it?"

A funny look swept Joe's face, or perhaps it was only my guilt that made it seem so. "Any man who can afford a hankie this fine won't miss it." He turned away to the rubbish bin.

I couldn't help myself. "Don't."

He turned back. "What's got into you?"

"Nothing. I just don't see why you're suddenly so keen on tidying. We'll keep it another day or two in case… he comes back. It's only good business."

Circling back, he dropped the handkerchief onto the countertop. "You sure that's the only reason?"

Trembling on the inside though I was, I made myself meet his gaze. "What other reason would there be?"

The clanging of the shop bell kept him off from pressing me further, my savior not a customer but Rivkah Katz. The Triangle tragedy had brought us closer, taking us from neighbors and fellow businesswomen to friends. It was a rare week she didn't stop by at least once, always bearing some delectable dish – the braided challah bread eaten on the Jewish Sabbath and holidays; blintzes stuffed with cheese and sometimes dressed in sweetened berries or drizzled with lemon curd; and, my favorite, the savory potato pancakes known as latkes. She claimed she came for the female company, the opportunity to "kvetch" away from her customers and family.

Carrying the familiar cloth-covered basket, she looked between Joe and myself. "I am interrupting?"

Joe grunted a greeting and headed upstairs, leaving us to ourselves.

She turned to me. "Oy, I *am* interrupting."

Stepping out from behind the counter, I struck a smile. "If you are, then it's a most welcome interruption. Only you mustn't feel obliged to always bring us something," I added, gaze going to the basket.

Today's offering was kugel, a pudding made of egg noodles. She pulled a serving spoon from her apron pocket and dipped it in the sizzling crust. "*Fress!* Eat! You are too skinny." She insisted the same on nearly every visit.

I took the spoon and carried it to my mouth. The kugel was indeed delicious, creamy yet crisp on top. "The children will love this, and so will Joe. I'll serve it for supper tonight."

Her gaze glided over me, the head-to-toe perusal sending me squirming inside my shoes. "You look… different. Younger, even prettier." Dropping her voice, she added, "Don't tell me that husband of yours has started staying home nights?"

Her matter-of-fact mention took me aback. I hadn't realized Joe's nocturnal habits were common knowledge among the neighbors. Considering I now had my own secret to keep, I'd do well not to let my guard down.

Feigning interest in my feather duster, I forced a shrug. "Must be the Ponds facial cream I've been using."

She sent me a look. "*Bupkes*! A luster like yours doesn't come from any jar. You're *verschupft*!"

I felt my face flame, not because she was wrong but because she was so very right. I might be chipping away at my immortal soul with every stolen kiss and sinful stroke, but my physical self was flourishing. The pinkish cheeks and bee-stung lips of my girlhood had returned overnight.

Dropping my gaze, I admitted, "Things are… better."

Grinning, she reached out with both hands and pinched my scalded cheeks. "Keep things interesting in the bedroom, and you'll be a mother again before I can say mazel tov."

The handkerchief episode stayed with me all that week, following me to The Hotel Chelsea, Adam's and my latest trysting spot. Kissing a downward path from my bare shoulder, suddenly, Adam stopped, pulling back to study me. "You're a million miles away."

I started to deny it, but he cut me off with a look.

"Joe found your handkerchief. I told him it must have been dropped by a customer."

"Think he believed you?"

I hesitated. "I think he *wanted* to. But he has suspicions. I can tell."

My slipup was a warning, or so it should be. If we were discovered, it wouldn't only be our two lives in ruin. Our children would suffer, mine most of all.

He raked hard fingers through his hair. "I don't want you going back there."

I gathered the sheet about me as if it were made of chain mail rather than coarse cotton. "I don't have a choice."

He cocked a sandy brow. "Aren't you the same woman who recently assured me there's *always* a choice?"

Confronted with my own words thrown back at me, I mumbled, "That was... different. I'm not free to go my own way."

"You could be. So could I."

"Divorce, you mean?" The very word smacked of irredeemable sin and shattered vows.

He didn't deny it. "I've spoken to an attorney about having papers drawn up. I planned to speak to Vanessa soon. Might as well make it tonight."

Stunned, I spotted my stockings nesting with the dust bunnies beneath the bedstead. Sitting on the side of the mattress to roll them on, I addressed the mustard-colored wall. "We can't go on like this. It's wrong. And dangerous."

He finished buttoning his trousers and sat down beside me, the cheap mattress squeaking beneath his weight. "Sweetheart, I know you're frightened, and I don't blame you. But I'm asking you to trust me. I swear I won't let you down this time."

Doing my level best to ignore the warmth of his hip pressing against me, I snapped the last of the silk into place. "It's not you I don't trust. Joe could fix it so that I never saw my twins again."

Joe might be a drunkard and a dirty politician, but he had powerful allies. His Tammany cronies had no shortage of judges in their pockets.

Adam turned my face to look at him. "I won't let that happen. The five of us will go abroad."

"Abroad?"

Caught up in the dream he was spinning, he nodded. "How's Paris sound? The French are a lot more broadminded than we are here. And I've always had a hankering to see the Eiffel Tower. Like us, it's beaten the odds and stayed standing." He smiled.

I tried to smile back, only my stiff lips didn't seem capable of lifting. "Leave New York? For good?"

His smile slipped. "So long as we have our kids and each other, what's to keep either of us here?"

I hesitated, for it wasn't only my family and faith I feared losing. It was Kavanaugh's. Left on his own, Joe would run the business into the ground inside of a year, I felt sure of it.

Coming from money, naturally, Adam didn't see these things as I did. "You're thinking of your store, aren't you?" It sounded almost an accusation.

I stood and finished doing up my shirtwaist, my trembling fingers making a hash of the eyes and hooks. "I'm thinking of my children's *future*."

Adam got up as well, though he made no move to help me with my buttons as he usually did. "You can start up somewhere else under your own name. Call it O'Neill's or… Blakely's, whatever you like. While you're at it, why not make it a dress shop like you wanted in the first place? No more compromises."

No more compromises. And yet, Life, as I'd come to learn, held little but.

I tucked the shirtwaist into my skirt band and threw on my coat. "You've no notion of what it takes to build a business from the ground up."

His eyes narrowed. "Right, I guess to you I'm just another spoiled rich kid." When I didn't rush to deny it, he added, "You're a worse snob than I'll ever be."

Joe had accused me of much the same. Coming from Adam, the remark cut.

"That's not fair. Or true." Grabbing my hat and handbag, I stomped over to the door and made a clumsy grab for the handle.

Adam stepped between it and me. "Don't leave like this."

"Like what?"

"Mad as blazes."

"I'm not—"

"I could light a match on your cheekbone. If you're going to fight with me, the least you can do is stick around for the making-up part."

In truth, already my anger was ebbing. His stab at humor drained the last of it.

"Guess we just had our first fight, huh?" he said, easing the purse from my hand.

"Our first as lovers," I agreed, remembering our rocky reunion in the Plaza tearoom. "And I don't think you're spoiled. You're the most caring, generous man I've ever known."

"If you do decide to start another business, I promise to roll up my sleeves and do whatever it takes to help… so long as no cows need milking. And I think we'll both agree fishnet mending isn't my forte, either."

We shared a chuckle.

Sobering, he said, "Come away with me to Paris, not someday, but tomorrow."

"*Tomorrow?*"

Earnest eyes answered. "I tried 'paving the way' once before and nearly lost you for good. I'm not inclined to repeat the mistake. And I'm sick of meeting in hotels. Bring the twins and whatever belongings you can't bear to leave and meet me this time tomorrow at the American Seamen's Friend Society Hotel at No. 113 Jane Street. The accommodations are on the spartan side, but it's decent and discreet and right across from the westside piers. I'll be waiting with Robbie. And our passages."

"Adam, I—"

"But if you don't come, I'll know it means you've decided to stay with him, that it's not 'go safely for now' but goodbye for good. Because, my darling, you're right about one thing – we really can't go on this way."

Chapter Thirty

By the time Adam stepped inside the mansion on Upper Fifth Avenue, Vanessa had gone to bed with a headache, an increasingly common occurrence. He eyed the closed door connecting their rooms. Ever since the night he'd walked in on her with Yvette and behaved so abominably, he'd stuck to his side of it. Eager as he was to put their misaligned marriage behind him, he would wait and speak to her first thing in the morning.

Instead, he went to look in on Robbie, wide awake and waiting up for him. In lieu of the usual bedtime story, he did his best to prepare the boy.

Sitting on the side of his son's narrow bed, he pulled an old picture postcard from his pocket. "See this photograph, sport? It's the Eiffel Tower. When it first went up, people said it was an eyesore. The design, pretty much everything about it, broke what they thought of as the rules. It was scheduled to be knocked down years ago. But over time, opinions changed, and the French government decided to let it stand. That's the thing, son. You can't always rely on rules alone. Sometimes, you've got to look deep inside yourself to know what's right. Understand?"

Snuggled beneath the down coverlet, dotted with leaping lambs, Robbie yawned, heavy-lidded eyes fighting sleep. "Kinda."

"Never mind, we'll talk more in the morning." Adam left the postcard on the nightstand and reached for the lamp. "Sleep tight," he said and bent to brush a kiss on Robbie's forehead.

When he got back to his room, he was shocked to find Vanessa settled into his armchair by the fire. She stood when he entered, loose hair spilling about her shoulders, her thin frame wrapped in a dressing robe of champagne-colored Chinese silk, lined in blush-pink taffeta, the romantic garment at odds with the sharp, purposeful look on her face.

"Yet another late night. Papa Blakely still putting you through your paces?" she said, taking in his loosened tie and rolled-up shirtsleeves.

Adam tensed. She'd had him followed once, before Robbie came along. Then he'd had little to lose. Not so now. "I'm just back from looking in on Robbie."

She cast him a quizzical look. "Is he ill? Nanny Chilton didn't say anything earlier."

The question was pure Vanessa. She trotted Robbie out for guests much as she showed off the Vermeer hanging in their drawing room or the Tiffany & Company stained-glass oriel window crowning their foyer; otherwise, she was content to keep him in the background.

"No, he's not sick," he answered, patience straining. "I always check on him before I turn in. It's part of being a parent."

Not that he'd been a very good one of late. Their father–son outings to Central Park had fallen off, a casualty of late nights at the office and rendezvouses with me. The last was more than a month ago when Vanessa was in Boston visiting a school chum. Somewhere between the goat-cart ride on the Mall and hot chocolates at the Dairy, Robbie confessed that a puppy wasn't all he longed for. He'd very much like a little brother to play with. If all went as Adam hoped, his son would have a stepbrother *and* sister to grow up with as soon as tomorrow.

"Since you're here, there is something I need to talk to you about." He waved her back to the chair, but she stayed stubbornly standing.

"Can't it wait 'til morning?" she said around a sigh. "I was hoping for company of the… non-talking kind."

Lest he miss her point, she untied the sash of her robe. A shimmy of white shoulders slid the garment off. Silk puddled at her feet. Beneath, she wore nothing but the pearls, their opulent luster accentuating her chalky pallor.

He hadn't seen her naked since the night he'd walked in on her with Yvette. Other than shock at her thinness, he felt no more moved than if a marble nude stood before him.

"Yvette's night off?" he quipped.

Her smile soured. "She's complaining of a cold, so I sent her off to bed."

"I'm sure she'll be good as new tomorrow."

She bridged the gap between them. "If you must know, our… friendship is worn rather thin of late. I'm thinking of letting her go."

Movement caught his eye. He sent a quick glance to the connecting door, a thin strip of light showing beneath. "Better not let her hear you say that."

"It's not Yvette I want. It's you. It's always been you. And you wanted me once, too, remember? Just a little. Just enough."

Adam shook his head. "I look back on that night with profound regret. And shame."

A smile played about her pale lips. "And yet for all your fine scruples, you went stiff as a plank."

"It's late. We'll talk in the morning." He picked up her robe and passed it to her.

Jamming her thin arms into the sleeves, she glared at him. "Must we always be at each other's throats? Can't we be friends at least?"

"I may not have shown much discernment in choosing a wife, but I'm still fairly selective when it comes to who my friends are."

Her face hardened. "Ah, yes, your many *friends*. The whore I understood, but I confess your recent conquest confounds me."

Adam froze. He might be willing to admit to adultery, but he'd be damned if he'd see me dragged through the mud. "Your paranoia must be getting the better of you."

"The woman in that dreary dry goods store on Grand, that's her, isn't it? The mick tart you met in Ireland. The 'Rose' you tried throwing me over for."

Adam felt as if he'd just been sucker punched. How much had she overheard that evening she'd followed him into the store? How much had she *seen*?

Cinching her sash, she sent him an acid smile. "I believe I'll pay Mrs. Kavanaugh a visit. I doubt her husband would appreciate his wife having a... shall we say 'admirer'? You know how hot-headed these Irish are. I shudder to think what he might do if he caught wind he was being cuckolded."

Adam's furious gaze flew to her bare throat – so slender and wringable. Imagining the satisfying snapping sound it might make, he advanced, gratified to see her back up an equal measure.

"Listen to me very carefully, Vanessa, because I'm only going to say this once. Stay away from that store. Stay away from that woman and her family. If I find out you've so much as set foot on Grand Street, I'll make sure you regret it."

She sent him a strange look. "Is your plan to beat me, then? Under certain circumstances, that might be… interesting."

He stared at her, feeling hatred so strong, it left him shaking. "No, I plan to divorce you." There, he'd said it.

She stared at him, mouth agape. "People like us don't get divorced."

She was mostly but not entirely right. "If the Posts can part ways, then so can we."

The heiress, Emily Post, had sued for divorce after a *Saunterings* column revealed her husband, Edwin's affair with a Broadway chorus girl. Such was the power of a columnist's poison pen.

Vanessa shook her head. "You'd never go through with it, if only for Robbie's sake."

Once that would have been true. Not so now.

"Seeing as you've never been much of a mother to him, I'm confident he'll recover." Adam crossed to the connecting door and opened it for her to go.

She tromped over. "I'm warning you, Adam, don't do this. If you do, I'll name your precious Rose as a co-respondent. She'll be ruined, and her paltry little store driven out of business."

The threat enraged Adam, but he had a trump card of his own to play. "How do think society would react to learning that Vanessa Carlston Blakely is a secret Sappho? Your name would be dragged through the sludge by every newspaper and scandal rag in this city. No matter what good you've done, how many philanthropic committees you've chaired, whoring yourself out to your maid is all anyone will remember about you."

She went pink to her scalp. "You wouldn't."

He blew out a breath. "It doesn't have to be this way. We don't have to go on hurting each other. I have every intention of being fair with you. Keep the house and everything in it. Anything you want, name it. Anything – except Robbie."

Her eyes widened. "You can't seriously mean to take him?"

"I *am* taking him. To Paris. See that Nanny has his belongings packed by noontime."

The face that society wags once likened to an angel's twisted into a witch's mask. "You'll be sorry for this, Adam. Sorrier than you ever imagined." She stomped out, slamming the door behind her.

That time, Adam made sure to lock it. Stepping back, he felt as if a noose had been lifted. Tomorrow, he'd leave with Robbie. Going forward, there would be no more nursery meals, no more rules against romping outdoors or keeping pets in the house. In Paris, he – *we* – would give Robbie the good, simple life he'd always wanted for him.

He changed for bed without calling for his valet, yet another stilted convention he'd no longer be bothering with. Unshackling himself from Vanessa meant freeing himself from the family financial empire as well. For years, his sister's husband, Roger, had been chomping at the bit to run things. Let him.

Turning down the lamp, he lay back and laced his hands over his chest. Sounds of furniture kicked and drawers slammed kept him awake for a while, but eventually, Vanessa spent her spleen and quieted. Likely she'd dosed herself with the laudanum he wasn't supposed to know about. Based on the bills crossing his desk, her use of the sleeping aid was a regular thing. She must be more miserable than she let on. Maybe in divorcing her, he was doing her a kindness.

Holding my image in his head, he drifted off. In his dream, we were back on the cliff on Inis Meáin, not the boy and girl we'd been but our present selves.

He reached out and cupped my cheek. "I told you I'd make you happy again. You are happy, aren't you?"

Banging bled into the dream as a roar of surf rushing into rock. The storm was coming. No, it was upon us! The tide rose, climbing the cliff wall to wrap foamy fingers about us. Fighting to keep his head above water, Adam strained to hold onto me, to keep us both afloat, but it was no use. I slipped through his fingers and disappeared, swept away by a pitiless ocean.

The gaveling stopped. A hand shook his shoulder. "Mr. Blakely, sir, wake up."

Adam opened his eyes to his valet's fraught face staring down at him. He bolted upright, tearing off the covers. "My boy—"

The valet shook his head. "Master Robbie is fine. It's Madam. She died during the night, and that foolish Frenchie maid of hers has gone and rung for the police."

In the few minutes it took Adam to throw on clothes and rush downstairs, Yvette Bellerose had installed herself in his front parlor, along with the two attending police detectives. Sipping a glass of water, she went silent when

213

Adam entered. Taking in the black looks bounced his way, he surmised that whatever she had said was far from flattering.

Much was made of the previous evening's argument she'd apparently overheard between he and Vanessa. Statements were taken from the rest of the staff as well, though as the household had retired early, no one else reported hearing anything untoward. Afterward, Adam invited the lead detective to his study. Yes, he and his wife had argued, he admitted, but afterward, she'd gone back to her room, and he'd remained in his for the duration of the night, end of story.

Only it wasn't. Not having called for his valet, there was no one to corroborate his account. Because Vanessa was young and healthy, beautiful and rich, there would be an inquest. The autopsy confirmed an overdose of laudanum as the cause of death. In the absence of a suicide note, the manner of death was deemed suspicious – and those suspicions all pointed to Adam.

Day and night, reporters camped upon the sidewalk outside his house, rushing the ironwork gate every time a door opened. At least one over-zealous newsman went so far as sifting through his rubbish. Someone broke into the garage in the mews backing the mansion and keyed "*Wife Killer*" onto the side of the shiny black Cadillac Frank took such pride in keeping just so.

Grief-stricken and needing someone to blame, Andrew Carlston exerted his influence with the District Attorney's office to press for an indictment. Adam was charged with first-degree murder and escorted to police headquarters at 300 Mulberry Street and from there to the municipal jail known as the Tombs. Upon receiving the news, Horatio Blakely folded to his office floor. Speechless and semi-paralyzed, he hadn't left his bed since, nor was he expected to.

The trial was set for two weeks from the discovery of Vanessa's body. Though the evidence brought up in the pretrial hearings was all circumstantial, the newspapers rendered their guilty verdict already. But then a rich, homicidal husband made for more sensational headlines than an innocent man wrongfully accused. And sensation sold papers.

"Looks like that Blakely feller may fry," Joe announced one morning, stepping inside our flat with a stack of freshly printed dailies tucked beneath his arm.

"What makes you say that?" I asked, struggling to steady my voice.

214

"See for yourself." He walked over to where I sat, nursing a cup of tea, and dumped the lot onto the kitchen table.

I grabbed a *New York Times* from the top. My eye flew to the space above the fold where Adam's case, already billed as "*The Trial of the Century*," was once again the headlining story.

"To think he stood downstairs just a few months ago, a cold-blooded wife-killer despite his pedigree and plump pockets," Joe opined, pouring himself coffee from the pot on the stovetop.

"You don't know that," I snapped, a headache striking the base of my skull. "Innocent until proven guilty, isn't that how it works over here?"

Despite the damning circumstances, I refused to believe Adam capable of cold-blooded killing. But how far would innocence carry him? I wasn't so naïve to believe it any guarantor of justice. The world wasn't always a fair place or a kind one. Good people, like Gerta, died through no fault of their own. Girls and young women slaved in sweatshops, such as Triangle, only to be done in by the greed of an entitled few. Adam wouldn't be the first to be wrongfully convicted and sent upstate to prison, or worse, the electric chair.

Joe carried his cup over to the kitchen table and sat. "Say, what'd he buy anyway?"

Reaching for a second paper to see if the coverage was any fairer, I looked over. "Sorry?"

"The day he came here looking for a gift. For his sister, he said. What'd he end up with?"

Wondering what he was getting at, I shook my head. "I don't remember. Why?"

"Just curious is all." He lifted the top off the sugar bowl and dropped three cubes into his coffee. Stirring it with his finger, a habit I hated, he added, "You're always such a stickler for recording every sale in that ledger of yours, I just thought you'd remember."

"Well, I must have forgotten. We're none of us perfect, after all," I snapped, slathering butter on a toast slice I couldn't think of eating.

Since his arrest, Adam had managed to get one message to me through his driver, Frank. Under no circumstance was I to go anywhere near the courtroom, no matter how bad things got.

The first morning of the trial, I waited for Joe to leave, then changed clothes and slipped out. Walking a few blocks off so as not to encounter any of my near neighbors, I flagged down a cab and directed the driver to the city courthouse at 52 Chambers Street.

Commissioned in the 1860s by Tammany's Boss Tweed, the Italianate-style courthouse was an imposing edifice as well as a bustling concern. Within the main rotunda hall, officers of the court, sober-suited lawyers, policemen, and sundry civilians milled about. Pulling my hat's veil low over my face, I joined those filing up the main staircase. At the top, a guard pointed the way to the thirty courtrooms. After a false turn or two, I found Adam's.

As befitted the "Trial of the Century," the wooden benches were crammed with family and friends, acquaintances and curiosity-seekers, newspaper reporters, and sketch artists. The Carlstons and their camp occupied the front rows on the prosecution's side, supporters of Adam the other. I crossed the aisle to the defense and slipped into a vacant spot at the back.

I'd no sooner settled in when a smartly dressed older woman entered, her tailored tweed suit of the finest fabric and fit, a black fox fur stole about her shoulders. I blinked, sure my veiled vision misled me. But no, it was Beatrice Blakely. Even considering the dozen years gone by, I was shocked to see her hair gone to silver, her stance stooped to the cane she clutched. Despite her past cruelty, I couldn't but pity her, for she stood to lose her husband and son both.

Finally, Adam was brought in. I'd steeled myself to see him shackled and clad in prison stripes. Instead, they'd removed the handcuffs and allowed him the courtesy of his own clothes. The sober gray pinstripe looked looser on him than I remembered, the lean-muscled body I loved lost inside the fine wool. Judging from his drawn face, he'd slept even less than he'd eaten.

Despite my shrouding, he spotted me easily, his step stalling on his progress down the center aisle. The bailiff nudged him on toward the defense table. I fixed my gaze upon the back of his bare head, silently telegraphing my love and support.

At nine o'clock, the twelve men of the jury were led in, working men shoulder-to-shoulder with dark-suited businessmen, one in a cleric's collar. Watching them file into the jury box and take their places in the high-backed seats, I scrutinized each's face to gauge how he might lean.

"All rise," the bullet-headed bailiff ordered.

The room stood as Judge Abernathy entered. He took his seat on the bench and bade us do the same. Fingering his gavel, he delivered his preliminary instructions to the jury and then called for opening arguments.

D.A. Edward Fellows rose from the prosecution table, doing up his jacket button and loudly clearing his throat before beginning. In his late fifties, of substantial girth with steel-gray hair, a closely clipped beard, and a magenta waistcoat that matched the broken veins in his nose, he was known as "The Verdict-Getter." His fiery impeachment of Adam as a cold-blooded wife-killer, uniquely possessed of both motive and opportunity, more than lived up to his reputation.

In contrast, Adam's attorney, Josiah Elgin, was rail-thin, clean-shaven, and sober-suited as a Puritan forefather. The cornerstone of his comments, delivered in a clear, monotonic voice, pointed to the paucity of evidence, and reminded the jury that the burden of proof lay with the prosecution.

A break for lunch was called, and the courtroom cleared. With nowhere to go and no appetite for food, I bided my time on a bench in the corridor, my veil drawn over my face and my rosary in hand.

The proceedings resumed with testimony from the witnesses. When the defense declined to call any – apparently, not even Adam himself! – the field was ceded to Mr. Fellows.

Fixing a steely eye upon the jury, he said, "The state calls Miss Yvette Bellerose."

Vanessa's maid sashayed up to the witness box as an auditioning actress might step onstage. Powdered and rouged, her décolletage indecently dipping for daywear, she turned to face the courtroom.

"Do you solemnly swear to tell the whole truth and nothing but, so help you, God?"

Hand upon the Bible, she nodded. "*Oui*, I do."

"Be seated, Miss Bellerose," the judge said.

She took the straight-backed chair provided, a process that involved a good bit of shifting of bum and jiggling of breasts.

Once she'd settled, the prosecutor began, "For the record, what is your occupation, Miss Bellerose?"

Fingering a bobbed brunette lock, she answered, "Lady's maid and companion to Madame Vanessa Blakely."

"How long were you employed by Mrs. Blakely in that capacity?"

She pursed her painted lips. "I first met Mademoiselle... pardon, *Madame*, when she visited Paris with her parents in... 1898."

"That would be prior to her marriage to the defendant, Mr. Adam Blakely?"

"*Oui, plus que treize ans...* More than thirteen years."

"That's a considerable time. Were the two of you close?"

"*Monsieur?*"

"Did she confide in you?"

From his seat at the defense table, Mr. Elgin called out, "Objection, leading the witness."

My gaze flew back to the bench.

"Sustained. Mr. Fellows, if you have an actual question for this witness, kindly get on with asking it."

"Right, Your Honor." Fellows pivoted back to the witness box. "Mrs.—"

"Alas, it is mademoiselle," she said, the correction accompanied by a winsome pout.

"*Miss* Bellerose, would you say you knew Mrs. Blakely well?"

"*Ah, oui.* Mademoiselle always said she would be lost without me."

"Would you characterize her as a happy person?"

From Mr. Elgin: "Objection, calls for speculation."

"I'll rephrase. Did she ever express to you that she was sad or... frightened of something? Or *someone?*"

"Mademoiselle was sunshine itself... until her marriage."

"*Until* her marriage, I see. And did she ever confide in you her reasons for her... dissatisfaction?"

"*Eh, bien*, she did, but I hardly like to say it."

Judge Abernathy interjected. "The witness will answer the question."

"*Monsieur* Blakely, he... how do you say *en anglais*... he cheated on her."

A gasp rolled through the room. Cheeks hot, I resisted the urge to shrink into my seat.

"Mrs. Blakely knew this for fact, or was she speculating?"

"*Mais, non*, she *knew*. She hired the..." She hesitated as if once again, searching for the English. "Private detective."

Mutterings of shock and condemnation ricocheted about the courtroom. I held myself board stiff, bracing myself to be called out as Adam's lover.

"She had this detective surveil... follow her husband?"

218

"*Oui*, for *presque*... almost one month."

One month – the very duration of our affair! I should have listened to Adam and stayed away. I'd been selfish not to. If my coming here brought more harm down on his head, I couldn't say how I'd live with myself.

"And what did he discover?"

"There was a woman, but this was years ago when Mademoiselle – Madame – was *enceinte* with Robert."

Jolted, I accidentally bumped the arm of the woman next to me. Murmuring apologies, I told myself there would be ample time later for sorting out my muddled feelings. For the moment, all that mattered was the trial.

Pivoting to hold the jury's gaze, Mr. Fellows asked, "Mr. Blakely was... carrying on while his wife was pregnant?"

Staying put in his chair, Mr. Elgin said, "Your Honor, again I must object. Mr. Fellows' narrative plays like a dime-store novel. Mr. Blakely's morals aren't on trial here."

The judge opened his mouth as if to sustain the objection, but Mr. Fellows intercepted. "Forgive me, Your Honor. My outrage as a Christian husband and father momentarily overcame my professional judgment. I'll withdraw the question." He turned back to Miss Bellerose. "Beyond Mr. Blakely's... infidelity, were there other causes for his wife to be dissatisfied... dare I say, *unhappy* with him?"

The query brought an emphatic nod. "*Monsieur*, he did not... share a bed with her."

At last, Mr. Elgin stood. "Objection. Again, calls for the witness to speculate. Many married couples of the Blakelys' social stature maintain separate bedrooms. In this instance, the two rooms are connected by a dressing closet. Unless we are to believe that the witness maintained round-the-clock watch, she cannot say with certainty that..." he cleared his throat, "conjugal relations did not occur."

Eyes darting between the two lawyers, Miss Bellerose broke in with, "Oh, but I can! Madame used to weep that Monsieur would not lie with her."

Judge Abernathy turned to the witness chair. "Miss Bellerose, going forward, you will refrain from any such outbursts and speak only when addressed, do you understand?"

Appearing duly chastened, she nodded. "*Pardon, Monsieur Le Juge.* My grief, it makes me forget myself."

219

Mr. Fellows resumed. "According to your sworn statement, you overheard the defendant, Mr. Blakely, arguing with Mrs. Blakely the night of her death. Can you walk us through the events leading to that argument?"

"*Monsieur* was out. Madame retired early. I came to her room as I always do, to help her undress, brush out her hair—"

"Objection," Mr. Elgin interrupted. "I fail to see what bearing this… recitation of the duties of a lady's maid has on the case?"

Fellows' dramatic sigh reached to the room's rear. "Your Honor, I am simply seeking to establish a timeline of events for the night of the mur – *decease* – of Vanessa Blakely."

The judge nodded. "I'll allow it, but for the last time, Mr. Fellows, come to the point."

"I will, Your Honor, thank you for your indulgence." Turning back to the Frenchwoman, he continued, "You helped Mrs. Blakely prepare for bed. Was there anything… different about her instructions that night?"

"There was one thing, but I do not like to say it."

Judge Abernathy interjected. "You are under oath, young lady. Answer the question."

"When I tried to help her on with her nightgown, she shook her head. 'I won't need that tonight, Yvette,' she said."

From jury to spectators, all of us were perched upon the edges of our pews.

"What happened next? Did she retire?"

"*Non, monsieur.* She put on her robe and went to the door of the dressing room."

"What, if anything, did you take that action to mean?"

"She hoped to seduce Monsieur so that she might have another baby."

"To your best knowledge, was she… successful?"

I steeled myself for her answer. As the other woman, I had no right to jealousy, and yet…

"*Non,* she was not. Monsieur told her to leave. And that… he desired the divorce."

Shock spilled through the gallery. Caught up, I had to remind myself to breathe. Adam had kept his word, and now he might… what word had Joe used – "fry" – for it.

"You know this how?"

220

"Through the door, I heard him say he would make her sorry if she stood in his way."

"Did you interpret it to mean that he would harm her in some way?"

"Objection, again calls for witness speculation."

The judge shook his head. "I'll allow it. You may answer, Miss Bellerose."

"*Oui*, make some violence against her." A handkerchief materialized in her hand, and she dabbed it beneath her eyes.

Fellows stepped back. "No further questions."

"Mr. Elgin, your witness."

Adam's attorney approached. "Tell us, Miss Bellerose, what time did Mrs. Blakely return to bed – that is, her own?"

"Close to ten o'clock. She was upset, crying. I tried to comfort her but *hélas*..."

"Did you see, or hear, Mr. Blakely enter her room at any time?"

"I had a cold, and she sent me to my bed. If I stayed with her, perhaps she would be alive." A tear slid down her cheek, cutting through the caking of cosmetics.

"So, that's a no?"

"*Non*. I took the tonic: Kimball White Pine and Tar Cough Syrup. It made me sleepy."

Mr. Elgin's face lit. "As a father of four, I'm quite familiar with that particular tonic. It contains both alcohol and chloroform. Under its influence, how can you be certain you didn't hallucinate or even *dream up* this entire story?"

Mr. Fellows erupted from his seat. "Objection!"

Judge Abernathy spared him but a glance. "Overruled. You'll answer, Miss Bellerose."

"I did not dream it."

Whether driven by devotion to a dead mistress or a desire to garner attention for herself in the press or both, Yvette seemed to have a personal stake in seeing Adam convicted.

"Did you see Mr. Blakely administer any food or drink to his wife that evening?"

"*Non*."

"Have you ever in your more than thirteen years in Mr. Blakely's employ seen him strike or direct any form of physical violence toward his wife?"

Yvette hoisted her chin. "I did not see but—"

"Did you ever observe any bruises or other violent marks upon Mrs. Blakely's person?"

"*Non.*"

Though Mr. Elgin's back remained to the room, the smile in his voice was impossible to miss. "No further questions."

Chapter Thirty-One

Risky as it was, I had to see Adam.

At five o'clock, the judge adjourned the proceedings until the following morning. Once Adam was manacled and led away, the room rapidly emptied. I quit the chamber and found the exit stairs leading outside to the covered walkway known as The Bridge of Sighs. At its other end lay the city jail, the Tombs – and Adam.

Contrary to its name, the eight-story prison was anything but silent. A hodgepodge of humanity circulated within – lawyers conferring with their clients; friends and family visiting incarcerated loved ones; uniformed keepers; court clerks; police officers, some with detainees in tow; and vendors peddling pies and other foodstuffs.

The passageway to the men's prison opened onto four stories of iron galleries divided into cells. Two keepers patrolled each tier, clubs at the ready. Occasionally, a hand or limb stretched out from the bars. Adam's leg? Adam's arm? Looking up, I wondered which was his.

Five dollars, discreetly palmed, bought me ten minutes alone with him in an interview room. Another five ensured the guard stood *outside* in the hallway.

Adam was brought in, still wearing his court clothes. He'd left off his suit coat. In vest and shirtsleeves, he looked every whit the gentleman at his leisure – barring the irons about his wrists and ankles.

He shuffled forward and took his seat at the table across from me, his expression one of tender frustration. "You'd have made a lousy soldier, you know that?"

I mustered a smile. "I never have been any good at following orders. How are you being treated?"

He shrugged. "It's not the Ritz, but the food's plentiful, and my cell has an iron bed with a surprisingly decent mattress, a chamber pot, and a window overlooking Centre Street. The accommodations on Murderer's Row are a lot less cushy, I'm told." His gaze dimmed. "Considering the less-than-savory parts of my past brought to light today, I wonder you can stomach the sight of me."

I reached across and touched his shackled wrists, no matter that physical contact was forbidden. "It's not my place to judge."

"Isn't it? All these years later, it isn't my wife I feel guilty for betraying. It's you. It's always been you. Even now, when it's likely too late to matter."

"Don't say that. You'll be found innocent. You *must* be."

He sat back, shaking his head. "Did you see the faces on those jurors? If they were being put to ballot today, I'd fry for sure."

Fry – how I was coming to hate that word! A sudden, dizzying image of Adam, *my* Adam, in the dreaded electric chair, scalp shaved, trousers slit up the sides so that the leads might be applied, flashed before my mind's eye, and I gripped the table.

"The jury's made up of regular, mortal men, not saints and not angels. As Mr. Elgin said, it's not your morals on trial."

"Aren't they?" His gaze honed upon mine. "This may be my one chance to say it to you face to face, so I will: I didn't kill her. Whatever I may have threatened in the heat of the moment, I didn't lay a finger on her. The last I saw her, she was alive."

"Of course she was. You couldn't commit murder. It's not in you."

"I'm not so sure about that." He blew out a breath. "Many times over the years I wished her dead. Now that she is, a part of me can't help wondering if this isn't some sort of divine retribution."

"Vanessa wouldn't be the first to misjudge her laudanum dose and die for it." One eye on the ajar door, I dropped my voice and added, "That maid, Yvette Bellerose, is entirely too keen on seeing you convicted."

His expression shuttered. "She and Vanessa were… close."

Still in the dark about the depth of that relationship, I said, "How do you know she didn't overdose Vanessa herself, deliberately or by accident?"

He considered that. "Before we argued, Vanessa said something about dismissing Yvette. If Yvette was eavesdropping, she may have overheard that too."

I sat up. "That might well be motive for murder."

"A shaky one, but yes, I agree."

"No shakier than the case against you. You'll speak to Mr. Elgin?"

"I will. I've already told him I want him to put me on the stand, but he says it's too risky. Seems adulterers don't make the most sympathetic of witnesses."

"Oh, Adam, I'm so sorry for… all of it."

"I'm not." Weary eyes met mine. "This last month has been worth a lifetime at least."

"Not if you're convicted it's not!"

"Convicted or freed, I'm done for. I'll never live this down."

"You mustn't worry about that now. Concentrate on being proven innocent."

He tried for a smile. "That's Elgin's job." Sighing, he shook his head. "Ironic, isn't it? Just when I finally get up the gumption to free myself from the prison of my marriage, I land in an actual prison."

"Not for long."

He squeezed my hand, the forbidden contact sending chains clanking. "You give me hope. I'm not sure if that's a kindness or a cruelty, but you do. You always have."

A cough came from close by, then the door opened, and the guard entered. "Time's up."

Adam leaned toward me, breath brushing my cheek. "If I'm convicted, promise me you'll watch over Robbie. Vanessa wasn't much of a mother, but she's the only one he's ever known. If I'm… taken, he'll be without a father too. It would help me face things if I knew you were there to look out for him."

Tears burned my eyes, blurring what might well be my last look upon him that wasn't from across a courtroom. "I will."

He hesitated. "I suppose it hardly matters now, and yet I can't help wondering… Would you have come? To Paris, I mean?"

I steeled myself for yet another lie, this one said in the service of love. "Yes, I would have."

The following day, Mr. Elgin relented and called Adam to the stand. The defense attorney's line of questioning was crafted to debunk the D.A.'s argument that Adam alone had motive for murdering Vanessa. Why should Adam dirty his hands with murder when he could simply move forward with a divorce? He even contrived to slip in Vanessa's possible plans to fire Yvette, though when asked what reason she might have for doing so, Adam answered with a stone-faced and not terribly convincing, "I couldn't say."

With his questioning concluded, Mr. Elgin returned to his seat, and the judge gestured to the prosecution. "Mr. Fellows, your cross."

The portly prosecutor stood. Hooking his thumbs in his bracers, he approached the witness box. "How are you today, Mr. Blakely?"

"I've been better."

"Yes, sir, I expect you have." A pause, a chummy smile, and then, "Kindly walk us through the events leading up to the argument with your late wife."

"I worked late."

"Where did you dine?"

"I had a sandwich at my desk."

"Can anyone corroborate that?" Fellows pressed.

"I'd think that would be your job."

Titters trickled through the courtroom.

The judge intervened. "Answer the question, sir."

"My secretary brought it to me," Adam said.

Fellows nodded. "Between work and home, any stopovers?"

Adam swiped a hand through the front of his hair. "I stopped for a drink."

"Where was that?"

"The Chelsea."

Adam's black Cadillac had been confirmed waiting on the street outside, Frank at the wheel, leaving Adam no choice but to admit to being there. Even knowing that in advance, I tensed, feeling as if I shared the witness stand with him.

"The Chelsea *Hotel*?"

Adam nodded. "Yes. Is that a crime?"

"Not a crime but certainly a peculiar choice. After putting in a long day at the office, you went all the way downtown to Twenty-Third Street to what, soak up the bohemian atmosphere?"

"I had a lot on my mind, and I wanted to go somewhere I wasn't likely to run into anyone I knew."

The prosecutor scoffed. "Smart, one might even say calculating. Did you meet with anyone while you were there?"

My heart leaped to my throat. As always, I'd arrived and departed separately, and I was reasonably certain no one had seen me enter or leave Adam's room. The hotel was, if not derelict, down-at-heel, its staff spread thin and not of the questioning sort. Still, if I'd thought revealing our affair would spare Adam, I would have done so in a heartbeat, no matter that it would mean living the rest of my life with the equivalent of a scarlet "A" stitched to my breast. And yet I had to think admitting to a second such liaison would do him more harm than good.

"No," Adam replied, adamantly as I'd known he would.

"No?" Fellows echoed. A studied half-turn toward the courtroom and then, "And yet, according to the hotel staff, a man matching your description arrived around six-thirty p.m., ordered a double bourbon from the bar, and booked a guestroom – Room 1017 to be precise – for which he paid in cash."

Mr. Elgin shot to his feet. "Objection, Your Honor, asked and answered. I fail to see what bearing any of this has on the case at hand."

Fellows looked to the judge. "It bears on Mr. Blakely's character as well as establishes a timeline of events leading up to the mur... demise of Mrs. Blakely."

"Overruled. I'll allow it, but tread carefully, Mr. Fellows."

Fellows turned back to Adam. "Did you take a room at The Chelsea, Mr. Blakely?"

Thinking back to our leisurely lovemaking and the stupid fight that had followed, I bit the inside of my cheek until I tasted iron.

"I did."

"For what purpose? Perhaps to entertain a... lady friend?" Mr. Fellows sent a sly wink out to the courtroom.

"Like I said, to think things over."

"Things such as... how best to go about killing your wife?"

"Objection!" Mr. Elgin cried out.

"Sustained."

Mr. Fellows gave the judge an amiable smile. "I'll withdraw the question." Focusing back on Adam, he asked, "How long did all this... *thinking* take?"

Adam shrugged. "Couple of hours. I've never had much of a head for liquor. I slept off the bourbon and then headed home."

"Would it surprise you to learn that, when deposed, your driver, Mr. Francis Cafferty, went on the record as recalling that stopover to be two hours and twenty minutes?" Not waiting for Adam's answer, the prosecutor whirled away and produced a slender transcript, which he waved about with a magician's flair. "Your Honor, I submit into evidence the testimony, under oath, of Mr. Francis Cafferty, chauffeur to the Blakely family, as Exhibit A."

I cast my gaze to the jury box. Judging from the stony countenances staring out, Adam's testimony wasn't settling at all well.

"Fellows swung back to Adam. "What time did you arrive home?"

"About nine-thirty."

"Walk us through what happened next."

"I went upstairs, took off my coat and tie and then checked on my son. When I got back to my bedroom, my wife was waiting."

"And that was unusual, was it?"

"Yes."

"She walked through the connecting closet?"

"I believe so, yes."

"To what purpose?"

A slight pink stain appeared on Adam's cheeks. "To… talk."

"Talk was all she wanted? Nothing else?"

"She wanted me to… take her to bed."

"And did you?"

"No."

"Instead, you argued, isn't that so?"

"Yes."

"Over?"

Seated at the room's rear though I was, I saw Adam redden. "I told her I wanted a divorce."

Hardly news, still necks were craned, spectacles and lorgnettes adjusted to improve views. Even the court stenographer stopped typing to stare.

"You told your late wife you planned to divorce her. How'd that go over?"

Fisting my gloved hands, I steeled myself.

"Not well. She was upset, angry. We both were. That doesn't mean I murdered her."

"Sure about that? You'd been drinking. You threatened her, said you'd make her sorry if she didn't fall in line and give you what you wanted – your divorce?"

"I recall saying something to that effect, but it was an exaggeration, a figure of speech."

"Were you planning to leave your wife, Mr. Blakely, or was that a 'figure of speech' too?"

"I was going to leave, yes."

"The next day, in fact?"

"Yes, but—"

"And did this plot... pardon me, *plan* include taking your son with you?"

"It did."

"And did Mrs. Blakely give any indication that she might consent to this arrangement?"

"Not at the time, but—"

"Did she, in point, swear to fight you every step of the way?"

Jaw clenched, Adam answered, "Yes."

"And so you took the only course left to you. You made certain she didn't wake up to see another day. You deliberately overdosed her with laudanum, isn't that so, sir!?!"

"*No!* If you'll let me explain—"

"No further questions."

From the bench, Judge Abernathy asked, "Any final witnesses, Mr. Elgin, before we move to closing arguments?"

It was the fifth day of the trial and the final witness for the prosecution. Adam's driver had just stepped down from the stand. Poor Frank. Pale as a sheet, he looked as though he were the one who stood accused of murder. Hard as he'd tried to "put in a good word" for his beloved Mr. B., short of perjuring himself, he couldn't give Adam the one thing he most needed: an alibi.

Mr. Elgin stood. "Your Honor, I call to the stand Dr. William Edmund Holtz."

Murmurs made the rounds for as of the day before, Dr. Holtz had not been included on the list of defense witnesses.

The doctor was sworn in, and Mr. Elgin ambled up to the box. "For the record, Doctor, please state your relationship to the deceased."

"I was Miss Carlston's... pardon me, *Mrs. Blakely's* physician. I've

229

treated her since she was a girl. Indeed, the entire Carlton clan has been under my care for nearly thirty years," he added, the mouth beneath the immaculately manicured mustache curling into a prideful smile.

Mr. Elgin nodded. "Given your longstanding physician–patient relationship, she must have trusted you, dare I say, implicitly?"

Mr. Fellows rose. "Objection. I fail to see what bearing this… reverie has on the case."

Steady as still water, Mr. Elgin ignored him and addressed the bench. "The defense means to demonstrate that Vanessa Blakely was not murdered but instead took her own life. Who better to speak to the deceased's frame of mind than her longstanding physician?"

"Objection overruled. Oh, do take your seat, Mr. Fellows," Abernathy snapped.

Mr. Elgin repeated his question, and the doctor's smile spread. "Well, yes, I like to think she trusted me to that degree."

"Don't be overmodest, Doctor. She might have seen any number of highly qualified physicians in the city, yet she continued to come to you after her marriage, isn't that so?"

"Yes."

"According to your appointment diary, she visited your office in mid-October, twice in November, once in December before the holidays, and lastly, January twentieth, two weeks prior to her death. That seems a considerable number of physician's appointments for a fit young woman. Can you tell the court the reason for such frequency?"

The doctor's smile flattened. He turned to the judge. "Your Honor, with all due respect, patient confidentiality is the cornerstone of a practice such as mine. Prominent persons rely not only on my medical expertise but also on my… discretion."

To the judge's credit, he didn't dither. "Mrs. Blakely is deceased, and a man, her husband, stands accused of her murder. You'll answer the question, Doctor."

Doctor Holtz faced back to Mr. Elgin. "Mrs. Blakely, though in her prime, suffered from advanced cancer of the breast."

Shock rippled through the room. Caught up in the current, I braced myself.

"Advanced cancer of the breast sounds grave indeed," Mr. Elgin said. "In layman's terms, how ill was Mrs. Blakely?"

"She was dying."

More rumblings and judge's gaveling before the doctor could continue.

"She'd discovered the lump by happenstance while bathing. Sometimes, if detected sufficiently soon, a cure can be achieved. The breast is removed through a procedure known as mastectomy. The surgery is long and difficult, as is the recovery, and the results are... disfiguring. Still, some patients and their husbands elect to pursue it."

"Did you recommend such a surgery to Mrs. Blakely?"

"I did not. I referred her to a colleague in Boston who specializes in cancers of the breast and female organs."

"Did she go to see him?"

"She did. I received his written report."

"And did he offer her any hope, perhaps propose an alternate diagnosis or suggest she undergo surgery after all?"

The doctor shook his graying head, which suddenly seemed as if it must weigh heavy indeed. "Unfortunately, his examination confirmed my diagnosis. Given the size and location of the tumor, her disease had progressed beyond the point where curative measures might be pursued."

"How much time did she have left?"

"A year, most likely."

Collective breaths were held, mine amongst them.

"And in such cases as Mrs. Blakely's, what is the prescribed course of treatment – if, indeed, *treatment* is even an accurate word?"

"Any prescriptive would be purely palliative – that is to say, administered with the sole purpose of managing the patient's pain, rather than prolonging life."

"Did Mrs. Blakely report any pain?"

"As yet, her symptoms were more in the way of discomfort, some localized tenderness at the tumor site, and swelling of the armpit. The swelling worsened at night, disrupting her rest."

"Did you prescribe any medication, a sleeping aid, perhaps?"

"Yes, laudanum."

"Laudanum, I see. Are you aware that an overdose of laudanum is the undisputed cause of Mrs. Blakely's death?"

Mr. Fellows, uncharacteristically quiet ere then, called out, "Objection," albeit with far less force than was his usual fashion.

"On what grounds?" the judge demanded.

Fellows coughed into his hand. "No one is disputing Vanessa Blakely died from a surfeit of laudanum in her system. The issue is who administered that fatal dose, not who prescribed it. Unless the defense intends to put Dr. Holtz on trial, Mr. Elgin is wasting the court's time."

"I'll be the judge of that, Mr. Fellows. You may proceed, Mr. Elgin but see that you tread... carefully." The judge shifted to the stone-faced doctor. "Answer the question, Dr. Holtz."

"I assure you I was very careful to instruct Mrs. Blakely, indeed all my patients, to take no more than the prescribed dosage."

"Did Mrs. Blakely indicate the dosage was sufficient to her needs?"

"Yes, for the time being. Eventually, the pain would have progressed, requiring more aggressive management."

"More laudanum?"

"Not necessarily. I would have placed her on a regimen of morphine injections, but as explained, she hadn't yet reached that stage."

"One final question, Doctor: did Mrs. Blakely ever do or say anything in your presence to indicate she might be considering ending her life?"

The doctor cleared his throat. "Suicide ideation is a common reaction among patients when first made aware their illness is terminal. Understandably, such news comes as a shock to the nervous system, especially when the patient is young and otherwise healthy as was Miss Carlston – forgive me, Mrs. Blakely."

"With all due respect, Doctor, that's not what I asked. Did Vanessa Blakely ever utter anything in your presence to indicate she might be contemplating suicide?"

Mr. Elgin looked to the judge, who intervened with, "Doctor, again I must remind you that you're under oath and obliged to answer."

Looking out to Andrew Carlston and his weeping wife, Dr. Holtz admitted, "Once. It was after my last exam. I had the laudanum dosage instructions written out and ready for her by the time she had dressed and joined me in my office. Picking up the note, she let out a little laugh and said, 'Hell's bells, Holtzie, if I'm a goner, I might as well have a say in the how and when and cook up some trouble if I can manage it.'"

"And you took that to mean?"

"Suicide, I suppose, but at the time, I assumed it was the hysteria speaking."

"Do you recall when that was?"

The doctor's brow furrowed. "January the twentieth, if I'm not mistaken."

"So, about two weeks prior to her being found dead of an overdose?"

"Yes, that's correct. There was an appointment scheduled for February but... she didn't live to keep it."

"I see. Thank you, Dr. Holtz, you've been most... illuminating. Your Honor, I have no further questions for this witness."

"Mr. Fellows, your cross," the judge said.

The prosecutor answered with a glum shake of his head. "The state rests, Your Honor."

"Very well, Doctor, you may step down. Court is adjourned until tomorrow morning at nine o'clock. We'll hear closing arguments then."

Chapter Thirty-Two

Doctor Holtz's testimony had tipped the scales in Adam's favor, but he wasn't in the clear just yet. The attorneys' closing arguments still must be made, and Mr. Fellows was nothing if not a compelling orator. Pondering all the ways he might poke holes in the doctor's statement made for yet another sleepless night.

At nine o'clock the next morning, the attorneys' closing arguments commenced. Mr. Fellows began by reiterating his "evidence", all of which pointed to Adam as a philanderer who'd resorted to murder to rid himself of an unwanted wife, not knowing that nature would soon do so for him. Pulling out all the stops, he even resurrected a case from 1891, "The People vs. Carlyle Harris" wherein Harris, a student at Columbia Medical School, had done away with his fiancée by feeding her morphine capsules.

Finally, it was the defense's turn. Mr. Elgin began by slowly, methodically rebuilding Adam's savaged character.

"Much ado has been made by the prosecution of Mr. Blakely's brief affair during the first year of his marriage. I but quote from the Book of John 8:7 the words of Our Lord and Savior who said, 'Let him who is without sin among you be the first to throw a stone…' I ask you today to apply those very words to my client. Should one brief indiscretion on the part of an inexperienced young man muddling through his first year of matrimony be held against him for the rest of his days? More to the point, should it be taken as cause for robbing him of his liberty, perhaps even sending him to his death? Since his son's birth, Mr. Blakely has behaved as a model husband and father…"

True enough, until that rainy birthday evening when he'd walked into my store and back into my life.

"While his... youthful error and heat-of-the-moment request for a divorce may bar him from sainthood, they do not make him a murderer. Who are we, sinners ourselves, to send him to his last account for a crime he did not commit, a crime that, indeed, did not occur at all?"

"Instead, let us examine the facts. Had Adam Blakely done away with his wife, would he return to his bedroom, a room adjoining hers to... *sleep* of all things! Is that the behavior of a man who's just committed murder? As a barrister in these hallowed halls of justice for more than a quarter of a century, allow me to assure you, it is not. On the contrary, a guilty man would have put as much distance, and as many witnesses, between himself and his victim as this fair city's considerable nightlife could accord. Instead, he stayed within his own house, laid his head upon his own pillow, and slept the slumber of the innocent – because he *is* innocent!"

"But there is one person who did indeed have ample cause to kill Vanessa Blakely... the lady herself! She'd seen two physicians: Dr. Holtz, whose testimony you heard, and an expert in Boston. Both medical men came to the same sad conclusion: her cancer was beyond cure. Both concurred her earthly time was winnowed to a year at most, and that she could expect those final days to be marked by terrific pain. She had access to the murder weapon: the laudanum. Lastly, she had motive, a motive with which we can all sympathize if not condone."

He concluded by cautioning against allowing any resentments they might harbor over the defendant's "privileged position" to lead them to condemn an innocent man, to deprive a motherless boy of his father and the city of one of its most generous benefactors, for though it was Mrs. Blakely who'd been chiefly visible in charitable circles, her philanthropy had relied upon her husband's "industry and civic-mindedness."

"In closing, gentlemen of the jury, I ask that you do the only moral thing, the only just thing, and that is to render a verdict of Not Guilty on all counts."

From the first drop of the gavel, Judge Abernathy had kept a tight grip on the proceedings, and his closing remarks to the jury proved no exception. Seeming to hold the gaze of each juror in turn, he began: "A young and beautiful woman, a pillar of this community, is dead and that is, without doubt, a great tragedy, and yet your duty today is not to affix blame based upon emotion but to follow the facts and deliver a verdict with as much moral certainty as your collective conscience will allow."

Further instructions were given pertaining to the balloting, and then the twelve jurymen were led off to begin their deliberations.

For the rest of us, there was naught to do but wait. We filed out into the corridor, the Blakelys and Carlstons taking up sides like opposing armies. Even were I not veiled, I doubted Beatrice Blakely would know me for the lowly Irish girl she'd driven from her home all those years ago; still, I kept my distance, seating myself on the bench farthest away. I'd just closed my eyes and settled back to pray when a woman's voice had me opening them again.

"Evelyn Moon reporting for... *The Brooklyn Eagle*. May I have a moment?"

A bespectacled brunette of thirty-odd hovered above me, her hair hidden beneath a dated and rather monstrous hat, her high-buttoned shirtwaist stretched taut across her formidable bust, the lace on the right sleeve stained with what must be ink. "Sob Sisters" they were sometimes called, or "The Pity Patrol", the Miss Moons of the yellow press specialized in the "human interest" piece. Sappy with sentiment and high on melodrama, such stories were assumed to appeal to female readers. I didn't fault her for going after her story.

I simply wasn't going to be the one to give it to her.

I stood, restoring us to eye level. "If it's a quote you're after, I've nothing to say."

Behind the thick-framed glasses, sharp eyes raked me. "And yet you've been here every day this week. You obviously have some stake in the outcome."

Refusing to rise to the bait, I sealed my lips and stared her down.

Undaunted, she plucked a fountain pen from behind her ear and opened her moleskin notebook. "I'll just take down your name if you don't mind."

"As a matter of fact, I *do* mind."

"You're Irish. That's interesting."

"And why is that?" I asked, not bothering to strip the irritation from my voice – my *Irish*-accented voice.

Rather than answer, she fired back with, "What's your relationship to the deceased?"

"I wasn't aware I had any."

"To the accused, then?"

I shook my head. But something, a slight hesitation, must have given me away.

Her dark eyes lit. "It *is* the accused, isn't it!?! You're that girl he kept on the side years ago, aren't you? The one who almost broke up his marriage?"

"I most certainly am not." Though I had indeed come close to doing just that, I was in no man's keeping and never had been.

The bailiff summoning us back saved me from saying more. A glance at the wall clock confirmed the jury had reached its verdict in just thirty-five minutes. How such swiftness boded for Adam we would soon find out.

With bigger fish to fry, Miss Moon scuttled inside. I wasn't far beyond.

Any priest worth his salt will counsel to never under any circumstance bargain with God. Pray, yes; beseech, perhaps but bargain – never. And yet, taking my place upon the wooden bench, I haggled like a Fulton Market fishwife.

Blessed Father, spare him, and I swear I'll spend the rest of my days as a true and faithful wife to Joe, no matter what. Spare him, and I'll find a way to strike the memory of not only our night on Inis Meáin but every sinfully sweet time together since...

"Foreman of the jury, have you reached a verdict?"

Hands clasped, I slipped to the edge of my seat.

A lanky man in a cheap, checkered suit stood from the juror's box. "We have, Your Honor."

Heart hammering, I watched the folded paper pass to the bailiff, who crossed to the bench and handed it to the judge. Judge Abernathy gave it a glance before addressing the jury foreman. "On the count of murder in the first degree, how find you the defendant?" he asked.

Fingernails gouging my palms, I steeled myself for the worst.

"Not guilty."

Tears sprang to my eyes. Adam's life was spared! Whatever followed, he wouldn't go to the electric chair.

"And on the count of murder in the second degree?"

I held my breath.

"Not guilty," the foreman repeated.

Fresh relief welled within me. Adam wasn't to be imprisoned for life, either.

Down the line, the same Not Guilty verdict was repeated for the lesser charges.

Like a theater audience moved to give a standing ovation, the court-room vaulted to its feet, myself with it. Adam and Mr. Elgin shook hands.

Well-wishers fanned about the defense table, including Beatrice Blakely who hobbled over. Reporters encircled Adam, Miss Moon among them. Taking in all the glad-handing and back-slapping, the crack and pop of the cameras, it was hard to believe that a day ago, the verdict was predicted to go in the very opposite direction.

How I ached to go to him! Instead, mindful of the vow I'd only just made, I slipped into the aisle, joining the flood of bodies clearing the courtroom. Almost to the door, I flagged down a passing page and pressed my hastily scribbled note into his palm. I lingered just long enough to see him push a path to the defense table and hand my folded message to Adam.

I hadn't signed it, but there was no need to. The single line would mean nothing to anyone beyond Adam and myself.

Go safely for now.

Out on the courthouse portico, I happened upon Frank. Accustomed to my heavy veiling from all those evenings of ferrying me home, he spotted me easily and threw up a hand.

I waited for him to make his way over. "You've heard the good news?" I asked once he'd reached me.

He took off his cap and scrubbed the back of one gloved hand across his forehead. "I don't mind telling you, I was worried for a while."

He wasn't the only one.

"Caddie's parked a block over. Can I drop you somewhere?"

I shook my head. "Thank you, but no. And... I'm afraid I won't be seeing you anymore."

"I'm sorry to hear that, ma'am." He hesitated as though he had something more on his mind. "You and Mr. B, well if you'll pardon my saying so, what the two of you have is something special, a once in a—"

"Take good care, Frank." On the verge of tears, I hurried off before I might spill them.

By the time I crossed the threshold to Joe's and my flat, I was decently dry-eyed and reasonably composed. I peeled off my gloves, hung up my coat, and unpinned my hat. The children would be at school still and Joe about his day, at a Factory Investigation Committee meeting most likely. Ordinarily, I treasured my solitude, a rare state in a household with young children, but that afternoon, I would have given an eye tooth to hear Moira thumping about or Joey honking on his clarinet.

I headed for the kitchen. A good, strong pot of tea might be no anti-dote for a broken heart, but a comforting cuppa had seen me through many a trying time.

Joe sprawled in one of the kitchen chairs. I gasped, nearly stumbling over my feet.

"You frightened me half to death." Recovered, I cut a look to the open bottle of whiskey and glass set out on the table.

"Does a man need an appointment to see his wife?"

If it was a fight he was after, for once, I was too spent to give it to him. I turned away to the stove, portions of my pinched face reflecting in the polished copper pots hanging above.

The scraping of the chair heralded him coming toward me. Steadying my breath, I concentrated on filling the kettle from the tap and setting it atop the stove burner.

His light hand landed upon my shoulder. "Don't ever leave me, Rosie. I couldn't stand it if you did."

I turned slowly about. "Who said anything about me leaving?"

His eyes, rimmed in red and dark as coal chips, met mine. "I know I haven't been the best of husbands, leastways not these past few years, but you must know how I feel about you. Christ, woman, you're my heart."

Though I would have sworn I'd spent all my sobbing in the cab ride home, I felt my eyes moisten. "Joseph Kavanaugh, sure you'll ruin us all with your blaspheming," I said, the scold sticking in my knotted throat.

"I mean it, Rose. I worship the ground you walk on. Always have, always will."

I looked up into his face, the crooked nose berry bright, the earnest eyes dulled by drink. What I wouldn't give to go back to our early days when a smile from me had sufficed to set things right between us. I had loved him then, only not in the way he'd wanted. Not in the way I loved, and would always love, Adam.

And yet, when Joe buried his head against my breast, his arms going about me and clasping me close, I couldn't help but feel as though I'd come home.

Exonerated, Adam was free to live his life. The Powers That Be had granted him a rare second start, and he was determined not to waste a single second. His first step was to tender his resignation to his father's board

239

of directors, for Horatio had lived only long enough to see Adam freed. The move sent company stocks plummeting for all of a fortnight, the shares recovering swiftly when his brother-in-law, Roger, took the helm.

Next, Adam put the "mausoleum" he'd shared with Vanessa on the market and moved Robbie and himself into a modest wood-frame house on Buckingham Road in Prospect Park, Brooklyn. Weary of living under so many watchful eyes, he pensioned off the older servants and let the younger go with letters of reference and generous severances – all except Yvette Bellerose. The lady's maid had vanished as soon as the verdict was announced. Missing with her were Vanessa's prized pearls.

The mansion sold quickly, its contents sold to private collectors, the artwork deeded to the Metropolitan Museum of Art. Watching as the last crate was carted away, Adam felt a rush of relief. Beyond his books, typewriter, and a few mementos, he was happy to let the lot of it go, including the Caddie. The flashy automobile was yet another vestige of the life he couldn't wait to leave behind. He resolved to give it to Frank, overriding the chauffeur's embarrassed objections.

"That's real generous of you, Mr. B.," Frank said as they stood under the garage shed in the mews behind the main house, taking cover from the light March drizzle. "and I appreciate it, I do. But I couldn't. It's too much."

Adam looked up from stubbing out his cigarette. "Stacked against a decade of loyal service, I'd say it's not nearly enough."

Frank answered with an anguished look. "But sir, the trial, my testimony… I never meant to get you into hot water. I should have thought ahead to what the coppers might ask and come up with a better story."

"No, you did right. Lying is a sticky wicket. No matter how innocent or well-intentioned, a lie only ever leads to another," Adam said with conviction, thinking of ourselves.

Frank tried again. "Why not hold onto it for Master Robbie? He'll be of age before you can blink."

The prospect of Robbie's boyhood flying by any faster only doubled Adam's resolve. He pushed a hand into the pocket of his mackintosh and brought out the second set of keys. "No, you take it, Frank. You're the one who's kept it tiptop all these years."

"But sir—"

"No more buts. I insist." He tossed the ring of keys.

Frank caught it. "All right, sir, seeing as you put it that way, thank you.

Fact is, I'd feel lost without the old girl. Driving, it's all I've ever known. Motorcar mad, that's what Betty calls it. She swears I have petrol for blood."

Lighting another cigarette, Adam asked, "Ever considered chauffeuring as a business?"

"Sir?"

Adam took a draw of his smoke, thinking aloud. "I suspect the big hotels would leap at the chance for their well-heeled guests to be ferried about in a smart car by a fine fellow like you."

Frank's beet-red blush greeted the suggestion. "I've been in service most of my life. Managing the bookings and accounting, the facts and figures, I'm not sure I have the head for it."

"Maybe not," Adam conceded, "but I'll bet Betty does."

Frank and the head housemaid, Betty, had been an item for years now. Neither was getting any younger.

"Why not turn over the business side of things to her and stick to what you do best – driving? Sounds to me like a match made in heaven… in more ways than one."

Stuffing his hands into his pockets, Frank rocked back on his heels. "Well, now that you mention it, she has been sore at me lately, swearing if I don't pop the question soon, she'll up and marry the grocer to save herself from being an old maid."

Thinking of me, Adam urged him, "Don't let her get away. If you do, you'll spend the rest of your days regretting it."

"It's not having anything to offer her that's held me back, but now… well, now the sky's the limit!" Frank hesitated. "You'll write me a reference, sir?"

Adam ground out his smoke. "I'll do better than that – I'll stake you." Reading Frank's fuzzy look, he added, "Front you the funds in return for a portion of the profits. How does five percent net for the first five years sound?"

Frank's face lit. "I'd say that sounds swell, sir!"

"No more 'sir' or 'Mr. B.' We're partners now. From here on, it's just plain Adam, deal?" Adam struck out his hand.

Beaming, Frank pumped Adam's palm as though it were attached to a petrol hose rather than a human body. "I can't wait to tell Betty."

Adam stepped back. "Don't wait. Go on to your girl. We can hammer out the details once the two of you talk things through."

241

Watching Frank head off, a spring to his step, Adam found himself smiling. Good-hearted and hard-working, Frank and Betty had more than earned their shot at the American Dream. It was a privilege to be able to help them realize it.

So far as his own dreams went, he'd resumed writing, not the same, sappy story he'd begun all those years ago, but a new novel filtered through the lens of a seasoned eye and a heart made strong through hurting. Pulling the garage door closed behind him, he took the path back to the house. One last walkthrough, and then he'd turn the keys over to the new owners.

It was time to let go of the past and live again.

Chapter Thirty-Three

On Sunday the 14th of April 1912, shortly before midnight, the luxury passenger liner, RMS Titanic, the pride of the White Star Line and advertised as "practically unsinkable," struck an iceberg off the Grand Banks of Newfoundland on her maiden voyage from Southampton to New York. A little over two hours later, the ship was sunk. Among the 1,500 lives lost were Isidor Straus, co-owner of the R.H. Macy & Co. department store, and his wife, Ida, and John Jacob Astor, one of the world's richest men.

Seven hundred-odd survivors were fished from the freezing waters. On reaching the Port of New York, the injured were taken to St. Vincent's, a hundred or so of the able-bodied to the American Seamen's Friend Society on Jane Street where I was to have rendezvoused with Adam.

In the months following his trial, I'd devoted myself to patching things up with Joe. For once, he met me midway. Though still immersed in Tammany business, the FIC especially, he spent more evenings at home. Sitting in our snug parlor, mending his shirts or sewing a button on one of the children's coats, I could almost believe those steamy, stolen afternoons with Adam had never happened.

When at first the queasiness came on, just for a short spell and mostly in the mornings, I told myself it must be nerves, a delayed response to all I'd gone through. But when I missed my monthly not once but twice, the truth could no longer be denied.

After all these years, I was pregnant again.

My new son arrived in the early hours of the 2nd of October 1912. Considering the circumstances of his conception, I supposed it only fitting that birthing him nearly killed me. My body felt as if a motor car had plowed through it, but the risk and pain proved worth it. My newborn was as healthy and beautiful as any mother might wish for. Cradling him close, I searched his tiny, reddened face for clues. Granted, blue eyes, button noses, and cherub's cheeks are universal features of babyhood; likewise, the dusting of reddish-gold hair upon his head might as easily have come from myself as Adam. But in my heart of hearts, I had my answer.

He was Adam's.

I called him Blake Donal, the first name a shortened version of Blakely. At first, Joe balked, swearing I couldn't have picked a more Prot-sounding name had I tried, but I held firm, pointing out he wasn't the one of us who'd labored for twenty hours.

Sitting by my bedside a few days later, his gaze wandered to the wall clock, "I was thinking I might join the fellas for a pint, but if you need me here—"

"Pat's bringing the girls by later," I broke in. "Joey or Moira can sit with me 'til then."

"If you're sure," he said, already on his feet and dropping a kiss on my forehead.

"Go on with yourself." Putting on a smile, I flagged him toward the door.

Watching him hasten off, I owned the idyll was over. It was back to the old ways. Back to boozy nights and lip-paint-stained shirt collars. Back to Tammany and all its trappings. Nothing truly had changed.

The passing of Tammany's "Big Tim" Sullivan in August of 1913 hit Joe hard. When I'd met Sullivan at College Point, he'd been in his political prime. It was to be a career cut short by hard living. Said to be suffering from late-stage syphilis, he'd been ruled mentally incompetent and committed to a sanatorium. On the morning of the 31st of August, he gave his keepers the slip. Hours later, they found his body on the railway tracks in the Bronx. More than twenty-five thousand mourners turned out for his funeral at Old Saint Patrick's Cathedral, Joe and I among them.

That November, Joe was elected city comptroller. The position hardly seemed suited to a man who, by his own admission, couldn't make heads or tails of a ledger sheet, but by then, I'd learned to pick my battles. The old pattern of late nights resumed full force. In lieu of complaining, I counseled myself to count my blessings: three healthy children and a thriving business.

After years of scrimping, I was finally able to pay off the bank note and own our building outright. Kavanaugh's now took up the entire terrace of shops. What had begun as a dry goods emporium was now a department store in all but name. Only our Grand Street address held us back. By then, midtown had eclipsed downtown as the retail hub of the city. Resolved that Kavanaugh's not stay stuck in the old century, I threw myself into scouting locations for a new, modern store. If I had my way, and I meant to, soon we'd be giving retail titans such as Macy's, Wanamaker's, and B. Altman's a run for their money.

With Joe's political star continuing to climb, more and more we found ourselves pictured in the papers and not only the Irish ones. Photographs of "the winsome Mrs. Joseph T. Kavanaugh" made their way into the dailies, with considerable copy devoted to my clothing. Once, I might have welcomed the notice, but now, the reporters with their notepads and pencils and flashing cameras carried me back to the dark days of Adam's trial.

On the upside, the press attention worked as unpaid advertising for the store. Well-heeled women I felt certain had never before set foot below 14th Street began showing up in our shop. Little did they suspect that the bespoke ladies' hats and other coveted accessories were cut and sewn by myself at night whilst my husband gadded about and my children slumbered.

"Don't ever tell a customer no," Rivkah counseled when I confessed to struggling to keep up with the mounting demand. "Say you're waiting on a shipment from your supplier – in Paris."

"But that would be dishonest," I protested, sucking on my sore thumb, made into a pin cushion by a late-night slipup.

She shook her kerchief-covered head. "No, shiksa, that would be business."

One crisp autumn morning, Adam sat on his front porch, working his way through a pot of French roast. Robbie raced up, arms full of the morning's mail, their golden retriever pup, Winnie, nearly grown now, imprinting the freshly painted floorboards with muddy pawprints. Dog and boy skidded to a stop, Robbie dropping the pile onto the wicker table.

Moving the coffee urn out of the way of Winnie's wagging tail, Adam glanced at the mail spilling over the table. "Anything good?"

Robbie nodded, blond hair flopping into his light blue eyes. "Sears Roebuck Company catalog and a coupla letters. This one's from Gram," he added, dipping into the stack.

Adam took another sip, the rich chicory flavor souring. Since his trial, he'd seen his mother only a handful of times, mostly brief hellos involved in handing-off Robbie. Every other Saturday, she sent her car and driver over Roebling's East River Bridge to fetch Robbie for the day. Though Adam wanted no relationship with her himself, he wasn't so cruel as to keep her from her only grandson.

He picked up her letter and broke the seal.

"What's it say, Pop?"

Shocked to see the once pristine penmanship reduced to a spidery scrawl, Adam quickly refolded it. "I'll read it later and let you know. Run inside and change for school."

"But—"

"Hop to. And wipe Winnie's paws while you're at it. If she tracks in mud again, Mrs. Purdy will have our hides."

He waited for the pair to clear the porch before returning to the letter.

> *My dearest Adam,*
>
> *I expect I'm the very last person from whom you wish to receive correspondence, and yet here I am, writing you anyway. As I never was one for dithering, I shall come straight to my point. I am ill, dying if my doctor is to be believed, which I expect he is. I know you think me selfish, heartless even, and I suppose I deserve your censure. I do deserve it and yet, in my defense, I was never made for motherhood as some women are. But know this: even at my worst, always I acted with what I believed to be your best interest at heart.*
>
> *Come to me, son, not for my sake but for yours. Wicked old schemer that I am, I am also...*
>
> *Your loving mother,*
> *Beatrice Louisa Blakely*

Once Robbie had left for school, Adam changed into what he'd come to think of as his city clothes and took the train in. Davis, now steel-haired and stoop-shouldered, met him at the mansion's entrance. Despite the years gone by, Adam had to fight the urge to throttle him for the part he'd played in Vanessa's elopement scheme. Granted, planting a punch in the butler's weathered face wouldn't rewrite history, but it would feel mighty good.

Crossing the threshold into his mother's rose-colored bedroom, Adam struggled to contain his shock. Her letter hadn't exaggerated. The shrunken woman propped upon the bank of satin-covered pillows scarcely resembled the steely society matron who'd ruled their family roost for as long as he could remember.

The corners of her thin lips lifted. "You came. I wasn't certain you would."

"That makes two of us." Chest tight, Adam approached.

"You're looking quite the bohemian," she noted, taking in his loose-fitting coat and trousers and the patterned scarf knotted about his throat. "Is Robbie with you?" she asked, peering past him to the door.

He fingered the goatee he'd recently grown. "No, but he can come Saturday if you like."

"We'll see." She settled back against the piled pillows. "Something tells me I may not be up to playing toy soldiers, though I expect he only still plays to humor me."

Nonplussed, Adam shook his head. "Once, you discovered a toy soldier hidden in my lap at dinner and called for Nanny Everett to toss the whole battalion into the trash."

Her gaze dimmed. "I thought I was making you strong, preparing you to take your place as a titan of industry. Now, I see all I accomplished was to make you hate me."

Pulling up a chair, he said, "I don't hate you."

She lifted a brow in the old imperious way.

"All right – not *anymore*."

She chuckled, a hearty, unguarded laugh such as he'd rarely heard from her. "Progress, I suppose." The smile on her lips disappeared as if vapor. "Hatred poisons the blood, feeds on flesh and soul until there's nothing left but rot. Hatred was Vanessa's downfall. Her cancer was rooted in hate, I firmly believe that."

He tensed. "So, what's eating you, Mother?"

She paused, smoothing a papery thin hand over the silk-embroidered coverlet. "Not hatred, if that's what you're hinting at. Regret. I only hope it's not too late to make things right."

247

In all Adam's years, he'd never heard her apologize. She must be dying indeed. "If you have something to get off your chest, I'm listening."

She drew a wheezing breath. "I've done you a great disservice, Adam, albeit for what I believed were all the right reasons. I didn't realize the depth of harm I'd caused until I read your book."

Of all the things he'd steeled himself to hear, that wasn't among them. "*You* read my novel?"

"Open that nightstand drawer and see for yourself."

He reached for the glass drawer-pull. Sure enough, a copy of *My Wild Irish Rose* lay inside, pages dog-eared. He closed the drawer and looked up. "I suppose I should be honored that my *scribblings* have found favor at last."

Gaze on his, she didn't bite. "You really are quite gifted. The character of the deceitful, scheming society mother was particularly well-drawn."

"Thanks. I had no dearth of material to draw from."

She snorted. "Funny, too. All these years, I never appreciated what a droll sense of humor you possess."

He folded his arms over his chest. "I'm sure you didn't ask me here only to compliment me on my craft."

"From your book, I gather you put together that it was I, with Davis's help, who intercepted your letters to Rose and hers to you, including… the one about the baby."

He nodded. "You were the one who insisted Davis drive us to the ball."

To her credit, she didn't so much as flinch. "What choice did I have? That Carlston butler was so ancient he creaked."

"All those weeks you pretended to be on my side, you were plotting with Vanessa," Adam said, the old rage rising. Fighting it down, he asked, "Did Father know? Hell, he probably helped you."

She shook her silvered head. "I told him I would take care of things, and he never questioned my methods." She released a rattling breath. "I thought once you and Vanessa married, you'd settle down to happiness, but seeing the misery your marriage became, I realized how wrong I'd been to play God with your lives. Only by then, it was too late. I know it scarcely signifies now, but I'm so very… sorry."

"An apology *and* an admission of guilt, this is a banner day. So, now, I'm supposed to forgive you, is that it?"

A thin smile answered. "That is how these things are usually managed, yes. If you can't forgive me for my sake, then do it for yours."

"Meaning?"

"My days are almost done, but there's still time left for you. And Rose."

Hearing my name on his mother's lips was very nearly Adam's undoing.

"She has more metal in her than I gave her credit for. Dragging herself and that horrid carpet bag to my doorstep took courage."

Adam felt his jaw give way. "What are you talking about?"

She took a moment to moisten her mouth. "Tampering with your mail and helping Vanessa kidnap you aren't the sum of my sins. On the day her ship made port, Rose came here, looking for you."

Adam dug a hard hand through his hair.

"You'd taken Vanessa shopping. I made sure to get rid of her before the two of you returned."

"How?"

"I showed her the Saunterer clipping of you and Vanessa at the charity ball and offered her money to go away and forget she'd ever met you. She turned me down – flat. Tore up the check and swore she'd be back, that she wouldn't believe any of it until she'd heard it from your lips. I lived on tenterhooks for weeks, expecting her to turn up at any time. She never did. And then you and Vanessa married, and I put Rose Kavanaugh out of my mind... for a while."

"She never told me," he said, thinking back to that afternoon at the Plaza when we'd spilled our souls to each another, or so he'd thought.

"No, I don't expect she would. Noble to her core. Proud, too." Rheumy eyes lifted to his. "Now that you know the whole truth, what will you do?"

Adam shook his head. "It's too late to do anything. She's married with children." Children who should have been his, starting with the little girl I'd lost.

"I may be soon to give up the ghost, but I do still take the dailies. Come up in the world though she has, she hardly wears the face of a happy woman. But then leg-shackled to that puffed-up Tammany blowhard, how could she be happy?"

"Your point?"

She speared him with a look, and he could almost believe they were back at that perfectly polished dining table, himself bracing to announce his intention to marry the beautiful Irish barmaid who'd stolen his heart. "Taking back what's rightfully yours isn't stealing. It's courage."

Emotions raw, Adam rose to go. "Let me send Robbie to you. He deserves a chance to say goodbye. He really loves you, you know."

Her eyes reaching up to his looked suddenly, suspiciously wet. "He's a wonderful boy. You should be very proud."

"I am." He hesitated and then bent to buss her cheek. Stepping back, he realized his eyes were damp. "Shall I come again?"

She shook her head. "I'd rather you remember me as lucid. But before you go, I have something for you, a parting gift." She slipped a hand beneath the coverlet and brought out a key. "In the top drawer of my writing desk, you'll find Rose's letters and yours to her. Take them. They're yours, after all."

He took the key, hands shaking.

A tear coursed down her creased cheek. "Have courage, Adam. Be bold for both your sakes. Do what you must to take back your life. And your Rose."

Chapter Thirty-Four

Brentano's Literary Emporium, 39 Union Square at 16ᵗʰ Street
Tuesday, 4ᵗʰ August 1914

Pushing Blake in his pram, Moira and I fought to finish our ice creams before the sun did the job for us. Despite dressing for the weather in light linen frocks, chip straw hats, and cotton crochet wrist gloves, we were melting apace with the frozen sweets. Done in, we took refuge beneath the cool blue awning of Brentano's Literary Emporium.

Pitching the remains of my soggy cone into the rubbish bin, I said, "Where to next?"

Moira flagged a hand in front of her flushed face. "Somewhere with a big bank of electric ceiling fans like the ones you're putting in the new store."

Recently, I'd closed on the purchase of a block-long parcel off Herald Square. If all went according to plan, we would break ground the following spring.

"We can go to the pictures," I suggested, not yet ready to toss in the towel on our mother–daughter outing. "There's a new Fatty Arbuckle film showing at the Bijou Dream."

She cast a skeptical look to the pram. With Joe visiting Kathleen at the Sea Breeze tuberculosis hospital and Joey at Coney Island with his cousins, we'd had to bring the baby.

"Bet you anything they keep it cool inside here, otherwise the pages would curl." Turning to squint inside the store window, she let out a squeal.

I followed her gaze to the sign taped inside the glass, and my heart stopped.

ADAM H. BLAKELY
reading from his literary debut

MY WILD IRISH ROSE

1 p.m., signing and reception to follow.

Below were fifty-odd copies of the novel clad in Kelly green dust jackets.

"We'd better get a move on if we want to catch that picture," I said, laying a damp hand on her arm.

Moira didn't budge. "A novel with your name on it, aren't you even curious?"

"Lots of Irish women are named Rose," I pointed out, jiggling the pram. Blake, bless him, woke as I'd hoped and let out a wail to raise the dead. "We can't very well take a bawling baby to a book talk."

She nudged me aside and commandeered the carriage. "You go. I'll push him in Union Square Park. He'll be out like a light in no time."

Panicking, I said, "Why not all go together?"

"Cripes' sake, Mums, you're always going on about how you don't have time for books and reading. Well, now you have a whole afternoon. Unless you have some deep, dark reason for not wanting to go in?" she added, big brown eyes raking me.

"Of course not. What a thing to say."

Left with little choice, I went inside, thinking to nip in, buy my copy, and leave before anyone – namely, Adam – was the wiser.

I entered to the whirr of ceiling fans, the breeze carrying the comforting scents of linseed oil and Moroccan leather. Hushed voices drew my attention to the rear of the room where a lectern and forty-odd folding chairs sat out, every seat occupied by patrons cradling copies of Adam's book. Adam himself was nowhere in sight. I suspected they had him stowed away in some makeshift greenroom, awaiting his grand entrance.

Turning away, I spotted more copies of *My Wild Irish Rose* by the register. I took one from the stack and handed it to the counter clerk, a young blond in a blue-striped pinafore.

She turned it over to check the price on the back. "That'll be two—"

"Ladies and gentlemen," a male voice boomed from the back of the store, "it is my supreme privilege to introduce the man of the moment, the master of the masterpiece, the author of the rip-roaring read of 1914, Mr. Adam H. Blakely."

Fierce clapping followed, my heart's thundering dissolving into the din.

I coughed to recapture the blond's attention. "I'm in a bit of a rush," I said, holding out my two dollars as Adam stepped up to the lectern.

A goatee graced his chin, and in lieu of a necktie, a patterned scarf was knotted about his throat. Smiling out into the assembly, he took a moment to settle on wire-rimmed spectacles before beginning.

"*My Wild Irish Rose* has been a long time in the making – sixteen years – and it's my privilege to share a short passage with you today. The story, though fictional, was inspired by my time in the Arans, a rare, unspoiled trio of islands off Ireland's southern tip. In the scene I'm about to read, the protagonist – I wouldn't call him a hero – has just told his girl, Rose, that he's going back home to America."

Fiction my foot. It was Adam's and my story. Plundering our star-crossed love for art – I couldn't yet say if I was flattered or furious. I only knew I had to stay and hear more.

I took my book and crept closer, intending to stay out of sight in the back. Alas, an elderly gentleman spotted me standing, and holding fast to the stubborn gallantry of an earlier era, insisted on giving up his seat. At first, I refused, but when he wouldn't accept no as an answer, I took it to quell the shushes and dark looks directed our way.

Seeing me, Adam sputtered to a stop, choking on a cough. "At least one reviewer was right on the nose – I really am eating my own words," he quipped, reaching for his water glass.

The audience's chuckling bought him a moment to muster his composure before resuming reading, "…'*If we've only the two days, then we'll make the most of them, won't we,' Rose said, slaying me with that wonderful, wistful smile that was so wholly hers. Locking her whiskey-colored eyes on mine, she stuck out her hand. I took it, the skin worn rough from days spent mending fishing nets and scavenging seaweed, and suddenly, it didn't matter that she was my dead buddy's sister and not yet eighteen. Or that another girl, a 'suitable' girl, waited for me back home. Or that my folks were certain to hate Rose on sight for no other reason than that she was born poor. And Irish. And pure-hearted. No, in that madcap, magical moment, I was too head over heels to give a damn about any of it. My fingers firmed about Rose's, and I admitted I was signing up for a great deal more than an unsanctioned holiday. I was signing up for her. For us. For hope and possibility. For love. And that the real adventure, ours, was just beginning.*"

Around me, people put their hands together and popped up from their seats. The store manager ushered Adam over to a table and directed those wishing to have their books signed to form a line. I hesitated, warring with myself. Now that he had seen me, shouldn't I at least stay to wish him well? In the end, I fell in queue and shuffled forward with the rest. When the gushing young miss ahead finally moved on, I steeled myself to step up.

Adam's features formed a polite, social smile, save for his bespectacled eyes, which burned like chips of blue fire upon my face. "This is a surprise."

"A welcome one, I hope," I said, wishing I were less wilted-looking. "I was passing by and spotted the sign." Catching his look of confusion, I added, "We're in Gramercy now."

Shortly after Blake's birth, we'd moved to a gracious Georgian-style brickwork townhouse on East 20th Street. The location, directly across from a gated private park, was also spitting distance from Tammany headquarters; the latter had brought Joe on board, for once, without a fight.

If Adam was surprised at how I'd risen in the world, he didn't show it. "I'm out in Brooklyn. Prospect Park. Plenty of open space, though once Robbie starts Groton, it'll be down to me, the housekeeper, and the dog."

So, he hadn't remarried. I should have felt sorry for it. I didn't. If the bevy of swoony female readers was any indication, bachelorhood was entirely his choice.

I hesitated. "I read of your mother's passing. I wanted to write you, but I wasn't certain I should."

Beatrice had died that fall. According to the obituary in *The Times*, her funeral was attended by what few of her circle remained in the city.

His expression shuttered. "We made our peace at the end. I'm grateful for that."

Turning the topic, I said, "The book looks grand."

A rueful smile answered. "About the title, it was my editor's idea. Hope you don't mind."

I managed to shrug. "As names go, Rose isn't exactly rare."

His gaze drifted downward, making me worry a button had come undone. "May I sign that for you?"

Belatedly, I realized I hugged the hardback to my heart. "Yes, please." Flustered, I passed him the book.

Opening to the title page, he bent his head, and I spotted several silver hairs threading the crown, a reminder that time was marching by for both of us.

He closed the book and handed it back. "From the papers, I take it you're set to open a new store in Herald Square?"

"I... *we* are," I amended, for Joe was still my husband and partner, on paper at least. "A proper department store – six stories, four lifts, an escalator even."

"Sounds terrific, very modern." His expression clouded. "But be careful not to get in over your head. This war in Europe, there are rumblings..."

European tensions had simmered since France lost its 1870 war with Prussia, giving birth to a unified Germany. The trouble was brought to a boil on the 28th of June with the assassination of the Austro–Hungarian heir to the throne, Archduke Franz Ferdinand, shot dead, along with his wife, by nineteen-year-old Gavrilo Princip, a Serbian nationalist, as their motorcade moved through the Bosnian city of Sarajevo. A fraught July followed, with Austria–Hungary demanding Serbia turn over Princip and the other plotters. Instead, Serbia called upon her ally, Russia. Austria–Hungary retaliated by declaring war on Serbia on the 28th of July, the one-month anniversary of the archduke's murder. Germany, an ally of Austria–Hungary, declared war on Russia and then France. What European power might fall in next had us all on tenterhooks, as did the possibility of America's future involvement.

My thoughts swung to Joey, thankfully too young to be conscripted. "President Wilson swears he'll keep us out of it. You believe him, don't you?"

Adam hesitated. "I believe he'll stick to his pledge of neutrality so long as it's in his power to do so. But if any of our direct allies, say England, declare war, the hawks in Congress will push for us to join in. And the press will back them. Wars sell even more papers than murder trials," he added, slanting me a rueful smile.

A loud cough had me glancing over my shoulder. The queue had grown again. Judging from the scowls and shifting feet, our tête-à-tête was testing everyone's patience.

I looked back to Adam. "I'm cutting into your custom and being terribly unfair to your admirers."

"Stay for the reception," he said, his neutral tone at odds with the hope in his eyes. "Afterward, we can go for coffee – sorry, tea – and have a real catch-up."

The last time we had caught up over tea, I'd ended the afternoon in bed with him.

Mindful of the promise I'd made that day in the courtroom, I shook my head. "I'll settle for reading your book."

A pained look passed over his face. "Fair warning, it gets pretty soppy in parts, especially the ending – happily ever after all the way."

A happily-ever-after ending. So, fiction, after all.

"I'll say goodbye now." I gave a wobbly smile and stepped away.

"Rose—"

I turned back. For a thrilling few seconds, I thought he might mean to come after me.

Instead, he stayed seated. "Not goodbye." His eyes took me in, regretful but resigned. "As a dear friend recommended more than once, better to say *go safely for now*."

That night, alone in bed, I finally found the courage to crack the book cover. Staring back from the dedication page was Adam's inscription:

> *To my Wild Irish Rose,*
> *she who blooms eternal*
> *in the garden of my heart.*

Undone, I slipped the volume into my nightstand drawer. I would read it another time when I could look back on our hours together with more happiness than hurt. Would such a time ever come, I wondered. I had to hope so.

The next morning, Wednesday, the 5th of August, we awoke to the following headline splashed across the front page of the *New York Times*:

ENGLAND DECLARES WAR ON GERMANY
British Ship Sinks; French Ships Defeat German; Belgium Attacked; 17,000,000 men engaged in great war of eight nations.

PART III: Tumult, 1915–1921

There is no room in this country for hyphenated Americans.
When I refer to hyphenated Americans, I do not refer to naturalized
Americans. Some of the very best Americans I have ever known were
naturalized Americans. Americans born abroad. But a hyphenated
American is not an American at all... The one absolutely certain
way of bringing this nation to ruin, of preventing all possibility of
its continuing to be a nation at all, would be to permit it to become
a tangle of squabbling nationalities... The only man who is a good
American is the man who is an American and nothing else.

Theodore Roosevelt, Speech to The Knights of Columbus,
October 1915

Chapter Thirty-Five

Though officially, America took a stance of neutrality, once our ally, Britain, entered the war, we began shipping horses and munitions across the Pond. Three-quarters of those shipments went by way of New York Harbor, making us a prime target for pro-German saboteurs.

On the 3rd of July 1915, German–American university professor, Eric Muenter set off a timed explosive aboard the Britain-bound arms ship, the SS Minnehaha, then made his way to Long Island, where he forced his way into the home of mogul J.P. Morgan Jr., holder of a monopoly on munitions exports to Britain and France. Shot twice, Morgan managed to pin Muenter and wrangle away one of his two revolvers whilst Mrs. Morgan and the butler disarmed him of the other, the butler hammering the would-be assassin's head with a lump of coal.

Just after two a.m. on the 30th of July 1916, a thunderous boom broke our sleep. Joe grabbed the bat he kept under his side of the bed whilst I raced down the hall to check on the children. The next day, we learned there had been an explosion at the transport docks. Fueled by two million pounds of stored explosives, the blast's force did substantial damage to the Statue of Liberty and caused Ellis Island to be evacuated. Nine deaths were reported, amongst them, a Jersey City infant catapulted from his crib. Blessedly, our losses in Manhattan, from Battery Park to Times Square, were material only, mostly blown-out windows, including the recently installed stenciled glass panes in the new Kavanaugh's.

In January 1917, British intelligence intercepted a coded telegram from German Foreign Minister, Arthur Zimmermann to Germany's ambassador to Mexico, Heinrich von Eckhardt. Should America enter the war against Germany, Mexico was to invade the border states of Texas, New Mexico, and Arizona, miring our forces and munitions at home. Whether or not Mexico's President Carranza would have bitten on the bait, the Zimmermann Telegram was the final nail in the coffin of American neutrality.

On April 6, 1917, the United States finally declared war on Germany. A nationwide draft was enacted on the 5th of June, calling all men between the ages of twenty-one and thirty-one to service. My Joey was about to turn sixteen and, like so many lads, eager to join the fighting and prove himself a man. He had taken to hanging about the 69th Regiment's armory on Lexington Avenue, drawn there by the big, splashy recruitment banner that hung over the front staircase. I consoled myself that Germany would be beaten well before he reached his majority. But as my son was swift to point out, boys eighteen and even younger were volunteering.

"I just need Pop to come with me to the armory and sign the waiver," he said, turning toward Joe, enthroned in his favorite armchair, head buried in an open copy of *The Irish-American*.

For once, Joe wisely kept mum, but then, Joey was my boy and always had been.

"Well, that's not going to happen," I said, fear toughening my tone. "The pair of you are staying put and that's that."

Joey turned pleading eyes upon me, his stricken expression making him seem closer to six than sixteen. "But Ma, the Gerries stand to take over all of Europe and maybe America too. The army needs men to go over there and show Kaiser Bill who's boss."

His simplistic view of war made me want to shake him. "Exactly – men, not *boys*."

It was, alas, the very worst thing I could have said. He puffed up, slender shoulders pulled back and narrow chest thrust forward. Defiance such as I'd never seen in him blazed from his darkening eyes. "Pop was in the ring when he was my age, weren't you, Pop?"

Out of the corner of my eye, I spied Joe shifting in his seat. "Your father fought one man at a time, not an army, and with fists, not firearms or… worse," I added, shuddering to recall what I'd recently read of the powerful new artillery and deadly mustard gas. "You'll just have to wait until you come of age before going off to be shot at."

"But Ma, that's *five* years off! It's sure to be over by then."

"From your mouth to God's ear," I shot back, thinking of the three thousand American lives, including Danny's, forfeited in the fight for

Cuba and the Philippines. That conflict, fewer than four months long, was a skirmish compared to the present worldwide war.

Angry eyes met mine. "Other mothers are proud to see their sons serve. You're being selfish is all, selfish and... unpatriotic." He spun away and stomped off.

Never had he spoken to me so. Accustomed as I was to butting heads with Moira, ere then, Joey had always been my sweet, biddable boy, my easy child. Cut to my core, I sank into the nearest seat, vaguely aware of Joe lowering his newspaper.

"You can't keep him tied to your apron strings forever," he said, not unkindly.

"Maybe not, but I can keep him safe at home until he's legal. After that, if the war's still on and he's called up, you'll just have to use your pull and see he's sent as far from the frontlines as possible. A posting to a headquarters office as a clerk or stenographer would suit him. He has my knack with numbers and the loveliest penmanship."

He studied me a moment. "Say I *could* fix it so that he sat things out on the sidelines, that's not what he wants. What he wants is the chance to prove himself."

I met his eye, never mind that mine were watering. "All these years I've stood by you through thick and thin – the drinking, the dirty dealings, the... women." Hardest of all, I'd given up Adam. "Now, I'm asking you to do your part and protect our son. You owe me that much."

Several weeks went by, then a few more. Family meals stayed strained, including the twins' sixteenth birthday, which we all spent pushing uneaten cake about our plates. Joey's sullen silences hurt me deeply, but at least there was no more talk of permission slips or glory fields. And then, one evening, I whisked in from a meeting with the architect and engineer for the new store to find Moira and Joe sitting silent in the front parlor.

I took in Moira's strained face and tight lips and dropped the rolled-up drawings on the console table. "You're home early. Don't tell me we've won the vote already?" I quipped.

When not in school, she all but lived at the Interurban Woman Suffrage Council, headquartered at the Martha Washington Hotel, where she and other volunteers dispensed pro-vote literature, slogan buttons, and signs.

She darted a look to her dad. "If you won't tell her, I will."

Fingers fisting in the folds of my skirt, I split my gaze between them. "Tell me what?"

Twisting her bottom lip beneath her teeth, she admitted, "Joey's… up and volunteered."

Woozy, I gripped the table edge. "That can't be. He's not of age, not even close. The only way they would take him is with… written permission of a parent." I swung about to Joe. "*You. Signed.*"

He had the audacity to shrug. "Has his heart set on going. There was no talking him out of it."

I shoved away from the table and rounded on him. "There was no need for you to talk him out of anything. You only needed *not* to sign. The one time in the whole of your miserable, misbegotten life when all you needed to do was… *nothing* and you couldn't manage not to muck *that* up."

He fortified himself with a slug of scotch and heaved himself to his feet. "To hear you talk, Joey's heading off to fight the Hun all by his lonesome. Tom Foley and George Washington Plunkitt and Charlie Murphy all have sons and nephews and kid cousins heading over too, and not all of them as conscripts."

Suddenly, I understood. "You signed off for our son to be shot at and gassed and… God only knows what else to curry favor with your Tammany cronies!"

Moira dashed across the carpet and put herself between us. "Mums, please, it's as much my fault as it is Dad's."

That she favored her father was a fact I'd learned to live with, but I was in no mood for her blind devotion. "Really, how so?"

She lifted watery eyes to mine. "The last time Joey walked me home from the Suffrage Council, he asked if we couldn't cut stop by the armory. Said he wanted to see if his buddy's big brother was there. I didn't think much of it at the time, said sure, I'd wait for him on the steps out front. He was in there over an hour. That must have been when he met with the recruiter."

I pressed firm fingers to my throbbing temples. "Thank you for telling me, but you're hardly to blame." I shifted to who was very much to blame. Joe. "First thing in the morning, we'll go to the armory together and withdraw permission, explain how this is all a dreadful mistake."

Joe stared at me as though I had grown a second head.

Moira spoke up. "I don't think it works that way, Mums. Joey's already been processed and assigned."

"*Assigned*? Where?"

She swallowed. "To, uh… an infantry regiment bound for France."

ENLIST TODAY IN THE 69th INFANTRY.

Go to the front with your friends.

Don't be drafted into some regiment where you don't know anyone.

Early the next morning, I marched myself to the 69th Regiment's armory on Lexington Avenue at 25th Street. After more than two hours spent staring at the waiting room walls, plastered with posters of Uncle Sam, white-whiskered, steely-eyed, and invariably pointing out from the frame, I managed to wrangle a private sit-down with the recruiter. First, I tried charm (feigned), and then tears (genuine), and lastly bribery – a gratis shopping spree at Kavanaugh's for his missus? But as Moira had foretold, nothing worked.

Gaunt-faced, he looked up from the papers piled high upon his desk. "I'm sorry, ma'am, but once the paperwork's processed, it's out of my hands."

"There must be *something* you can do, Sergeant. My husband didn't know what he was signing." Reckoning this was no time for pride, I added, "He drinks, you see. I'm afraid our son took advantage of his… intoxication to prevail upon him to come in and sign the waiver."

It was, if not the absolute truth, a near neighbor to it. Were Joe not blinkered by decades of dissipation, he never would have signed off on sending our underage son to war. For the time being, I held onto that belief as if it were my rosary.

But if I'd hoped to sway the sergeant with my sorry circumstance, I was to be disappointed, sorely so. "Mrs. Kav-a-naugh," he said, patience straining, "I know you think your son's case is unique, but I'm here to tell you it's not. If I listened to every sob story from every mother who crossed my threshold, I'd have no men left to send over."

Thinking of Joey with his fuzzed upper lip and innocent eyes, I clenched the handle of my handbag. "But that's the very thing. My son isn't a man. He's a boy, a sixteen-year-old *boy*."

He set aside his fountain pen and laced together his hands. Regarding me over their steeple, he expelled a heavy sigh. "The current law states that a minor of at least sixteen years can serve with a parent's permission. Your son, Joseph, is sixteen, and his parent, your husband, gave his consent in writing."

"Then tear up the bloody paper!"

I scoured the stacks spread across his desk, wondering if the sheet with Joe's signature might be among them. Were I to spot it, I'd tear it up myself. Let them toss me in jail and throw away the key. Let them drag me before a firing squad, for that matter. So long as my son was safe, I'd gladly suffer whatever consequences came my way.

As if reading my thoughts, he slid the stack nearest me to the blotter's far corner. "Young *men* like your son are willing to risk their lives to ensure a free Europe and the continued safety and liberty of Americans at home and abroad. Instead of trying to stop him, you should feel proud to support the sacrifice he's making."

Beaten, I scraped back my chair and stood. He started up as well, but I'd no use for his petty politeness or superficial chivalry.

I glared down at him, pinning him with the force of my mothers' fury. "I carried that boy and his twin sister inside me for nine months. So, you'll forgive me, Sergeant, if I'm not all that interested in how *you* think I should feel."

Joey's orders were to report to Camp Mills, an army training camp on Long Island's Hempstead Plains, by September 13th. There, he and his fellow National Guardsmen would prepare for deployment to Europe with the 42nd Rainbow Division of the American Expeditionary Forces under Brigade Commander Douglas MacArthur.

The eve of that dreaded departure arrived all too soon. Pacing brought me to Joey's empty bedroom. He'd dropped in at the armory earlier and from there, gone on to say his goodbyes. An army issue haversack, packed, sat out on the foot of his bed. Beside it lay a pocket-sized copy of *The Soldier's English–French Dictionary*. The sight of that small, brown-covered book laid a stone-sized lump in my throat. My son was a soldier now. Try as I might, I still couldn't grasp that my gentle boy with the soulful eyes and hesitant smile would soon be exchanging gunfire and grenades and mustard gas with other boys and young men who'd happened to be born in the Rhineland.

Joey returned in the early evening, wearing his uniform – olive drab wool breeches and tunic, leggings, and wide-brimmed campaign hat – and a manly confidence I hadn't seen in him before.

Sitting waiting in the parlor, I put on a smile and beckoned him over. "You must be starved. I'll warm something up."

Smile hesitant, he shook his head. "Thanks, Ma, but I'm meeting a few of the fellows at McSorley's. They're giving away a turkey dinner to any soldier shipping out."

The East Village alehouse where Danny and Adam were to have toasted their homecoming remained a popular watering hole. Patrons could count on complimentary platters of cheddar cheese, crackers, and sliced raw onion; the latter had sent many a wife and sweetheart dodging her man's embrace. I should know. McSorley's was a favorite haunt of Joe's. Only now, our kissing days were behind us, and our son was headed there with his fellow doughboys for a send-off supper. It seemed only yesterday he'd been Blake's age, a little boy for whom soldiers were toys made of tin, and battle but a game.

I couldn't help it. I broke down. Tears overflowed my lower lashes and spilled down my cheeks.

"Geez, Ma, don't cry." He dropped to his knees and hugged my skirts as he had when little, only now, it was me who laid my head upon his shoulder, my tears wetting the wool. He drew back, scouring my face with his big, earnest eyes. "I'll stay home, and we'll play Trip 'Round the World and Old Maid and Topsy Turvy like we did when me and Moira were kids."

Wishing for a hankie, I wiped my wet eyes on my sleeve. "I won't have you wasting your last night playing parlor games with your watering pot of a mum." I set my hands atop his shoulders and held him at arm's length, his newly shorn head making me think of the sheep we'd counted when he was small and couldn't sleep. "Go enjoy yourself with your mates. And mind you clean your plate, Mr. Finicky-Faddle. Once you sail, turkey dinners will be all in the past."

"That's right, I'll be dining on… *poulet* with the Frenchies." He grinned, pleased with himself for remembering the French for chicken.

My sweet, brave boy, he hadn't a notion of what lay ahead. "Let's hope so," I murmured, though from what I'd heard of trench rations, tinned meats were the best he could hope for.

He got to his feet. "Guess I'll be going, then?"

265

I nodded. "Mind you don't drink too much. You have a big day tomorrow."

"I'll stop at two ales, promise. McSorley's serves 'em in pairs, you know."

"I do," I said, thinking again of Joe, who'd likely never stopped at two drinks at McSorley's or any other saloon in his life.

Halfway to the hallway, he turned back. "You're coming to the armory in the morning with Moira and Pop, aren't you?"

"Of course I'm coming," I said, though I wondered how I'd bear it, lining Lexington Avenue with all the other families, waving our boys off as they marched north to the 34th Street ferry slips.

His expression eased. "Then we'll have plenty more time for talking at breakfast and in the cab over."

I struggled on a smile. "That we will, my love."

Yes, we'd talk in the morning but of trivial things. If he had room in his haversack for a second muffler. What weather he could expect upon landing in France. Speaking of anything more, anything of substance, we were past that now. With the swipe of a pen, Joe had sent our son off to war. It fell to me to piece together a life in the aftermath.

Chapter Thirty-Six

On the 25th of October 1917, Joey and the 42nd Division quit Camp Mills and traveled by train and then ferry to the Port of Hoboken where they boarded a troop ship bound for "Somewhere in France." Much later, we'd learn he'd landed at Brest.

On Election Day, November 6, 1917, New York passed a pro-suffrage referendum granting women the ballot in state and local elections, making us the first eastern state to fully enfranchise women and the fifteenth in the union to do so. Irish-born though I was, never was I prouder to call myself a New Yorker.

Charlie Murphy's Tammany Hall had had a substantial hand in getting out the vote. As it had in the aftermath of the Triangle fire, the Society weighed in on the right side of history.

"Even you have to admit Tammany's influence isn't all bad," Moira wheedled.

"I suppose I can give the devil his due this once," I conceded, "though I still hold that NAWSA and your Mrs. Chapman Catt are the true heroes of the day."

In response to the opposition's charge that most women didn't wish to vote, Carrie Chapman Catt and volunteers from her National American Woman Suffrage Association, Moira amongst them, had spent more than a year going door to door, polling women in every city and town in the state. The suffragists were intrepid. No tenement was too menacing, no farmstead too far afield. The petition drive paid off. The NAWSA collected more than one million signatures, more than sufficient to get suffrage on the ballot.

Moira's smile slipped, the first flush of triumph giving way to the familiar frustration. "Now, if only Wilson will keep his word and endorse the Constitutional amendment."

267

"Perhaps he will," I said, thinking President Wilson would do well to stop dragging his feet lest he have a second war on his hands, this one on home soil.

Earlier that year, in January 1917, a splinter group of the NAWSA, the National Women's Party led by Alice Paul, began posting picketers outside the White House gates, the first-ever protests of the presidential mansion. In June, the arrests began. Nearly five hundred Sentinels of Liberty were taken into custody, with one hundred and sixty-eight women jailed. The horrific stories of hunger strikes, forced feedings, and beatings by guards had leaked to the press, increasing public support for the brave suffragists.

At home and abroad, upheaval seemed to be in the air. In Russia, Bolshevik revolutionaries led by Vladimir Lenin launched a leftist coup against the provisional government they themselves had put in place. Among Lenin's first actions as de facto dictator was to make peace with Germany. Weighing what the loss of Russian military support might mean for Joey and his fellow doughboys ratcheted my worrying.

Thanksgiving and then Christmas came and went. Though we did our best to keep the season, Joey's empty seat at supper was impossible to overlook. How could we tuck into our roast turkey with any real relish knowing he and his fellows were making do with potted meat eaten from the tin?

Not that my darling was one to complain. Be he encamped, entrenched, or en route to the front, he swore he was "swell", "in the pink", and "fit as a fiddle." His army-issued postcards presented an unflaggingly cheerful picture of soldiering life: waiting in the "chow line" for "slum", a stew concocted of whatever the camp cooks had on hand mixed with the previous meal's leavings; playing cards in the YMCA hut; and listening to music from the officers' gramophones, carried into the dugouts to lighten the mood. Trench foot, "cooties", and dysentery were brought up but briefly and always with humor, the death and carnage not at all. But what he left out, or the military censors blacked out, the newspapers covered in lurid detail.

The calendar turned to 1918, and still, the war wore on. Every day, the death toll and casualties climbed. The Army Medical Department took over the hospital on Ellis Island to treat wounded servicemen, men, and boys left limbless from the landmines, faceless from exploded bombs, or with lungs so scarred from mustard gas that they coughed and wheezed and fought for breath like old men.

The country pulled together as never before. Women on both sides of the suffrage issue led the relief efforts for the widows and orphans of occupied Belgium and Northern France. Both the Boy Scouts and Girl Scouts organized Liberty Loan drives. The boys trawled the streets in their army green woolens touting, "Every Scout to Save a Soldier." The girls tended victory gardens, drove ambulances for The Red Cross, and sold their first-ever Girl Scout cookies.

Film stars brought their glamour to bear on the war effort. Martha Mansfield walked the Manhattan streets peddling dollar doughnuts for the Salvation Army. Douglas Fairbanks, Mary Pickford, and British-born Charlie Chaplin all hosted bond rallies in cities around the country, including New York.

Needing to do *something*, I threw myself into the war effort, buying a small fortune in Liberty bonds and putting up posters encouraging our customers to do the same. Otherwise, I kept myself busy with preparations for opening the midtown store. The new Kavanaugh's, as I envisioned it, would be both a temple to timeless elegance and a marvel of modern ingenuity, its twenty-five sales departments kitted out in ornate plasterwork, luxe marble, and beveled mirrors and lit by electrified crystal chandeliers. A wooden escalator would ferry shoppers from the main sales floor to the rooftop restaurant. Or they might ride the lifts staffed by all-female operators, their free-flowing "jersey dresses" designed by an up-and-coming young French designer, Gabrielle "Coco" Chanel.

By the time I walked in at night, Blake was in bed and Moira out with her suffragist friends. That left Joe. As I saw it, his going behind my back to sign Joey's waiver was the final nail in the coffin of our marriage. Seizing upon his snoring as an excuse, I had his things moved to a bedroom down the hall. For the first time in years, I didn't have him stumbling in and waking me at all hours. Now, I had my nightmare for that.

Ever since Joey had shipped out, I'd been beset by the same dreadful dream. Like a newsreel played in the movie houses before the picture began, night upon night, it unfurled in grainy grayscale inside my head. Artillery fire sparking a barren sky, silhouetted with tanks and broken trees. Stone houses barricaded by sandbags. A battered bridge. Though I'd never actually heard the *brat-a-tat* of machine guns, my dream-self summoned what the awful sound must be like. The driving rain swelling the river to a roiling cauldron of clay, the fields and footpaths melted to bogs. Joey and his fellow doughboys going over the trench top and fanning across the shell-torn field, rifles raised and bayonets at the ready.

Only Joey wasn't moving forward with the others, not anymore. Rain lashing me, I fought to reach him, the muck sucking at my soles, my sodden skirts weighing upon me like an anchor. I made a funnel of my hands and called to him in the same fond, firm tone I'd brought to bear when he was a sleepy-headed little boy slow to school.

Joey, love, you mustn't drag your feet. March toward Mummy like a good little soldier.

A good little soldier.

Suddenly the sky split, an arc of unholy light. Keening drew my eye to the barbed wire, and a lone figure staked out like a strawman.

Joey!

I dropped to the ground and commenced crawling. *I'm coming, son.* Reaching him, I pulled myself to my feet.

He lifted his sagging head and looked at me with the desperate eyes I'd seen on hares caught in a hunter's snare. "Ma, is it you? *Ma!*"

"Yes, Joey love, it's me – Mummy's here," I crooned, caressing his bloodless cheek, sweat-slick and icy. "Close your eyes and—"

"*Maaaaaaaaaaaaaa!*"

"Mums!" I came awake to Moira's arms about me. "It's just a dream," she assured me.

I dragged a trembling hand through the damp tangle of my hair. "Is it?"

"Yes, of course it is." She turned up the lamp and settled in beside me. "Dreams are our unconscious mind working to resolve what's troubling us."

She'd been reading Freud again. I could always tell. The doctor's theories on the machinations of the human mind sometimes made for racy fare, but Moira always was mature beyond her years.

"I'm sure you're right," I lied, lest I spook us both from further sleeping. She eyed the space beside me where once Joe had slept. "I'll stay if you want."

Tempted though I was, I shook my head. "I'm counting on you by my side tomorrow, rested and bright-eyed, for Kavanaugh's grand opening." She hesitated. "Is Dad coming?"

I stiffened. "Your father's plans are his own, but I suppose he'll be there."

Being a silent partner seemed to suit Joe. So long as Kavanaugh's bankrolled his politicking – his last campaign had cost us dearly in Delmonico dinners – he kept his word not to interfere with the store. But even an animal knows better than to bite the hand that feeds it. Under my steady hand, Kavanaugh's fed, clothed, and shod him exceedingly well.

The following day, Saturday, the 10th of August, I stood onstage with Moira, Blake, and Joe outside the main entrance to the new store, the Grecian-styled pillars bedecked with pink bunting, the brass-and-etched glass revolving doors wrapped in ceremonial pink ribbon.

Despite the heat, spectators gathered three-deep, many savoring the complimentary strawberry ice creams and pink lemonades passed out by waitresses from our rooftop restaurant. An all-girl brass band uniformed in rose-striped pinafores kept the crowd entertained while we waited for Mayor Hylan to arrive and cut the ribbon. As Hylan was a Tammany man, I suspected I had Joe to thank for his agreeing to attend, though these days, gratitude was the very last sentiment I had for my husband.

The speeches made and the ribbon cut, we ushered Hylan and our other VIP guests inside for a champagne reception – *pink* champagne, of course. Giant ice sculptures flanked the foot of the spiraling grand staircase. The rose-pink carpet runners were so plush, our soles sank into them. Every sales counter was bound in pink satin bows, every plate-glass countertop and frosted glass mirror stenciled with "*K&C*" – Kavanaugh & Company, a touch I'd borrowed from the Plaza. In the main gallery, a tuxedoed pianist stroked the ivories of a Steinway grand. Arrangements of pink roses were put out in every department and alcove. We even wore them as corsages, the conceit, Moira's contribution.

"It's Dad's name on the door, but everyone who's anyone knows Kavanaugh's is your creation," she insisted when I wondered aloud if it wasn't all a bit much.

Joe stayed for the duration, bending the mayor's ear and mugging for the cameras. Despite the champagne he put away, he was on his best behavior.

Monday morning, our official opening, started out sultry with threats of rain. I looked over at Moira, calmly spreading marmalade on her toast. "What if no one turns out?"

"Honestly, Mums, you're worse than an ingenue on opening night. You saw the turnout on Saturday. People are chomping at the bit to see inside."

Belly full of butterflies, I pushed my plate away. "Yes, but how many were curiosity-seekers, there for the free food and entertainment? We need serious shoppers if we're to keep open."

Less than an hour later, I drove up to find a block-long queue wending from the main store entrance, most women and girls but a few men as well, mopping their faces and fanning themselves. Once the opening bell rang and the doors opened, they rushed the sales counters. Cash registers dinged as sale after sale was rung. Cosmetics were sampled, laces and scarves handled, hats tried on before beveled mirrors. Solicitous salesclerks circulated the various specialty areas. Couture-clad models paraded along the aisles like pretty pied pipers, leading ladies over to the fashion department where the latest evening gowns, day dresses, and sportswear might be tried on in the privacy of curtained dressing rooms.

Looking on from the mezzanine, gripping the gilded rail, I could scarcely credit my eyes. Nearly twenty years in the making, the vision I'd sacrificed and fought for had all the markings of a smashing success.

The rest of the week followed in a similar vein, the sales so robust you'd never know a war was on. I made it my practice to arrive each morning before opening and conduct a counter-to-counter tour, chatting up the department heads and sales clerks and weighing in on the displays. My royal progress, or so Moira called it. She could tease all she liked – it was a friendly way of keeping staff on their toes. A week in, I hadn't caught so much as a glove out of place.

By the second week, things were running close to clockwork. I stepped inside the Gramercy house earlier than ordinary, looking forward to a cold glass of lemonade and to putting my feet up. Moira met me inside the foyer. Eyes streaming, she held out a tan-colored card, stamped "*Govt.*" A Western Union telegram.

As if suddenly transported beyond my body, disconnected and floating, I looked on as a hand, mine, reached out to take it.

Deeply regret to inform you Private Joseph D. Kavanaugh
killed in action France July 30th crossing the Ourcq River to
break through German lines. Letter to follow.

I folded to the floor, hugging myself hard, nails biting into the sleeves of my jersey dress.

Moira dropped down beside me. "Oh, Mums," she said, rocking me as though I were a hurt child.

Through the fog, I remembered my other son. "Blake?"

She managed to get me up and over to the hallway bench. "I took him to the neighbor's. He doesn't know yet. Neither does Dad. He's still at Tammany. I'll call over. Better yet, I'll walk over now and bring him h—"

"Stay put," I snapped, finding strength in anger. "He'll hear it from me when he comes home tonight."

Moira's mouth dropped open. "But he might not come home for hours."

I stood and dragged myself to the stairs without replying. That time when Moira tried to help, I waved her off. Climbing up, I leaned on the banister, feeling an old woman for all that I was still two years from forty.

I reached my bedroom. Catching my reflection in the dresser mirror, I realized I still wore my hat. Pulling out the pin, I tested its sharpness, pricking my glove to be sure, half-amazed I could still feel. Moira was likely right. Joe wouldn't come home until later. When he did, he would almost certainly be drunk. And I would be waiting.

Joe walked in a bit before midnight. Out in the foyer, he struggled off his hat and coat, colliding with the console table. Muttering curses, he scrubbed at his shin.

Other than a lone lamp, I'd left the parlor dark. Sitting in the armchair he favored, I waited for him to make his way over to me, or rather the liquor cabinet I'd put myself in the path of.

Midway in, he spotted me. "Christ, woman, you gave me a start. What are you doing sitting down here in the dark?"

"Waiting. To give you this." Rising, I flung the telegram at him.

Like a fish, his mouth opened, but no sound came out.

"Joey's dead. Yes, that's right. *Dead.* Thanks to you, we're the parents of a dead soldier instead of a living-and-breathing boy with the whole of his life ahead of him."

Throat working, he scraped a shaking hand through his hair. "He was my son too."

"Was he? From the first, you treated him more as a foundling than your own flesh and blood. And then, come the day you finally take notice of him, what do you do – you take him to the feckin' armory and sign away his life!"

"Rose, I—"

I pounded my chest, hitting my heart hard. "He was my boy, *mine*! I'm the one who carried him inside myself, who rose in the middle of the night to chase away the goblins and sing him back to sleep!"

I dug my hand inside my robe pocket and pulled out the hatpin. Brandishing it, I took a step toward him.

Eyes wide, he backed away, bumping into the flocked-paper wall. "Rosie, put that down. You're not yourself. You don't know what you're doing."

"Don't I? All these years I've tortured myself because you weren't my first, told myself your boozing and whoring were my just desserts. But I'm done with paying for my past. Now, it's your turn to pay for all the pain you've brought."

I lunged. Despite the drinking and weight gain, his boxer's reflexes didn't desert him. He sidestepped my sloppy blow and caught my wrist.

"Drop it, Rosie. Drop it or, God as my witness, I'll crush your bones to powder."

For all my bravado and grief, I was but a being forged of flesh and bone. A final spasm saw my fingers unfurling, the hatpin pinging to the floor.

He released me and hooked his hands about my throat. Frozen to tableau, we faced each other, his heavy puffs of breath scoring my nostrils.

"Go ahead and finish me, you son of a bitch!" I screamed, past caring what became of me. "Or are you too much of a coward?"

My goading galvanized him. His big thumbs moved over my windpipe, pressing inward. His face closed in upon mine, so near, I could have counted every berry-hued broken vein.

"Take it all back. Take it back, and I'll let you loose."

"N-never," I rasped, feeling as if my throat must be caving.

The pressure mounted. Black dots danced before my watering eyes. My chest tightened, my starved lungs clamoring for air. I couldn't be sure, but I thought my feet left the floor. A strange peace settled over me. I'd be seeing Joey soon, sooner than I'd supposed.

Feet pounded toward us. "Dad, stop! *S-t-o-p!*" Moira latched onto her father's forearm. "Let her go – *now!*"

Blake ran up as well, pummeling Joe with small frantic fists. "Stop hurting my mommy!"

Joe's hands fell away. Gasping, I folded over. Moira wrapped an arm about me, keeping me from falling. Bawling, Blake clasped my leg.

Joe stared as if awaking from a bad dream. "I didn't mean it. Sweet Jesus, Rose, are you all right?"

Gulping air, I managed to grind out a single word. "*Go*."

Muttering, "Sorry, so very sorry," he backed out into the foyer. The sound of the front door closing was the first peace I'd known since the telegram had ripped all our worlds apart.

Chapter Thirty-Seven

The next morning, I found the black dress I'd worn for Kathleen's funeral and put it on, never mind it was a half-decade out of date. A jet-beaded scarf about my throat hid the bruises, black-and-blue marks the circumference of Joe's thumbs. Decently done up, I went downstairs and spent the morning draping black bunting about the front door and gate. Moira begged me to come inside and rest, but I waved her off.

"If you want to be of help, see to Blake," I said, voice still rusty. "He's too little to understand what's happened."

She stared at me. "*I* don't understand. What was that last night? And where's Dad? He still hasn't come home."

I turned away. "This isn't his home anymore."

"But Mums—"

"Your father and I are married for the duration, but this house stopped being his home the moment that telegram came. If you decide you'd rather live with him, I'll be sad, but I won't stop you. But so long as you're beneath this roof – *my* roof – you'll abide by my rules. He's not to cross the threshold. There's nothing more to be said on the subject."

Poor Moira. In less than a day, she'd lost both her twin and the father she adored. Later, I'd look back and wish that instead of laying down edicts, I'd opened my arms and taken her into them. Instead, I stood with hands upon my hips, holding firm until she burst into tears and ran inside. I went back to my wreathing. Passers-by paused to express their condolences. Neighbors came by as well, carrying covered dishes. I acknowledged their offerings with spare thanks and not only to save my voice.

I had nothing left to say.

* * *

Joe turned up a week later, sober and contrite. From Moira, I knew he'd taken a room at the Veteran Firemen's Association on East 10th Street; still, his reappearance scarcely surprised me. I'd known it was only a matter of time.

I met him outside at the top of the front steps. "Come for your things, have you?" I said, positioning myself between him and the door. "They're packed and ready. Wait here, and I'll have the gardener help you carry them to the curb. Or I can have them sent to you at the VFA, whichever you'd rather."

Several steps below me, he lifted his incredulous gaze to my face. "Things got… out of hand the other night, and I couldn't be sorrier. Nothing like that will happen ever again, I swear."

Arms folded, I let silence stand as my response.

"I haven't touched a drop since, and I won't go back to it. I'm a changed man. You have my word."

After twenty years of broken promises, I weighed his word on par with fool's gold. "I won't take your word, but I advise you to take mine – as final. You and I are finished."

He tore off his hat and smashed it to his breast. "If I had it to do over, I'd never sign that waiver. I'll regret it for the rest of my days. Believe me, if I could trade my life for his, I would."

I did believe him, not that it mattered now. Little did.

"Shutting me out won't bring him back," he went on. "You and me, Moira and Blake – we're still a family. Together, we can see our way through this, I know we can."

For years I'd put up with his drinking and bad behavior, resolved to hold my family together. Now, I owned that living under the same roof as a drunkard had done us all more harm than good. If I'd taken the children and left when I'd had the chance, gone to Paris or Timbuktu or even the other side of town, Joey would be alive now.

"Goodbye, Joe."

I turned to go in, but he reached for me. "Rosie, please!"

I glared down at his hand on my sleeve. "Decided to turn my bones to dust after all?"

His fingers fell away. Dropping down a step, he looked up at me with anguished eyes. "Please, Rosie, I want to come home."

"Mind you don't call me by that idiotic name again." *Rosie* was a relic of another time, a time when being happy together had still seemed possible.

"And this isn't your home, not anymore. If you want to see Moira and Blake, I'll arrange for them to visit."

"*If* I want to see them!?! They're my flesh and blood." His gaze darkened. "So, this is it, huh? Giving me my walking papers? We're man and wife. Or is your plan to divorce me? I wonder what your precious church would have to say about that?"

How like him to throw my faith in my face. "We're married 'til death parts us, but make no mistake, our days of sharing a roof are done."

"What's to keep me from walking inside that door – *my* door? Not the law, that's for damned sure. It's my name on the deed."

Once, such a threat would have cowed me. Not so then. "Give me trouble and I'll march myself into the newsroom of *The Times* and *The Herald* and oh, *The Evening Post*." Fundamentally Republican, *The New York Evening Post* was by far the most vociferous of the Society's critics. "I suspect the journalists will be all ears for the dirty dealings you and your Tammany chums get up to, the vote tampering you gents brag about among yourselves when you're in your cups. Tammany man or not, the Police Commissioner will be obliged to investigate. If it comes to it, I'll take the train out to Oyster Bay and make my case to President Roosevelt himself." Though in poor health and retired to his family home, Sagamore Hill, the former President was still a formidable figure as well as no friend of Tammany's.

He went white except for his ears, which burned bright red. "You're bluffing. Giving me up would mean seeing all your grand schemes go up in smoke, your precious store ruined."

"Exactly – *my* store, the business *I* built from scratch and can just as easily smash to smithereens if I choose. What, you don't believe I'd do it? Try me and you'll see just how little Kavanaugh's means to me now that there's no Joey to pass it on to."

He stared at me as if seeing me for the first time. In a way, he was. Not the green girl he'd wed, or the adulterous matron weighed down by guilt, but the steely businesswoman forged from nearly twenty years of standing alone at the helm. The mother who'd just lost the son she'd spent nearly seventeen years raising. No threat he threw at me could move me now.

"You must really hate me," he said, fierceness fading.

"No, Joe, I don't hate you. If I did, there might be hope for us. The God's truth is I don't feel anything for you at all."

278

I stayed on the stoop, watching him carry his suitcases down the brick footpath and out the ironwork gate. Sapped, I shuffled back inside and started up the stairs, my head feather-light, my legs nearly weightless. Midway up, I sank to my knees. Past pride, I took the remaining steps on all fours.

Moira met me at the top. "Mums!" she cried, gathering me against her.

I opened my mouth to answer, my tongue coarse and clumsy, my mind suddenly, frightfully fogged. "B-bed... Get me to bed."

Named for its flagship *Trip To The Moon* ride, Luna Park in Coney Island was a glittering, electrified wonderland, wildly popular with working people. Strolling the park with a blond taxi dancer from the Bowery, Joe confided, "Used to bring my wife out here when we were courting. Not to Luna, wasn't built then. To the beach."

"*Courting*, huh?" The chippie, Dottie, shoved a stick of Wrigley's chewing gum between her cherry-painted lips. "That's real sweet, Joe-Joe."

"I was never all that crazy about the water, but Rose is a regular mermaid." He took another pull from his flask. "We met at The Windsor." Noting her blank look, he clarified, "A big fancy hotel on Fifth Avenue."

Cracking her gum, she brightened. "Take me there sometime?"

"Can't, s'gone now." Soused though he was, he could still see it, every detail burned into his brain. "It was St. Paddy's Day. Me and the fellas were marchin' down Fifth when the flames shot out. Rosie was on the fifth floor, given up for a goner, but I wasn't having it. Climbed up and carried her down."

"Course you did, big strong feller like you." She gave his bicep a squeeze.

They came up to a mock Turkish minaret bursting with white light-bulbs, and for the first time, Joe looked, *really* looked at her. Peering past the face paint to her soft, babyish features, he said, "Say, Dot, what year were you born?"

Fingering the spit curl bisecting her forehead, she answered, "'Ninety-nine, why?"

Christ, she was just a kid, not much older than Moira. Thinking how he'd felt her up on the train ride out, he cringed inside. "Better get you back to the city."

"Don't be a party pooper." Her gaze drifted off. "Ooh, this looks like a hoot!" She picked up her heels and peeled off.

Gouty leg barking at him, he caught up with her at the velvet-covered entrance ropes to one of the fieldstone pavilions, *Fire and Flames* chiseled into the frieze-work.

"Only costs a measly 'ole quarter." She pointed to the slate sandwich board with the toe of her tango shoe. "Next show starts in five."

Wiping his damp forehead, he said, "Won't your, uh, mother worry where you are?"

She snorted. "Old bat's back in Frisco with sugar daddy number three." Taking his arm, she tugged them toward the ticket taker. "Got someplace better to be?"

The question brought him back to the recent ugly scene with me, and he shook his head. "Nowhere. Nowhere at all."

LIAR, LIAR?

TAMMANY BIGWIG CAUGHT WITH PANTS ON FIRE
CITY COMPTROLLER MOONLIGHTS AS CARNIVAL
CLOWN

City comptroller and Tammany Hall insider, Joseph "Killer" Kavanaugh, found himself once more in the limelight, only this time, with his pants on fire (literally!) after storming a Luna Park stage during the recreational park's popular "Fire and Flames" disaster extravaganza. The program, which plays twice daily during the summer months, depicts the burning of a replica four-story tenement house. The carnival conflagration had just erupted when Mr. Kavanaugh leaped from his seat in the audience and bounded onto the platform, barreling into the faux firemen, rescuers, and horse-drawn fire trucks. In attempting to climb the ladder, a stage prop unequal to his weight, Mr. Kavanaugh crashed through the rungs and fell backward into a burning beam, igniting his posterior. The breeches blaze was extinguished by a fast-thinking stagehand, and the victim led off amidst a shower of jeers and rotten tomatoes from the stands.

It will be recalled that Mr. Kavanaugh, a former foreman of Engine Company No. 6, received the Bennet medal in recognition of his bravery during the Windsor Hotel fire of 1899. He showed similar brio at the tenement house fire at 105 Allen Street of 1905, for which he was lauded as a hero.

Mr. Kavanaugh, who owns Kavanaugh & Co. depart-
ment store with his wife, Rose, attended the performance in the
company of an Anonymous Young Woman. According to several
eyewitnesses, including Yours Truly, the Tammany politico, of Irish
descent and Lower East Side provenance, appeared belligerent and
babbling, a condition attributable to the spirits flask from which
he was seen to refresh himself prior to The Incident. Alas, how the
mighty have fallen!

—Yours,
The Saunterer

The column in *Town Topics* was but the beginning. The story of Joe's disgrace was picked up by every Republican-leaning daily in the city and several Democratic ones too, igniting another sort of firestorm, one not so easily extinguished as his trousers.

The times were changing, and Joe's revered Tammany Hall was changing apace. With organized labor on the rise, the Society was having to compete for its constituency. It was one thing for its chiefs to carouse in the vice districts under the organization's aegis, quite another for one of them to put his buffoonery on parade for the public. In breaching that unspoken understanding, Joe had committed the only truly unpardonable sin.

He'd made not only himself but the Machine a laughing stock.

The following day, he presented himself at the Tammany to beg forgiveness of the big boss himself. Only Charlie Murphy refused to see him. The members of Murphy's inner circle took their cue from their leader and shut Joe out as well. Proclaimed unfit for office by his own, he was left with little choice but to tender his resignation. Overnight, he became persona non grata. Men who once hailed him on the street now looked the other way. But as he later would confess to Moira, the snubbing paled to insignificance compared to losing us, his family.

Alas, he couldn't rewrite the past – the last years were a boozy blur of back-slapping and balloting – but he could do something about the present and, God willing, the future. He poured his liquor stash down the sink, no matter that Prohibition would soon make those bottles second to gold.

Staying on at the VFA hadn't proven possible, not with so many pensioned-off smoke eaters in need. He'd moved to rooms on Hester Street, spitting distance from the tough, teeming streets where he'd been born.

To stave off temptation, he started working out at the gym, reviving the training routines of his prize-fighting days. Gloved fists plowing into the medicine ball, sweat sliding down his slimmed body, he felt fitter than he had in a decade. He began to recognize the man staring back at him from the moisture-spotted shaving mirror, older to be sure but still the same Joe Kavanaugh who'd run into fires, not because it made him a hero but because saving lives was what he was born for.

Gainful employment was what he needed to feel like a man again. Returning to the business that bore his name was out of the question. Even were he to invoke right of law and force his way back in, the sleek, six-storied department store was as a foreign land to him. He'd be lost in it.

Instead, he used what pull he still had to petition for a place on his old engine company. The current crew was made up of mostly unfamiliar faces, men young enough to be his sons, but there were a few old-timers left, Pat amongst them. Whatever black marks he'd racked up in recent years didn't take away from the lives he'd saved, the genuine good he'd done, or so his supporters argued. In the end, the ayes carried. Humbled, he accepted the well-wishes of those who'd championed him, not with speechifying but with sincere gratitude. Begging off the bottle passed about in his honor, he headed for home, humming *Rose, Sweet Rose* all the way.

A letter from Joey's commanding officer, Major "Wild Bill" Donovan, fleshed out the circumstances of my son's death. According to the major, the Old 69th took up position above Chateau-Thierry at Viller-sur-Fere on the Ourcq River. The primary objective was a fortified German position, Meurcy Farm, which the Irish lads called Murphy's Farm. Joey was cut down by enemy fire on the 30th of July whilst advancing across the river to rout the German forces. According to Donovan, death had been instant, a blessing I latched onto. Unlike in my nightmare, he hadn't suffered.

Learning I wouldn't receive his body was another bitter blow. He'd been laid to rest in a military cemetery not far from the battlefield, his grave graced by one of the thousands of slim white crosses hallowing France.

In the fortnight that followed, I teetered between despair so deep I thought I might drown in it and a near-narcotic numbness in which I might float for hours on end. When I wasn't pacing, I passed hours in the rocking chair where I'd nursed and crooned to all three of my babies. Hugging Joey's infant blanket to me, I stared out the window to the gated park, watching the tree turn from green to golden.

Moira took charge of my care and feeding, ferrying in countless cups of tea and plates of thickly buttered toast, ordering me to "Drink!" and "Eat!" as though I were the child and she the parent. In a way, she was, mothering not only me but also Blake. Looking back, it hurts me to think how alone she must have felt.

Had a placid autumn followed, I might yet be in my dressing robe with unwashed hair, picking at plates of invalid fare and humming snatches of lullabies to an empty lap. But as is often the case in life, it took a fearsome threat to jog me from my limbo state.

The Spanish Flu.

Chapter Thirty-Eight

The "Spanish Flu" tore through Europe and the United States, the sobriquet sticking despite the disease being no more widespread in Spain than elsewhere. The first wave, generally mild, struck in the spring. The infected suffered the usual chills, fever, and fatigue, most recuperating within a few days to a fortnight. Autumn 1918 saw a virulent resurgence wherein a victim might fall ill in the morning and be dead that night, skin blued and lungs fluid-filled. Unlike prior influenzas, the scourge was as apt to fell those in their prime as it was infants, the elderly, and infirm.

On the 4th of October, New York City health commissioner, Dr. Royal S. Copeland, ordered businesses, including department stores, to open and close on staggered shifts to minimize crowding on trolleys and subways. Additional ordinances required people to cover their noses and mouths when coughing or sneezing and banned spitting in the streets. Service workers were advised to wear gauze masks. Most were happy to do so.

Despite all the precautions, hospitals overflowed with flu victims as did morgues, funeral parlors, and cemeteries. Gymnasia, armories, schools, and other public buildings were pressed into service as treatment centers. Young and old, rich and poor, Republican and Democrat, newcomer and nativist – no one stood beyond the disease's deadly reach.

Unable to sit on the sidelines any longer, I shook off my blankets, bathed, dressed, and came downstairs. The piled-up newspapers confirmed the worst. Not about to risk another son, I pulled Blake out of St. Ann's Academy that day. Until the scourge subsided or a vaccine was found, I would oversee his schooling at home.

I was at the dining room table when Moira walked in. Spotting me, fountain pen in hand and luncheon plate cleared of all but crumbs, she drew up.

"Mums, you're… up." She ran her gaze over my washed and neatly pinned-up hair and crisp shirtwaist as though afraid to believe her eyes.

"I am. Shall I have Cook make you something?"

She shook her head. "I'll grab a sandwich later." Settling into the seat across from me, her gaze went to the curriculum I was marking up. "What's that?"

"Your brother's program of study." I briefly brought her up to speed on my plan.

"Of course I'll help," she said once I finished. "Though I don't know how much use I'll be with mathematics. Numbers never were my strong suit."

"I remember," I said, hiding a smile, for neither she nor Joe ever could tally two and two and come up with four. "If you'll tackle history and literature… and French, we should be all right. Oh, and Latin." It was a lot to ask, I knew.

She glanced away. "I don't have any Latin, but I have a friend who does."

Given the bookish set she ran with, all suffragists like herself, I wasn't surprised. "Brilliant," I said, pleased to see the subject settled. "So far as I can tell, the lessons are mostly to do with conjugating the verb 'to be' – he is, after all, just five."

Fiddling with my fountain pen, she asked, "Did you see this morning's *Times*?"

I glanced to the stack of back editions I was still working through. "Not yet, why?"

She picked up the paper and handed it to me. I took it, my eye honing upon the headline above the fold.

FIGHT STIFFENS HERE AGAINST INFLUENZA.
COMMISSIONER COPELAND APPEALED TO
TAMMANY HALL'S EXECUTIVE COMMITTEE TO USE
ITS PARTY MACHINERY TO SEEK OUT INFLUENZA
CASES.

"Bully for Tammany," I said sourly, not yet ready to make peace with my old rival.

She shot me a look. "Dad's volunteered as a home inspector – in the *eighth* district."

285

The Lower East Side district, once primarily Irish and German, was now home to Jews who'd fled Russia and Eastern Europe. Canvassing households in that densely crowded quarter was a highly risky undertaking.

"I wouldn't worry for your father. He has the constitution of an ox," I added, thinking of the prize-fighting moniker in which he'd taken such unseemly pride. "I've never known him to be sick a day, barring a bout with the bottle."

Moira leaned in, eyes entreating. "Is it so hard to believe he's changed? If only you'd hear him out, you'd see that he has."

I clanked my teacup upon its saucer, sending tea slopping. "I've given your father nearly twenty years *and* my first-born son. I don't intend to sacrifice a single moment more to him."

"You can't go on blaming him for Joey forever," she said, tone gentling.

"Can't I?" I snapped, hating how easily the tears still came.

"Joey wanted to go. It was all he talked about. If Dad hadn't signed off, he would have found another way."

"Stow away on an army transport, you mean? I doubt he would have managed, no matter how keen he was. The one time he tried running away, he got no farther than the front walk."

He'd been about Blake's age, a gentle little boy with a fondness for picture books of puppies. And now he was gone. Dead.

"He couldn't be more broken-hearted about Joey, about... well, all of it."

Eyes swimming, I shook my head. "His being sorry won't bring back your brother. If he's looking for absolution, let him seek it in church from a priest."

It was advice I'd do well to put into practice myself. I hadn't been to Mass since Joey's memorial, a bitter reminder he was "Somewhere in France" and would stay so.

She stood with a sigh. "Fred and Harry are waiting for me."

I didn't have to ask what Moira and her friends, Fredericka and Henrietta, were up to. I'd spotted the stack of Sanitary Department leaflets out on the hallway table when I'd brought Blake home from school. As with the war effort, the public pitched in, posting placards and passing out literature on stemming the spread of the disease.

"Mind you wear your mask. And tie it on tight. I don't know what I'd do if I lost you or Blake. You two are... my world."

Once, I would have included Adam in that select sphere. Now, I couldn't bear to think of him beyond hoping he and his son were staying free of the flu.

One foot in the hallway, she turned back. "Everything's going to be all right, you'll see."

I forced a smile. "Yes, of course it will be."

I only wished I could bring myself to believe it.

As the death toll mounted, New York was as good as a ghost town. Though Commissioner Copeland refrained from mandating commercial closings, the city's theaters, restaurants, cinema houses, pool halls, and saloons served stragglers at best. A few stalwarts stubbornly stuck to their routines, Joe amongst them. When he wasn't on shift at the firehouse or canvassing for flu cases, he could be found at Grupp's Gymnasium on West 116th Street in Harlem. The trolley ride uptown helped clear his head, or so he swore.

It was a Friday afternoon in mid-October. Despite the popular day, the gym floor and gallery were mostly empty, the fighters, trainers, fans, sports reporters, bookies, and fight-fixing mobsters all lying low. The diehards had dwindled to four: the owner, Billy Grupp; Joe's former trainer, a dwarf who went by Shorty; Declan Ryan, a hulking Irish kid from Hell's Kitchen who'd run with the Eastman gang as an enforcer; and Joe.

It was Joe and Ryan in the ring. Joe wasn't crazy about the kid, who he saw as too swaggering and tough-talking to come to anything other than a bad end, but given the slim pickings of sparring partners, he couldn't be choosy.

"Think you still got it, 'Killer?'" Ryan taunted, dancing on his toes like a "damned debutante", or so Joe would later tell it.

Fed up with youngsters like Ryan going on as though they'd invented the sport, Joe held up his hands, laced into the mandatory five-ounce mitts. "In my day, we fought like men. With our bare knuckles."

"I'll go no-gloves if you will, old man." Defiant, Ryan undid one glove and then the other and dropped the pair in the corner.

Three rounds into the agreed-upon four, Joe owned he'd underestimated his opponent. Thirty years his junior, Ryan slipped through his defenses and struck hard, Joe's legendary crouch-and-rush style no match for the kid's fleet footwork and lightning punches. Too proud to bow out, Joe went blow-for-blow, absorbing punches to his head, chest, and solar plexus and sweating profusely. Ryan landed two shots in a row, opening a cut over Joe's eye. Fighting the pain, Joe reminded himself he had just one more round to make it through. If he could keep on his feet until the final bell, a draw would be called, and he could walk away with his dignity.

"Break it up!" Shorty slipped between the ropes, a towel about his neck. "S'enough for today."

Scowling, Ryan kept up his guard. "We agreed to four rounds."

"You deaf? I said you're done, so scram." Shorty waited for Ryan to clear the apron, then shepherded Joe over to the bench. "Christ, kid, you don't look so good. Where's it hurt?"

Mopping his face with the towel, Joe snorted. "Ask me where it doesn't hurt. It'll be a shorter answer."

The beating he'd taken wasn't the worst of it. Since waking that morning, he'd been beset by a full-body ache, the drumming in his head reminiscent of his drinking days, though for two solid months, he'd stuck to root beer.

Shorty laughed, but his eyes stayed worried. He might be pushing seventy with a gamey leg and grandchildren whose names he didn't always remember, but he had the peepers of a young buck and those darting, deep-set orbs didn't miss Joe's glassy gaze or grayish pallor.

"Get yourself a rubdown and then wash up and go home," he said, handing Joe a bottle of Sloan's Liniment.

Joe took it, squinting to read the label. "'Good for man and beast.' Seeing as I'm a bit of both, I'll expect a complete cure," he said with a chuckle.

Sloan's balm didn't begin to put a dent in the godawful aching, which grew worse as the evening lengthened. Pain-racked and shivery, Joe forced down a bowl of barley soup his landlady had left him, not because he was hungry but because a full belly had always been his cure-all. Inside of an hour, his stomach heaved, bringing up the soup and the ginger ale he'd washed it down with. By midnight, his fever spiked to 104 degrees Fahrenheit. Fearful that if he lay down he might never get up again, he piled on blankets and sat in the chair, teetering between teeth-chattering chills and surges of heat so intense the soles of his feet swam inside his house slippers.

Around dawn, nature's call had him hoisting himself to his feet. Heavy-headed and sweating, he navigated his leaden legs to the toilet. Gripping the edge of the porcelain sink, he stared into the moisture-spotted mirror, hardly recognizing the damp, ashen face as his. Something he'd eaten? The mishmash he'd consumed in the last twenty-four hours alone would test any man's mettle, even one who prided himself on a cast-iron constitution. Before the soup, there'd been a pickle from a pushcart vendor on Hester Street, a savory pie of dubious provenance from a stall on Essex Street, and a plate of raw clams from an Italian peddler on Mulberry Street. Small wonder his guts were grumbling.

Another spasm struck, doubling him over. He emptied his stomach into the sink and then scrambled to the toilet to void his bowels. It wasn't until he rose again on wobbly legs that he looked back to the bowl and saw it. Blood.

That's when he finally conceded he had It. The Flu. The Grippe. The damned Spanish Influenza. He who'd never been sick a day in his life, leastways not the sort of sickness that didn't come from the bottom of a beer keg or bottle, was weak as a newborn babe, shaky as a palsied codger.

He didn't see anyone for two days until Moira came, her regular Sunday stopover, not that I knew about it then. "Dad, it's me. Open the door, these groceries are heavy."

Through the flat door, he answered, "Daddy's down with... a cold. Leave the bags in the hall. I'll get 'em once you're gone."

The flimsy excuse didn't fly with her. "You sound rotten. Are you on the sauce again?"

"No! I swore to you I've stopped, and as God is my witness, I have. I'm under the weather is all. Give me a few days, and I'll be good as new."

Setting down the bags, she was struck with a sinking in her stomach, not the influenza, praise God, but a sudden, fearful surety. "You have it, don't you? The Grippe's what's making you sick, isn't it?"

Silence, so unlike him, answered.

"Don't lie to me, Dad. Not now, not after... everything."

"Moira, lovey—"

She smacked her open hand hard upon the door. "Daddy, please!"

"All right, yes. Yes, I'm pretty sure I do."

"*Pretty sure?* What does the doctor say?" She pressed her cheek to the peeling paint and held her breath.

A pause and then, "Any doctor with a grain of sense has hightailed it to the country, and the ones still here are caring for cases worse off than me."

"A nurse, then?"

Again silence.

"Dad!"

"Whatever you do, don't tell your mother."

Thankfully, she came to me straightaway, though not entirely by choice. When she opened our front door, she found me standing on the other side.

"Jesus, Joseph, and Mary, where have you been?" I demanded, whisking her within and helping her off with her mask. "I've been pacing holes in the parlor carpet for the past two hours." Taking in her pale face, I fitted a hand to her forehead. The skin beneath my palm was blessedly dry and cucumber cool. Relieved, I dropped my arm and stepped back. "No more leafleting, no more meetings, no more volunteering of any sort until this pestilence is in the past. You're putting yourself and the entire household at risk, and I won't stand for it any longer."

Her eyes filled. "I didn't go leafleting. I went to see Dad."

"You didn't take the streetcar, did you? Please, tell me you didn't?"

She shook her head. "Taxi."

"Thank God you had that much sense."

Dark eyes narrowed. "Aren't you even going to ask how he is?"

I bristled. "Soused, I suppose, or recovering from his latest binge."

She speared me with a look. "He's sick. With the Grippe."

That my big, bullish husband could be felled by something as innocuous as a germ had never entered my mind. As the shock wore off, worry took root.

I clutched her shoulders. "How close did you come? Tell me you didn't catch his breath."

"He wouldn't open the door so much as a crack. Oh, Mums, he's in there all alone!"

A sudden calm came over me. I released her and turned away to the stairs, mentally tallying the supplies that would be needed.

She followed me up. "Where are you going?"

"To pack. Your father needs nursing, and I'm rather good at it."

"But what if you catch it too? I could lose you both."

Stepping off the upper landing, I headed for the linen press. "I'm healthy as a horse."

She groaned. "That's what Dad always says."

Taking out a stack of folded sheets, I said, "Keep a close watch over Blake whilst I'm away." All it would take was one of his schoolmates luring him beyond the gate for a match of marbles or stickball, and he too could come down with this. "And mind you stay indoors as well," I added, filling her arms with a second set of bedding.

Watching me, she shook her head. "Honestly, you two are ridiculous. After everything that's happened, you kicking him out, why would you risk yourself to go take care of him? It makes no sense."

"Perhaps not," I conceded, counting out towels. "But that, my girl, is marriage."

Chapter Thirty-Nine

I had the housekeeper call for a car. A half-hour later, a shiny black Cadillac rolled up to the curb. Keeping watch at the front window, I felt my heart hitch. Once, Adam had kept such an automobile.

I fixed on my white cotton mask and turned to Moira, waiting at the window with me. "Likely your father will be fine. But if aught should happen to either of us, promise you'll take care of Blake. You'd be... the only family left to him."

Another of my lies. Blake had a father and a half-brother too, or so he would if only I broke my silence and admitted the truth.

Her face crumpled, making her look a little girl again. "Of course I'd take him. He's my brother."

I gave her blotchy cheek a light pinch. "It may not be the influenza your father has. You know how men are when it comes to sickness – babies, the lot of them. Or, if it is the flu, it could be another, less dangerous... variety." What was that word that kept coming up in the newspaper reports? *Strain.*

A suitcase in either hand, I descended to the sidewalk where the flashy automobile idled. Seeing me, the dark-suited driver got out and hurried over.

"Here, ma'am, let me get those," he said through his mask, commandeering my bags and opening the rear passenger door.

Slipping into the back seat, it struck me. "Frank?"

The eyes above the mask smiled back at me. "Miss Rose! Not in a million years did I expect to lay eyes on you again."

"Nor I you." Mindful of Moira watching from the stoop, I pulled the door closed.

Sliding in behind the steering wheel, Frank asked, "Where to?"

"Hester at Norfolk," I said, meeting his eye in the driver's mirror.

Despite improvements in living conditions since my tenement days, the Lower East Side was still a hotbed for disease, the flu especially. If Frank declined to drive me there, I wouldn't fault him for it.

"Buckle up and enjoy the ride," he answered, his old unflappable self.

I relaxed back into the buttery leather, the plush interior bringing back a bevy of bittersweet memories. "How've you been keeping, Frank?" I asked once we were underway.

"Never better. Betty and I tied the knot a while back. No kids so far, but we're still hoping."

Thinking of Blake, my surprise baby, I smiled. "None of us ever knows what life will bring. I'm glad to see you doing so well for yourself."

Eyes on the road, he nodded. "Thanks to Mr. B, I am. Before he moved out to Brooklyn, he gave me this beauty and staked me and Betty in our chauffeuring business. Added two more automobiles since, not quite a fleet but getting there. Both my drivers are flat on their backs with the flu, so it's just me right now."

How like Adam that sounded. Throat thickening, I shifted to look out the rolled-up window as we turned onto Broadway, quiet as a country lane. What few traffic police I spotted wore white medical masks and worried looks. Once we crossed Delancey, traffic picked up, still, the narrow streets had a sluggish feel, the sidewalks cleared of all but a few sellers' carts. No one loitered. Ordinarily, a shiny black Cadillac in that part of town would draw considerable notice, but beyond moving out of our way, no one paid us much mind.

We pulled up to a dilapidated brownstone, masonry crumbling, the street number matching what Moira had given me. Sagging stone steps led up to the entrance, a peeling mustard-yellow door with graffiti scrawled across. A dull-eyed young mother sat on the stoop, rocking a small child in her lap. On the step below, a girl of four or so poked a stick at a dead rat.

Frank switched off the ignition and got out to open my door. "I'm happy to wait."

Stepping out, I said, "Thanks, but I'll be staying."

He popped the boot and took out my bags. Despite my assurances that I could manage, he insisted upon carrying them inside, sidestepping the family camped out on the steps.

The entrance hallway was dank and dun-colored, the stained wallpaper in various stages of peeling off. Setting my cases at the foot of the metal stairs, Frank dove a hand into his coat pocket and brought out a card case. "Call this number any time, day or night, and I'll come in a jiff," he said, passing me a card.

Frank's Limousine & Car Service.
Established 1912.
we do the driving so you don't have to.

"Thank you, that means a great deal." I slipped the card inside my handbag and reached for my wallet to pay him, planning to add a generous gratuity.

He shook his head. "On the house."

"No, that isn't right. You drove all the way down here and under the worst possible circumstances. There's your time and petrol and—"

"Any friend of Mr. B's is a friend of mine. For life."

Seeing he wouldn't be budged, I put away my purse.

He handed me the bags one at a time, carefully, as though they carried china instead of sickroom supplies. "Those are steep-looking stairs. Sure I can't—"

"Absolutely not!" I cut in, refusing to let him risk himself further.

"Then I'll say goodbye." He tipped his hat and headed for the door.

"God bless you, Frank. All the luck."

Joe's flat was on the third floor, one of three units. Lugging my cases along the silent hallway, I spotted it straightaway, for taped below the scratched metal doorplate was a placard proclaiming:

INFLUENZA!
keep out of this house by order of board of health.
Any person removing this card without authority is liable to prosecution.

I reached out and rapped. "Joe, it's Rose."

After my first few knocks went unanswered, I began banging in earnest. "Joe Kavanaugh, open this minute," I demanded, neighbors be damned. "I know you're in there."

From the other side of the door, a hoarse voice finally answered, "Go away."

"I will just as soon as I've seen you." Another lie. The stuffed satchels at my feet weren't going anywhere and neither was I.

"I'm not much to look at," he said, a hint of the old humor in his voice. Despite all that had happened between us, I caught myself smiling. "You never were, so you might as well let me in."

"I mean it, Rose, go away." That time, he sounded serious.

But so was I. "I'm not leaving, so you'd best make up your mind to open that door."

A sigh made its way out to me, A moment later, he relented. "Let me get my mask on."

The door inched open. I picked up my bags and stepped quickly inside, the staleness striking me in my stomach. Joe's hangovers hadn't made for a pretty picture, but not even the worst of them prepared me for the sight of him.

Waxen-faced, glassy-eyed, and greasy-haired, he stood back, wearing a white cotton undershirt gone gray and baggy trousers held up by bracers. "Satisfied?"

"Not yet, but I will be once we've gotten you fed, bathed, and back in bed." I set my burdens by the door and turned to close it.

Sick as he was, I felt his gaze going over me, stopping at all the spots that in the past, he'd done more than admire. "You look good, Rosie. Are you?"

"Not good but... better." I turned to face him. "You've lost weight."

He followed my gaze down to his sagging waistband. "It's not all the influenza's doing. I'm back to boxing. Not to compete – too long in the tooth for that. For the exercise. And it keeps my mind off... things." His gaze settled on the satchels I'd set down. "Traveling light, I see."

"I brought a few things from... home." My home, not his. Not anymore. "Belladonna, Moore's Throat Lozenges, Vicks VapoRub, Bayer aspirin, tea and honey, Bovril – and clean linens."

The flat was fetid, fertile ground for the germs we were all so keenly conscious of. I made a mental note to send to the store for bleach, ice, and one of the new Westinghouse electric fans to circulate the air.

I reached up to unpin my hat, trying to recall into which case I'd packed my apron. "Small wonder you're sick, living in this sty."

He leaned back against the cracked plasterwork as if needing help holding himself upright. "I had a woman in to clean for me, but she came down with it too."

"Half the city's sick." I hesitated. "Moira says you're one of the volunteers going door to door."

He shrugged. "Keeps me out of trouble." His face tensed. "Moira's all right, isn't she? And Blake?"

"They are. I took Blake out of school. Moira has strict instructions to keep him and herself indoors."

He nodded his approval. "You always were the brains of us."

I didn't answer. Spotting the small kitchen, I headed toward it, rolling up my sleeves as I went. "I'll put the kettle on. Once the water's boiled, we'll see you washed and fed, and then you'll have a nap whilst I scour the place from top to bottom."

He chuckled. "Bossy as ever."

I didn't deny it. "Were you expecting otherwise?"

He shook his head. "I've missed your bossiness. I've missed... lots of things."

The admission threatened to take us to terrain I wasn't yet ready to navigate. I jerked my chin toward a half-open door from which I glimpsed a metal-framed mattress and the tail of a balled-up blanket. "Back to bed with you. I'll bring your tea as soon as I see things sorted."

He hesitated. "Between my stomach and my bowels, I don't know which is emptier. I'm starving, but I can't keep anything down. Or in."

I found my apron and tied it on. "We'll start you off with broth. If that stays down, there'll be toast and jam later." I spoke to him as if he were one of my kids.

His gaze dimmed. "I should never have let you in."

"Well, you have, and now, I'm here for the duration. I won't be setting foot outside this palace 'til you're on the mend." *And I'm past the point of contagion,* I added to myself, for I wasn't about to carry this plague home to the children.

"And what then?"

I hesitated. "Get well, and I suppose we'll see."

Hope sparked in his eyes as I'd known it would. Another lie so he'd fight his way back to health, or was I truly considering taking him back? I didn't know the answer any more than he did. I only knew we had twenty years and three kids binding us. Like it or not, he was family and always would be.

He tucked into the broth I'd heated, draining the bowl, despite my warning to start with small sips. Within the hour, he brought it all back up again, head buried in the porcelain basin.

I set the foulness aside to be dealt with later and guided his damp head back to the pillow. "You went at it too fast, that's all."

He snorted. "To think I've looked at the world from the bottom of a bottle for most of my life and never known a day's sickness, and now that I finally find the gumption to give up booze for good, I'm laid flat. If that's not the luck of the Irish, I don't know what is."

He let out a rusty laugh, the rattle in his chest bringing on a bout of coughing. When he'd finished, blood flecked his lips.

"Hush, you'll waste yourself." I snatched a clean cloth from the bedside table and blotted his mouth then quickly refolded it so he wouldn't see. "Close your eyes and have a rest. We'll try again later."

Days passed, the hours marked not by sun or city lights – for he begged me to keep the blinds closed, swearing the glare hurt his eyes – but by the crowing of Kathleen's old cuckoo clock. Too exhausted to bother making a proper meal for myself, I subsisted on the invalid fare I served him – broth and toast and heavily honeyed tea. For once, I was sorry there was no whiskey in the house. I could have done with a drink. No matter how many cool cloths I pressed to his brow or spoons of ginger ale and broth I slid between his cracked lips, he was worsening. The big, bluff, barrel-chested Joe I'd known all these years, the man with whom I'd built a business and brought up a family, was wasting away before my eyes. And there wasn't a bloody thing I could do about it.

Talking quietly together whilst holding my hand seemed to comfort him the most. Sometimes, he asked me to sing to him, and though I'm as tone-deaf as a person can be, my warbling never failed to bring out his smile.

I'd just finished another rendition of *Rose, Sweet Rose* at his insistence when he lifted his head to look at me. "What a pair we make," he said, fever-parched lips parting on a smile.

"We've known the two days," I agreed, the Irish saying for "the good and the bad."

"You're more beautiful now than you were on our wedding day."

"I didn't know the influenza brought on blindness too."

He rolled his eyes, the whites the color of egg yolk. "Why do you always have to make it so hard?"

"Make what so hard?"

"Loving you. I still do, you know. Always have, always will." He pressed his clammy palm to my cheek. "Soon, I'll love you from the grave."

I caught his wrist and held his hand in place. "Now that you've quit drinking, sure you'll see eighty at least."

"I'm done for, and we both know it. But God be willing, you have a long life ahead, not with me but with him. Adam."

Shock struck me momentarily dumb.

"He's a fortunate fellow, Mr. Adam Blakely. Some men are born lucky. The rest of us, we've to make our own luck. And now, Rosie Girl, mine is about run dry."

I opened my mouth to protest, to swear he had it all wrong. Before I could, I stopped myself. I'd spent the past two decades in deception. Did I really want to waste these last days together keeping up the same tired lie?

"What gave me away?" I asked, thinking back to how I'd stupidly held onto Adam's handkerchief. Perhaps a part of me had wanted to be caught.

"One night, after the fire, I was sitting by your bed at St. Vincent's when you called out his name in your sleep. Much as I tried telling myself he must be a sweetheart back in Ireland, I knew better. Not many Irishmen are baptized Adam. And then, during the trial, I saw his full name in print. Adam Horatio Blakely, same as the A.H.B. on that hankie. Coincidence maybe, but I didn't think so."

"Oh, Joe, I wish things had been different. If I could go back, I'd be kinder, less critical—"

"Hush, you were as good a wife to me as you could be and, God knows, a better one than I deserved. A lesser woman would have walked out on me years ago, even one who loved me."

I shook my head, tears splashing the sheet. "I did love you. I *do* love you."

He reached up and wiped the side of my eye with his thumb. "Don't waste so much as another teardrop on me, Rosie Girl. I've had a good run of it. I climbed faster and higher than I ever dreamed to and fell just as fast and hard, but that's life, isn't it? And now, God's stepping in to do what I should have done years ago. Set you free."

"Don't say such things." I touched his thin shoulder through the sheet. "Moira and Blake need you. *I* need you."

He cast me a look. "No, my love, you don't. Between the two of us, you've always been the strong one, the beauty *and* the brains. Now, make me a promise so I can lay my head and be at peace."

Swallowing a sob, I nodded.

"Once I'm gone, don't waste yourself on mourning me. Swear you'll seek your happiness with him or another man worthy of you. Though at times I've had a strange way of showing it, happiness is all I've ever wanted for you."

"Joe, I—"

"Swear."

I gave in. "All right, Joe, I swear."

I laid him to rest in Old St. Patrick's Cathedral in a crypt close to that of "Honest" John Kelly, another of his Tammany idols. Standing back as he was sealed away, I took heart that, in the end, he'd died not only sober but as the brave hero I'd first met and married.

Moira was a watering pot as was to be expected. Though she'd come to terms with her childhood champion having feet of clay, Joe was still the father who'd showered her with the devotion most men reserve for sons. Blake, bless him, bore up despite brimming eyes. Unlike Moira, he didn't have memories of Joe at his best. Still, he too had lost the only father he knew.

I went through the funeral Mass and interment dry-eyed, not because I didn't grieve him – I did – but because by then, I felt as if every teardrop had been wrung from me. For nearly twenty years, my life had been joined with Joe's for better and for worse. Now, he was gone. The freedom I'd so often fantasized for myself was finally mine. Only, I didn't feel so much free as I did... adrift.

Chapter Forty

Monday, the 11th of November 1918, we awoke to the best early Christmas present possible: the surrender of Germany. Berlin was in the grip of revolutionaries, the ousted Kaiser in flight to neutral Holland. The War To End War was finally finished, the map of Europe redrawn in the Allies' favor. And now, our boys were coming home. Other mothers' sons, not mine. Every time I spotted a returned soldier, a red chevron discharge stripe sewn onto his left sleeve, my heart hitched.

On the 10th of September 1919, we in New York heralded our heroes: General John J. Pershing, Commander-in-Chief of the AEF, and 25,000 of his soldiers in trench helmets and full combat gear filing down Fifth Avenue from 107th Street to Washington Square. White-clad war nurses passed out blossoms. Marching bands competed with the city-wide clamoring of bells. A wood-and-plaster Victory Arch rose over 24th Street. The general and his staff passed beneath it at full salute. Most poignant to me were the front-row seats set up along the parade route for those doughboys too ailing and crippled to march.

It wasn't only the war's end we had to celebrate. Finally, the flu was on the wane. Suddenly, travel was possible again. From Colm's letters, I knew our father was growing evermore fragile. And there was a new generation to greet. Whilst Colm had stayed a bachelor, between Ronan and Keira in Dublin and Killian and Úna on Inis Mór, I had nieces and nephews and grandnieces and grandnephews galore, none of whom I'd set eyes on beyond their baptismal photographs. It was past time Moira and Blake met their Irish relations, past time I shucked off my Yank trappings to walk barefoot upon that dearly missed quay.

Buzzing with excitement, I brought up my plans to Moira and Blake over breakfast one morning, "Darlings, I have a surprise."

Blake's head shot up from his bowl of Kellogg's Toasted Corn Flakes. "A puppy?"

"No, my love," I admitted, steeling myself for his crestfallen face, for he'd been asking the same for nearly a year, "but I promise we'll take a drive to the country and pick one out just as soon as we're back."

Moira stopped beating the teaspoon about her coffee and looked up. "Back from where?"

"Ireland. A change of scene will do us all a world of good."

Judging from Moira's fallen face, she didn't agree.

"Do they have puppies there?" Blake asked. Like all my children, he had a one-track mind when he wanted something.

"I'd be surprised if they didn't. There are plenty of other animals too – cows and chickens and donkeys, and a goat named Willy. He's kin to the first Willy we kept, the one I helped birth when I wasn't much older than you are."

His eyes rounded. "That must have been a *long* time ago."

I let out a laugh, my first in some time. "Indeed, my love, it was."

"When are you leaving?" Moira broke in.

"The ocean liner tickets are booked for two weeks from today."

Her jaw dropped. "But I can't just pick up and leave."

I set my teacup upon the saucer. "I don't see why not. You don't start college until the fall." To my great pride, she'd been accepted into Vassar.

Blake turned to his sister. "C'mon, Mo, it'll be fun."

"Mind your sister's name is *Moira*, at least within these four walls," I said. Moira and her suffrage friends thought it great fun to adopt male nicknames, but the practice set my teeth on edge. "And gather your books and have Mrs. Gentry walk you, otherwise you'll be late, and Brother Andrew will keep you after to pound his erasers."

"Chalk makes me sneeze," he said, scooting off his chair. More and more, he resembled Adam, not only in looks but in mannerisms, the lopsided smile especially.

"Not so fast. Where's my kiss?" I asked, unable to resist calling him back.

He groaned and trudged back over. Wrapping my arms about him, I inhaled his little-boy scent: clean hair and cotton school sweater, the tang of the lemon drops on his breath explaining why most of his cereal remained in the bowl. Before I knew it, he'd be sneaking cologne instead of candy, growing peach fuzz on his top lip, and making a fuss about a family trip abroad as his sister was doing.

301

I waited for him to clear the room before turning back to Moira. "I see now that springing this trip on you wasn't the best way to go about it," I conceded, "but I do hope you'll make the best of it. Once you start college, we'll only ever have the summers together as a family."

She stared down into her undrunk coffee. "I'm not sure I'll be going to college."

Blindsided, I drew back. "But it's all you've talked about, worked for."

She shrugged. "Things have changed."

I reached for her hand. "I'm sorry, I've been too caught up in my grief to help you through yours. You've been strong and brave for the both of us, but you don't have to be, not anymore. I'm better now. You can talk to me, tell me anything."

Her eyes filled as if I flagged onion slices beneath them. "I'm not strong or brave at all. I'm stupid and selfish, and I've made a horrible mess of my life."

Unlike some her age, Moira wasn't one for melodrama. "Surely, it can't be all that bad?" I fished, hoping that were so.

She puckered her lips as she'd done when she was little. "All those nights I said I was studying at the library or stuffing envelopes at the Suffrage Council office, I've been seeing someone. A man."

So, Moira had a secret beau. "Why all the sneaking about?" She didn't answer, and a fresh fear swamped me. "Oh, Moira, he isn't married, is he?" Having trod that tempestuous path, I knew full well the heartache it held.

"No, of course not."

I fell back against the chair, limp with relief. "Then why not have him to the house?"

"Rob comes from a very prominent family – a *Protestant* family," she added.

"It's not... ideal," I admitted, "but provided he doesn't demand you give up your faith, there may be a way to manage matters down the road. If you love him. Do you?"

"Madly! Rob is the sweetest, most wonderful man. Feeling and brilliant and *gorgeous.*"

Her rapturous description had me smothering a smile. "How did the two of you meet?"

"Through Joey."

Tears sprang to my eyes. Blinking them back, I asked, "Your young man was a friend of Joey's?"

"Not exactly. They met at McSorley's the night before they shipped out. All the doughboys hung their turkey wishbones on the lamp over the bar and pledged they'd come back and collect them after the war. Once he was sent home, Rob took down his and... Joey's too. Joey had mentioned having a twin sister who was a suffragist, and he tracked me down to the Martha Washington. When the secretary said I had a gentleman visitor, I couldn't think who it could be. We don't get all that many men. I got up from my desk, and our eyes met, and it sounds crazy, I know, but we both just *knew*."

"I don't think it sounds *crazy* at all," I said, thinking of Adam's and my first meeting.

"We've met nearly every evening since. He comes by as I'm finishing up and takes me to the Garret."

"The Garret?" I echoed, struggling to keep up.

"A coffeehouse off Washington Square. Afterward he... drives me home."

The coffeehouse sounded on the seedy side, but it was her mention of the car that had me fretting. "Has his own automobile, does he?" Taking in her flushed face and lowered eyes, I suspected she and her young man had got up to a good deal more in that machine than motoring.

"A Rolls Royce. It was a gift from his grandfather."

"That's quite a gift."

"His father is well off, but his grandparents are lousy rich."

I sat back. "Don't tell me he objects to you continuing your education?"

"Not at all. He's quite modern that way."

Thus far, her mystery beau sounded close to perfect. Perhaps too perfect. "Then what's the problem?"

Her face crumpled. "Oh, Mums, I've gone and gotten myself preggers!"

Braced though I'd believed myself to be, still the news came as a blow. "I doubt you're the sole one responsible," I murmured. "Any idea how far along you are?"

"About two months, I think."

Panic ebbing, my mind moved toward the practical. The new flapper fashions were short on hemlines but long on waists. That elongated silhouette could conceal a world of sins, including an early pregnancy.

She hiccuped out a laugh. "Ironic, isn't it? All the time I've put in passing out contraband copies of Mrs. Sanger's *Family Limitation* and *The Birth Control Review*, and now, I'm caught myself."

I winced. "What does Rob have to say?"

"I... haven't told him yet."

"Oh, Moira."

"I keep meaning to, but every time, I chicken out."

"He has a right to know." *And a responsibility to fulfill.*

"I'm meeting him tonight. I'll do it then, promise."

"No, my darling, you won't."

She blinked.

Since losing Joey, I'd focused my attention on Blake, my baby chick. About to fly the nest, Moira hadn't seemed to need me as once she had. Too late, I owned the disservice I'd done her.

"From here on, Rob will call for you here at the house."

"But—"

"No buts. Until your marriage vows are made, you'll carry on your courtship to the letter of propriety. No more motoring about the city consorting with impoverished poets and Bolsheviks and whoever else dines at that dive he's been taking you to."

Her mutinous look told me she was feeling nearly herself. "But that's hypocrisy."

"Call it what you will, but unless you want whispers of a shotgun marriage to follow your child all his or her life, you'll do as I advise."

Reminded that she hadn't only herself to consider, she subsided into her seat. "What about Ireland?"

I reached over and tucked a loose lock of hair behind her ear. "I don't suppose Ireland's going anywhere, and neither am I. Not until I hold that sweet babe of yours in my arms. He or she is my first grandchild, after all."

Now that the initial shock was easing, I realized I rather fancied the idea of having a baby about again, one I could love and spoil to my heart's content.

An idea occurred to me. "Why not ring Rob and invite him to supper tonight?"

"Tonight?"

I nodded. "Ask his parents too, that is, if they won't mind breaking bread with a Papist. And a tradeswoman," I added, only partway joking, for all the money I'd made couldn't blue my blood.

"Rob's mother died when he was little, but he can ask his father. He's out in Brooklyn," she added, as though a sea separated us instead of only the East River.

"Surely, he's not too busy to cross a bridge to toast his own son's engagement?"

"He's a writer, so he makes his own hours. Come to think of it, you met him years ago, the summer before the war. We had Blake with us, and we stopped by that bookstore off Union Square."

I swallowed a gasp, the effort sucking the moisture from my mouth.

"You went in to buy his book. It had your name in the title. My... something Irish Rose, I think it was."

Finding my voice, I said, "*My Wild Irish Rose.*"

She nodded. "Yes, that's it. *My Wild Irish Rose* by Adam Blakely."

Chapter Forty-One

Out in Brooklyn, Adam was having parental troubles of his own. Just that morning, Robbie announced he wouldn't be going back to Harvard. Instead, he meant to start at Carlston Enterprises, formerly Carlston *Blakely* Enterprises, at the month's end.

"With all due respect, Dad, it's my life, and I have to live it as I see fit."

Giving up on the eggs cooling on his plate, Adam threw down his napkin. "And *this* is what you choose?" He started to say more but ringing from the butler's pantry cut him off.

Their housekeeper, Mrs. Purdy poked her head inside. "Master Robbie, telephone for you. A *young lady*," she added, tossing a wink Adam's way.

"Thanks, Mrs. P." Robbie rocketed from his seat. Glancing over at Adam, he asked, "Mind?"

Adam waved him off. "Don't keep a lady waiting on my account. But come find me after. This conversation is far from finished."

In his attic office, Winnie draped over his feet, Adam tried losing himself in the publisher galleys for his latest book. Stuck on a sentence that still wasn't right, he finally gave up and set the page aside for when his mind was less muddled.

With the war over, he'd hoped he and Robbie might spend more time together, maybe take a camping trip to the Adirondacks as they'd used to. Instead, his son frittered away his free time tooling around town in the Rolls his Carlston grandfather had given him. Adam didn't begrudge his son a splashy car, but he would have liked for him to have earned it.

Now, Robbie was poised to enter the dog-eat-dog world of industry from which Adam had done everything in his power to preserve him. Not because anyone was making him but because he *wanted* to. Such a choice was, to Adam, unfathomable. And yet, looking back over the past decade, he supposed it made a strange sort of sense. Facts and figures, absolutely everything to do with the making and managing of money were Robbie's strong suits since he'd set up his first sidewalk lemonade stand. It seemed the famed Blakely Midas touch hadn't died out after all.

It had just skipped a generation.

A throat being cleared brought him back from his brooding. He looked up to Robbie on his threshold. Taking in his son's troubled expression, he surmised the phone call must have been a doozy.

"Have a seat, son."

Robbie walked up to the desk. "If it's all the same to you, sir, I'll stand."

Sir. The frosty formality was an unhappy reminder of his relationship with his own father, a legacy he liked to think he'd spared his son. But perhaps not entirely.

"Suit yourself," he said and reached for the humidor of Cubans. Though he'd given up cigarettes years ago, cigars were one of the trappings of most male rites of passage. Judging from Robbie's lifted chin and squared shoulders, such a milestone moment seemed to be afoot.

"Everything all right?" he fished, flipping back the box lid.

Waving off the smokes, Robbie said, "I've met a girl. Not just any girl but *the* girl."

That, at least, Adam could wrap his mind around. "That was her on the telephone?"

Robbie nodded. "I'm going to ask her to marry me. Tonight."

Adam started to say… *something*, but Robbie held up a hand. "I know we must seem young and rash to you, but we're old enough to know our own minds – and hearts."

Paraphrased prose from *My Wild Irish Rose*, his words thrown back in his face. Being cast as the disapproving parent had Adam feeling depressingly old.

"I see." Gathering himself, he took his time in trimming his cigar.

Robbie hesitated, wearing the same look he'd had as a kid when he'd wanted to ride the pony in Central Park but hadn't liked to ask. "I'd like to give Mo Mom's ring, the one from Gram. But if you won't give it up, I'll ask Granddad Andrew for an advance and pick out a new one from Tiffany's."

Adam lit his cigar, struggling down the acid reply that rose to mind. This was Robbie's moment, ill-conceived though it might be, and he wouldn't sour it by bringing up ancient family history. "Relax, sport, the ring's yours."

Robbie's eyes lost some of their mutiny. "Mean it?"

Adam nodded. "Your mother and grandmother would want you to have it. *I* want you to have it. I'd give you your mother's pearls, too, if they hadn't gone missing."

Truth be told, Yvette's stealing the necklace had done him a favor. More so than any engagement ring, the pearls symbolized the lie he'd let himself be roped into leading.

Adam took a soothing drag of his smoke. "I guess I should count my lucky stars you two didn't up and elope."

"We thought about it," Robbie admitted, running a hand through his hair, the same wheat-colored blond Adam's once was, "but Mo doesn't want to disappoint her mother."

Hoping Mo's mother wasn't a harridan on par with his own, Adam asked, "Has her heart set on a big church wedding, does she?"

"A *Catholic* church wedding," Robbie said, sounding grave.

Such an announcement would have put off many a Protestant papa, but not Adam. "I hope you know that doesn't make any difference, not to me."

"I didn't think it would, but it's good to hear you say so. They lost Mo's brother in the war, and her mother's taken it hard. Anything other than a Catholic wedding would kill her, Mo swears it."

"Outliving your child is every parent's worst fear," Adam said, thinking of my Joey and all the others who never made it home. Robbie's stint in the ambulance corps had nearly started him smoking again. "Once you have a family of your own, you'll understand what I mean."

Robbie slipped two fingers beneath his shirt collar as if the stock were suddenly uncomfortably tight. "There's something else you need to know. I just found out myself."

"I'm all ears," Adam answered, wondering how many more white hairs Robbie meant to give him.

Robbie regarded him with a stiff upper lip – and eyes liquid with pleading. "Mo and me, we're having a baby."

Standing on Adam's front porch early that afternoon, I lifted the door knocker. Since learning Moira's Rob was Adam's Robbie, I'd known

308

I couldn't let Adam walk into my impromptu dinner party and be blindsided.

A friendly-faced matron with gray-streaked hair answered. "Can I help you?"

"Mrs. Joseph Kavanaugh." I reached inside my handbag and brought out my card. "I'm not expected," I admitted, kicking myself for not having rung ahead. Hopelessly old-fashioned, I still didn't entirely trust the telephone or, more properly, the gossipy lady operators who worked the switchboards. "Is Mr. Blakely at home?"

She nodded. "Holed up in that attic that does for an office. I'll tell him you're here if you don't mind waiting."

"I don't mind, thank you."

I entered the modest foyer, aware of her darting looks from my card to myself. "Pardon my asking, but you wouldn't be any relation to that Irish family that opened the new midtown department store, would you?"

"I'm Rose Kavanaugh, yes," I admitted, wondering if she'd had a less than satisfactory customer experience.

A smile broke over her face. "I hope you won't think me forward if I say what an inspiration you are to us all. I'm Irish myself – Irish–American, anyways, first generation. So was my late husband. I can't tell you how nice it is to see our people opening something other than saloons, not that there's anything wrong with a good, stiff tipple every now and again. But here I am blabbering on and forgetting my manners. Parlor's down the hall, first door on the right. Make yourself comfy, and I'll bring Mr. B. straightaway."

Too antsy to sit, I passed the wait at the parlor mantel, studying the framed photographs of my future son-in-law from babyhood to young manhood. A photograph of Robbie in uniform sitting behind the wheel of an army ambulance seemed to be the most recent. Blond-haired, blue-eyed, and lanky, he was indeed Adam's boy.

Feeling eyes upon me, I put the picture back and turned to Adam entering. Despite the gray threading his hair, the fine lines bracketing his eyes, and the awful jacket – a tweedy affair, thin on threads and patched at the elbows – I didn't have to look far to find the beautiful boy I'd first fallen for.

"You've done away with the goatee," I said by way of a greeting, for the brief bookstore meeting was the last time I'd laid eyes on him.

He touched his chin, the stubble glinting more of silver than gold. "One of my better decisions, I'm told."

He stayed where he was, but his eyes moving over me seemed to be making up for lost time. Though my black dress's mid-calf-length hemline was modest by the modern standards, I felt suddenly, embarrassingly bare.

"You must be wondering why I've come?"

He crossed the sun-faded carpet toward me. "Life has taught me never to look a gift horse in the mouth. But yes, I am asking myself why today of all days should turn out to be so lucky. It certainly didn't start out that way."

I came to my point. "I'm here about my daughter."

He cast me a quizzical look. "The precocious imp I met at your store all those years ago?"

"Not so impish any longer. She's coming on eighteen and about to begin college, or so that was our plan before... the baby news."

"Baby news?" He stared as though I'd sprouted a second head. "Sorry, I don't follow."

I might have loved him for the lion's share of my life but in that moment, I was entirely a mother. "She and your son spoke about it on the telephone this morning."

He hesitated. "Rob did take a call from his girl, Mo. Come to think of it, I never got around to asking what the nickname stands for."

"Moira," I supplied, wondering if the silly sobriquet wouldn't follow us all to our graves.

He shook his head as if there were cobwebs in want of clearing, but then, I had given him not one shock but two.

"We'll sit, shall we?" I suggested, moving to the serpentine-backed sofa.

"Yes, of course." He followed me over and took one of the pair of comfortably worn armchairs.

We had no sooner settled when Mrs. Purdy entered with a black-lacquered tea tray. She set it on the teakwood table in front of me and took off, sending me shy smiles over her shoulder. I poured coffee for Adam, adding two sugar lumps and a dash of milk without having to ask.

He leaned in to take it. "We're going to share a grandchild. I used to think of us having a family, but this wasn't at all what I pictured."

"Not much in life ever is." I glanced to the Nabisco biscuits on the tray, and a lump lodged in my throat. "My Joey loved these. I tucked a tin in the last care package I sent him. I wonder if he ever got it. I suppose I'll never know." I sipped my tea, seeking to loosen the familiar stuck feeling.

Adam's eyes sought mine. "I'm so sorry, Rose. I can't begin to imagine what you've been through."

"Thank you for that. And for your flowers and kind note. I should have replied."

"I'd hoped to hear from you but didn't really expect to." He scraped a hand through his hair, the mannerism evoking a multitude of memories.

I lifted my cup and took another swift sip. "Will Robbie's Carlston grandfather object to them marrying, do you think? Moira's hardly a pauper, but she is Irish, Catholic, and the daughter of a tradeswoman."

The war had changed a lot, but it hadn't changed everything. Snobbery, though subtler than before, still existed.

"My son is his own man. As of this morning, he's in possession of the family engagement ring. He plans to pop the question tonight."

Sitting back, I felt as if a weight were suddenly lifted. "Will they... be all right, do you think?" I added, wondering if I ought to offer Rob a position at the store, at least until he and Moira found their feet.

Adam's confident nod set the rest of my worries to rest. "Rob is heir to two substantial fortunes. Your baby chick will be not only loved and cherished but kept in a finely feathered nest. Heck, they can have a brood of babies if they're so inclined, send the boys to Groton and the girls to European finishing schools."

I smiled. "Grand as that all sounds, I'm afraid my daughter fancies herself something of a socialist."

He let out a laugh. "My parents must be thrashing in their tomb. I like your girl already."

"Make no mistake, she's Joe's daughter down to the dimple in her chin."

He set his cup aside. "When Frank told me how you shut yourself in to nurse him, it was all I could do not to head downtown and carry you out of there. I reminded myself I didn't have the right."

"You didn't," I agreed, studying my cooling cup.

"And now?"

Not waiting for my answer, he rounded the table and slid in beside me. His hand on my nape was all it took to bring me to him. I lifted my face to his, and his mouth met mine in a gentle kiss, our lips as perfect a match as ever.

I sat back, bemused by how easily he could still melt me. "I came for my daughter, not... this."

"Mo... Moira's a grown woman about to start a family of her own. Isn't it time to start thinking of yourself for a change?"

Watching his face, I said, "I have another child, a little boy who's still grieving his big brother and father. His name is Blake."

"I didn't know," he said. "I'll look forward to meeting him tonight."

"You're still coming to supper then?"

"Wouldn't miss it."

"Grand, I'll see you at seven." I stood and started for the door whilst my rubbery legs still carried me.

He walked me out into the hallway. "I'd drive you, but I don't keep a car anymore."

I almost brought up his generosity to Frank, but knowing how he hated a fuss, I kept mum. "The train suits me."

"You'll need a taxi to the station. I'll have Mrs. Purdy telephone."

"Thank you."

We reached the front door. Wondering if he meant to kiss me again, I stepped back before he could.

If Adam was disappointed, he didn't let on. "I'll bring a bottle of champagne tonight... unless you'd rather I didn't," he added, sensitive to how I'd suffered with Joe's drinking.

"I'm still a publican's daughter, aren't I?" I said, wanting things to be friendly and natural between us for Moira's sake. "Seeing as we're celebrating a wedding *and* a grandchild, best bring two."

Chapter Forty-Two

We celebrated Moira and Robert's wedding at St. Ann's, our home parish since the move to Gramercy. Below in the choir room, I helped her on with her gown, a confection of cream-colored satin and tulle, spangled with silver bugle beads and descending into a handkerchief hemline. The dropped waistline, in keeping with the current flapper fashions, camouflaged the baby bump beautifully.

I finished pinning her lace cloche cap veil in place and stood back. "You're everything a bride should be and more, my darling."

Her smile met mine in the dressing mirror. "You're the stunner, Mums. If you were anyone else, I'd be green with envy."

After considerable back and forth with Moira – "Really, Mums, these days, who's even heard of *half-mourning*?" – I'd agreed to a mauve tulle frock festooned with metal foil sequins. The slit sleeves and calf-length skirt didn't seem quite the thing for a widow creeping up on forty, but Moira insisted. A hair fascinator of silk roses studded with seed pearls and brilliants, my own creation, crowned my newly shingled hair.

I slipped my arm about her. "My sweet girl, all eyes will be on you exactly as it should be."

Her mouth turned up. "I can think of one pair of eyes that are certain to be on you alone."

"I'm sure I don't know what you mean." Feeling my face heat, I broke away and busied myself with fluffing her train.

Since my visit to Prospect Park, Adam's courtship campaign had moved toward a full-blown siege. One morning, I stepped into my office to find it blanketed with crimson roses. On another occasion, a teal-blue Tiffany & Company box was left out on my desk. Within was a gold and mother-of-pearl seashell pin, a shameless harkening to our island days.

"I'll give you a hint." Eyes alight, she grabbed both my hands. "His initials are A.H.B., and he's very shortly to become a member of this family. Come to think of it, that's two hints."

Were we truly so transparent? Then again, Moira never had missed much.

"You always did have an active imagination," I demurred, not yet ready to give in. "Now take a twirl. I want to see how that train is draping."

Wedding day or not, like a dog with a juicy bone, she wasn't about to let up until she'd picked the subject clean. "The first time the four of us sat down to supper, he could scarcely keep his eyes off you. Then again, it's not every day a man finds himself about to become in-laws with his first love – and muse."

My gaze flew to hers. "How long have you known?"

"That you're the Wild Irish Rose? Our dinner got me curious, so I... borrowed the copy from your nightstand. The inscription cinched it."

"How far did you get?" I asked, dreading her answer.

"Far enough to know that it's not a novel, not really. More of a memoir disguised as fiction. Except for the ending, but we can work on that."

Done in, I fitted a hand to my brow.

She gently pried away my fingers. "I wouldn't say a word if he wasn't eligible and kind and clearly smitten with you. Good-looking too, in that distinguished, older gent sort of way."

Distinguished, older gent. To me, Adam was eternally twenty-three with sun-streaked hair and the bluest eyes I'd ever looked into.

"Above all, I think you love him back. You do, don't you?"

Rather than deny it, I asked, "Wouldn't you and Rob find it awkward seeing us together? As a couple?"

She shrugged. "Rob's memories of his mother are foggy, mostly her whisking into his nursery for a goodnight kiss before going off to one gala or another. So no, I don't think he'd mind."

"And yourself?"

Eyes on mine, she answered, "Dad didn't make you happy. I understand that now in a way I couldn't have before Rob."

I reached out and cupped her cheek. "Your father and I had some good years. Above all, he gave me the two of you."

"The *three* of us, you mean."

Too late I realized my slipup. That Blake almost certainly wasn't Joe's was the last of my secrets, one I still resolved to carry to the grave. Covering, I said, "I didn't want to make you sad by bringing up Joey."

Tears welled in her beautiful, black-brown eyes. "I miss him so much. And Dad, too. I'd give anything to have him here to walk me down the aisle. He'd know just what to say so I wasn't nervous."

For once, I found my handkerchief straightaway. Dabbing her cheek, I said, "I believe they *are* here with us and as proud of you as I am. Now, no more crying. You won't want to meet Rob at the altar red-eyed and blotchy."

Later, looking on as she and Rob exchanged their vows, I sent up a silent prayer that they would know true and lasting happiness. Despite the topsy-turvy ordering of things, there was no doubt they were marrying for the best of reasons. Love.

A reception at the Waldorf-Astoria followed, the very hotel where Adam had attended the fateful charity ball all those years ago. Frank's fleet of limousines ferried the wedding party and guests from the church. Assembling at the hotel, we paraded down the magnificent three-hundred-foot marbled and mirrored corridor known as Peacock Alley, coming into the Palm Court where the wildly popular, and soon-to-be illegal, cocktails were served. Fortunately, the new federal prohibition against selling spirits wouldn't take effect until January. In more ways than one, I'd put on Moira and Rob's wedding by the skin of our teeth.

Like me, Adam was kept busy greeting guests. More than once, I caught myself seeking him out from the side of my eye. He cut an uncommonly fine figure in his formalwear, the black wool tailcoat with ribbed silk lapels, black waistcoat trimmed in silk braid, and fitted black trousers the perfect foil for his tall, fit form. Nor was I alone in thinking so.

Though I'd kept the reception details out of the wedding announcement, a handful of reporters caught wind of the arrangements and wrangled their way inside, including the indomitable Evelyn Moon. Though I hadn't seen her since Adam's trial, I recognized her at once, her figure slightly fuller, her dark hair shot with silver.

The cocktail hour concluded, we proceeded to the Empire Room for a lavish sit-down supper, commencing with the eponymous Waldorf salad of chopped apples, celery, grapes, and walnuts dressed in mayonnaise, a curiously appealing combination. Subsequent courses followed, all in the French fashion. Croustade of mushrooms Bordelaise. Medallion of sea bass a la Joinville. Filet de boeuf with haricots verts. We finished with an assortment of cheeses, petits fours, and chocolates, coffees, and cordials. Thinking of my and Joe's simple wedding, our union toasted with California "champagne" drunk from tin cups, I couldn't be but grateful for the bounty Kavanaugh's had brought us all.

The finale, a four-tiered wedding cake, was rolled in. Before it was cut, white-gloved waiters carried in trays of champagne, the fluted glasses passed out in preparation for the toasts. Custom dictated the father of the bride give the first speech. Instead, I stood to give it.

"To my darling Moira, who's always made myself, and her father, nothing but proud. And to Robert, who in a short while has become more son to me than son-in-law. Love, long life, and much happiness, my darlings. May your troubles be few and your blessings plenty."

The traditional Irish toast met with hearty applause. Adam's tribute followed, so funny and eloquent and heart-warming that we were all crying and laughing at turns.

With the meal concluded, the tables were pushed aside to make room for the dancing. In lieu of opening with a waltz – the Austrian-originated dance had fallen out of favor since the war – the band struck up a lively jazz number.

Adam slipped into the vacant seat beside me. "They look good together."

"They do, indeed," I agreed, following his gaze to the dance floor where my thoroughly modern Moira hiked up her hemline to shake, shimmy, and kick in sync with her new husband.

Adam leaned closer. "We should join them. People expect it."

The first and last time we had danced together was Samhain all those years ago.

Finishing off my wine, I admitted, "I'm afraid my ballroom dancing ends at the One Step."

He cracked a smile. "I have it on good authority the next number will be more our speed."

Against my better judgment, I let him guide me onto the dance floor. I might be the mother of the bride and a successful businesswoman, but the first, thrilling press of his hand to the small of my spine brought me back to that love-struck girl again. Stepping into his arms, I took a moment to place the music, but once I did—

316

My gaze flew to his. "*My Wild Irish Rose* – you really are relentless, aren't you!?"

Lips brushing my ear, he admitted, "What five bucks will buy in New York never ceases to amaze me. I like the hair, by the way. Very chic."

I ran a gloved hand along my shingled nape, not yet used to the bareness. "Moira's idea. She thinks me hopelessly Victorian."

He laughed. "If only she knew."

Thinking of his book, which she'd admitted reading, I felt myself blushing.

All too soon the music ended. I slipped my hand from Adam's and stepped back.

Warm blue eyes brushed mine. "Thanks for the dance. I wouldn't mind doing it again... among other things."

I left the broad hint unanswered.

We'd just reached the edge of the dance floor when Miss Moon walked up. Despite her horrid puce frock, a good five years out of fashion, I conceded her voluptuous figure was holding its own.

Behind the spectacles, her gaze glided over Adam. "I absolutely adored your last novel. The characters are so vividly drawn and your prose sublime."

I'd venture his prose wasn't all she found sublime.

I sent her a stinging look. "If you'll excuse me, I have guests to see to – *invited* ones."

Going through the motions of mingling, I owned the unflattering truth. I wasn't only put out that Miss Moon had crashed my daughter's wedding. I was jealous. Jealous of any woman who might lay claim to Adam's attention, no matter how fleetingly.

Later, I helped Moira out of her gown and into her traveling suit. She and Rob would leave by train that night for their honeymoon in Niagara Falls, yet another unwitting homage to their parents' histories. We saw the happy couple off amidst a shower of rice and rose petals. Soon after, the room began to clear.

"Off duty at last." Adam walked up, carrying a bottle of Veuve Clicquot and two fluted glasses, one tucked into each jacket pocket. "Have a drink with me."

I touched my temple where the makings of a headache had begun. "I've already drunk more than I should."

"In that case, one more won't make much difference. C'mon, a last hurrah before Senator Volstead and his cronies have us all toasting with teacups."

The sense of being studied drew my eye out to the cloakroom where Miss Moon lingered despite having collected her wrap. Our gazes caught, and a strange smile lifted her lips.

Defiant, I turned back to Adam. "All right, one drink."

Back stairs brought us to an empty upstairs parlor decorated in the Turkish style. Taking in the fringed draperies, Persian carpets, and Moorish-inspired furniture piled with pillows, I felt as if I were entering an *Arabian Nights* tale.

I took a seat on a brocade-covered settee whilst he opened the champagne. My gaze rested on his gloveless hands, the backs broad, the fingers tapered. Remembering the feel of them on my body, warmth swept through me.

The cork's popping shocked me back to the moment.

Holding out the frothing bottle, Adam passed me a full glass then dropped onto the cushion beside me.

I touched my glass to his. "To our children," I toasted, thinking not only of our newlyweds but also Blake, his son too, though he could never know it. "Think they're at Grand Central by now?" I asked, resolved to stick to safe subjects.

He glanced at the shiny new Rolex banding his wrist. "Should be boarding any time." He set his glass aside and reached for mine to do the same. "Hard as this may be to imagine, I didn't ask you up here only to congratulate each other on our progeny."

He set his mouth to mine, and suddenly, I wasn't the mother of the bride anymore but that reckless, mad-in-love girl again. I kissed him back as I had in the cave on Inis Meán when I'd thought never to see him again. As I had that December afternoon at the Plaza when we'd buried our scruples beneath hotel bed linens.

The sense of the world tilting had me opening my eyes. I was on my back, Adam braced above me, silvered hair falling over his brow. "Tell me you don't want this, and I'll stop."

I couldn't, not with any honesty. Instead, I said, "I'm to be a grandmother."

His gaze slipped over me, and his mouth lifted. "You don't look like any grandmother I've ever met."

Imagining the salacious scene we made, I lifted myself on my elbow. "Carrying on this way, at our children's wedding, no less. What if your Miss Moon or some other reporter were to walk in?"

A sandy eyebrow arched. "She's hardly *my* Miss Moon, and if I thought compromising you would get you to marry me, I'd have arranged for the entire staff of *The Tribune* to lie in wait. With cameras."

"Adam, I'm being serious."

"So am I. I eloped once before. I've a mind to try it again with a bride of my choosing."

"I can't just... run off. I have Blake, the store—"

"Kavanaugh's has a full-time manager, and I can send Mrs. Purdy over to stay with Blake until we get back. She practically raised Robbie. Your boy will be in the best of hands. And so will you." He kissed me again, playing his fingers upward along the seam of my stocking.

A thud brought me back to myself. I tore my mouth away and looked to the overturned bottle, champagne overflowing the tableside and sopping the carpet.

That time, I found the fortitude to shove down my dress and struggle to my feet.

Tucking in his shirt, Adam got up as well. "What are you so afraid of, Rose?"

"Afraid, I'm not," I insisted, only I was, though not in any way he likely imagined.

I hadn't been a good wife to Joe. Could I trust myself to do better with Adam? Lately, the thought had crossed my mind that perhaps I wasn't cut out to be a wife at all. If I was married, it was to Kavanaugh's. Could I honestly expect another man, even one as modern-minded as Adam, to play second fiddle to the business that bore my late husband's name?

He raked a hand through his hair. "If two wars and an influenza epidemic have anything to teach us, it's that life is too short and precious to waste. Marry me. Once Moira and Rob have their baby, we can go away, anywhere you want. We'll bring Blake with us, sail the seven seas."

How simple he made it all sound. "I have a life here and a business. Kavanaugh's is positioned to be the Selfridge's of New York. True, I'm not needed to count out the cash drawers, but I am still needed."

"Fine, we'll stay put. I'll rub your feet when you come home after a long day, pour you a sherry, and lull you to sleep with reading aloud my latest manuscript pages."

Despite the lovely picture he painted, I didn't entirely believe him. "Since I've known you, you've done everything in your power to get away from New York. With Rob wed, you're finally free to go anywhere you fancy. If you stayed stuck here for my sake, you'd come to resent me for it. And that I couldn't bear."

I expected him to soften. Instead, he went rigid as ironwork.

"That's quite a speech, but I doubt you believe it any more than I do." His mouth pulled tight. "I've loved you most of my life. I've waited for you for most of my life too. Marry me or don't but know this: if I walk out of here, I'm as good as gone. No more 'go safely for now'. It's flat-out goodbye. Oh, you'll still see me at family gatherings, that's unavoidable. But I won't come to you again, not like this. Is that really what you want?"

Adore him as I did, I wasn't about to be bullied. "I can't marry you right now. I can't marry anyone right now. Someday, perhaps, but not now. It's nothing to do with loving you. I do, very much."

I reached for him, but he tore his arm away, chest heaving as though he'd run a race. "Oh, you love me all right, but not nearly as much as you do your precious store. Ironic how I could hold my own against the man but not the business that bears his name." He locked his angry eyes on mine and waited.

One final chance to speak up. One final chance to stop him.

Stubborn as ever, I stood my ground in stony silence.

He wheeled away and flung open the door.

Only after his footsteps faded did I reflect that my stubborn pride had proven a far fiercer foe than Beatrice Blakely ever had.

August 1920

Moira and Rob's baby came at the end of June, a fine, strapping boy who looked so much like Joey had as a newborn, I could almost believe he'd come back to us. They baptized him Neil Joseph, the former a nod to my maiden name, the latter for his deceased grandfather and uncle. I stood as godmother; Adam as "Christian witness", the closest to godfather we could come considering he was a Protestant and the ceremony was performed at St. Ann's.

Afterward, I hosted a luncheon for the family and a few friends. Once the last guests left, the four of us brought the baby onto the back patio to catch the late afternoon breeze. Fittingly, Moira and Rob shared the loveseat. Blake, flopped upon his belly, shot marbles at our feet. Adam and I occupied the pair of facing wickerwork chairs. Neil, still in his baptismal finery, napped upon his grandpapa's chest.

Looking over at Adam, Moira bit her lip, "About the naming, I hope you don't feel… Well, in any way left out."

Adam shook his head. "I'm just relieved Horatio has died a long overdue death."

We all laughed.

"But seriously, Dad," Rob said. "Me and Mo… Moira," he amended, glancing my way, "agree the next boy will be Adam."

Moira poked her elbow into his side. "The next boy, or *girl*, will have to wait until I graduate college."

"And after?" Adam asked, for by then it was clear to all that, much as Moira adored Robbie and their little boy, she was the sort of woman who needed a career to feel complete. My daughter, indeed. "Now that you ladies finally have the vote, I'd think the sky's the limit."

The ink was still drying on the 19th Amendment. Signed into law on the 26th of August, it proclaimed that, "*The right of citizens of the United States to vote shall not be denied or abridged by the United States or any State on account of sex.*" For the first time in our young nation's history, women would vote not only in selected municipal and state elections but in national ones too. It was progress I felt privileged to be alive to witness.

"I'll apply to law school," Moira said, looking from Rob to me, ere then the only two privy to her plans. "Fordham and Columbia began admitting females a year or two ago. Yale, too, though I wouldn't want to be so far away from the baby. Or Rob," she added, slipping her hand into his.

Adam stood, Neil in his arms. "I've laid away a 1911 cuvée for a special occasion, and I can't think of a better one than this. Rose," he said, gaze flickering to me, "if you'll take the baby, I'll go get it from your Frigidaire."

The new electric appliance wasn't the only source of frostiness that day. Hating the chilly civility with which we now treated each other, I shook my head. "Stay put, I'll bring it."

A few weeks later, Adam embarked on the first of his solo travels, taking the Orient Express from Paris to Istanbul. I told myself it was better this way. Neither of us were tied down. But whilst being my own mistress had its merits, it also made for a lonely life, especially as Kavanaugh's now ran so seamlessly without me. Though I still weighed in on sales campaigns, fashion displays, special events, and pricing, my retail manager and chief operating officer, both hired away from Chicago's Marshall Field's department store, had matters well in hand. My pre-opening promenades, which I still stuck to, were no longer strictly necessary.

For the first since departing Ireland, I had time on my hands. Unsure of what to do with myself, I reprised my travel plans. I no sooner got off the telegram to Colm when fresh violence broke out between Irish nationalists and British security forces.

The Irish War of Independence ended in a truce on the 11th of July 1921. Signed the 6th of December 1921, the Anglo–Irish Treaty ended British rule in twenty-six counties. Banded together as the Irish Free State, they would be granted dominion rule, whilst the remaining six northeastern counties would remain in the United Kingdom. The peace, though imperfect, meant I could finally go home. Home to Ireland.

PART IV: Full Circle, 1922

Go to the land whose love
Gives thee no rest;
And may Almighty God...
Bring thee through mist and foam
To thy desire,
Again to Irish land.

Anonymous, Medieval Latin lyric

Chapter Forty-Three

April 1922

Queenstown, rechristened Cobh, wasn't nearly as big or as bustling as I remembered it, the chorusing of cathedral bells falling upon the hush of quaint cobbled streets. Unlike my previous visit, I'd no need to make do with stale oatcakes or rely upon the generosity of strangers. Blake and I supped on fish and chips in the hotel's dining room, our window table overlooking the harbor.

"People here talk funny – funnier than you, even," he whispered once our waiter stepped away.

Smiling, I said, "Would you believe when I first came to New York, I could scarcely make heads or tails of what people said to me because of *their* accents?"

Whilst Cobh hadn't much impressed my New York born and bred boy, the view from our train window the next day held him in wonderment.

Nose pressed to the glass, he exclaimed, "Those are real-live cows, aren't they?"

Following his gaze to a field of grazing milchers, I nodded. "Indeed, darling, they are."

The modern, motorized ferry took us from Rossaveal to Inis Mór in little more than an hour. "A grand soft day," as we Irish are fond of saying, the rain fell in buckets, the fog thick as blankets. Hunkering with Blake beneath the canvas deck cover, I strained to see through the soupiness.

Closing in on Kilronan, the skies cleared, showing the harbor dotted with fishing skiffs, the pier peppered with people. I bit back my impatience as the anchor was dropped, the gangplank lowered, and the luggage brought up.

Stepping off with Blake, I spotted a big, barrel-chested man pushing forward to us. "Colm!" I cried, abandoning our bags to meet him.

It was himself all right, softer about the middle, and his walrus mustache gone mostly gray, but otherwise, the same bluff big brother of my memory. We clasped each other close, the old enmity forgotten.

He held me at arm's length, taking in my shingled hair, smart coat, and high-heeled shoes. "Look at yourself, all grown up, and a grand lady too."

Moist-eyed, I let out a laugh. "I don't know about grand but grown up certainly. Forty-two and a grandmother."

"What if you are? You're still my little sister." He dropped his gaze to Blake beside me. "Might this braw lad be my—"

"Blake, sir," my little man answered, sticking out his hand.

Squatting, Colm took it with a mien of amusement. "Call me uncle."

Blake's solemn expression eased into wonder. "I've never had an uncle before."

A wiry man with a cap of messy salt-and-pepper curls shouldered his way up to us. "Well, now, you have three."

"Kil!" I launched myself at my baby brother, reaching out to ruffle his hair, pulling back before I did. "You're all grown up."

He chuckled. "With six kids and a grandbaby on the way, I'd better be."

Colm looked between us. "Between Killian here and Ronan in Dublin, sure we O'Neills are breeding the other families outta Ireland."

Killian commandeered the larger of my cases, moving us along. "Úna's back at the pub putting on the dinner."

"I hope she didn't go to any trouble," I said. After all these years, I still wrestled with the fact that the prickly schoolmate of my memory was wife to my sweet brother.

Killian rolled his eyes. "She's a woman, isn't she? She's been cooking these two days."

Not one to be overlooked, Blake piped up with, "Mommy says you have lots of animals."

Smiling overtop my son's towhead, I explained, "Other than in the zoo, we don't see many big beasts beyond horses. With automobiles all the rage, even those are becoming scarcer."

Colm winked. "I'll take you to the croft for a wee look-in if it's all right with your mam."

Face lit, Blake looked to me, eyes beseeching. "Can I, Mommy?"

"Change into your play clothes first," I said and pointed out the pub from the cluster of like-looking limestone cottages.

"Yippee!"

I watched him tear up the footpath, then turned back to my brothers. "Where's Da?"

Colm and Killian exchanged looks, their sudden silence making a knot of my belly.

Killian reached for my hand. "He tried his best to hold on, but he was too weak."

A tear slipped from my eye, and I didn't bother with wiping it. "When?"

Colm spoke up. "Sunday last," he said and gave my shoulder a squeeze. "Said he was feeling stronger and that he'd come down to the taproom and sit a while. We found him that evening in his chair by the settle. His pipe had gone out and himself with it."

Killian squeezed my hand. "Colm wanted to send you a telegraph on the ship, but I told him to hold off until we could break the news in person. Was I wrong?"

"Yes… no. I suppose it hardly matters now." I blinked hard, sending tears sprinkling. "What matters is he passed peacefully, surrounded by family and friends, everyone but… myself."

Colm's eyes met mine. "You never left his thoughts, not for a single day these four-and-twenty years. 'What time is it in New York?' he must have asked a half-dozen times a day. He was fierce proud of you. 'I always knew things would come right for our Rose,' was one of the last things he did say to me."

"If only I'd made it back to see him before…"

Colm's hand on my shoulder tightened. "Quit racking yourself, will ya? You can't hold yourself at fault for a war, not to mention two of 'em."

"Can't I? If only I hadn't been so caught up with the store, the kids…" *With Adam.*

Colm shook his head. "That's life, little sister. It creeps up on you and then races by. Da loved you with the whole of his heart, as you did himself. At day's end, who can ask for more than that?"

Colm threw open the inn door, painted green rather than the rooster red I remember. "We're electrified now," he announced, punching the button on the brass wall plate with a showmanship worthy of P.T.

Barnum. A fizzle and flicker, and then bright beads of light poured down upon us.

Killian lumbered over to the stairs with my luggage. Despite my pleas, he carried both cases up himself.

The delectable aroma coming from the kitchen suggested Úna still labored. Rather than look in and risk encroaching, I stayed in the taproom and took stock. A fancy brass bar rail. The wattle walls painted white, not peat-stained as I remembered. A homey hearthrug rolled out by the settle. My gaze stopped at Da's empty chair. His clay pipe and tobacco box were laid out on the table as though he might walk in at any moment.

I turned back to Colm. "Place looks grand."

"We keep things sharp," he said, clearly pleased by my praise. "With the new motorized ferry, we get more tourists than we used to. Yanks especially do fancy their comforts."

"And their privacy," Killian added, stepping off the landing.

"We built a guestroom off from the kitchen," Colm continued. "The Yank put up there now is a queer hawk but quiet as a mouse."

Killian joined us. "'Twas my Úna who settled him on Thursday last. Asked for his meals to be left on a tray outside his door. Don't think he's come out since, but the food disappears, so we ken he's kicking."

Only half listening, I wandered over to the bar. "Would you believe I haven't been behind the stick since I left?"

Colm joined me. "Lost your touch, have ya?" he asked, tone tinged with the old challenge.

I looked from him to Killian, and suddenly it was as if we three were kids again, my big brother baiting me, the littlest one egging us on. "I'll wager I can still pull a better pint than the pair of you with one hand tied behind my back."

"Try it with two, only mind what you draw flat, you drink," Colm said, lifting the pass-through.

Stripping off my traveling gloves, I walked through and sidled up to the taps. "I've never drawn flat in my life, Colm O'Neill, and I don't suppose I'll start doing so today."

Grinning, Colm tossed me an apron. "Good to have you back, little sister."

Tying on the apron, I smiled. "It's good to be back."

And it was.

328

Visiting with family and neighbors took up a full fortnight. In the taproom, I spotted familiar faces, toughened by the years. Sadly, Tam McGhee had passed a few weeks before my father. I liked to sit at the settle and imagine the pair of them smoking their pipes and trading fishing stories in Heaven.

To my delight, Blake embraced island life as if born to it, shucking off his shoes and digging for limpets with his cousins, as well as milking a cow far better than Adam ever managed. At night, we shared my narrow bed beneath the eaves, cuddling beneath the covers.

One predawn morning, we were awakened by Colm bellowing from the bottom of the stairs. "Rose. *Rose!*"

I pulled on my wrapper and padded out to the upper stair landing. "What's so important it can't wait 'til breakfast?" I called down, still half-asleep.

"Come down and see for yourself," he answered, maddening as ever.

Peeved as I was, my curiosity proved more potent. Bidding Blake go back to sleep, I went downstairs.

Colm stood in the center of the taproom with a middle-aged couple in their traveling clothes, trunks at their feet. I looked among the three of them, wondering why I was being called to play hostess in my night-clothes, when it struck me.

I sprung off the landing. "Ronan! Keira!"

"We are, unless you have another brother and sister-in-law by those names?" Ronan held me tight, then passed me to Keira, who did the same.

Far from minding, I hugged her just as heartily.

She drew back to look at me, gaze going to the silk butterflies embroidered upon my robe. "I hardly recognize you, such a grand lady you are."

Too embarrassed to know how to answer, I looked back to Colm. "I take it this explains all the whispering between you and Killian these past several days?"

Ronan jerked his ginger-whiskered chin to his wife. "Blame herself. She insisted on keeping it a surprise."

Keira linked her arm through mine and led us toward the kitchen. "Come along, dearling, we've a world of catching up to do."

Once the tea was steeped and poured, the subjects of marriage, childbirth, and babies were quickly exhausted. Hands laced about our steaming mugs, we stared at each other with stupid smiles.

Despite grayed hair and spectacles, Keira seemed much as I'd left her, whereas nearly a quarter of a century away had changed me in ways I still struggled to admit. For good or ill, New York was my home now. I missed the energy in the air, the sidewalks clogged with crushing crowds, the honking horns and blaring sirens, even the hurry everyone seemed always to be in. My first few nights on the island I'd lain awake, the silence roaring in my ears. Above all, Moira and Baby Neil were in New York as was… Adam. How close I felt to him here, on this sandy soil and rocky turf where our love was seeded.

That evening, Colm joined me at the pier, my old watchpoint. He lit a cheroot, and we stood in silence, watching the sun sink below the horizon.

Emboldened by the waning light, I said, "You were wrong about him, you know."

He didn't have to ask who I meant. Adam, of course.

"He didn't desert me. His family kept my letters from him and his from me."

Exhaling a ring of smoke, Colm took in the news with a nod.

I might have left it there but being back on my home soil had cracked something open inside me. "After Joe… passed, Adam asked me to marry him. I turned him down."

That time, Colm turned his head to look at me. "Why'd you do that for? You've been mad for him since you were seventeen."

I hesitated, searching my memory but most of all, my soul. "I've loved him for so long, how'd I bear it if our marriage was anything less than a marvel?"

Once the words were out, relief washed over me. My admission amounted to a clearing of the air, even if Adam wasn't there to witness it.

Colm's gaze went back to the bay. "He'll ask again."

"He won't. He warned me he wouldn't, and he won't."

"Not everyone's as stubborn as yourself."

The soft strangling sound I let out was equal parts laugh and sob. "He is."

"Then ask him."

"I will not!"

He snorted. "You've got the vote now, don't you? Might as well put on trousers and make it official."

Glad Moira wasn't there to hear him, I said, "I've a mind to see Inis Meán before I go. Have one of the lads take me out tomorrow, will you?"

He stubbed out his smoke. "No need. The ferry calls at all three islands now."

Happy to hear I could come and go on my own, I made my goodnights and went inside.

Snuggling Blake against me, I slept in snatches. Dawn lights saw me slipping out of bed to bathe and dress. Downstairs, I made a light meal of tea and toast and then hurried down to meet the first ferry. Or so that was my plan. I'd scarcely cleared the yard when Úna rushed after me, begging me to mind the oven whilst she ran a swift errand.

Úna's errand was anything but swift. By the time she returned, the ferry had pulled out, not to return until noon. Resigned to waiting, I rolled up my sleeves and helped her turn out the loaves.

When the ferry returned, I was pacing the pier. Other than a middle islander making her way back from the mainland, I had the deck to myself. The crossing was tame and efficient, the boat's motor cutting through the whitecaps with ease. Remembering Adam working the oars through those same choppy waters, the spindly cradle of Colm's currach all that stood between ourselves and the icy sea, I considered it a mercy we'd survived to see all these years.

The middle island was only slightly more populated than I remembered it, most paths still tracts of beaten earth. My years as a city dweller had made me tentative and tender-footed. Taking the footpath to the lookout point, I registered every stone and shell. The climb up the cliffside seemed steeper than before, but then there was no Adam beside me to pass the time talking. Nor was I seventeen anymore.

Fortunately, my islander instincts hadn't deserted me entirely. Hugging the rocks, I managed to find the cave entrance, the moss-covered stones clear of overgrowth as if someone had taken clippers to them. Ducking, I breathed in the loamy pungency as another might a fine perfume. A single blind step steered me into what must be a spider's web. Wiping the sticky skein from my cheek, I dug the electric torch out of my bag.

"If we find ourselves stranded a second time, I can't promise I'll act the gentleman."

I dropped the torch and wheeled about.

Adam stepped clear of the shadows. Staring, I half wondered if I wasn't having one of Dr. Freud's hallucinations. But no, the figure a few feet away was no figment of my fancy but the flesh-and-blood being I'd spent the whole of my adult life loving.

Finding my voice, I said, "I don't recall you acting all that much of a gentleman the last time."

"Fair point." Reaching me, he opened his arms.

I stepped into them and set my cheek upon his chest. "You're the Yank recluse Colm made mention of?"

Tender fingers stroked my hair. "I am."

"And you followed me here?"

"To be absolutely accurate, I *preceded* you here. The head start is all thanks to Moira."

Moira!? Of course. My daughter was one of the few people with my itinerary and the only to know me as Adam's Wild Irish Rose.

I drew back and looked up at him. "But how did you know I'd be coming here today? Don't tell me Colm—"

"Not Colm, Úna. She recognized me when I first arrived. Once I assured her my intentions were honorable, she agreed to help in any way she could."

"By making a baker of me?"

He gave a sheepish nod. "She tipped me off you'd be taking the first ferry out, and I asked her to see to it you were delayed. I needed time to prepare."

Before I could ask what for, he broke away to pick up the torch, shining it on the cave wall. Not an oilskin but a proper picnic cloth was spread out, a food hamper, and an old-fashioned spirit lamp set atop.

Turning back, he slanted me a smile. "I figured if I was going to eat crow, I might as well do it in style. And wash it down with some of your brother's excellent poteen." Before I could answer, he dropped down on one knee. "Moira Rose O'Neill Kavanaugh, will you marry me? For the record, I don't give a damn whether we travel or not or where we call home, though I've grown rather fond of New York. My son and daughter-in-law are there, my grandchild is there, and above all, you're there."

"Oh, Adam."

Wincing, he shifted knees. "I don't know how many more years I'll be fit to go down on bended knee like this, so if you love me even a little, say yes – quickly."

If I loved him! "As it happens, I love you rather a lot."

"So, it's a 'yes'?"

Staring through misty eyes, I nodded. "It is."

He rose, arms going about my waist, mouth fastening upon mine, the kiss slow and deep and thorough, filling me with hope for all the happy years ahead.

I can't for certain say how long we stood together like that, kissing like courting kids, but eventually, reality, or certainly motherhood, intruded, and I found the will to move away. "Mind, our marrying will mean adding another chick to your nest, one who won't be flying away for quite some time."

He touched my cheek, a glancing caress that sent my senses spinning and laid the worst of my worries to rest. "Robbie's boyhood went by far too fast. Fact is, I'm looking forward to being a father again, and Blake is a wonderful boy. We've been fast friends for a while now. Once we're all under the same roof, I'm sure I'll grow to love him like he was my own."

I pulled a deep breath, girding myself to let go of the last of my secrets and lies, as yet unsure of the consequences. "Blake *is* yours. Your son."

He stared back, mouth working but no words coming out.

"I should have told you years ago. But I knew if I did—"

"I'd never let the two of you go."

Put that way, how selfish and small-minded my secret-keeping seemed.

"And now, I never will." He hugged me hard, his arms an anchor I never wanted to cast off. "This time, I'm not taking any chances. Tomorrow, I'll bring a priest over from the mainland. We can hold the party afterward in the pub, if your family's agreeable."

Lightheaded with relief, I drew back to look at him. "*Agreeable?* Mind we're not the only ones who've waited nearly a quarter of a century for you to make an honest woman of me. Colm will be beside himself."

His cautious smile stretched into a grin. "Good, because I'm counting on him to give the bride away."

And all at once, we were lovers again, our love tested by time and seasoned by suffering. Standing in the safe harbor of Adam's arms, I knew we'd both finally found our way home.

Epilogue

Saunterings, June 1922

*Wedding season is upon us, gentle readers! And who among this
season's crop of cherry-lipped debutantes will be the latest in what
promises to be a long and wearying parade of blushing, bobbed-
hair brides?*

*No debutante at all, but retail maven, widow, and grand-
mother, Rose O'Neill Kavanaugh! The founder, with her late
husband, of the eponymous department store, tied Cupid's knot
earlier this month while visiting her ancestral pile in the Emerald
Isle.*

*And the fortunate groom? No husky Celt swain or Paddy
Prince but New York's own blue-blooded, blue-eyed, best-selling
novelist, Adam H. Blakely.*

*Oui, mes chères, s'truth. The estimable Irishwoman, an erst-
while emigrant to these shores, is now Rose O'Neill Kavanaugh
BLAKELY.*

*It will be recalled that the couple shares a grandson as well as
an acquaintanceship of more than twenty years. At the December
1919 wedding of their children, an elegant, albeit hurried affair,
that positively poured with pre-Prohibition bubbly, they were
observed to disappear together to one of the Waldorf's private
salons.*

*Most recently, the latecomers-to-love met up "by chance" on
the largest, and most thoroughly unpronounceable island of Mrs.
Kavanaugh Blakely's native Arans. The rustic wedding took
place at the bride's family's harborside hotel where, one can hope,
toasts were raised with actual glasses, not teacups. A whirlwind*

*honeymoon on the Continent – Rome, London, and Paris – is
taking place even now.*

*Devotees of this column will recall that it debuted with an
engagement, also Mr. Blakely's, but well, no need to dredge up all
that now. And so it seems fitting that it, and I, should close with a
wedding, also his.*

*Recent events have inspired this intrepid reporter to retire her –
yes, HER – steno pad and trusty Underwood No. 5 to seek out,
if not a like late-life love match, a country cottage where she can
rusticate in peace. Or perhaps a Paris pied-a-terre from which she
can kick up her T-straps amongst the smart set of Montmartre.
Quel choix! Either way, without further ado…*

Au Revoir,

The Saunterer

Evelyn Moon AKA the Saunterer AKA Yvette Bellerose unfurled the
typed sheet from the roller and blew on the ink. Pulling on the pearls
tucked inside her blouse collar, she sat back to give her final column a
good glance-over, making sure she'd sprinkled in just the right amount
of French to be droll. But not too droll.

The real her was as American as apple pie and Yankee Doodle.
Fortunately, she'd had a knack for disguise and sufficient French to plant
herself as a maid in a boutique Paris hotel catering to wealthy Americans.
If Elizabeth Cochran writing as Nelly Bly could get herself committed
to the Women's Lunatic Asylum on Blackwell's Island to break her story,
surely Evelyn could teach herself to use curling tongs?

Early on, Vanessa had found Evelyn's typewriter and latest poison pen
piece and pressed for answers. What business had a humble French maid
moonlighting as a society wag? Left with little choice, Evelyn had dropped
the accent, admitted all, and braced herself for dismissal or worse, exposure.
Fortunately for her, Vanessa had recognized in Evelyn a cunning kindred
spirit. Admiration replaced her ebbing anger. Instead of ordering Evelyn off,
she'd proposed a partnership. Together, they'd come up with the Saunterer,
a powerful persona whose pen would serve Vanessa's interests, namely
nabbing Adam Blakely once he got back from playing soldier in Cuba.

Serve Evelyn had, starting with whipping up that first charity ball
story, which Vanessa had made certain was picked up by *Town Topics*, the

first in what would become her regular column. Over the years, Vanessa's dishing up the dirt on her rivals ensured Evelyn a steady stream of material. Evelyn would have been content to carry on her twin lives indefinitely. As the waspish Saunterer, she was free to speak her mind, as Yvette, to indulge her carnal side. Her dual identities brought the best of both worlds – until Vanessa discovered she was dying and decided to mend fences with Adam, beginning by ridding herself of Evelyn.

It hadn't been hard to slip in the fatal drops of laudanum. Still raging over the argument with Adam, Vanessa had downed the drug in her mug of cinnamon-spiced warm milk as she did every night. Eternal slumber was quick in coming.

In Adam, Evelyn had the perfect patsy – the cheating cad pressing for divorce. Only at the last minute, that cursed doctor had come forward and spoiled everything. True, his testimony lent plausibility to Vanessa's death being by suicide, but Evelyn couldn't risk that someone in Vanessa's family or Adam himself might put together the pieces at some point. Even if not, in attempting to frame Adam, she had made a powerful enemy.

Rather than tempt fate, she'd taken the pearls and disappeared. Or rather, Yvette disappeared. Evelyn simply returned to her rented flat across town, burned Yvette's wig and clothing and cosmetics, and resumed life as a full-time reporter. Until recently, she supposed she'd die in her swivel chair, stale coffee, and a wax-paper-wrapped sandwich set out on her desk.

She'd had a good run. Skewering the filthy rich in print was both a social service and rollicking good fun. Not to mention she'd gotten away with murder – literally. But no one's luck lasted forever. The popular taste was changing. Sordid society scandal wasn't selling as it once had. The old moral outrage was missing. With the proliferation of speakeasies and jazz joints, everyone – rich, poor, or middle-class – was a not-so-secret sinner.

She finished reading. The copy was good. Better than good, pitch perfect. A fitting swan song, it struck all the right chords. She reached for the brown paper mailer, slid the column inside, and sealed it.

Adieu, New York.

She pulled the chain on her desk lamp, pushed back her desk chair, and stood.

On the office threshold, she turned back inside. And sketched a bow.

THE END

Acknowledgments

Every book is a journey, not only for the reader but for the author also. My journey with Irish Eyes was a saga unto itself, the odyssey made smoother and infinitely more fun by the friendship and fellowship of the following kind and talented author tribe: Leanna Renee Hieber, Fiona Davis, Jessica Gibbons (w/a Jess Russell), Nancy Bilyeau, Finola Austin, Suzan Colón and Mary Browning Rodgers.

My sincerest gratitude to Julie Miesionczek and Mary Browning Rodgers, who gave their time and talent to weigh in on an early version of the novel. Ladies, your insightful notes were invaluable in honing a behemoth of a book into a publishable manuscript.

Heartfelt thanks to Fred Rappoport and David Fisher for their stalwart championship of the book and my writing career, and to Barbara Biziou and Arathi Rao for their mentorship and encouragement over the years.

Huge thanks to my two "subject matter experts" with hearts of gold. The first, Captain Paul Hashagen, a third-generation New York firefighter, whom I found through his fascinating non-fiction book, A Distant Fire. A History of FDNY Heroes. Paul not only answered my questions on the design and proper use of nineteenth-century scaling ladders, sundry horse-drawn fire apparatus, and the particulars of the Windsor Hotel Fire, covered in his book, but also read my pages to do with the fire and offered a diplomatic yet detailed critique.

On the military history front, I am so very lucky to have crossed paths with Bert Cunningham, New York Army National Guard 69th Infantry Regiment Veterans Corps Historian. I met Bert on Kevin Fitzpatrick's excellent World War I-themed walking tour of Manhattan. When I told him I was writing a novel that spanned the Spanish American and First World Wars, and that I had *questions*, rather than run for the hills he volunteered to answer *all* my military queries and vet my pages, which he did.

Any errors are entirely my own.

Many thanks to the talented team at Lume Books, especially Aubrie Artiano, Head of Publishing, and freelance editor, Miranda Summers-Pritchard for midwifing my story. Owing to your insights and thoughtful notes, the book was brought into the world in infinitely better shape.

To my mom, Nancy Louise Tarr, who, based solely on my phone sum-up of the plot, exclaimed Irish Eyes was the best thing I'd ever written. From your mouth to God's ear, Mom!

Last but never least, to my husband, Raj Moorjani. As Rose would say, "We've known the two days." Every moment of every day is made inestimably better by having you to share it.

Hope C. Tarr

New York, New York

Author's Note

Joe's rescue of Rose from the Windsor Hotel is based on the real-life heroics of fire Captain William Clark. Clark carried out several daring saves at The Windsor, notably climbing to the second floor on a standard ladder, then using a hand-held scaling ladder to reach the third floor, and lastly levering himself to a fourth-floor window to reach a woman trapped inside. Clark was awarded the James Gordon Bennett Medal in 1900, then the sole decoration for valor within the Fire Department of the City of New York. Today, the FDNYC's Board of Merit continues the annual tradition, awarding this most senior of medals for outstanding acts of heroism.

The firefighters called to 105 Allen Street on March 14, 1905, also used scaling ladders to reach trapped tenants. Joe's saving the left-behind child draws upon the real-life rescue executed by Officer Dwan, who ran through the burning building, uniform afire, with a little girl clinging to his neck. Dwan fell from the fire escape, but the child landed safely atop him. Unlike Joe, who got off lightly, he sustained a broken shoulder, fractured hip, possible internal injuries, and numerous cuts and burns. Happily, he lived to receive a commendation from the people of the Lower East Side. It wasn't until after 1911, a year that saw two tragic fires: The Triangle Shirtwaist Factory in Washington Square (March 25th) and the Dreamland amusement park in Coney Island (May 26th) that what we've come to think of as modern fire codes would be enacted.

Further to being afire...

Town Topics: The Journal of Society was a sizzling weekly scandal sheet that put New York's elite in the proverbial hot seat. In 1891, Colonel William d'Alton Mann took over the publication from his brother. For "Saunterings," its most popular feature column, Mann aimed his poison pen at those occupying the very pinnacle of society. His most famous target was Edwin Post, husband of Emily. When Post refused to pay hush money, Mann exposed his affair with a Broadway chorus dancer, leading to the couple's 1906 divorce.

Book Club Guide

1. *Irish Eyes* is told in Rose's voice, the story seen through her eyes. Throughout the novel, much is made of the class difference between herself and Adam. Does this reflect a realistic perception of the mores of the time or her own insecurities?

2. At the start of the story, Adam travels to Ireland to keep his "soldiers' promise" to his fallen friend. He later asks Rose to marry him when he could have easily left the island and picked up his easy life in New York. Yet, like Rose, he also proves to be more human than always heroic. He gets back at his wife by keeping a mistress. He laments being an often absent father to his young son and yet takes no real steps to alter the arrangement. He despises working for his family's firm, and yet it takes a devastating blow for him to strike out on his own. To what extent did you empathize with him despite his flaws? Do you consider him heroic despite his failings?

3. Adam proposes to Rose and almost immediately asks her to stay behind in Ireland while he returns to New York to "pave the way" with his family. Outcome aside, do you think his was a reasonable request given the class constraints of the era?

4. Once arrived in New York, Rose and Gerta are processed through the temporary Emigrant Landing Depot at the Battery. Several times, Rose likens the newcomers to cattle being herded through one chute to the next. Both women pass inspection, but not without enduring ethnic prejudice and misogyny. Do these scenes have any parallels to how immigrants are treated today?

5. Though Rose never encounters a "No Irish Need Apply" sign, her Irish accent and appearance elicit implicit forms of prejudice from the moment she first arrives. Put yourself in her shoes – better yet, *pampooties* – and imagine walking into a store to ask for work, knowing that your speech and clothing, hair, and face instantly brand you as Other.

6. Joe Kavanaugh has been called a "striped character" – equal parts hero and antihero. As a fireman, he repeatedly demonstrates selfless bravery, but as a politician and husband, he can be selfish, bigoted, and at times, cruel. By the end of the novel, does he redeem himself or is it a case of too little too late?

7. Throughout the twenty-five years covered in the book, Rose's choices are often at odds with her core convictions. She marries one man but continues to love another. She supports female enfranchisement but not "birth prevention" despite having gone through an out-of-wedlock pregnancy. She is a devout Catholic who refuses but ultimately engages in an extramarital affair. To what extent are you able to empathize with Rose despite her flaws? What might she have done differently? To what extent is she the heroine of her own story?

8. Moira's commitment to the cause of women's suffrage is a thread that runs through the latter part of the story. Given the global Women's March movement, do you see parallels to today's world?

9. Several times, Rose acknowledges that she is married first to Kavanaugh's the store, second to Joe Kavanaugh, the man. To what extent do her struggles to balance her roles as wife and mother with her ambition as a business leader mirror the work–family issues women face today? Do you admire her for growing the store from dry goods emporium to luxury department store? Or should she have found a way to strike a better balance and worked harder at her marriage?

10. At the heart of *Irish Eyes* is the Adam–Rose–Joe "love triangle." Both men struggle to free themselves from their backgrounds – Joe as a "dumb mick boxer" from Orchard Street and Adam from the codified constraints of high society in the age of Mrs. Astor's "Four Hundred." Which man do

you think had the most to overcome? To what extent was each a prisoner to social expectations and male gender roles of the era? Who, if either, did you root for to win Rose – are you Team Adam or Team Joe?

11. America's entry into The Great War – World War I – has a profound effect on Rose and her family. The war effort saw women entering public life in new and visible ways, notably in the workforce as they took up jobs and roles traditionally exclusive to men. In the U.K. and U.S., to what extent did the war help bring about passage of laws enfranchising women?

12. Until the Covid crisis, the influenza pandemic of 1918 was arguably the most destructive "plague" since The Black Death of the Middle Ages. While the actual death toll remains unknown – numbers reported at the time are generally believed to be gross underestimates – it may well have topped 100 million. Then, everyday people from all walks of life and political persuasions pitched in to enforce health code requirements and promote responsible behavior such as masking, refraining from shaking hands, and so forth. How and why does this response differ from our own during Covid?

13. Several historical figures appear throughout the book, including Tammany Hall kingpins "Boss" Charlie Murphy, Timothy Sullivan, and Tom Foley, whose names are still seen on many of the buildings, streets, and squares of present-day New York City. Even humble Irish-born fruit-seller, Jane Noonan, is taken from real life, depicted courtesy of first-person accounts and a surviving photograph of Jane presiding over her stall outside the Castle Garden gates. Do you enjoy "meeting" real-life characters from history in the pages of fiction? Or do you prefer that the characters in a novel be purely made up?

14. How does Rose and Moira's relationship change in the course of the book? Was Moira's reaction to learning her mother was "The Wild Irish Rose" realistic to her personality? To the era?

15. Tammany Hall is integral to the second half of the book, so much so that "The Grand Old Machine" is almost a character in its own right. To what extent are the "greed and graft" engaged in by certain Tammany

leaders specific to the organization versus a sign of the times? Did Joe's endorsement of "honest graft" surprise you? Had power corrupted him from the man Rose first met and married? Or was his reaction consistent with his hard-knocks upbringing? How much, or how little, have politics changed from the early 1900s to now?

16. Despite her difficult beginnings, Rose ultimately achieves her American Dream through hard work, tenacity, and intelligence. The novel likewise references several real-life immigrants, such as Isidor Straus, the Bavarian-born co-owner of Macy's department store, who rose to prominence and great fortune by building retail and other business empires. How likely are such rags-to-riches stories today?

17. Did you find the ending of *Irish Eyes* satisfying? Realistic or fairy tale? What would you have liked to see happen for the core characters?

About the Author

Hope C. Tarr is an award-winning author, screenplay writer and journalist whose articles have appeared in *The Irish Times, USA Today*, and *Baltimore* magazine. She cowrote and developed a podcast series, "The Triangle Shirtwaist Fire of 1911: An Emigrant's Experience" with the Irish History Podcast. *Irish Eyes* is her historical fiction debut and the launch of her *American Songbook* series.

Prior to commencing her writing career, Hope earned a Master of Arts degree in Developmental Psychology and a Ph.D. in Education, both from The Catholic University of America. She is a founder and curator of the original Lady Jane's Salon® reading series in New York City, which ran from 2009 to 2020 and donated its net proceeds to Women in Need, a charity supporting survivors of domestic abuse and homelessness.

A lifelong animal lover, Hope built a national grassroots coalition of animal advocates, breeders and veterinary medical organizations and successfully petitioned the U.S. Postal Service for a commemorative stamp to encourage responsible pet ownership and connect low-income pet parents with free and low-cost spay and neutering services.

Hope divides her time between Manhattan and the Jersey Shore with her husband and their rescue cats. Visit her at https://hopectarr.com for updates and https://hopectarr.substack.com/ where she writes *History with Hope*.

Printed in the USA
CPSIA information can be obtained
at www.ICGtesting.com
LVHW030043210324
775030LV00005B/347